BURNING SORROW

BURNING SORROW

TED SIMON

Random House
Toronto

Canadian Cataloguing in Publication Data

Simon, Ted, 1948-
Burning sorrow

ISBN 0-394-22115-X

I. Title

PS8587.I56B8 1990   C813'.54   C90-093169-8
PR9199.3.S55B8 1990

Jacket Design: David Wyman
Jacket Illustration: Tony Hamilton

Printed and bound in the United States

PART ONE

1938

Vinaroz

April 15, 1938

Vinaroz was burning. The offshore wind drove long skeins of gray and black smoke across the waterfront quays and out over the bay; on the bay itself two fishing smacks lay awash and sinking, hulls shattered and pierced by cannon and machine gun fire as the crews tried to evacuate a few of the defenders of the town before it fell. The pair of Messerschmitt 109s that had strafed the smacks was roaring back into the sun to wait for more targets.

SS-Major Erich Starke stood in an olive grove that crowned a knoll about two thousand meters from the outer defenses of Vinaroz. The sun was climbing toward mid-morning, and it was already quite warm; the rain had stopped just before dawn and the raw earth of the trenches and shell craters in the olive grove now steamed gently in the gathering heat. Some of the olive trees had been uprooted and splintered by shell-fire in yesterday's attack, which had driven the Republicans from their positions back onto the town itself, but there was still enough of the grove standing to provide a reasonable amount of cover.

Starke, however, was not taking advantage of the concealment the trees offered. He leaned against one of the intact trunks, steadying his binoculars on the silvery-gray bark, examining the town. He could hear regular and heavy firing from the outskirts, and the dull thump of a mortar that seemed to be near the church or the town hall. The Republicans wouldn't last much longer; they had to be nearly out of ammunition, and the Nationalist soldiers attacking them were

3

fresh *regulares,* Moroccan Riff tribesmen commanded by Spanish officers. The *regulares* were dreaded by the Republicans for their battle practice of castrating enemy dead and, from time to time, enemy wounded.

If I were facing them, Starke thought, lowering the binoculars, I would make sure that I kept back one bullet for myself. When this is over, Franco ought to send all of them back to the desert. They're sub-humans. But I suppose when you're fighting Communists and Jews, that's appropriate. Use the trash to eliminate the trash, better than spilling good blood.

There was a bunker dug among the olive roots two meters behind Starke. Half its roof had been blown off by a shell. Yesterday morning it had been a Republican bunker, this morning it was a Nationalist one. Starke gave the civil war in Spain about a year more to run, before Franco's legions managed to suppress the last of the Republicans. In the meantime, it was a wonderful place to test weapons and battle tactics. The success of the big spring offensive, which had reached the Mediterranean here at Vinaroz and in so doing split Republican territory in two, was the direct result of the new technology and military thinking. The Bf109s that had strafed the fishing smacks were perfect examples of the improvement in equipment, and the German Condor Legion that fielded those planes and the new Stuka dive bombers was gaining priceless operational experience for the big war that was coming. The ground forces were learning a great deal, as well. Combined-arms tactics, with tanks, infantry, aircraft, and artillery all cooperating, was the wave of the future. And the German Reich, thanks to the intervention on the side of the Nationalists, was going to know more about modern warfare than anyone else in the world. When the time came—

Enough dreaming, Starke told himself. You're here to do a specific job. Concentrate.

He turned around and slithered down into the damaged bunker, which was squelching with mud. A Spanish artillery captain and a signalman were hunched over a field telephone, trying to persuade it to work; the bunker was serving as a gunnery observation post. There were two other men squashed into the bunker besides the artillerymen and Starke: Colonel Eugenio Davila of the

Falange Security, and Lieutenant Colonel Heinz Teichmann, one of the German Wehrmacht officers posted as advisers to the Spanish Nationalists.

"Well?" Teichmann asked. He eyed Starke with distaste. Teichmann was Regular Army, and had little use for the upstart SS, especially upstart SS officers who appeared from Berlin with what amounted to *carte-blanche* in dealing with the Spanish. And what Starke was at Vinaroz to accomplish didn't improve Teichmann's mood, no matter how justified the accomplishment was to be.

"I'll go in soon," Starke said. "Just as soon as the Stukas leave." The air bombardment was scheduled for 1015 hours, whereupon the *regulares* were supposed to overrun the dazed defenders and begin taking their battle trophies. They'd been promised twelve hours' sack of the town, as well as the use of the women remaining in it.

"Very well," Teichmann said. "And suppose the Stukas put paid to him?"

Starke shrugged. There was nothing he could do about that. He said to Davila, in the reasonably good Spanish he'd picked up during his months in Spain, "Is he still where he was this morning?"

"He's in the church bunker, we know that much," Davila answered in the same language. He spoke little German, and disliked using it; some obscure form of Spanish pride. "He won't go far from it, he can't and maintain control of what men he's got left. The town's small. And he'll survive the bombs if he stays in the bunker."

The man to whom they were referring was Philipp Ernst von Lynchen und Friedland. His family was old Prussian aristocracy fallen on hard times, and he'd been one of the most brilliant infantry officers in the new Wehrmacht of the Third Reich. Six months after the Spanish Civil War began, he'd been found to be plotting an attempt on Hitler's life. He'd evaded the Gestapo and surfaced later in Spain, where he joined the Republicans and exerted his considerable military talents on their behalf. His skill was responsible for thousands of Nationalist deaths in the Brunete offensive and the battle of Teruel. Those deaths, however, were not the reason for Starke's presence outside Vinaroz: von Lynchen's treachery had apparently sent Hitler himself into a maniacal rage. Not trusting the army to dispose of the traitor, he had given the SS the task. The orders

were precise: von Lynchen und Friedland was to be captured, dragged back to Berlin, stripped of his rank, interrogated, tried for treason by a People's Court, and hung from a meathook until he was dead. *Pour decourager les autres.* Starke had been tracking him for five months, with the help of Davila's network of Falangist agents. Now Starke had him, or almost.

But it wasn't going to be easy to extract him from Vinaroz, not in one piece, anyway. Starke would have preferred to wait, but the Fuehrer was growing impatient, he'd been told, and in any case it wouldn't serve any purpose if von Lynchen died heroically defending Vinaroz to the end. It would be worse if he slipped away by sea; Starke would have to start looking for him all over again. This wasn't the perfect situation, but it would have to do, and Starke was experienced. He mused on it. Having to preserve a man's life for later disposal was a new twist; his earlier kills had been just that. There had been four of them, two in Czechoslovakia, one in Poland, one in Austria. Five, actually, if he counted the Austrian's wife, although she hadn't been politically important, she'd merely been there. Starke had used her to get at her husband, and she'd never suspected a thing, not until the end when her husband was bleeding to death over the picnic basket and the knife blade was sweeping toward her own slender throat, up there in the wood in the Austrian Tirol.

If it had gone on much longer she'd probably have been in bed with him. Starke knew she'd been considering it, which wasn't unusual with women. He looked a good four years younger than his real age of twenty-seven, and was long-legged, slender, with clear dark eyes and a mop of thick brown hair that curled delicately around his ears. He had a full mouth, which would have been almost feminine had it not been for the strength of the chin beneath it, and had a knack of projecting a fresh-faced innocence that made women want to mother him and men trust him. He'd been only just tall enough to meet SS recruiting standards, but even that height was a mild disadvantage in his work, and he'd developed a stance that made casual observers think he was shorter than he actually was. He was far stronger than his fine-boned body made him appear.

The artillerymen had finally got the telephone working. The captain was gabbling into it in Spanish. Twenty meters away a 75mm

field gun of one of the support batteries banged unexpectedly; the report made Starke blink. The captain screamed a cease-fire order into the telephone and laid the receiver down on a broken crate. The instrument looked like a small black animal, shot through the head and dead.

Starke looked at his watch. Ten-thirteen. He climbed out of the bunker and went back to his tree, scanning the sky. Southward, above the coast, he could make out a dozen black dots: eight larger, four smaller. The bigger ones would be the Stuka dive bombers, and the others the Bf109s of the fighter escort. The Republicans still had a few Rata fighters, supplied by the Russians. The Ratas were based up north toward Barcelona, but they hadn't been interfering lately, partly because of the bad spring weather, partly because the Republican pilots were losing their enthusiasm.

Starke narrowed his eyes against the sun. Now there were two more dots, these out to sea past the burning town, flying toward the Stukas and their escorts. With some difficulty, Starke managed to locate them fleetingly with the binoculars. Jug-shaped fuselages, big flat noses, stubby wings and spatted fixed landing gear: Ratas. Not all the Republican Bolsheviks were staying home.

Starke lost the planes and lowered the binoculars. As he watched the sky, two of the Bf109s peeled away from the Stuka group and sailed toward the Ratas. The dots twisted and turned about each other, intermittent vapor trails scratching across the Spanish blue. One of the vapor trails turned gray, then black, and the dot at the tip of it began to fall. Starke found it with the binoculars; it was one of the Ratas, fire pouring from the engine cowling. He followed it downward for perhaps ten seconds, until the entire fighter was enveloped in a tapered sheath of flame. Then it blew up. Starke took the binoculars from his eyes. The second Rata was already on its way down, smoking. The Bf109s returned to their charges, which were by now at an altitude of about three thousand meters and almost over the town. One by one the Stukas rolled into their dives, plummeting toward the Republican-held positions around the church, the town hall, and the harbor quays. The howl of their engines and the shriek of the slipstream around their dive brakes drowned out the small-arms fire from the town; Starke could just make out the specks of the

bombs as they left the Stukas' bellies and wings and plunged into their targets while the dive bombers, relieved of their loads, pulled out at no more than a thousand meters and clawed for altitude. Huge gouts of smoke and wreckage boiled above the rooftops as the bombs detonated.

Time to go, Starke thought. He returned to the edge of the bunker, where the artillery captain was shouting into the field telephone again. The 75mm guns started banging. Davila was already scrambling out of the bunker, his SI35 submachine gun slung over his right shoulder, Starke's weapon in its leather case in his left hand. Starke took it from him, unzipped the case and took out the gun. It was an MP28, one of the expensively tooled submachine guns produced for the Wehrmacht in the early thirties and much superior to the new mass-produced MP38. Starke had modified this one himself, to reduce the likelihood of jamming. He gave the weapon a brief check—he had stripped and cleaned it earlier in the morning—and headed with Davila toward the rear of the olive grove, where an armored car was tucked behind a stone wall. The vehicle was a light two-man SdKfz 221 provided for Starke, reluctantly, by Lt. Col. Teichmann. Two *regulares* were sitting on the rear fenders; they were part of what Davila termed euphemistically his "special squad." They grinned at Starke out of their dark faces, teeth gleaming.

Monkeys, Starke thought. He got into the vehicle with Davila and started up, following the road around the olive grove, accelerating hard as the town came into view around the bend. The armor was proof against small-arms fire at this distance, but there was no sense in remaining in the open any longer than necessary. Above Vinaroz the smoke and dust clouds from the bombs and the fires were still climbing into the air; as they roared closer to the outskirts Starke could smell the damage, swept inland by a vagary of the wind: plaster dust, high explosive, burned wood and paper and tar, carrion.

They reached the edge of the built-up area and stopped at the Nationalists' forward command post, a shell-riddled house perhaps fifty meters along the winding main street. The street led eventually to the town square and the church where, according to Davila's sources in Vinaroz, the German renegade could be found.

Inside the command post, Davila quizzed the officer in charge. The man was at least equal to Davila in rank, but he knew who Davila was and the knowledge made him more than cooperative. Starke listened, following most of it despite the speed of the interchange. The idiomatic parts of it he didn't get; five months in the country hadn't allowed him to become fluent.

"What's the situation here?" Starke asked when Davila turned away from the other colonel.

"Resistance has almost collapsed. Most of the last defenders, and what civilians are still here, are in the houses down by the water. The only others are in and around the church, where the central command post was."

"How close can we get?"

"The bombing raid wasn't all on target. The street's blocked by rubble two hundred meters from here, and there are fires. We should go on foot. Colonel Escobar estimates there are no more than a dozen men, if that many, still in the church positions. We are digging them out, one by one."

"It is important that von Lynchen not be killed along with the others," Starke said sharply. "That is the whole point of my being here."

Davila did not quite shrug. He didn't care whether von Lynchen was killed or captured, as long as he was no longer available to the Republicans. He was cooperating to this extent purely for that reason. "We will try," he said. "But fortune is capricious, especially in battle."

Starke thought: spare me your military philosophy. He followed Davila back into the sun-drenched street, where they took extra magazines and a supply of grenades from the armored car. The *regulares* were no longer grinning; their faces had taken on a hungry, feral look. Starke said, "Let's go," and the four men set off along the rubble-strewn street.

The gunfire wasn't nearly as heavy as it had been before the Stuka raid, although it was keeping up a steady tempo. It was punctuated by distant and not-so-distant screams, some masculine, some feminine. The Riff tribesmen would be running loose in an hour or less, as soon as organized resistance ended. Starke hoped to be on the way to the

Nationalist rear and the plane to Berlin before that happened; even their officers had trouble controlling the Moroccans once they had been turned loose to pillage. Their ferocity had to burn itself out before they were safe to handle.

Starke and Davila led the way, one on each side of the street, keeping close to the walls and running in alternating dashes from door alcove to rubble pile to alley mouth, covering each other as they went, with the Moroccans doing the same behind them. Bodies sprawled in the street, both Nationalist and Republican. Some had been fragmented by shell fire, and spatters of blood and tissue flecked the cobblestones and nearby walls. Lying around the bodies were broken rifles, a smashed mortar tube, scraps of uniform, big black flakes of burned paper, shell cases gleaming brightly in the sun, empty ammunition belts, chunks of plaster chipped from the walls by gunfire. Occasional wounded Nationalists stumbled back toward the rear, but there was no sign of civilians; they'd be hiding in the cellars or the rubble. Once Starke and the others passed a supply detail hauling ammunition up to the forward edge of the battle area, but it wasn't until they were only about fifty meters from the church—Starke could see its badly damaged tower looming above the rooftops ahead—that they came across Nationalist combat troops. Urban fighting was like that, Starke knew; a pitched battle could be going on but the men involved would hardly ever be in sight.

A Nationalist light machine gun nest was just ahead, dug in behind the shattered wall of a house, its muzzle pointing through a tiny gap formed by a barricade of broken timbers. Beyond the barricade was a small square with a bomb crater in the middle of it, and on the far side of the square was the church. Its wooden front door had been blown off its hinges by the bomb. The Stukas, here at least, had been extremely accurate.

A Nationalist captain was crouching behind the barricade, next to the machine gun crew. Davila, bent low, scuttled up beside him; Starke followed. A bullet passed overhead with a snap and thudded into a brick wall a few meters behind. The gunner fired a two-second burst in reply. When the echoes died away Davila said in a low voice, "They're in there?"

The captain nodded. He had a three-days' growth of beard and

looked exhausted. "A few left," he said. "Six tried to break out to the harbor a few minutes ago but we got them all."

"Was there a German?" Starke asked, frowning. This was what he'd been afraid of. In a pinch, he could bring von Lynchen's body home, but it would really be a failure of the mission. There might be repercussions for Starke if von Lynchen weren't taken alive.

"I don't know," said the captain. "You can look at the bodies, but they're in the open. You might get shot doing it."

"Never mind," Davila said. "He's probably in there. We'll have to go and see. Are you ready?"

The captain nodded. "We were instructed to wait for you. Everything's ready. There are two men in the shell hole out there, in grenade range of the door. That's our artillery."

"Go, then."

The captain nodded and put a whistle to his lips. He took a deep breath and blew into it. The noise was shrill, earsplitting. Starke, peering between two balks of charred timber, saw the heads and shoulders of two men rise out of the shell hole in front of the church door. They made throwing motions, and the machine gunner simultaneously began firing a long burst into the open church door to cover the grenadiers. Six grenades flew into the church's dark interior and detonated in a ripple of flashes and echoing bangs. At the same instant, the Nationalist infantrymen who had been concealed around the square leaped out of cover and dashed for the gaping entrance to the church. The machine gun fell silent, to avoid hitting them.

Now, Starke thought. He scrambled over the barricade and pelted toward the church door on the heels of the Spaniards, his MP28 held ready in the regulation manner. Adrenalin flowed through him in a breezy rush, the sun was bright, he felt exhilarated. This was what he was meant for, what he was meant to do. He sensed Davila and the pair of *regulares* hot on his heels and then he was at the church door, down in the fighting crouch, scuttling sideways as soon as he was through the door into the gloom within.

There was a series of bangs and crashes from the church transept. In the dim light Starke saw pews jumbled together in piles of boards and broken supports. The gunfire echoes were deafening, mixed with the zing of ricochets. He dropped behind a smashed pew, waiting for

grenades to signal the next rush. Another shot from the direction of the apse. They were making a last stand behind the altar. Starke sensed the Nationalist troops infiltrating up the side aisles toward the Republican position. He had to try to get them to hold off, take von Lynchen alive if he was there. The gunfire stopped for a moment, as men on both sides worked out what to do next. Without raising his head, Starke shouted in German:

"Von Lynchen! It's over! Surrender now and we'll give you the honors of war!" A lie, but it might appeal to the Prussian sense of military fitness. If nothing else, an answer would help pinpoint the man's position, assuming he was in the church.

An answering shout, also in German. It reverberated inside the nave, making it impossible for Starke to locate the exact position of the speaker.

"Go to hell, whoever you are. You and your Fuehrer both. Tell them in Berlin there's some of the real army left."

He'll have to be dug out, Starke thought. Damn. "Honors of war, von Lynchen," he called back. "I guarantee it."

The only answer was a burst of submachine-gun fire. One bullet clipped a board not ten centimeters above Starke's head. He was baiting me, he thought as he rolled sideways. Trying to fix my position.

The Spaniards had opened up again, ignoring the dangers of ricochets. Somebody screamed and then gave a bubbling moan. Grenades banged around the altar. That's done it, Starke thought. The fucking Spaniards forgot their orders. No wonder their war's gone on this long.

The echoes died, to be replaced by a silence punctuated by faint scuffling noises and the distant snap of small-arms fire elsewhere in the town. Starke got carefully to one knee, keeping his head low. "Von Lynchen?" he called. There was no answer, no firing. Starke took a chance and ran, doubled over, toward the altar. Boots and wood scraped on stone: the Nationalists were moving up as well.

The transept was lighter because of the apse windows high up in the thick walls. Starke reached the pillar closest to the altar, which put him ten meters away from it. There was one body with Republican badges sprawled on the floor, half behind the altar, face up. It wasn't

von Lynchen. Starke stepped carefully from behind his pillar and walked toward the body, the MP28 ready. Davila was emerging from the shadows on the other side of the nave, with his Moroccans behind him. Other Spaniards slowly materialized out of the gloom.

There were two more bodies behind the altar. One was Spanish, and the other was von Lynchen. He was leaning against the altar's chipped stone, a Star submachine gun across his lap, with his eyes closed and blood trickling from the corner of his mouth. There was more blood on his ragged battledress tunic, but he was still breathing.

Good, Starke thought, lowering the muzzle of the MP28. Now if I can just patch him up long enough to get him to Berlin—

Von Lynchen's eyes flew open and the Star's barrel came up, tracking toward Starke's belly.

Starke hadn't lowered the MP28 all the way. He snapped off a single shot that slammed into von Lynchen's upper right arm and knocked the Star sideways before the other German could aim properly. Von Lynchen was already pulling the trigger, though, and the gun hammered, the bullets flying uselessly toward the roof. Then his body jerked convulsively as a burst of gunfire from behind Starke hit him. Blood spattered from von Lynchen's chest and he fell sideways onto the paving stones, his gun silent and dropping with him. Starke looked up. Davila had stopped firing but his gun was still aimed at the dead German.

"Pigshit," said Starke furiously. "God damn you. What in hell did you do that for?"

"I beg your pardon, Major?" Davila said, his voice sharp and angry. Starke knew he had badly insulted the Spaniard. "He was trying to kill you. What did you expect me to do?"

Davila's Moroccans, their blood up and alerted by the anger in their commander's voice, were watching Starke hungrily. He had to apologize and back off. The tribesmen would kill him at Davila's smallest gesture.

"Thank you," Starke said evenly. "I regret my hasty temper and my words."

Davila nodded, although he continued to look surly. "Very well. You wish the body carried back?"

"If you would be so good," Starke answered in polite formality.

Davila barked an order in the tribesmen's language. The two Moroccans grabbed von Lynchen's body under the armpits and started dragging it out of the church.

Outside, in the square, the sun was momentarily blinding. Most of the shooting had stopped, to be replaced by the rumble and crackle of flames and a steady background racket of shouts and shrieks. The Moroccans had been turned loose.

Starke and Davila, the *regulares* trailing along behind with their burden, skirted the crater and clambered over the barricade into the street leading back to the main command post and the armored car. The machine gunner and his loader were smoking cigarettes; the captain was nowhere to be seen. Davila took a wrinkled cigarette from his own battledress pocket and paused to light it. His face was still sullen; he hadn't forgiven Starke for the outburst back in the church.

The street beyond the barricade wasn't deserted any more. Small parties of looters ran in and out of the houses; some were Spaniards, more Moroccans. Some of the bodies had already been mutilated by the *regulares*; Starke glanced down an alleyway as he walked and glimpsed a pair of the Riff tribesmen bent over a prone and half-naked form, knives busy. Disgust swept through Starke as one of the men triumphantly held up a bloody fragment of flesh. These people were not long out of the trees.

A little farther on, three Nationalist soldiers had dragged a middle-aged man out of a house and were beating him with their rifle butts. He was screaming in short, hard bursts. "A Red," Davila said as they passed. The sight seemed to improve his mood.

They were a hundred meters from the command post and their vehicle when they heard screaming and a wooden door in the wall ahead of them flew open. Through it ran two women, naked from the waist up, skirts torn. Half a dozen *regulares* boiled through the door after them. One of the women—neither was more than seventeen—saw Davila's uniform and European complexion and ran to throw herself at his feet, wrapping her arms around his knees. The other prostrated herself in front of Starke, and he felt her fingers clamp around his right ankle. Both were crying out for help, the words

broken and fragmented with hysteria. The one clasping Davila's knees had a deep, bleeding cut in her right breast: a knife wound. Davila tried to kick her off, but she only clung tighter. The Moroccans had stopped a few meters away, muttering, their eyes narrowed and angry. All of them had slung their rifles and were carrying long curved knives. Starke cocked his MP28 and held it not exactly pointing at them, but ready.

"Get *off*, you Red slut," Davila snarled. He beat at her arms with his fist and she let go, slumped and sobbing in the dust. He looked at Starke, "Be careful with the gun," he said. "They'll bring others and kill us if you interfere. Leave them alone, and they'll leave us alone."

The girl at Starke's feet was whimpering raggedly, still clutching his ankle. He shoved her off and turned his gun muzzle away from the *regulares*. They grinned at him and moved forward.

"This was a Red town," Davila said. "These two sluts would be shooting at us if they could."

He smiled and gestured the Moroccans forward, saying something in their own language. They grinned even more ferociously and ran up to the women, dragging them away from Starke and Davila. The girl at Starke's feet grabbed desperately at his leg and clung for an instant until a knife came out of nowhere and slashed at her wrist. She let go, howling madly.

"Come *on*," Davila hissed urgently. They hurried up the street, their own two Moroccans following reluctantly with von Lynchen's body. After a few meters Davila had regained his composure, and seemed positively good-natured. Screams echoed from the walls behind them, cascading down into moans. Starke looked back. There were at least a dozen *regulares* back there now; he couldn't see the women among them, although from the sounds he knew they were there.

"They'll last about two hours, if they're lucky," Davila said cheerfully. "If they're not lucky, it could go on for three or four." He exhaled a long gust of cigarette smoke. "There won't be any Communist brats coming out of *that* pair. Ever."

Starke nodded. He agreed, but considered that the Red women should have been simply shot. Allowing even savages to run wild like

this was bad for military discipline. He thought about suggesting this to Davila, but decided against it.

"Are you interested in a woman?" Davila asked. "They'll be around for the taking for the rest of the day."

Starke shook his head. Rape for its own sake didn't interest him, and he didn't find grubby Spanish peasant women attractive anyway. "Thank you, no."

"Whatever you like," Davila answered indifferently. He stopped as they reached the armored car and issued a sharp order to the Moroccans. "Let's get your package back to the lines."

Istanbul

May 27-28, 1938

Marc Rossi leaned against the balustrade of the upper level of the eastern end of the Galata Bridge, watching the evening sun go down. The air smelled of coal and wood smoke, salt water, drying seaweed, cooking oil, frying fish from the vendors' stalls on the bridge's lower level, and decaying fruit. Beyond the far end of the bridge, across the darkening waters of the Golden Horn, lay the Stamboul shore and the ancient city of Constantine and the Ottoman sultans. Outlined against the inflamed sky, Istanbul was jet black and without detail: Yeni Mosque, looming over the bridge's western end, the domes and minarets of the Suleimaniye Mosque far away to the northwest on the crest of the Third Hill, to the southeast of the bridge the great curved bulk of Haghia Sophia, and on from that again the spires of Topkapi Sarayi, the palace of the Sultans, deserted now and falling in on itself, stone by stone and tile by tile, under the indifferent neglect of Kemal Ataturk's new Turkish Republic.

In the shadows under the far shoreline, and a hundred meters south of the bridge, the Turkish steamer *Yildiz* lay at anchor; Rossi could just make out the grimy buff of her superstructure and her white funnel band against the lights scattered along the waterfront. When the sun came up again she'd be gone, outward bound to deliver her cargo of Jewish refugees either to the shores of Palestine or to the untender mercies of the British immigration patrols.

Rossi stopped leaning on the balustrade and straightened up, flexing the stiffness out of his shoulders; he'd been waiting for some

17

time. He was better off, though, than those people out on the freighter. Some of them had been aboard for days, waiting first until their number was made up, and then until some fault with the steamer's ancient engines was repaired. She was under German charter this time, or more precisely under the charter of the Central Office for Jewish Emigration. The racial policies of the Third Reich had made strange bedfellows: the emigration office as part of Reinhard Heydrich's *Sicherheitsdienst*, or SD, the security service of the SS. Heydrich was responsible only to Himmler, chief of the SS itself, and Himmler had given the SD head the responsibility of removing all Jews from the Reich. Thousands and thousands, their possessions confiscated, with no resources and nowhere to go, had been dumped over the borders into the reluctant care of Germany's neighbors. The Zionist self-defense organization Haganah, and the refugee escape network Mossad, were trying to get as many as possible to Palestine, but the British—who controlled the region under the mandate given them after the World War—were vigorously trying to keep the refugees out. This the British did because they were worried about Arab loyalties in the event of another war, and many Arabs resented Jewish settlement of Palestine. The most virulent opponent of Jewish immigration was the Arab Mufti of Jerusalem, spiritual leader of the Palestinian Muslims, whose men had murdered scores of Jewish men, women, and children over the past year. The British had thrown him out of Palestine in 1937, but he was now in Damascus and continuing to orchestrate ever more violent terrorist operations against the settlers. The British seemed unable, or unwilling, to stop the violence. Rossi thought they might be allowing it to continue in order to frighten Jews out of coming to Palestine.

If they were, the maneuver wasn't working. Rossi was completing another shipload tonight. It would leave before dawn tomorrow.

The sun had dropped behind the skyline, and Rossi looked at his watch. Cohn was late, just a little. A freighter horn boomed downstream toward the Bosporus, echoing among the hills. When the sound faded Rossi heard the *tunk-tunk* of a single-cylinder boat engine from the upstream side of the bridge, and leaned expectantly over the balustrade. A few seconds later the bow of an open boat slid from under the bridge arch, to be followed by the rest of it, with Avi Cohn

in the stern holding the tiller. Cohn leaned over to shut off the fuel tap to the inboard engine, and expertly swung the bow toward the landing stage by the bridge. Rossi left the balustrade and hurried down the stairs to the lower level.

Cohn was already ashore and tying the boat up when Rossi reached the quay. Most of the vendors had packed up for the evening and gone off to their hovels; the dozen that were left were going through the sunset prayer, arms outstretched toward Mecca. Rossi and Cohn made themselves unobtrusive under the shadow of the bridge pier. "Everything all right?" Rossi asked. He spoke in fast, idiomatic Italian.

"That engine's not long for this world," said Cohn, in the same language. He had a Pisan accent. "It's why I'm late. We'll have to look for another boat. There's something else, too, more important. There's a warning out on Arab opposition. Remember that rumor? That the Mufti was sending discouragers out to interfere with the escape routes?"

"I remember."

"Apparently it's true. Bliewas says as far as he knows they're not moving yet, but he said for us to be careful."

"Fine," Rossi said. "We'll be careful."

"We're going to have to do something about the boat, Arabs or not," said Cohn. "Or the engine, at least."

"Tomorrow we can look for something," Rossi said. An unseasonably cold wind was blowing up the Golden Horn this evening; Rossi closed the collar of his battered leather jacket and brushed a lock of black hair away from his forehead. He was just under six feet tall, lanky and lean from hard living and erratic nourishment, with an oval face, olive skin, and a high-arched Roman nose. If his features had been only a little harsher it would have been a cruel face, but it was saved from this by the wide-set brown eyes under dark lashes. His hands, which he now thrust into his jacket to warm them, were broad and tough: peasant's hands, although he was not of peasant stock. He was a tenth-generation Italian Jew, or would have been had his parents not emigrated to New York a quarter century ago, when he was three.

He looked down at the boat bumping its rope fenders against the

stone of the landing stage. "Will the engine get us over to *Yildiz?"* He asked Cohn. The refugees were being put aboard at night to reduce the chance of British intelligence finding out that another load of would-be immigrants was on the way.

"I hope so," Cohn said. Unlike Rossi, he was a northern Italian Jew, whose ancestors had come over the Alps from the Austro-Hungarian Empire a couple of centuries before. There was Caucasian back in his genes somewhere; he was fairer than Rossi, with light brown hair and brown eyes. But he was just as thin as the other man, with the same look of rawhide about him. They had both been working with Mossad for three years, helping move the refugees through Turkey and Rumania and Yugoslavia; Rossi had been into Palestine twice, once to Jaffa and once to Netanya, the new settlement founded by the Bene Binyamin organization in 1928. *Yildiz* was going to Netanya, or as near as possible without running into the British.

"If it doesn't," Rossi said, meaning the engine, "we'll have to row. It won't be much of a load, there're only four of them."

"They were lucky the steamer was delayed," said Cohn. "It could be a couple of weeks before there's another charter ready. What time will you bring them down here?"

"Midnight." The four members of the Berger family were tucked away in a Mossad holding house near the Galata Market; they'd arrived late last night, exhausted, distraught, and half-starved, having come down the Vienna-Belgrade-Constantsa escape route all the way from Berlin. It had taken them a long time. The Rumanians, under British pressure, were making transient movement difficult again.

"Fine," Cohn said. "I'll be here. As soon as it's dark I'm going out to the freighter, but I'll be back before twelve."

"Midnight, then," Rossi said, and went back up the stairs to the main bridge level. The light was fading quickly. He walked along Karakoy Avenue past the lower terminus of the Tunel, the underground funicular railway that carried passengers to the heights above the eastern side of the Golden Horn. This side of the Horn was once the old Italian quarter of Galata, where traders from Genoa had settled under the protection of the Byzantine emperors in the twelfth century; later, under the Ottoman sultans, it became the general

European quarter of Istanbul. The Turkish Republic now called it Beyoglu, but everybody still referred to it by its old name. Rossi's quarters were part way up the hill near the Galata Tower, part of the old Genoese fortifications and now used as a fire-watch position. Galata had a history of burning down every so often.

He turned north along Voyoda Avenue and followed it to the flight of steps that ascended to the lower end of Kulesi Street, which wound steeply up the hill toward the Tower. An alley just south of the Church of Saints Peter and Paul led off to an old han, a two-story house built around a courtyard. The han was rented by Mossad through a Turkish intermediary; Rossi and two other men of the escape organization lived here while they were in Istanbul. The other two were away at the moment. Cohn wasn't one of them; he stayed over on the Stamboul side, near the railway station. The field men avoided forming large groups; they had to remain unobtrusive. For the same reason, the refugees didn't share quarters with them.

Rossi took the outside stairs to the second level and let himself into his room. There wasn't much in the way of furniture: a cot with blankets; a bureau with most of the paint peeling off, surmounted by a mirror tarnished gray-green; a wardrobe whose door was held closed by a twist of wire; and a wobbly wooden table with three chairs around it. One of the chairs was missing its back; a dozen books were piled on the table next to an oil lamp. In the corner stood a brazier for driving the chill off in cold weather. None of the men who stayed in the han, including Rossi, ever did any cooking; they ate what the street vendors offered, or sausage and bread in their rooms.

Rossi tossed his jacket onto the cot and sat down at the table, fishing among his books for the letter. He found it where he'd left it, slipped into an English copy of Procopius's *Secret History of the Empire*, which was lying underneath the 1896 edition of Grosvenor's *Constantinople*. Rossi was fascinated by the history of the ancient city. If and when he had a chance to resume his education, he intended to make himself a historian. He'd had to leave Brooklyn College after two years' study, when the Depression really hit and work was almost unavailable. In the meantime, he read.

He opened the letter and smoothed it out. It was from his mother; he'd read it four times since picking it up from the *poste restante*

yesterday morning. He hadn't set foot in America for nearly three years, and he was sometimes so homesick he felt ill. Being abroad hadn't affected him during the first two years, but now. . . .

He pushed the feeling away and began to read. Most of it was simply news about neighbors and friends up and down the street, and gossip from across the back fence. Who was getting married. Who wasn't married, but should be, who'd died, who'd been sick but was recovering. His father was still working, he'd found work just before the bank was going to take the house away, better than the Goldmans down the street who were turned out by the bailiffs last week. It was a Jewish neighborhood, mostly Central Europeans and Russians, but there were a few Italian families like his own. The Rossis had lived in an Italian neighborhood for a few years once, but the Italians had all been Catholics, unsurprisingly, and it had been difficult. Matters improved after Rossi's father moved them to Brooklyn, since Jewishness seemed to cement over the cracks between nationalities. That was even more true now, with the Nazis in power and going from strength to strength. Rossi's mother rarely mentioned European affairs in her letters; neither did his father, who wrote rather less often. They both had a vague idea of what he was doing at the far end of the Mediterranean, and kept any hint of their knowledge to themselves.

The last paragraph:

> You remember I told you that Tamara was engaged last September to Theo Berman, they were married on Monday just gone by   They are going to have a short honeymoon I don't know where the money came from but it's up in the Adirondacks somewhere. She was very happy. She told me the day before the wedding to send you her best   I think she's over it now, I hope so because   It will be bad for them if she still thinks about you   I guess she understands now why you did what you felt you had to but you must remember it was hard for her at the time so thats why she was so angry for so long. But your Father and I understand, dont ever forget that.

Rossi folded up the letter, replaced it in its envelope, and sat back in

the chair, his eyes fixed upon nothing. One more link broken, although he'd known for three years that it was really already severed. There'd been never a word exhanged between Tamara and himself since the night he'd told her he wasn't going to ask her to marry him, that he was going to Europe. Everybody'd been in an uproar over it, except his father, who somehow had seen it coming. He'd left a week later: then work in Rome, Trieste, Fiume, Vienna, Istanbul, Belgrade, Sofia, Bucharest, even Berlin, once. Three years.

The worst of it was that she'd been a very good woman. He hoped Theo Berman, who was nice enough in an ordinary way, realized his luck. But Rossi hadn't been in love with her; there was a space in him that she simply didn't *fit*. He hadn't been able to explain it then, even to himself, and he still couldn't. But he regretted the long silence. He and Tamara had once been the best of friends.

He put the letter back into the copy of Procopius, left the table, and stretched out on the cot. After setting the battered alarm clock, he closed his eyes and instantly fell asleep.

He was suddenly and completely awake five minutes before the alarm went off. It always happened that way; the clock in his head was just as reliable as the machine, which he set only out of habit and against the day his internal sense might fail him. He fumbled matches out of his pocket, lit one, and carefully guided the flame to the oil lamp on the table. After taking a few bites of bread and a gulp of thin Turkish wine from the small store he kept in the wardrobe, he moved the wardrobe half a meter away from the wall and opened the compartment under the floorboards. Inside were a 9mm Browning automatic pistol and several spare clips of ammunition, as well as a long slender knife in a leather sheath. Rossi replaced the boards, carefully brushing the dust and dirt back into the cracks to conceal the panel, and stuffed the Browning and two clips into his jacket; the sheath knife he snapped onto his belt at the small of his back. He extinguished the lamp and was ready to go.

The outside air was cold, much colder than it usually was at this time of year. Rossi made his way down Kulesi Street to Voyvoda, and headed for the Galata Market area to the northwest. The streets were

deserted. Everyone had gone to bed, even the beggars Rossi could occasionally hear snoring in the door alcoves.

After a few minutes' walk, he reached the east side of the market building and paused outside one of the line of vaulted stalls that ran around the exterior of the huge square building. There was something wrong, somewhere; he sensed that he was not the only walker in the night. He might have heard a sound, at the subliminal edge of hearing, somewhere behind him.

He faded into the shadows of the arch, loosening his jacket to reach the knife more easily, and waited, peering back up the street. Nothing happened; all he could hear was a barking dog somewhere, the faint, never-ceasing rumble of shipping moving about in the harbor, and waterfront voices calling far off.

Rossi readjusted his jacket and went on, keeping to the shadows. He was keyed up, as he always was when he was moving people, and prone to imagine things.

The refugees were being kept in a han south of the market building, only a block from the shoreline of the Golden Horn. Rossi entered the long, narrow courtyard from whose center a stairway led to the upper floor. At the top of the stair he passed along the gallery with its pointed arches, stopped at the third door, and tapped the code: shave and a haircut, two bits. No Turk or Arab would ever be likely to use it; it was too American.

The door opened quietly. Inside the room a lamp was burning, but turned very low. Eli stood back to allow him to enter. "Any difficulties?" he asked. Eli was a Jew whose family had lived in Istanbul for nearly five hundred years; he was twice Rossi's age, balding and tubby.

"No," Rossi said. He had decided not to mention his unease outside the market, especially since the Bergers were here in the room with Eli. The four family members all looked at Rossi, apprehension and hope mingling in their expressions: husband and wife in their early thirties, two girls about eleven and ten.

"Good evening," Rossi said in German. He'd picked up a lot of it in his three years of working the escape lines. "I'm here to take you to the ship. We'll be leaving immediately. Is there much to carry?"

"No," Berger said. He was thin and very dark, with bushy eye-

brows and a sallow face. "Most of it was taken from us on the way."

Rossi nodded. Traveling Jews had little defense against the petty extortions of border police and the bureaucrats who handed out transit visas. "That's not unusual," he said. "I can only promise you that things will be better from here on. You're from Berlin?"

"Yes. I'm Leopold Berger. Esther is my wife. This is Anna"—indicating the elder child—"and this is Rebecca."

The two children looked at Rossi without smiling, their eyes hollow and haunted. They were terribly thin. Rossi silently cursed the Nazis, the SD, and the British into eternal damnation. "I'm afraid I can't tell you who I am," he said. "I hope you understand."

Berger nodded. "Yes."

"Come, then."

They had four wretched bundles among them, three tied up in scraps of cloth and the last a disintegrating fiberboard suitcase. "We had decent luggage when we left," Berger explained, in an attempt to salvage some of the pride he had been forced to shed little by little over the past few weeks, "but the Rumanians at the border took them away to look for contraband, and we never saw them again."

"And most of our clothing," Esther said bitterly. She had a deep, voice, beautiful despite its overlay of exhaustion and tension.

"It's better to travel light," Rossi said comfortingly.

He took them down into the courtyard. "We have to travel fast and quietly," he said to them at the bottom of the stairway. "We have several blocks to go. Please don't talk unless it's absolutely necessary."

Berger nodded, just visible in the dark. Rossi led them out into the street and down to the avenue that ran along the shore of the Golden Horn. Ahead, the Galata bridge with its strands of lights stretched toward the Stamboul side. *Yildiz* was anchored on the far side of the bridge and Cohn, God willing, was waiting in the boat at the landing stage.

They reached the bridge and hurried through Karakoy Square, and then down the steps past the lower pedestrian level of the bridge to the landing stage. To Rossi's profound relief, the boat was there, bobbing in the chop rolling up the Golden Horn from the Bosporus.

"I brought life jackets from *Yildiz*," Cohn said in a low voice as he helped the Bergers into the boat. "It's getting choppy."

"Engine okay?" Rossi asked as he got aboard.

"So far. Get the life jackets on them while I start up."

Rossi did so while Cohn hauled at the flywheel. After several hard yanks the engine popped, snapped, and settled into its hollow *tunk-tunk*. Cohn swung the tiller to point the bow toward the far side of the Horn and *Yildiz*'s anchorage. The Bergers huddled amidships; Rossi went up into the forepeak to watch ahead for floating debris, which was a constant menace to small boats. As he went he thought he saw a light gleam from the shore astern of them, but when he looked again it was gone.

The boat thumped steadily through the black chop of the harbor. Reflections of the lights on the far shore glittered and fragmented on the surface, shook themselves apart and composed themselves again. *Yildiz*'s white masthead light drew very slowly closer; Cohn would be using it as a navigation mark.

They were halfway across. Rossi didn't relax, though. He felt unusually keyed up, as though part of him were expecting something abrupt to happen. He put his hand into his leather jacket, nervously touching the butt of the Browning to make sure it was still there.

There was something low and black on the water off the starboard bow, almost under the arches of the bridge. Distances were hard to judge at night; it might be a log close by, or something large farther off. Rossi couldn't tell. It vanished as he strained his eyes at it. Shadows on the water, nothing more? The boat thumped valiantly on.

He watched the surface ahead, squinting hard. There it was again, nearer this time and more clearly outlined against the lights of the Stamboul side. There was a white gleam at one end of it.

A bow wave. It was another boat, traveling fast.

For a split second Rossi thought it might be the Turkish harbor police, and just as quickly realized it couldn't be. They'd have their running and masthead lights on. This boat wasn't showing so much as a glimmer. He strained his hearing, but the engine of their own boat was too loud for him to hear anything else.

"Avi," he called. He took out the Browning and snapped off the safety catch. "There's somebody out there. *Speed up*."

He heard a muffled curse between the beats of the engine, and then the beats speeded up. Spray snapped over the bow as the craft plunged her forefoot into a wave, but she wouldn't go much faster than she already was.

Without warning, the other craft loomed out of the darkness, swinging onto a parallel course and closing. Rossi could hear the drum of her engine now; she was bigger than their own launch, and a lot more powerful. He couldn't see who was aboard, and there was only a suggestion of a dark hump near the stern, where the tiller would be. He tried to sight the Browning on the hump, but the pitch and roll of both boats kept throwing his aim off. He swore under his breath. He couldn't fire anyway, not until he knew who they were. "Leopold!" he hissed. "Get your family down into the bottom. *Quickly!*"

They went down, and just soon enough. The other craft turned suddenly and nosed in at them, only five meters away now, closing, closing, a meter away. Rossi fired at what he thought was the helmsman, saw the figure slump. Then the port bow of the other boat slammed into the gunwale of their own, almost knocking Rossi into the bilges, but he got his balance back just in time to see four shadows rise up from the enemy launch and grab for the gunwale of Rossi's craft.

Stand by to repel boarders, he thought irrelevantly as he fired again. This shot hit and its target fell backward into the opposing craft. He heard another bang, somebody shooting, maybe Cohn, and then one of the remaining attackers cannoned into him and slammed him back against the port gunwale before he could fire again. The man was almost on top of him and Rossi could smell fear-sweat and mutton grease and the sickly herbal odor of hashish. The *Hashshashin*, the Assassins. The Old Man of the Mountain back again, in the person of the Mufti of Jerusalem.

The man had Rossi's gun hand by the wrist. He was dreadfully strong; Rossi couldn't bring the muzzle to bear. He heard another shot from the stern of the boat, Cohn firing, and then he rolled sideways, reaching back for the knife, there it was, out of the sheath and sweeping up under the assassin's arm, bedding itself between the ribs. Gasp and shriek and the grip on his gun hand loosened.

Where are the others—

He twisted onto his back and saw the man just in time; he was kneeling on the forepeak thwart, the knife in his hand already in its downward plunge. Rossi twisted sideways, trying to free his gun arm from the weight of the first man, and the knife blade seemed to brush his shoulder as it missed him and slammed into the hull planking. The point stuck there and the man grunted as he twisted at the hilt to pull the blade free. Rossi shot him in the stomach, and then in the middle of the chest. As the assassin collapsed Rossi struggled to his knees, looking frantically aft to see what had happened to Cohn. The other Mossad agent was slamming his boot into the face of the last attacker who was half over the gunwale, the rest of him draped outboard into the water. The man gave a muffled yelp and slipped over the side. Cohn bent down, grabbed up the pistol he must have lost in the fight, and leaned out and fired once into the water. The other launch drifted beside their own, pilotless.

"Avi?"

"I'm all right," Cohn's voice came back, breathless.

"Leopold? Leopold?" called Rossi. There might have been stray shots he hadn't had a chance to hear.

Berger's voice: "I think . . . Esther? Anna? *Anna*? Thank God. Rebecca." Rossi heard sobs. "We're safe," Leopold said. His voice shook.

Rossi realized suddenly that their engine had stopped. "What's our condition, Avi?" He clambered over the thwart, leaving the two bodies behind him, and made his way to the stern. Cohn used a flashlight, shading its lens with his fingers as he examined the engine.

"Fuel line's buckled," he said after a few seconds' inspection. "The bastard fell on it before I threw him overboard. I can straighten it out. I think. Who were they?"

"The Mufti moved faster than we thought," Rossi said. "They were on hashish. Did you smell the hashish?" He was feeling sick and light-headed and trying not to show it. He'd never killed a man before. And he hadn't even hesitated about doing it.

Cohn grunted. "No. But it explains what was the matter with them. A good thing they were using the stuff. They were too ceremonial for their own good. Bringing knives to a gunfight, stupid. Maybe they thought we were peace-loving Jews and wouldn't be armed."

"Maybe." Rossi's left shoulder was stinging badly, where the knife had brushed him. "Give me the light. I think I got cut."

They inspected the shoulder. The leather had turned the blade somewhat, but the sleeve was gashed open and blood was oozing steadily from Rossi's upper arm.

"It's not deep," Rossi said. "There's not much blood." The nausea was passing, but he still felt peculiar, as though a large part of his character had suddenly been rearranged.

"You'd better clean it out with disinfectant," Cohn told him. "And well. There's no telling where that blade's been."

"As soon as I can. Avi, we'd better see if they were carrying documents." He turned to the frightened refugees. "Leopold. Don't worry. You'll be aboard the ship soon."

The two men Rossi had killed were wearing nondescript clothing, trousers, shirts, jackets. There was nothing in the pockets of the man Rossi searched. Cohn found something, though. He turned the flashlight on it and whistled. "Marc. Look at this."

Rossi looked. It was a photograph. Of him, walking along Voyvoda Avenue. It was slightly blurred, as though it had been taken from a slowly moving car, but the features were more than clear enough.

"Shit," Rossi said. "I've been under surveillance. Damn. *Damn.* They must have seen us together at the bridge yesterday, and waited for us to make a run. We were a perfect target."

"Not perfect enough," Cohn said. He looked over the gunwale. "What should we do with the other launch?"

Rossi considered. "Stuff all the bodies under the thwarts and sink it. The longer they don't know what's happened, the better."

"Good. Let me try the fuel line."

Cohn cursed over the bent copper tubing for three or four minutes while Rossi used one of the oars to paddle the boat over to the attackers' launch. It was hard work, because of the wind and the choppy water. There were two bodies in the craft, the helmsman and one of the boarding party. The Mossad men checked the launch over quickly. A small sack of hashish and a Thompson submachine gun lay in the bilges. Rossi shook his head. If they'd used the gun, instead of following their knife tradition—

He shrugged; it didn't matter now. "Will the engine run?" he asked Cohn.

"It should. Let me get the hatchet."

They put the other two bodies into the launch and Cohn got their own engine started while Rossi chopped a hole in the launch bilges. Then they stood off a few meters and watched it sink. Nothing came up. There was a body drifting somewhere, the man Cohn had shot in the water, but he might not be found for a while.

"You're going to have to leave Istanbul," Cohn said as the boat thumped toward *Yildiz* once again. "You're marked."

"I know." Rossi shivered. His shoulder was burning. He hated to leave because it felt as though he were running away; but if he stayed he might lead the Mufti's Arabs to other targets. Even, God forbid, to innocent refugees.

"We'll put the Bergers aboard and go on to my side of the Horn," Cohn was saying. "The Mufti's people may know about the Galata safe house. There are people to warn, and we'll have to make arrangements to get you out."

"What about you? They might have seen you with me yesterday."

"There was no picture of me, though. And the bastards who had yours are all dead, I hope. I'll take my chances for a while."

"All right."

An hour later, Rossi was in the relative security of Cohn's quarters, over the south flank of the Second Hill not far from the Mosque of Mehmet Pasha. Cohn had a telephone, which he used while Rossi stripped out of his jacket and shirt and cleaned the knife wound. It wasn't very deep, and had almost stopped bleeding. He bathed it with dilute iodine and held still while Cohn bound it up. "I'm going out for a while," Cohn said. "Get some sleep. You may need it."

Rossi threw himself onto Cohn's bed and drifted off quickly; the last thing he remembered was regret at leaving his books and his family's letters behind in the safe house. When he awoke again, gray

dawn light was filtering in through the narrow latticed window, and Cohn was standing over him.

"It's all fixed," Cohn said. "You're taking the Orient Express as far as Trieste. It leaves in an hour. Donati will meet you at the station and move you along to Rome. He needs somebody there, they're short-handed."

"Documents?" Rossi asked. He touched the money and document belt he always wore under his trousers; his American passport was in it, as well as his Turkish visas and various permits for other countries. Not all of them were real.

"Your own, the usual method. American going to Rome for business purposes. It'll give you three months there, and Donati can grease the right palms as long as we need you in Italy. We'll have somebody on the train to watch your back as far as Trieste, in case the Mufti's people decided to take another whack at you. I brought you a bag from Eli's. Take some of my clothes and my razor. We're about the same size."

"Good," said Rossi. "Thanks." He levered himself up from the bed. The cut felt both numb and hot at the same time. "I guess we'd better get out of here."

Berlin

May 29-30, 1938

The driver of the Horch staff car had rolled his window down—he'd asked Starke's permission to do so when they left the Lichterfelde SS barracks—and warm night air swept into the rear seat where Starke sat alone and puzzled. He'd been cooling his heels at the barracks for the past six weeks, waiting, as Heydrich had instructed, for further orders. He was not quite under open arrest, not quite.

He'd managed to return to Berlin, with von Lynchen in a box and beginning to get a little whiffy, within thirty-six hours of leaving Vinaroz and an angry Colonel Teichmann. Teichmann had wanted his armored car back, and Starke wouldn't give it to him. They'd almost come to blows before Davila had intervened, with his Moroccans, on Starke's side. The Spaniard, after several months of helping Starke look for von Lynchen, was sick of both of them and wanted both Germans, the quick and the dead, off his hands. So Starke had got the armored car. The recollection made him grin to himself in the darkness in the rear seat of the Horch.

Heydrich had been annoyed at his failure to bring von Lynchen back alive, but no more than annoyed. The people who *were* more than annoyed were Hitler and the SS-Reichsfuehrer Heinrich Himmler, who was Heydrich's superior. They'd been looking forward to a wonderful public spectacle of treason and retribution, to the further discomfiture of the Regular Army, which was Hitler's objective, and to the further glorification of the SS, which was Himmler's.

"We'll have to keep you out of sight for a while, Starke," Heydrich had said in his office in the Prinz-Albrecht-Strasse SD headquarters. "I didn't think there was much chance of your getting von Lynchen alive, given the circumstances and the resources you had to work with. But I can't tell Himmler that. So there'll have to be some form of perceived punishment, until I can smooth some ruffled feathers." The long beaky face of the SD chief exhibited a faint smile; Himmler had once been a raiser of chickens.

"As for the Fuehrer," Heydrich had continued, "he's got other things on his mind at the moment, since the *Anschluss* with Austria back in March. Anyway, von Lynchen's dead, which is the main thing. The other matters were just icing on the cake, as far as I'm concerned. I'm sending you out to the Lichterfelde barracks for a while. Stay there. Don't communicate with anybody. Wait until I summon you. There are other things that need to be done, and I'm not going to lose one of my most resourceful men over an appropriately dead traitor."

And that had been that, as far as Starke was aware. He hadn't been reduced in rank, or clapped into the cells for dereliction of duty, so Heydrich must have gotten round both Hitler and Himmler somehow. Another agent might have been severely punished. For Starke, there were great advantages in reporting directly to the SD chief; Heydrich protected him from the vagaries of politics, and field security was a lot tighter.

The Horch was turning into a side street. Starke wasn't exactly sure where he was; down in the Charlottenburg district somewhere, he thought. He didn't know this part of Berlin well. He had been born on June 10, 1910, in the north German port city of Kiel, where his father was an engineer in the dockyards that built the great battleships and battlecruisers of the Kaiser's High Seas Fleet, the fleet that had battled England for mastery of the seas.

And which had lost that battle, as so much else was lost in 1918, including his father's job. In 1922 the unemployed elder Starke moved his family to Hamburg and found work as a common laborer there in the dockyards. The family, which had once been solidly middle-class, was now poor, and became poorer still in the great in-

flation of 1923; Starke's younger brother Karl died of malnutrition-related pneumonia during that bitter time.

Matters improved somewhat after 1924, and Starke's father found engineering work with a shipping construction firm, Geppert de Hamburg. By 1929 he had gotten the family back on its feet. Then came the market crash and the onset of the world economic depression, and Starke's father lost his job yet again. In despair, he shot himself.

Starke managed to finish his education, but had great difficulty finding enough work to support himself and his mother. In 1932 he joined the Nazi Party, and shortly after Hitler took power in January 1933, he was accepted into the SS. After two years' service, he was noticed by Heydrich and invited to join the SS security service, the SD. Heydrich quickly recognized in the younger man a ruthlessness that equaled his own, as well as great resourcefulness and intelligence; by early 1936 the SD chief was using him as a precision instrument to remove threats to the new Reich.

Starke jerked himself out of his reverie and peered into the gloom of the summer night beyond the window glass; the Horch was slowing to a stop. A few meters back from the street, set behind a high iron railing, was a large, nondescript house with heavily curtained bay windows on either side of a massive oak door.

"Here?" Starke asked. He had no idea what the place was, nor why Heydrich would want to meet him away from the Prinz-Albrecht-Strasse headquarters.

"Yes, Herr Sturmbahnfuehrer," the driver said, not turning his head to look at Starke. "You are expected. Just use the bell-pull on the right of the door."

Starke got out of the car, straightening the knot of his tie against the collar of his dress shirt. He'd lost weight in Spain and the brown suit was a little too big for him. He wondered for a moment when he'd put on the SS black and silver again; nearly two years had passed since he'd been in full uniform. In Spain he'd worn mufti, or Wehrmacht sergeant's kit.

There was an iron gate in the railing. He touched it and it swung open silently on well-oiled hinges. Carefully shutting it behind him,

Starke mounted the steps to the front door. As he gave the bell-pull a yank, he heard the Horch move quietly away from the curb into the night.

After a moment the door swung open, just as silently as the gate. Behind was a dim foyer, closed off from the rest of the house by a set of double doors with stained glass panes in their upper halves. Silhouetted against the colored light from within was a large, male figure.

"Yes?"

He'd been given another name to use. "Herr Dorf," Starke said.

"Go in, Herr Dorf." The man opened the door, and gestured. Starke left him behind in the foyer, and the stained glass doors closed quietly.

He found himself in a large, high-ceilinged room with luxurious though worn furnishings: there was a fireplace on one wall, with a big gilt-framed mirror above it. To Starke's right, a wide curving stairway led upward into dimness; straight ahead of him, another door led to the interior of the house. The lights in the room were shaded by cranberry-glass globes, casting a rosy pink light over the Kashan carpets and the crushed velvet upholstery of the sofas and overstuffed armchairs. The air smelled of old cigar smoke, perfume, and good cognac. One item conspicuous by its absence was a picture of the Fuehrer; there were other pictures on the walls, but Hitler's wasn't among them.

What the hell is this? Starke thought. Did Heydrich move?

He moved farther into the room and took a closer look at one of the pictures. It was oriental, beautifully detailed, and very explicit: a naked man in the embrace of two naked women. Next to it was a similar one, except that the male-female proportions were reversed. He glanced around. The other framed prints dealt with the same subject matter.

Ah, Starke thought. So that's where I am.

He'd heard rumors that the SD had taken over Chez Kitty, a brothel favored by the elite of Berlin, and also by their foreign guests. This must be the place, and the women would be on the SD payroll. They'd be ordered to report any useful pillow talk they might hear from their

clients. The rooms would have microphones, and perhaps provision for cameras. There didn't seem to be anyone here at the moment, though; the house was utterly silent.

The silence was broken by the sound of the interior door opening, and Starke turned quickly to face it. A woman of about fifty came into the room. She was still beautiful, although she'd taken pains to hide the aging of her complexion with powder. "Herr Dorf?" she asked.

Starke nodded. "Yes."

"I am Madame Kitty. I have a message for you."

Starke nodded. "Go ahead." He tensed, waiting; it was an odd way to transmit orders, but he wouldn't be surprised at anything Heydrich did. The man had a severely skewed sense of humor.

"I am to say," she began, furrowing her brow as though giving a memory recitation in primary school, "that after your long fast you must be very hungry. No man should have to work on an empty stomach. In this case, pleasure must come before business. Feel free to indulge."

Starke laughed, causing an expression of surprise to flit across the madam's face. "It's funny?" she asked worriedly.

"No," Starke said. "It's characteristic. Never mind. I presume the table is, or will be, set?" He felt the stir in his groin. Heydrich was right; it *had* been a long time. Starke had the ability to close off that section of himself for long periods and not be bothered by it, but when he wasn't working, his urges were as strong as any man's, if not stronger.

Relief showed on Madame Kitty's face. "Yes, of course, Herr Dorf. I've selected one of my best girls for you. She's upstairs, third door on the right. It's at the back of the house, so any noise. . . ." she gestured knowingly.

"Only *one*?" he asked. "I've been away for a long time."

She smiled delightedly, as though impressed. Starke didn't believe for an instant that she was. Women who worked in brothels were singularly immune to male boasting.

"What *is* Herr Dorf's pleasure, in that case?" she asked. She'd be reimbursed from the SD coffers for any extra services; no wonder she looked so delighted.

"I'd like two *Berliner*, to start with," Starke smiled, punning on the

idiomatic word *Berliner*, which referred to a jam-filled pastry. He reflected as he spoke that this wasn't actually unlike making an order in a confectioner's shop, with someone else paying the bill. He'd frequented brothels before, when his need was extreme, but never one of this class. Heydrich was good to his subordinates.

"Perfect!" Madame Kitty exclaimed, clapping her hands. "I have exactly what you need. Two wonderful girls from here in Berlin, very professional. Just go on upstairs, as I said, and your order will be brought immediately."

Starke nodded and climbed the long stairs to the second floor. The hall was long and dim, with lights burning low in brass wall sconces. There really was no one else here, as far as he could tell, unless the walls and doors were unusually soundproof. Perhaps they were.

He stopped at the door next to his and quietly tried the knob. It turned easily. He took a look inside; the bed was empty. Starke nodded to himself and let himself into his own room. Like the downstairs, it was lit by a rosy glow and furnished with comfortable ottomans, small tables, and a pair of armchairs. Through an open door on his left he could see the outlines of a white bathtub.

"Good evening," said the woman lying on the bed. She sat up as Starke entered. A long silk robe fell from her shoulders. It was strategically slit, offering glimpses of dark silk stockings and a garter belt, a lace brassiere.

"Hello," Starke said. "Who are you?"

"Sofia. And you are Herr Dorf."

"Yes."

Sofia smiled at him, displaying perfect teeth behind dark red, rosebud lips. She was perhaps twenty-five, which was older than he'd expected, with dark chestnut hair cut neatly around the ears and the back of the neck, and an oval face and perfectly clear skin: the type to turn heads on the Ku-damm, there was no doubt about that. Starke crossed to the bed and sat down on it next to her. The bed was canopied. He looked up and saw a huge mirror built into the underside of the canopy. When he looked back, Sofia was smiling at him. "Everything you might want, my love," she said.

"I'm not your love," Starke said bluntly. "We're both here on business. You're aware of it, I'm aware of it. Let's not confuse matters."

She blinked at him, but retained the smile. Top-class whores were very adaptable, a quality he admired, just as he admired their ability to wear the variety of masks their profession demanded. He was a specialist in masks and deceit himself, although for much different and higher purposes, and to some degree he empathized with such women.

"I'm sorry," she said. "I'm not really completely polished at this. It's more of an avocation, rather than a vocation."

"What do you mean?" Her accent was more educated than he'd thought at first.

She leaned forward to place her forehead on his shoulder. "It's a little embarrassing," she said. "You see, I do this because I like to. My husband is much older than I, and my appetites are . . . large. I have a taste for variety, shall we say. So I spend a few evenings a month here."

It was a ploy he hadn't run across before, but it was well calculated to awaken male interest. Starke observed, with clinical detachment, the evidences of his body as it became aroused. After a moment he decided to go along with the game, although he didn't believe for an instant that she was anything other than a full-time employee of Chez Kitty. "Does your husband know of this?" he asked.

"Of course not. But he is away on business frequently, and I tell him I stay with a friend. My friend keeps my secrets. She has a lover of her own." Sofia raised her forehead from his shoulder. "It's nothing very profound. I merely have a taste for men. So, despite what you said, it *is* a little more than business for me." She studied him in the dim light. "You are very good-looking."

Starke shrugged. She was an extremely accomplished actress; she ought to be on the stage. "You must have to put up with, shall we say, unattractive clients from time to time," he said.

"I like men," she told him earnestly. "The maleness is what's important to me, not the wrappings. Although because of who I am, I have the right of refusal. Sometimes I exercise it." She gestured at a wine cooler sitting on the bureau next to the bed. "Would you like champagne?"

"Later," he said.

"You're certainly in no hurry."

"Someone's joining us."

"Oh? I wasn't told about that."

"I made the arrangements after I arrived."

She looked interested. "A man?"

"No. A woman. One of your colleagues."

She laughed. "I see. You've been without for some time, then."

"Yes, for some time. I was—" *God in heaven*, he thought as he bit the words off. I nearly said I was in Spain. How could I make such a mistake?

He looked at her with new respect. He hadn't even realized she was slipping inside his guard. She ought to be working for Heydrich, if she was consistently this good.

"—not much in the company of women," he finished as smoothly as he could.

She was looking curiously at him, as though she didn't understand. But before she could say any more, the bedroom door opened and the other *Berliner* entered.

"Lock the door," Starke said.

"I already have," she said, holding up the key. "Good evening, Herr Dorf. I'm Gudrun."

She was twenty, perhaps, blond, a sleek Aryan specimen if ever there was one. She looked like one of the Teutonic warrior maids in the bad paintings a lot of Nazi Party members liked to hang on their walls, and was wearing a white robe that set off her Junoesque proportions. "Champagne?" Starke asked.

"Please," Gudrun said. She curled up in the middle of the bed while Starke opened the bottle of Dom Perignon. It was the real thing, of course; Madame Kitty's wouldn't try to fob off some carbonated vinegar on the kind of clientele that passed through its doors. He noted that Gudrun and Sofia had exchanged only a murmured greeting; like the good professionals they were, they would take their lead from the client.

They drank the champagne in relative silence. Starke lay on his stomach on the bed between the two women, propped on his elbows, contemplating first one, then the other. It was going to be a challenge to tell when he'd actually *reached* either one of them; tarts might wriggle and gasp in feigned passion, but rarely (in Starke's

experience) were they really involved physically. Most pretended involvement only to make the man climax as fast as possible, to get it over with. On the other hand, women at this level might be more outgoing. He'd have to find out. He was determined to make both of them respond, whether they wanted to at first or not. The male and strong dominated the feminine and weak: that was the correct way of man and nature, and women who consumed men's vital energies without submitting to being satiated themselves were, as far as Starke was concerned, in some fundamental way perverted.

He finished the last glass of champagne and rolled over to face Gudrun, propping himself on his right elbow. He felt Sofia move softly behind him, and then the press of her breasts against his shoulder blades as her arms went around him and her mouth pressed against the back of his neck. He reached out and undid the tie of Gudrun's robe.

Somewhere a bell tolled two in the morning. Starke lay naked under the coverlet, looking up at the mirror in the canopy of the bed. In its reflection he could see, dimly, his own face and on either side of it those of the two women; one bright head, one dark. They were both asleep.

He permitted himself a small grin of satisfaction. As far as he could tell, he'd achieved what he'd set out to do with the women, as well as satiating himself completely. He'd kept at Gudrun until he was quite certain he had broken through, and that she was no longer in control of her reactions. Then, to her surprise and distress, he had withdrawn himself without completing the act, and turned to Sofia. She had given a good simulation of delight, but the simulation had turned to reality in short order. The enforced celibacy of Spain had helped; he'd had enough of everything for both Sofia and Gudrun.

They won't dry out for a couple of days, he told himself, enjoying the crudity of the thought. Sofia really was remarkable. Her whore's reserve had hardly seemed to be there at all, even when he first entered her: another example of her expertise.

I really must speak to Heydrich about her, he thought. She could be extremely useful in certain areas.

He heard a tap at the door. Sofia raised her head, and then slid from under the covers to pad across the carpet, drawing on her robe as she went. Starke returned his gaze to the reflections above him. Gudrun was opening her eyes.

He heard a whispered conversation at the door, and then Sofia came back. "Herr Dorf," she said, "I apologize, but it is necessary for you to see someone. In half an hour. I will draw a bath for you."

Starke nodded; in a few seconds he heard water running into a tub. He got out of bed and followed Sofia into the bathroom; he didn't bother to put on any clothes.

Steam was rising from the water as it poured into the white enamel tub. Sofia had dropped her robe and Starke could see the smooth ripple of the muscles in her back as she leaned over to test the water temperature with the back of her hand. He felt a stirring in his groin; even in its satiated state, his body responded to hers.

"I will bathe you, if you wish," she said, rising.

"No," Starke said. He preferred privacy in his bath. "You and Gudrun may leave."

"Yes, Herr Dorf," she said obediently. But perhaps sensing his renewed interest, she made no move to go.

I could probably take her right now, Starke thought. Here on the bathroom floor. But Heydrich, I think, is coming. Not a good idea. "Sometime again, perhaps," he said. "Thank you."

She nodded and left. Starke closed the door and lowered himself into the steaming water.

When he came back out into the bedroom to dress, both women were gone, the bed was made, and someone had brought a fresh ice bucket with more champagne. And two clean glasses. Starke sat down in an armchair and lit a cigarette, which he had smoked almost to the end by the time the hall door opened. The man who entered the room was in civilian clothes, but there could be no mistaking that face. It was vulpine, the pale bony features under the blond hair, the ice-blue eyes and the hatchet-blade of a nose that made the chin, despite its natural prominence, appear to recede: the face of SS Lieutenant

General Reinhard Tristan Eugen Heydrich, chief of the SS *Sicherheitsdienst* and confidant of Heinrich Himmler himself.

"Well, Starke," Heydrich said, closing the door and crossing the room to inspect the ice bucket, "have you been treated well?"

"Yes, Herr Obergruppenfuehrer Heydrich," Starke said. He was already out of his seat and standing to attention. "Very well indeed."

Heydrich waved a hand and began working at the wire securing the champagne cork. "Dispense with military formalities. Sit down." He popped the cork expertly and poured. "You still haven't stopped smoking?"

"No, sir."

"It's bad for you, you really should try." Heydrich passed Starke a glass and sat down in the other armchair. "Well, Erich. Have you released all those necessary animal spirits?"

"Yes, sir. Thank you."

"I thought that after Spain and then six weeks of enforced idleness, you deserved a release. For your health, if for no other reason. And this place is secure, which is the other reason I chose to meet you in it." Heydrich frowned slightly. "I'm actually quite disappointed in the results it's brought. Men don't drop secrets on the pillow in quite the way they're rumored to do. Not with whores, anyway."

"They're likely more forthcoming with mistresses," Starke ventured. He thought about mentioning Sofia's talents, but decided it would wait.

"Yes. That's true." Heydrich sighed. "Maybe we should get rid of the place. It's a financial drain . . . but it might be useful one day, one never knows. However, to business."

Starke nodded, and sipped the champagne. There was a slight ache behind his eyes, the aftermath of the earlier bottle. His body was tired, but his mind was not.

"You're out of the soup with Himmler and the Fuehrer, by the way," Heydrich said. "I can't get you a decoration, however. I hope that's not a disappointment, although I imagine you can understand why."

Starke nodded again. Bits of shaped metal weren't particularly important to him; he knew what he'd done even if few other people did.

"Good," said Heydrich. He glanced at his watch. "I have a new assignment for you. Erich, it is the most important and difficult task you'll ever have undertaken for the Reich. It is going to require a great deal of preparation, and it is extremely dangerous. So much so that I am going to give you the right to refuse, before I tell you even part of it. And only part, I'm afraid. You'll only be told what to do after you're in position. Do you wish to refuse?"

"Of course not," Starke said. It surprised him that Heydrich should have even considered that possibility.

"Even," Heydrich said carefully, "if the preparation causes you some considerable humiliation?"

"Even then, sir."

"Very well. Don't say I didn't warn you. I have it on good authority—" Heydrich smiled microscopically—"that you are circumcised."

Starke felt his eyebrows rise involuntarily. "Yes, sir. But it was an anatomical problem when I was a child, not—"

"I wasn't accusing you of Jewish taint," Heydrich interrupted, holding up a hand. "It's a convenience, no more." He stopped, studying the younger man. The silence continued for some seconds.

"I do, however," Heydrich said at last, "want you to *appear* to be a Jew."

"Oh," Starke managed. "I see. That is, that is what you mean by humiliation."

"Are you still agreed?" The blue eyes had become glittery.

"Of course, Herr Obergruppenfuehrer." There'd be no overt punishment if he said no, Starke realized, but he'd spend the rest of his SS career behind a desk, as a major. "I'm quite willing."

"Good," said Heydrich. "I see I didn't misjudge you." He took a slip of paper out of his pocket and handed it to Starke. "Report to this address at noon tomorrow, after you've had some sleep. You have a long training period ahead of you. Civilian clothes, and bring only what you stand up in. No kit. Understood?"

"Yes, sir."

Heydrich stood up. So did Starke. "Good," Heydrich said. "The car that brought you will be at the door in a couple of minutes; it'll return you to Lichterfelde. The security on this is several grades

above top secret. For the time being you will report only to me. Understood?"

"Yes, sir." Heydrich was already at the door. "With your permission, Herr Obergruppenfuehrer—" Starke began.

Heydrich turned. "Yes?"

"One of the women here tonight may be useful. Her name is Sofia."

"Go on," Heydrich said, hand on doorknob.

"She is extremely talented physically, and a consummate actress. She pretended to me that she was married, and that she made her services available here to meet her sexual needs. It was so skillfully done that she had me almost believing it. A skill of that order—"

He stopped. Heydrich was grinning at him.

"Starke," he said, "for once your perceptiveness has let you down. Every word she told you was the truth. She is doing exactly what she said she was. Don't worry about it. I am aware of the lady's tastes. Good night, or rather good morning."

The door closed behind him. Starke stood nonplussed for a moment, and then put his head back and laughed.

Rome

August 22, 1938

The courtyard was already warm, although the morning sunlight had as yet reached only halfway down its western wall; the table where Rossi sat was near the east side of the court, and still in deep shadow. When Rossi looked up from the orange he was peeling he could see, just above the courtyard's north wall, the tree-clad crest of the Pincian hill with its great park. Rome was already awake, but here in the courtyard of Donati's house the hum of traffic was distant and muted.

He finished peeling the orange and sectioned it. A pip jumped away under his fingers and struck his coffee cup with a faint *tink*, almost inaudible in the twittering of sparrows in the eaves above. Two of the sparrows were sitting on top of the wall, watching him; Rossi took a few crumbs of bread from his breakfast plate and tossed them in the birds' direction. The sparrows fluttered down to the courtyard flagstones and began to tussle over the fragments.

He ate a section of the orange and returned his attention to the newspaper. It was Telesio Interlandi's *Difesa della razza*, which had begun to appear at the beginning of the month, and which was virulently anti-Semitic. It clearly had the tacit approval of Mussolini's Fascist government, which was another sign of the direction the government was taking. Rossi perused the Fascist papers as a matter of course, reading between the lines to sense how far the Fascists were prepared to go. It appeared that they were prepared to go a long way. Back in July, the inoffensively named Central Demography Office

had been transformed into the more sinister Office of Demography and Race, and only this month the office had ordered a census of all Jews in Italy, foreign and native. The government had also announced that no Jews would be allowed to study or teach in the public schools, and that no new Jewish students would be admitted to the universities.

Currying favor with Berlin and the Nazis, Rossi thought. How could Italians put up with it, or with the imperial posturings of Benito Mussolini? He was afraid it was going to get worse long before it got better. There were rumors of even more stringent controls on Jews to be imposed in the autumn.

The sparrows suddenly fluttered up from the pavement and disappeared over the wall. Rossi turned to look at the door leading into the house, expecting Donati to join him for coffee. Instead, framed in the doorway, was a young woman he'd never seen before. An expression of apologetic confusion was spreading over her face.

"I'm sorry," she said in American-accented Italian. "I didn't know someone was out here—"

"You're not intruding," Rossi said. He'd felt like company a few minutes ago, but now, perversely, he wanted to be left alone with the orange and the newspapers. "Come and sit down," he added, reluctantly.

She approached the table with some hesitation. She was extremely tall for a woman, only a couple of centimeters shorter than Rossi. She was also extremely thin, certainly too thin for her height, and angular into the bargain; she seemed to be all arms and elbows. A long cream dress hung from her shoulders as though it were on a hanger; on her feet were low-heeled summer sandals.

That's to disguise her height, Rossi thought as she jackknifed, not gracefully, into the chair opposite him. Her hair was cut quite short, into a smooth dark helmet framing a face that was almost as thin as the rest of her. She had a wide mouth, though, with just a dash of lipstick, and fine brown eyes, all of which gave her a sort of exhausted allure. Rossi judged by the delicate lines at the corners of her eyes that she was at least as old as he.

Donati shouldn't have let her into the courtyard without warning him. Rossi wasn't exactly underground, but he didn't want his

presence in Rome widely known. "Coffee?" he asked, indicating the pot. "I think it's still warm. I can find you a cup."

"No, thank you," she said. "Mr. Donati said we will be leaving in just a few minutes." The Italian was far from idiomatic, but fluent. "I'm Julia Belmont."

"You're from the United States?" Rossi said. He didn't switch to English.

"Yes. Newark, New Jersey, to be precise. It's a city near New York." She obviously thought he was Italian. "And you're Mr.—" she added tentatively.

He didn't answer. What now? he thought. I suppose I'll have to be rude.

He was saved the decision by Donati's appearance in the doorway. "Oh, hello, Marc, I didn't realize you were out here. This is Julia Belmont. She's from America—"

"Claudio?" Rossi said, a question in his voice.

"It's all right," said Donati. "Miss Belmont is from the United Jewish Conference in New York. She's here with some information that might help us move the Church authorities in a favorable direction."

"Oh," Rossi said. "I see." He was annoyed with Donati, and with the Belmont woman, for having made him feel like a boor. Nearly three months of enforced idleness were grating on his nerves.

Although, he reflected for a moment, he was probably lucky to be alive. That was mostly Donati's doing. By the time Rossi reached Trieste, the knife wound the Arab had given him out on the Golden Horn had turned dangerously septic. There must have been something on the blade. Donati got him to Rome in fairly short order, but by that time Rossi was nearly out of his head with pain and fever. He'd seemed to improve after a few days under the care of Donati and his long-suffering housekeeper Teresa, but then blood poisoning had set in. His body was already weakened by three years of bad nourishment, little rest, and nervous tension, and the doctor Donati used was afraid Rossi was going to lose his arm. That didn't quite happen, but Rossi didn't throw off the infection completely until late June, and by that time his arm had suffered some temporary tissue damage. Donati wouldn't send him out again with a bad arm—there was always some danger of violence—and he'd spent the weeks until

now helping Donati deal with paperwork and organizational matters, while his flesh restored itself. He was back to normal now, though, and was going to Trieste tomorrow to start field work again.

"Marc is working with the refugees," Donati was explaining to Julia. "Like us, he's Jewish."

She looked at Rossi. "Oh. But you're Italian as well. I see."

"My last name's Rossi," he said. "I actually grew up in Brooklyn. My parents came to the States when I was three." He was going to apologize for his earlier reserve, but then decided not to.

"Brooklyn. Oh, then you speak English. Why didn't you. . . ." Her voice trailed off.

"Marc prefers not to come to the attention of the authorities," Donati said. "He didn't know who you were. I'm sorry, Miss Belmont, I should have brought you out here myself." His face reflected deep concern at this inexplicable social gaffe. It was an expressive face, topped by thinning black hair; below the wide forehead was a pair of brown basset-hound eyes separated by a good solid Roman nose, and below that, a full mouth. He was a bit jowly, being around fifty-five, and portly in a way suitable to a successful Roman lawyer. He also had a puckish sense of humor, which had helped pull Rossi through some bad spots over the last couple of months. Rossi liked him a great deal.

"That's all right," Julia said.

"Your Italian's good," Rossi said. "Where did you learn it?"

"From my parents. The name was actually Belmonte, but they shortened it when they came to the States. We were a Genoan family."

The house door opened again and Teresa the housekeeper put her head out. "Telephone, *padrone*."

"Excuse me," said Donati. "I'll be back in just a minute." He disappeared into the house after her.

The silence stretched after he left. Julia was plainly ill at ease in Rossi's presence. "Have you been to Rome before?" he asked, to make up for his earlier brusqueness.

"No. I've never even been out of the States. I arrived three days ago. Just staying in a hotel."

"Can I ask what brings you here?"

She looked embarrassed. "I really ought to check with Mr. Donati first."

"Okay," he said in English, and smiled at her. She regarded him seriously; she didn't return the smile.

Donati came back out of the house and stalked angrily across the flagstones to throw himself into the chair next to Rossi's. "Not today," he said bitterly. "That was Pacelli's secretary. Our appointment's been postponed."

"What?" Julia's dark eyes widened in disappointment and a flash of anger. "But he told you—"

"Cardinal Pacelli's not going to be available for another four days," Donati said wearily. "We're now scheduled to see him Friday morning."

"But why can't he see us today? He said he would."

"The secretary wouldn't tell me. The Vatican never tells anyone anything, Miss Belmont, unless it wants to. I'm afraid matters don't work here quite the same way they do in the United States."

"Obviously," she said sharply. Rossi was somewhat surprised; there seemed to be more to her than gawkiness, and what he'd taken to be diffidence.

"What's the matter?" Rossi asked. He hadn't realized that Donati had been trying to see Pacelli, the Vatican's Cardinal Secretary of State and the most powerful Church official after Pope Pius XI himself. Claudio moved in more exalted circles than Rossi had known.

Donati turned to face Rossi, the basset-hound eyes more weary than ever. "We've been trying to get a private audience with the Pope," he said, the *we* referring, as Rossi knew, to the Italian Jewish Conference. Donati was chairman of the Conference, which was his public persona. Behind that, and secretly, he was also head of the Mossad division that coordinated the movement of Jewish refugees through Italian territory to Palestine.

"Pius *must* speak out against what's been happening in Germany for the past five years," Donati was saying, "and against what's beginning to happen here. What he did last year wasn't enough. It made the Nazis take notice at the time, but now they're up to their old tricks again."

Donati was talking about the Papal encyclical *With Burning Sorrow*, which Pius XI had had smuggled into Germany in March 1937, and which had been read from all Catholic pulpits there on Palm Sunday. It was a powerfully worded assault on the Hitler regime—attacking its neopaganism, its oppression of the Church in Germany, its education of the young, its pseudo-myth of blood and soil—and on Hitler himself, referring to him as a "mad prophet possessed of repulsive arrogance." But there had been no mention of the persecution being inflicted on the Jews of Germany; the encyclical was principally directed at the defense of German Catholicism. It had infuriated the Nazis, and had forced them to back away somewhat from their attacks on the German Catholic Church. But it hadn't led them to moderate their treatment of German Jews.

"What do you expect him to do?" Rossi asked.

"Another encyclical, if possible, but this time directed against racial persecution. I've been working for months to get Pacelli to agree to let us put our case to the Pope. Cardinal Mondolfo got in the way as much as he could, but I've been able to bypass him, finally."

"Who's Cardinal Mondolfo?" Julia asked.

"He's Secretary for Extraordinary Ecclesiastical Affairs," Donati told her. "Very powerful, although he's a rank below Pacelli. Giuseppe Mondolfo doesn't like Jews."

"Oh."

"Anyway," Donati went on, "the delay may have been a good thing in the long run. The evidence about what's happening in Germany is building up. Miss Belmont has brought some of it with her. If anything helps persuade Pius to act, that will."

Rossi turned questioning eyes on Julia. "Photographs and depositions," she told him succinctly. "A man who managed to emigrate to the States a few months ago was collecting everything he could about the concentration camps. He turned it over to us. There's no word for what's been going on there. Except, perhaps, inhuman." She was quite a different person when dealing with matters of business; the shyness he had first noticed in her was well hidden.

"In the meantime. . . ." Donati frowned. "Miss Belmont, would you consider moving in here? Staying in a hotel makes no sense, when

I have extra room. I hope I don't insult you by making the offer. My housekeeper lives in, so. . . ."

She nodded seriously. "I'm not worried about my reputation suffering, if that's what you mean. I'll have my things brought over here tomorrow morning, if you're sure you don't mind."

"Not at all. Since we are going to be under the same roof, perhaps we could dispense with some formality. Would you be offended if I asked you to call me Claudio?"

"Of course not. And I'd be happy to be Julia."

Rossi watched this with detached amusement. Donati was as courtly as an Italian could be, but his charm was meant to charm, not to seduce. His wife had died four years ago, and during the past three months Rossi had never seen him in the company of a woman other than Teresa, who was at least seventy.

Donati stood up. "I must go over to the office and continue to pursue Pacelli." A mischievous light appeared in his eyes. "Marc, why don't you take Julia out to see a little of Rome? You need to get away from the desk for a while, I think."

Rossi didn't know what to say for a moment. He glimpsed Julia out of the corner of his eye. She had turned slightly pink.

"Perhaps she'd rather not?" he said. It came out hopeful.

"Nonsense," said Donati. "Later in the day it will be too hot. Now is the perfect time. Julia, go on with Marc. He will take you wherever you wish to go."

Damn Claudio, Rossi thought a few minutes later, as he and Julia climbed into Donati's Fiat. What's he think he's doing, turning me into a tour guide for this woman?

Donati had insisted they take the car, despite the perpetual shortage of gasoline. Julia was folding herself awkwardly into the tiny passenger seat; she'd hardly spoken since Donati shooed them out of the house. She was carrying a white sun hat with a large floppy brim, which she arranged on her lap.

Rossi started the engine. "What would you like to see?" he asked. "There's an awful lot of it. Museums? The Vatican?"

"I'd like to go to the Forum," she said. "If it's not too far away."

"It's not a long way," Rossi said, and slipped the Fiat into gear. He drove along Via Margutta, where Donati's house was, and then jogged and jogged again to bring them out onto the Via Babuino. The traffic was mostly trams and buses, with occasional army trucks loaded with glum-looking soldiers. Military service wasn't a favorite career among male Italian youth. Rossi thought even Mussolini wouldn't be berserk enough to get into a European war, given the state of the Italian armed forces. They'd had a bad enough time in the invasion of Abyssinia in 1935, although they'd finally managed to win.

"Is that the Spanish Steps?" Julia asked suddenly.

"Oh. Yes. That's the Steps," Rossi said as they passed them. He was concentrating on maneuvering around a tramcar.

"Look," she said, "you don't have to take me anywhere at all if you don't want to. You could drop me back at my hotel. I'll just tell Claudio I wasn't feeling well."

"I'm sorry," he said. "It's fine, really. I've just got a lot on my mind." You idiot, he thought, what's the matter with you? A bright morning in Rome, nothing special to do, and the company of a moderately attractive woman. Stop being so grumpy.

With an effort he dismissed his irritability and began pointing out sights to her as they passed along the streets. At length they reached the foot of the Victor Emmanuel monument, where Rossi found a parking place. They got out of the car. Above them, the monument's white Botticini marble glared blindingly under the sun.

"It looks like somebody's idea of a wedding cake," she said, gazing at it from under the brim of her hat. "What a lot of *things*. Sacconi really let himself go on this one. It's awful, but I bet he had a wonderful time putting it together."

Rossi glanced at her. "You know architecture?"

"Bits and pieces," she said.

"Where from?"

"I studied art history at Brandeis."

"Oh," Rossi said. He felt a jab of envy. Her family had money, then. He'd suspected it from the clothes. "Up this way," he said. "It's a bit of a hike."

They walked round past the left side of the monument and skirted

the flank of the Capitoline Hill, coming out at the Piazzo Senatorio and the western end of the ancient Forum of Rome. Stretching away from them in the blaze of the morning sun were fallen stones and column drums, broken lintels and fragments of pavement, walls of Roman brick stripped of their marble facings. Just ahead rose the last three standing columns of the Temple of Vespasian, and beyond those the hulking mass of the Arch of Septimius Severus, the ruins of the Temple of Saturn, the Arch of Titus, columns, walls, fallen pediments, platforms, stairs leading nowhere like those in a Piranesi drawing, all jumbled together in an indescribable archaeological anarchy.

"My God," she said. "It's wonderful. Can we look?"

"Sure." Despite himself, Rossi was beginning to enjoy the morning. He'd poked around the Forum alone several times before, feeling a sense of wonder and thinking about the men who had piled stone on stone and brick on brick to build it, and about the men who had later put it to the torch. It was still fascinating, regardless of the hours he'd already spent here.

They trudged down into the wilderness of ruins. Julia found it confusing; the cyclic destruction and reconstruction of centuries had jammed monuments built hundreds of years apart into, around, and above each other. On the floor of the Basilica Emilia were green stains left by copper coins melted into the marble pavement when Rome fell to Alaric the Visigoth in 410 A.D.; not far away stood the Temple of Romulus, whose bronze doors, made a hundred years before Alaric was born, were still in place on their hinges.

Rossi stopped her near the eastern end of the Forum. "See that?" he asked.

It was the Arch of Titus. She nodded, frowning, trying to remember her history.

"Emperor Domitian built it," Rossi said. "To commemorate his father's victory in the Judean wars. Titus's soldiers sacked Jerusalem and destroyed the Temple."

"The Diaspora," she said quietly. "It began then."

They went to stand under the arch itself. The great curved mass of masonry loomed over them, brutal, pitiless, the insupportable weight of Imperial power suspended above their heads.

"See there?" Rossi pointed. "On the right side? The spoils of

Jerusalem that Titus brought back here to Rome. The altar from the Temple, and the Temple *menorah*."

She regarded it in silence for a few moments. Then she said, "Titus is gone, and so's his empire. But we're still here."

It was a thought that had occurred to him as well. She was muttering something. "What?" he asked.

"*Ozymandias*," she said. " 'Look on my works, ye mighty, and despair.' "

He finished it for her.

> Nothing beside remains. Round the decay
> Of that colossal wreck, boundless and bare,
> The lone and level sands stretch far away.

They looked at each other, embarrassed. "Too melodramatic," Rossi said. "Rome does that to people."

"It seems to. Could we go back now?"

They puttered along in the direction of the Piazzo Senatorio. Rossi was surprised at how long they'd been in the Forum; nearly two hours had passed and the sun was near zenith. The heat reflected from the stones around them and brought perspiration to their foreheads. Julia's hair had turned into damp points above her eyebrows, despite the shade of the sun hat.

When they reached the car he said, "Would you like to go back to your hotel? I can take you there." He felt he ought to take her to lunch, but he didn't want to. He still felt foolish and adolescent, quoting Shelley at her under the ruined Arch of Titus, even if she'd started it. She probably thought he'd been trying to impress her. The idea brought his grumpiness back.

"Thank you," she said. If she was disappointed at his dismissal of her, she didn't show it. "I think I'd like to lie down for a while."

"Good idea."

"I'm staying at the Raphael."

Rossi started driving back. There was road work on the Corso Venezia and the inevitable traffic jam, so he went around into the side streets to the west.

"Claudio said you helped refugees escape," she said as the Fiat bobbed along.

He didn't want to tell her very much. "Yes. There are several lines."

"Where do they go?"

"Often to Palestine. The British don't like it. What about you? Why did they send you here to help Donati with the Pope?"

"Instead of sending a man, you mean?"

"I didn't mean it that way." Lord, she was prickly. Maybe she used it to cover up her shyness.

"Okay," she said. "I've been working with the American Jewish Conference ever since I graduated from Brandeis. I guess I've got a knack for getting things done. And for persuasion. The Conference committee in New York wanted this very unofficial, very low-key. You know how you get more results, sometimes, if you work behind the scenes."

"I know," Rossi said.

"Also, I speak Italian, and it was I who gathered most of the information we want to give to the Pope. There were two of us up for the mission, me and a man. They probably would have sent him although I'd done the work, but he decided to get married, and so they had to settle for me."

"Oh. You're not married?" He didn't think she was; she wasn't wearing any rings.

"No."

"Never?"

"No." The prickly edge was back in her voice.

"I'm not prying," Rossi apologized. The sooner I've got her back at her hotel the better, he thought. We really rub each other the wrong way, somehow.

"What's going *on* up there?" she exclaimed suddenly.

He'd seen it too. A knot of men had gathered in the narrow street ahead. Arms waved violently about. Rossi heard shouting and slowed the Fiat down; the men were blocking most of the pavement. He saw a black shirt, then another.

"Damn," he said. "*Fascisti.*"

"What are they *doing?*"

She was answered by the crackle of breaking glass. One of the blackshirts had thrown a rock through the window of one of the small shops lining the street. Rossi could see the three balls above the entrance; it was a pawnshop. "*Pogrom.* They're after a Jew." He could see now that there were five of the blackshirts, and one civilian, a woman about Julia's age. Another stone flew to crash through the glass of the shop door, and two of the blackshirts started kicking at it. The woman began trying to shove the thugs away from the entrance. The men cuffed her aside as they continued their battering. She slumped against the wall, stunned.

"We've got to help," Julia cried.

"What?" Rossi had stopped the Fiat a dozen meters from the pawnshop, trying to work out what to do. They were five to his one, the police might show up at any moment, and if they checked his papers carefully he might be deported. And he had to be in Trieste. But the men had smashed the door's window glass in, and one of them was reaching inside to turn the handle. "The police—" he said.

"Damn the police," she snapped, and was out the car door before he could stop her, racing along the cobbles toward the pawnshop. He swore, reached under the seat for the tire iron Donati kept there, and followed. Faces turned toward them as he ran after her. One of the blackshirts had already been inside and was dragging the pawnshop's proprietor out onto the pavement. Blood sheeted from a gash in his forehead. He was at least seventy. The woman—it might have been his daughter—was still lying against the wall, weeping.

Julia was only a few meters from the thugs now, shouting at them. Rossi couldn't believe what he was hearing.

"Stop! I'm an American citizen! You can't do this! Stop!"

She's crazy, Rossi thought as he slowed down to stand beside her where she'd stopped a little way from the blackshirts. These people don't care who she is. Doesn't she have any idea what she's up against?

Two blackshirts were holding the old man by the upper arms. The other three slowly formed into a line facing Rossi and Julia. The one in

the center of the line seemed to be in charge; he was heavy and muscular, his head shaven bald like Mussolini's. His black shirt gaped open over his belly, straining at the buttons. "Keep your fucking noses out of this," he said. "Are you Yid-lovers, or what?"

Don't let her say it, Rossi thought desperately. Give her some sense. He took a better grip on the tire iron, wishing for a knife. They'd have knives.

"I'm an American," she hissed at him. "*And* Jewish. You'll be in trouble with the American authorities if you don't get out of here."

Rossi realized suddenly that she was horribly afraid under her fury, and that she was depending on him to back her up. She'd assumed he'd be as enraged as she was, and as ready to intervene. He cursed her naivete.

"Jewish, she says," said the man on the leader's right. "Good looking, for a Jew. Not too greasy." He wet his lips.

"Don't get too eager, Luigi," said one of the two holding the pawnshop owner. "You never know where a Jewish cunt's been." He laughed, hauled his fist back, and punched the old man in the stomach. The man doubled over and began to vomit on the pavement, causing the blackshirts to curse and let go of him.

"You *bastards*," Julia screamed at them. Their faces stiffened at the insult and two of them stepped forward. The word was far more offensive to an Italian than to an Anglo-Saxon, and Julia should have known it; or perhaps she did. Did she really expect to face them down with sheer nerve, and an American passport?

Rossi knew it wouldn't work, not now; their honor wouldn't let them accept such a taunt from a woman. He lunged forward, swinging the tire iron, and slammed the heavy bar into the leader's testicles. The man yelped and went down. Rossi took one step back and swung again, this time to his left, smashing Luigi across the hand that was already reaching inside his shirt. Luigi screamed and bent over, clasping his broken hand between his knees.

He was after a knife, Rossi thought. We're going to be lucky to get out of this one. He pivoted and jabbed the end of the tire iron into the midriff of the man on the leader's other side and heard the breath

leave him in an explosive gasp. A siren whooped somewhere away down the street; somebody'd called the police. That was almost as bad as the blackshirts.

He'd put three of them down, but the other two had been out of his reach, and the first three wouldn't take long to recover. The two left standing had their knives out and were advancing on him. He moved away, the iron ready, keeping his back to the wall. "Get back to the car," he said to Julia in English, keeping his voice low and even. "Lock the doors."

"No. I'm not moving. The police are coming."

"I don't *want* the goddamned police. We have to get out of here. *Go and get in the car.*"

The two blackshirts had heard the siren as well, and were looking doubtful. Maybe it would slow them down. Julia had apparently listened to the urgency in his voice, and was running toward the Fiat. Rossi remembered that in his hurry to follow her he'd left the keys in the ignition. Maybe she'd have sense enough to use them.

The leader was back on his feet, although his face was still contorted with pain. In his hand was a long knife with a wicked serrated tip, like a fish-knife. "Don't touch him," he snarled to the others. "I want him." He advanced steadily on Rossi, bent low in the fighting crouch of the Roman street thug. Rossi began backing steadily away, keeping out from the wall to give himself room to swing the iron. The man's honor had done him a favor; if they'd all gone after him at once he'd be as good as dead.

He heard the Fiat's door slam and then the grind of the engine starting. What was she going to do now? He didn't really believe she'd leave him in the lurch, but she might panic and decide to go look for the police.

The sirens were closer. The blackshirt leader feinted at Rossi. Rossi dodged, almost getting the man's wrist with the iron.

He heard the Fiat's motor just over his left shoulder, and then the end of its hood popped into his peripheral vision. She'd moved the car within his reach. The other four blackshirts started hurrying forward to do something about it.

Rossi flung the tire iron in the leader's face, simultaneously wrenching the Fiat's door open with his left hand. As he threw himself

into the car he glimpsed the iron slam into the man's nose, and a bright spurt of blood. Julia was already accelerating, straight at the other blackshirts, who were screaming curses at her as they dodged. She actually seemed to be trying to run them down. One of them grabbed at Rossi's door handle as the car passed, but he'd already locked the door. In seconds, the Fiat was away from them, past the pawnshop and down the street. Rossi looked through the rear window. A police car was visible a block behind. Four of the blackshirts had already disappeared, and Rossi glimpsed the fifth vanishing into an alley.

"Turn left, there, quick," he told her. "We have to get out of sight." He slumped into the seat, flooded first with relief, and then with fury. "First of all, thanks. But for God's sake, *don't* do something like that again. Don't you know what could have happened?"

She stiffened, involuntarily swerving the Fiat as she turned at the intersection. The wheels bumped the curb. "They were attacking that old man, and the woman. Were you just going to *turn around*?"

"I don't know. There's more going on here than you know about. It could be awkward for other people, if I got into trouble with the police here."

"That's disgusting. How could you even consider it? Not helping, I mean."

"Look, Miss Belmont," he said, biting back the anger, "this is not nice safe Newark, where you can whistle up a cop and he's on your side. Most of the police are Fascists, too. *We* might have been the ones arrested, and the old man into the bargain. Your American citizenship doesn't protect you or anybody else over here. You can't wave your passport in a blackshirt's face and think he'll run away with his tail between his legs. He won't. That's just stupid arrogance."

Her cheeks flushed with anger. "So we just run away? I thought you were—" She stopped.

"You thought I was what?"

"It doesn't matter."

"It does damn well matter. If we hadn't been lucky back there, do you know what would have happened?"

"They would have just beaten us up. But at least we'd have been defending our own people."

"Have you ever seen somebody who's been *just* beaten up?" he snarled. "It's not a few cosmetic bruises like your movies back home. It's broken bones and blood and vomit and internal bleeding. Nerve damage, a limp you'll have the rest of your life. This is not a place where the cavalry comes over the hill at the last minute. What would have happened, if we hadn't gotten away, was I'd have had a knife in me, and you. . . ." He stopped.

"What?"

"You insulted their manhood. They don't like women standing up to them. They would have raped you after dealing with me. All of them. They *might* have let you live. You might not have thanked them."

"It didn't happen," she snapped at him. "I deal with what is, not with what might be."

"My God," he said, "you're pigheaded."

She wrenched the wheel over and slammed on the brakes. Rossi almost flew into the windshield. "What the devil are you doing?" he yelled at her.

"You drive," she said, opening her door. "I don't know the city. I don't want any dents in Claudio's car. It might upset you."

He took a deep breath. "Okay. Let's stop fighting. We're supposed to be on the same side. Just *please* don't take any risks like that again. You won't be much use to Claudio from a hospital bed."

"If you say so," she said, looking at him with cold disdain. "Very well. No more fighting. Please take me to my hotel."

I hope, he thought as he changed places with her and put the Fiat into gear, that by the time I get back from Trieste she's left. Preferably for Newark, where she can't cause any more trouble. The woman's a menace.

They didn't do any sightseeing on the way to the hotel.

The Reich

August 22, 1938

The trucks came in the very early morning. Samuel Levy knew this because he heard the Johanniskirche bell striking three just as he was dropping off to sleep after making a trip to the bathroom, and the bell's last stroke was dying away as the sound of heavy engines rumbled in through the open bedroom window.

He sat up to listen. Beside him, sleeping lightly as she always did, his wife Rose stirred and muttered. There was no doubt about it; at least one large vehicle was pulling into the tiny square in the center of Altgarten's equally tiny Jewish ghetto.

He got out of bed and went to look out the narrow window that overlooked the square. Below him, lit by a wan moon and the streetlights, a car and two big trucks were already drawing to a halt on the cobbles, and two more trucks were following them. Their bulk almost filled the small open space tucked away among the old houses. Men were already jumping over the tailgate of the lead truck; they were uniformed and armed.

Oh, God, Levy thought. They've come. Why? What's happened? What have we done?

He ran over to the bed and shook Rose's shoulder. "Wake up, love. Wake *up!*"

She wriggled reluctantly until the fear in his voice penetrated. Then she sat up so quickly her head almost rammed into Levy's chin. "What's the matter? *Fire?*" She had a dread of fire.

"No. Nazis. They've brought trucks."

"Dear God." She struggled clumsily from under the bedclothes. Her five months' pregnancy was already making her movements awkward. "Samuel, what are we going to do?"

"Dress. Quickly. They'll probably come into the houses. Don't light the lamps."

He ran back to the window to look out again. The uniformed men were already in motion, striding toward the houses around the square. Levy frantically began to drag his clothes on. As he slipped his feet into his shoes, he heard a thunderous battering from the shop downstairs. Someone was pounding, with what could only be a rifle butt, on the door.

"Open up in there! *Raus! Raus!*"

Levy left Rose doing up her skirt and ran, shoes unlaced, down the stairs to the shop and its smells of spiced sausage and smoked beef and fish. The pounding on the door was heavier, as though it would burst the old wood from its hinges.

"I'm coming, I'm coming," Levy shouted as he fumbled with the bolts. The hammering stopped and he timidly opened the door. Two uniformed men stood outside. One was holding a rifle, the other a sheet of paper on a clipboard. SS, Levy realized, with a lurch of fear. Altgarten was too small to see much of them, but he recognized the uniforms. Out in the square behind them, Levy could see a black SS staff car.

"Get some lights on in here," snapped the man with the clipboard. He was obviously an officer. He stepped forward over the threshold, followed by the rifle-wielding soldier.

Levy ran to snap on the single light over the cutting bench, and turned to face the two Germans in the dim yellow light. The officer was wrinkling his nose. "Stinks in here, doesn't it?" he said to the soldier. "You can always tell a Yid meat store by the stench. Kosher, isn't that what you call it?" He prodded Levy in the stomach with the corner of the clipboard. Levy nodded, his throat constricted with fear.

"Christ knows what they put in the sausage," said the officer. "Dog and cat, likely." He turned businesslike and consulted the clipboard. "This is the Levy household?"

Levy nodded.

"*Speak* when you're spoken to. Have you put your own tongue into that sausage you sell?"

"Yes, sir. No, sir."

"That's better. Residents here are Samuel Levy, wife Rose, elder Levy, Aaron?"

"Yes, sir." Levy wondered whether his father had woken up yet, in his room at the back of the house. He was only sixty, but his hearing was poor.

"Good. You have fifteen minutes to gather belongings for a three-day journey. Bring only what you can carry yourself, the trucks aren't for your convenience. In fifteen minutes I want everyone in this house assembled in the square for an announcement. Get going."

He turned on his heel and stalked out of the shop, followed by the soldier. Levy remained still for a moment, hardly able to stay on his feet. His body didn't feel as though it belonged to him. They were taking him and his family away, away from Altgarten and the shop his grandfather had started. Three generations of stability erased by a typewritten list.

He made his knees work again and stumbled up the stairs as fast as he could go. On the landing, he almost ran into his father. Aaron must have heard something, despite his poor hearing.

"What's happening? Why are you downstairs with the light on?"

"Nazis, Father. We have to go. They've brought trucks."

"What? Why? Where are they taking us?"

"Father, I don't know. But we have to get ready. They've only given us a quarter hour."

"They can't do this."

"*Please*, father," Levy said desperately. "They have guns. You've heard what's happened in other places. Rose and the baby. If the Nazis were rough—"

That reached Aaron. He had been awaiting the arrival of his only grandchild with almost as much anticipation as Rose. "Yes. What are we to do?"

"Bring things for a three-day journey, only what we can carry."

"Nazi pigs," his father hissed, but turned and headed for his room.

Levy went to his own bedroom, where he found that Rose had

turned the light on and was picking aimlessly through a bureau drawer. Tears were streaming down her face.

"Rose—"

"I heard," she said. "I was listening on the stairs. Samuel, what have we done to deserve this?"

"I don't know. We have to go. We can't take much."

"I don't know what to bring. I can't think. How can they treat us so? We're *Germans*."

"We're Jews," he said flatly. "Think of what we took with us when we went to Baden after we were married. Choose that. I'll find the valises."

The sixty-four Jews of Altgarten were three minutes late assembling in the square. The officer Levy had encountered paced impatiently up and down in front of the lead truck, watching the deportees form into a ragged semicircle around him, their bundles and suitcases lying forlorn on the cobblestones at their feet. Levy watched how the lamplight gleamed on the polished black leather of the officer's jackboots and picked out the SS lightning-bolt insignia on his tunic collar. The high peak of his cap made him appear even taller than he was; he dwarfed all but a few of the men in the small crowd before him. Among the few tall Altgarteners were Levy and his father. They were standing with Rose at the back of the group; Levy sensed the watchful presence of the SS troopers behind him.

"Shut up, all of you!" the officer shouted, to silence the frightened murmurs of the men and women in front of him. A child was crying and would not be stilled. The officer scowled in the direction of the sound and it was abruptly cut off by a parent's hand. In the silence, the SS man climbed easily onto the bumper of the truck and looked over the small congregation of Altgarten's last and only Jews.

"You do not need to be frightened," he said, pitching his voice to carry. The accent and tone were educated. "I have good news for you, and better for the Reich, for that matter. You have all been approved for exit permits. From here you will be taken to a temporary camp, where you will remain until your passports and other documents

have been issued and arrangements have been made to receive you in Italy. From Italy, you will be allowed to emigrate to Palestine."

A low murmur broke from the crowd. The child wailed again.

"Be *silent*! I have not yet finished. In order to facilitate matters on your arrival in Palestine, an advance party of four men will be sent on ahead. These men will leave tonight. Passports will be arranged for these four in Vienna, tomorrow. I will now call their names. As each name is called, the person will come forward and stand by the front of this truck."

The officer consulted his clipboard, squinting at it in the poor illumination from the streetlights. "Jakob Waldstein!"

Waldstein stumbled forward.

"Theodor Schechtman!"

Please don't let me be one of them, Levy prayed. I have to stay with my father and Rose and my unborn child.

"Moritz Blau!"

"Samuel Levy!"

The others were moving toward the truck. Levy couldn't make himself budge.

"Samuel Levy! Where is Samuel Levy? Answer *now*!"

Levy raised his hand. "Sir, please substitute someone else, please. My wife is expecting a child—"

Something hard and heavy slammed into the small of his back. He yelped and almost fell to his knees, hearing Rose scream as he went down. But before his knees touched the ground a hand grabbed him by the collar and propelled him irresistibly forward toward the others waiting by the cab of the truck. The officer turned to watch. "Thank you," he said sardonically. "There are *no* substitutions. Someone in back. Bring him his luggage."

Rose crept forward with his valise. Her face was white and terrified. "Don't worry," he whispered as he took it from her. "I'll be waiting for you in Palestine. Our child will grow up free. I love you."

She nodded, unable to speak, and crept away again.

"Everyone else, into the trucks. You four. Identity check, then in as well. You're going straight to the railway station."

The officer verified who they were from their identity papers. Levy looked over at the staff car and saw his reflection in the driver's

window. Then he realized it wasn't a reflection; in the poor light, the face of the man behind the wheel resembled Levy's to a surprising degree, except that it was the face of a half-starved Levy.

He didn't have time to be curious about it; the soldiers were pushing him and the others toward the truck's tailgate. Levy hauled himself into the cargo space, wincing from the pain in his back where the rifle butt had struck him. Four SS men climbed in and sat on the benches at the rear, leaving the Jews on the floor. The truck's engine ground into life, and the big vehicle lurched into motion.

"Why is it so sudden?" Jakob Waldstein asked Levy. Waldstein was a tailor, a couple of years younger than Levy. He wasn't married. "We—"

"No talking, there!" snapped one of the SS men. "Keep your mouths shut. You can talk when you get to the Promised Land."

The four men on the floor of the truck rode in silence as the vehicle drove out of Altgarten and took the Regensburg road. Every kilometer that passed under the wheels added to Levy's agony of loss, even though the loss was supposed to be temporary. He was only a kosher butcher, who had wanted nothing more than to stay in Altgarten for the rest of his life, be with Rose, and raise children. He wasn't a Zionist. He had no desire to make the return to Palestine; it wasn't a return for him. His ancestors had been in Europe for nearly two thousand years. Dust and heat were alien to him. The only thing he knew about Arabs was that they rode camels and hated Jews. But then, everybody seemed to hate Jews.

What kind of animals would they have in Palestine? Would it be easy or hard to make the arrangements to be a kosher butcher? He'd heard that a lot of Jews who went there ended up farming, and he didn't know anything about farming. Rose and the baby might starve because he was so ignorant. Even though it was dark he put his forehead on his knees to hide the tears that leaked from under his eyelids. He didn't want the Nazis to see his weakness.

The truck grumbled through the night for almost an hour, and then they were passing through the outer part of Regensburg. The SS men, who had seemed asleep, stirred themselves and took up a more watchful attitude. The truck drove through the empty streets for a little while, and then stopped. Levy could hear the chuff and rumble

of switching locomotives; they must be near the railway yards.

They all waited in silence, the Jews and the SS men, for about half an hour. Then the officer appeared at the tailgate; he must have ridden ahead of the truck in the staff car.

"All right. Out."

They got up stiffly and climbed out of the truck, the soldiers first. Dawn was still a good ninety minutes away, and the Regensburg railway station was no more than a dim bulk above them, its doors and windows dully lit.

"I will escort you inside," said the officer to the four Altgarten Jews. "Your tickets are prepared. You're catching the Berlin-Vienna express at track two. In Vienna you'll be met and taken to the Trieste train. Don't deviate from the route, or try to come back. If you do, not only you but your relatives will be dealt with severely. Understand? Good. Come with me."

They obediently followed him into the echoing railway station and out to the platform. The train was already there; to judge by the people getting off, it had just pulled in from Berlin. The officer chivvied them into the rearmost car, and into an empty compartment.

"Stay here until you reach Vienna," he said, after giving them their tickets and documents. "There will be routine police checks on the way. Don't try to leave the train, or it will be known." He slammed the compartment door on Levy and the other three, and left. A couple of minutes later, Levy saw him outside under the platform lights, on his way back into the station. They were finally alone. But they weren't, really. If they tried to disobey their instructions, the vast police apparatus of the Nazi Reich would know about it in hours if not minutes, and hunt them down. What would happen then was a subject for their imaginations.

"Palestine," said Moritz Blau wonderingly. "We're going to Palestine."

"That's what they *say*," mumbled Schechtman. "If you can trust a Nazi."

The train shuddered and began to move out of the station. Blau, Schechtman, and Waldstein carried on a half-hearted conversation for a few kilometers. Levy didn't join in. He felt sick, lonely, and

exhausted. Then they all fell silent, watching their dim reflections in the window glass beyond which a few lights gleamed in the pre-dawn darkness.

They'd been traveling for perhaps thirty minutes when the train slowed down suddenly. Levy peered into the night. They seemed to be on the edge of a small town. The train slowed to walking speed, then to a crawl. It was pulling into a deserted station. On the platform were three men in raincoats, although there wasn't a sign of rain.

The train stopped and Levy and the others heard the clunk of doors opening and closing. Footsteps sounded in the corridor outside their compartment, and then the compartment door slid open. The three men Levy had seen on the platform were standing in the corridor.

"Contraband check," said one of them in a flat voice. "Open your bags."

"But we just were put on the train by the SS," Waldstein said plaintively. "We haven't any contraband."

"We're emigrants," put in Blau.

"I'll tell you who you are," said the policeman. "You're Yids, so shut up. Put your bags on the seats and open them. Then give me your papers." *Gestapo*, Levy thought.

He took his valise down from the luggage rack as the others hurried to imitate him. When the bags were open they stood quite still, stiff and obedient. The Gestapo man finished looking through their identification and travel documents.

"Levy, that's yours?" he asked, gesturing at the battered valise.

"Yes."

"Each of you point out your own luggage."

They complied.

"Get out into the corridor."

They won't find anything, Levy thought. It's just a waste of time. Why didn't the SS tell them about us?

He heard mutters from the compartment, and then:

"Look at this, Captain. The little Yid shits. Three out of the four of them."

The Gestapo captain came back out into the corridor. "Blau, Waldstein, Schechtman, you assholes, you didn't show me your currency export permits. Where are they?"

The three Jews looked at him, stunned. "What?" Blau asked. "I haven't any currency."

"Well. I see. What about you two?"

Schechtman and Waldstein shook their heads dumbly.

"Fine," said the Gestapo leader. "Off the train. You're under arrest for currency violation."

"But we weren't taking any money—"

"Shut up. Come here. What do you think that is?"

He shoved a roll of Reichsmarks under Blau's nose. "Sewn into the lining of your suitcase. How stupid do you think we are? Suitcase lining, for God's sake. You've probably got diamonds up your asshole. Same for you other two. Eight thousand marks among the lot of you. Get your bags and get out." He turned to Levy. "You kept your nose clean, did you? You're lucky."

The two policemen inside the compartment threw the luggage out into the corridor. Tears were running down Blau's face. "It's not true, it's not true," he stammered. "You put it there."

The Gestapo captain backhanded him across the mouth, knocking Blau's head against the corridor window. Blau stood with his face averted, eyes closed, his lips quivering. "Defamation of a Reich officer in the performance of his duty," the captain said. "That's good for another year. Anybody else have anything to say? No? Good, get on with you."

The policemen hustled the three Altgarten Jews away down the corridor toward the far end of the coach. Levy stumbled back into the compartment. Could it have been true? Were the others trying to get money out of the country? He couldn't believe that; everyone knew how dangerous that was. But why had the Gestapo let *him* go on? He couldn't understand it, unless there *had* been contraband. Maybe there had been. Maybe the others were desperate enough to take the chance.

The train had begun to move again. Outside the window Levy could see a line of pinkish gray on the horizon off to the east. The sun was coming up.

He hunched miserably in the seat while the train rumbled slowly onward. He was horribly thirsty, but neither he nor Rose had thought to put a bottle of water in the luggage. There'd be water for the

passengers somewhere on the train, but he didn't dare leave the compartment.

The train slowed down again. Now what? They didn't seem to be near any habitation; as far as Levy could tell in the near-darkness outside, the tracks were passing through a stretch of fields and broken woodland. He felt the train jolt to a halt. Perhaps a door opened and closed somewhere, but he couldn't be sure. He put his head against the back of the seat and closed his eyes.

He opened them in surprise and fright to see the compartment door sliding open again. Standing in the doorway were two men, but not the Gestapo officers. Without a blink they walked into the compartment, grabbed him under the armpits, and dragged him into the corridor. He tried to cry out, but as he opened his mouth a fist smashed into his midriff and drove the words out of him. The men slammed him up against the corridor wall and before he knew it they'd dragged a hood over his head. A hand dug into his pockets, searching, looking for and finding his documents. Then they were dragging again; he heard the *clunk* of a door opening, and felt a rush of cool morning air on his face. Suddenly he was *in* the air, falling, it seemed a very long time to fall, but then he smashed into the cinders of the track bed with a blow that drove the breath out of his body. The door clunked again, closing, and he heard the rolling squeak and clatter of the train beginning to move once more.

He was stunned and only half-conscious of being bundled into a vehicle, and of the sway of it as it began to move. Minutes passed. The air inside the hood grew stifling. He couldn't get his breath back.

"What are you doing with me?" he managed, at last.

"Be quiet. We're taking you back where you came from."

Back to the others? No. Not this way. They were going to kill him, of that he was sure. But he didn't know why. It was desperately important for him to understand why, otherwise his life didn't make any sense.

"Please tell me."

"Shut up."

"*Please.*" For an answer he got a blow across the mouth. He slumped, hopeless. There was no meaning in anything.

The car stopped and he heard doors opening. They dragged him out.

"Take the hood off him," somebody said. "We might need it again." A snicker.

The hood was yanked from his head. Levy stared wildly around. The men had taken him to what looked like a construction site in the middle of a forest. It was deserted. Stacks of lumber and bricks and concrete-mixing equipment stood around in the pale luminosity of very early dawn.

"Over there."

Levy walked ahead of them. Before him was a deep, narrow trench lined with boards: a form for pouring concrete. The bottom was sand. He stood at the edge of it. A hard cold circle touched him behind the ear.

"Pleasant journey," said a voice.

They put his body into the deepest part of the trench, and covered it with half a meter of sand. The concrete was to be poured this morning; the Jew would never be found. He'd eventually have lots of company though; when finished, the place was going to be a concentration camp.

The train was moving swiftly through the brightening morning. It had already crossed the now nonexistent border between Germany and Austria, and was no more than an hour and a half out of Vienna. Inside the compartment at the rear of the train, Starke was finishing his perusal of the Jew Levy's personal effects.

A razor and shaving brush (but no soap), a towel. Hairbrush, with a silver back, probably an antique. Two pairs of trousers, a thin, worn overcoat, two shirts ditto. A black tie. Underwear. A half-loaf of bread wrapped in a scrap of white cloth.

Starke wrinkled his nose at the underwear; it looked clean, but he wasn't going to wear it, no matter what his cover demanded. He opened the compartment window and threw the garments out, as well as the bread. He hesitated over the razor and shaving brush, but decided he'd better keep them, and closed the window.

Now for the papers. They were all in order, as far as he could tell. He drew the false Levy passport out of his jacket and compared its information to that on the genuine personal papers and the exit permit; he didn't think Heydrich's support people would have messed up, but it was better to be sure.

Everything was fine. From here, and for a while longer at least, he was on his own. Starke liked the feeling. It was like diving from the high board, the leap and the plunge, the free-fall. The inevitability of gravity, like the inevitability of history. The feeling had started this morning, when he'd accompanied the special unit for the collection of the Altgarten Jews; Heydrich had demanded that, for purposes of authenticity. If anyone asked Starke/Levy how he and his neighbors had been rounded up, he'd be able to tell them exactly how it had happened. No Altgarten Jew would be running around loose to identify him, either. They were all in a special isolation camp by now, and would stay there until the operation was over. Starke had even glimpsed Levy, back there in Altgarten, and had been gratified—in a way—at the resemblance between them. The Jew must have had some good Aryan blood back there somewhere. It was another one of Heydrich's careful touches. Starke was most unlikely to run across anyone who'd known Levy by sight, but if he did, the resemblance was close enough to get him by.

As far as Starke could see, Heydrich had covered every eventuality, right down to removing three of the four "advance party" and sticking them away in a jail somewhere. If necessary later on, they'd give evidence that Levy was indeed on the train to Vienna. It was part of the trail Heydrich was establishing.

Starke looked out the window, humming cheerfully to himself. Out there in a field beside the tracks, a farmer was haying. The horses drawing the mower were big bay creatures; their flanks shone in the morning sun. The long grass dropped in swaths as the mower blade sliced through them and the following rake pulled the cut hay into ridges across the stubble, up and down the field. The scene dropped away behind as the train whistled its way around a bend, thundering toward Vienna.

Starke was glad to be moving at last, far more than glad. Now that he had some leisure to do so, he wondered whether he might

have refused the assignment if he'd known what was going to be involved. Unlikely. He was SS, and held to the SS oath: My honor is loyalty.

Loyalty even in the matter of seeming to become a Jew. He'd never had to don a cover of this depth. His earlier identities had been superficial by comparison: a businessman, a student. Three months of absorbing the Jewish way of thinking, if it could be called thought, Jewish culture, if it could be called culture. The Torah. The sayings of the rabbis, like Hillel. He'd even learned a chunk of Yiddish, that bastardized version of German and God only knew what else, a perversion of the tongue of Goethe and Heine. Everything the Jews touched they made reek, and he'd been required to breathe that reek twenty-four hours a day, make it stick to him.

There'd been a bad moment about three weeks in, when he didn't think he'd be able to go through with it. The old Jew Heydrich had assigned to teach him had forgotten himself and shouted at Starke for some crack Starke made about a commentary by Rabbi Ben Eleazar. Starke'd hit him hard, three times, and gone to Heydrich. Heydrich had just looked at Starke with those freezing blue eyes of his and said nothing except:

"Not good enough to do it, Starke?"

Starke had gone back to his instructor.

He looked down at his thin wrists. At least, when he reached Palestine, he'd be able to start eating again. He'd intentionally lost a lot of weight over the summer, to deepen his cover; he didn't want to look too fit and healthy when he presented himself as a refugee headed for Palestine. The Jews running the escape routes were suspicious, Heydrich had told him, and a solid SS physique would be entirely too conspicuous. He could also produce a racking cough whenever he needed to. Four days' stubble on his cheeks and chin completed the transformation of his appearance.

He wondered how long he'd have to hang around in Palestine before he received the signal to go ahead. That would be interesting. He judged from the evidence so far that it was going to be an assassination, but he didn't know who the target was, nor where he'd have to go to reach him.

All in good time.

He was sure it would be a beautiful operation, though, worthy of Heydrich. The consequences would be explosive; Heydrich wouldn't be going to these pains for anything less.

Rome—Berlin

August 26, 1938

Julia was perspiring slightly, from both nervous tension and the August heat. Donati looked composed and calm as he walked beside her, although he was clearly feeling the heat as well; there were beads of perspiration on his upper lip.

How can he be so detached? Julia wondered. But then, she reminded herself, he's a lawyer.

They were passing under the inner end of the great curved colonnade of St. Peter's; behind them, the vast ellipse of the square shimmered with heat waves in the blinding noon light. In front stood the great bronze doors fronting Bernini's long gallery: the entrance to the Vatican itself.

They walked into the gallery and stopped just inside the doors. Julia could see, far ahead, a great flight of steps leading upward.

"The Scala Regia," Donati said, following her gaze. "They go to the Sistine Chapel, among other places."

The vastness of the place was already beginning to oppress her: the gallery stretching interminably away toward the stairs, the statues along its wall gazing with petrified eyes into alien Christian distances. She moved a little closer to Donati.

"We must be early," he said, frowning a little. "Wait. There's someone."

A man in a black robe and a low-crowned hat was gliding toward them; he seemed to have materialized in the gallery, rather than entered it. He came up to Julia and Donati and said:

75

"Mr. Donati and Miss Belmont?"

"Yes."

"Please come with me."

They followed. Julia realized now where he'd come from; there was a flight of steps, invisible from her previous vantage point, leading out of the gallery about halfway along it on the right. The priest—Julia thought that was what he was, or something like it—led them up the stairs into the depths of the Vatican Palace. Corridors, doors, more corridors, more flights of steps leading up and down. They came out into a long gallery, which had glass windows on one side overlooking St. Peter's Square; on the side of the gallery opposite the windows, the wall was lined with painted maps. On the ceiling above were more paintings, of biblical scenes and prophets and martyrdoms and Christian saints. They looked down at Julia with curious faces, the questions gliding from their painted eyes into her own.

Little Jew, why have you come here, to the center of our Christendom, you who have rejected us for so long? What do you want of us?

Human charity, she felt herself answer. My Messiah is not yours. But I am still human. Can you accept that in me?

The voices didn't reply. Stop letting your imagination run away with you, Julia snapped at herself. You're here to help Claudio persuade a man to do something. That's all.

The priest opened a door in the wall of the gallery and motioned them through. They traveled along some distance farther, and then entered a loggia, an anteroom with a vaulted painted ceiling, its walls lined with high-backed chairs. The floor was tiled in intricate geometric patterns. Light from arched windows fell across the tiles, and across a wall painting of a woman in a white robe, with a white hood over her hair: the Madonna.

A Jewish woman like me, Julia thought. The Christians conveniently forgot about that, and turned her into something else.

"Please be seated," the priest said. "I will tell Secretary Pacelli that you are here."

He opened a dark wooden door and vanished through it. Julia sat gingerly down on one of the chairs. The anteroom was curiously silent, as though Rome itself had vanished and there was nothing left

in the universe but the vault of the ceiling and the wall paintings and the tiled floor with sunlight pouring blindingly across it.

Donati remained standing. He was examining the frescoes. "I've been up here before," he said. "Raphael himself painted these. It was a commission from Pope Leo the Tenth."

Julia imagined the painter's brush moving in silence across the plaster, the woman's face gliding from his mind through the nerves and tendons of his wrist, through his fingers, through the stem and tip of the brush, thought becoming form on this wall across from her, for her to look through, the telescope reversed, into the mind of Raphael. Vertigo swept through her. She seemed to be seeing with two sets of eyes. She closed the pair she normally saw with, and the feeling slowly went away.

"Are you all right?" Donati asked. Julia opened her eyes. The lawyer was looking down at her with some concern.

"Yes. I'm fine. The sun was awfully hot, that's all." She felt a little dazed. There were ghosts in this place. She hoped they were more benign than not.

The door through which the priest had gone swung open again. Julia stood up as the Vatican Secretary of State, Cardinal Eugenio Pacelli, entered the loggia. He was carrying a buff accordion folder tied up with pink ribbon. Donati gave a brief, correct bow.

"Mr. Donati and Miss Belmont, I am pleased to see you. His Holiness will see you now in the library."

They followed Pacelli through more mazes of rooms. Julia had expected a great deal of ceremonial trappings with Swiss Guards and Noble Guards everywhere, but the corridors were quiet and deserted. The rooms seemed unused; dust filmed the window sills. Eventually Pacelli stopped before a small wooden door, drew a key from his robe, and turned it in the lock.

"Please go inside."

He followed them into the room. It was small and smelled of old leather. Light fell through two high narrow windows onto a wooden desk with a crucifix on it, and four hard-looking chairs with cane seats. There were bookcases lining the walls; it was from the bindings of the books that the smell of leather came. An ornately carved table,

dark with centuries of use, was the only other furnishing in the room. In the wall across from Julia was another small door, which was closed. Sitting at the desk, his white robe luminous in the sunlight falling across it, was Pope Pius the Eleventh, Supreme Pontiff of the Roman Church, Vicar of God, successor to the chair of Peter, and spiritual head of every Catholic *in orbis terrarum*. He was leafing through a small stack of papers, but looked up when he saw Pacelli and the two visitors.

"Good day to you both," he said without smiling, his small eyes intent and appraising behind the ovals of his gold-rimmed glasses. Julia realized, with a curious sense of wonder, that behind this portly man in the hard wooden chair lay the unbroken succession of the Papacy, almost twenty centuries of office, all the way back to a Jewish fisherman who had been the companion of a young rabbi from Nazareth.

Donati had spent several hours briefing her on the man in the chair. Before he became Pope, Achille Ratti had spent the first forty-five years of his career in the Vatican libraries and in teaching theology. He might have remained obscurely among his codices for the rest of his life had not Pope Benedict plucked him out of that obscurity and sent him as an Apostolic Visitor to Poland in 1918. There, in the carnage of the Polish-Russian war of 1919-1920, Ratti had first encountered the savagery of the Bolsheviks toward Catholicism. From that time on he had feared what might happen if Russian communism ever came to dominate Western Europe. That fear shaped his foreign policy, even to the extent of enacting a concordat with the Fascists of Italy in 1929, and another with Nazi Germany in 1933. The concordats, which had resulted in a surrender of some of the Church's power in return for permission to continue its evangelical mission, hadn't prevented either Mussolini or Hitler from continuing to nibble away at that power. The concordats, especially the one with the Nazis, had been to the Vatican's disadvantage. Pius was no longer enamored of the Germans, even as a shield against the Bolsheviks.

Donati was making a bow, precisely correct for a person not of the Pope's faith. There hadn't been any discussion of protocol, so Julia simply bobbed gently in acknowledgment of the position of the man before her.

"Sit down, please," Pius said. "Secretary Pacelli, you too. We will need your assistance in this matter."

Remember, remember not to be clumsy, Julia told herself fervently as she sat down. As usual when she was on edge, she felt composed exclusively of angles and protrusions.

"We have considered for some time the matter you have brought before us," Pius said. "We look upon the actions of the German government with grave concern. Secretary Pacelli informs us that you have given him further information about conditions inside Germany."

"Yes, Your Holiness," Donati said easily. "We have. I would like your permission to discuss it with you."

Pius turned to the secretary of state. "Have you looked at this material, Pacelli?"

The long, aquiline face with the deep-set eyes remained perfectly composed. "I have, Your Holiness."

"Is it of the significance Mr. Donati and Miss Belmont are suggesting?"

"I believe so. To some degree."

To some degree? Julia thought. Is that all? To *some degree*?

"Permit me to see it for myself, then, Pacelli," Pius said. He glanced at Donati. "I have not yet had an opportunity to examine it. Excuse me, please."

Pacelli handed over the folder he had been carrying. In it, Julia realized, were copies of the depositions and photographs she had brought from America. Julia herself had translated the depositions into Italian. The documents had been in Pacelli's hands since Monday, the day the first audience with the Pope was cancelled. Apparently he hadn't showed them to the Pope.

With the quick, trained eye of an archivist, Pius went through the material. His brow furrowed from time to time, and once he gave a palpable wince. Finally, he finished and closed the folder.

"Permit us to put some questions to you," he said.

For the next fifteen minutes he quizzed Julia and Donati on the sources of the documents, what they represented of Nazi policy, how the American Jewish community was reacting to the persecution, what the American government thought of it, how Italian Jews were being treated, what the British were doing about immigration into Palestine. Finally he turned to the secretary of state and said:

"Pacelli, I believe this makes it necessary to act as we were planning. Do you agree?"

Pacelli inclined his head ever so slightly. "Yes, Your Holiness. I do. But with circumspection."

"We have been circumspect too long," Pius said sharply. The schoolmaster-martinet showed through for an instant. "Being circumspect has not been enough. *With Burning Sorrow* was not enough. We must make that Satanic prophet in Berlin sit up and take notice."

"As you will it," said Pacelli, with a faint air of long-suffering. Donati had told her that Pius had a reputation for stubbornness, and that he did not always take the advice of his underlings, or even want to hear it unsolicited.

"Your Holiness," Julia ventured quietly, "may I ask what you are planning to do? It would relieve the minds of many of our people if they knew they could expect support against the Nazis."

Pius looked at her with a faint surprise. He'd obviously not expected the woman to speak without being spoken to, or at least not to speak so bluntly. Pacelli and Donati were both looking pained at her forthrightness. Julia didn't care. American women were different from those these men were used to, and they'd have to put up with it.

The Pope's penetrating eyes softened a little, as though they perceived a glimmer of the pain she felt. "There are limits to what you may know, Signorina."

"I understand that, sir."

"I have been composing a document which affirms the unity of the human race."

"Your Holiness," Pacelli said warningly.

"Pacelli," said Pius, "one of our apostolic duties is to provide comfort where comfort is needed. Even to those not of our flock."

Pacelli subsided with plain irritation. Julia thought: I am to be comforted, even though I am a Jew. Am I Jewish first, and human after?

Pius regarded her. "We had not decided whether to actually deliver such an encyclical. These things you have brought have made us decide to do so. For some time we have regarded, with mounting

concern, the German emphasis on biology and race as a measure of human worth. This must end. We are all human."

"Does this mean," Julia asked boldly, "that the encyclical will condemn the Nazi and Fascist actions against Jews here and in Germany?"

Pacelli emitted a grunt of annoyance. Pius shot him a barbed look and said:

"It will include that, among other condemnations of other things they have done. And are doing. Not only Jews are being persecuted in what that demagogue Hitler pleases to call the Third Reich. It is our intention to condemn biological racism as a whole, not only that directed at the Jews. Those who have ears to hear, let them hear."

"The Nazis do not have such ears," Julia said. "They may refuse to hear."

Pius favored her with a wintry smile. "When our words are read from every pulpit in Germany," he said, "the Nazis will hear. And they will wish they did not. But they *will* hear, I promise you. One third of the population of Germany is Catholic. Even Hitler cannot ignore *that* voice. And here in Italy we are all Catholic. There will be an end to such things as the Duce's Office of Demography and Race."

I hope he's right, Julia thought. How far does the power of the Church run? I'm not a Catholic, I can't sense it. But why could he not say outright that the Jews are the target of this biological racism, that it is aimed specifically at us? Why not? He *is* being circumspect, after all. But perhaps, just perhaps, the Nazis will finally be forced to pay attention to something outside themselves.

"Thank you, Your Holiness," she said. "We're very grateful."

Pius nodded in acknowledgment. "Thank you for assisting us in coming to this decision," he said.

Pacelli stood up, smoothing his robe, and led them out of the tiny room. Outside, the door closed, he stopped and turned to face them.

"What you have learned is to go no further," he said. "If you publish this abroad prematurely, it can only reduce its impact. You've been favored more than you realize in coming here. Few people know of that room, nor the way to reach it. His Holiness instructed me to

bring you this way, because he also is concerned about watching eyes and listening ears. There are men who do not want such a document published, and some of them are within these walls. I am not one of them, although I have reservations about the manner of execution. Do you understand?"

Julia and Donati both nodded. Then Julia said, "When? When will he speak?"

"When he is ready," Pacelli told her. "It will take time. But it will be done. His Holiness is a very determined man. Now please come with me."

The Vatican Secretary for Extraordinary Ecclesiastical Affairs, Cardinal Giuseppe Mondolfo, sat alone in his office, with his elbows on his desk. As he often did when deep in thought, he was stroking the prominent mole on his cheek just in front of his right ear.

The office's austerity reflected that of its occupant: there was no carpet on the polished marble floor, and the white plastered walls were bare of any ornament except for a black crucifix hung where Mondolfo's eyes would rest on it whenever he looked up from his desk. The cardinal often wore a hair shirt under his robes, and it was rumored that when he arrived at the Vatican in 1920 he'd looked upon bathing as an indulgence of the flesh closely approaching a venal sin. According to the story, Pope Benedict himself had had to gently advise Mondolfo—much to the relief of those who had to work with him—that God would overlook such indulgences.

Mondolfo was contemplating the information that had just reached him, via a sympathetic associate (spy was much too strong a word), from the offices of the secretary of state. It appeared that Pius had actually gone ahead and seen the two Jews, and in extreme secrecy at that. Pacelli had at least agreed to the meeting, if he hadn't actually promoted it. The audience was another sign of the direction Pius's thought was taking, and Pacelli's foreign policy with it.

Blast Pacelli, Mondolfo thought. For all his vaunted skill at diplomacy, the Cardinal Secretary of State couldn't see which way the wind was blowing. He was going to let the old man come out with

some violent attack on the Nazis, probably defending the Jews into the bargain, which would infuriate the Germans much more than had the *Burning Sorrow* encyclical. And at a time like this, with the socialists and communists on the move everywhere, the Germans were crucial to the defense of western Europe against Bolshevik atheism. It was bad enough to put the German Catholic Church into more danger by offending the Nazis further, but to do so and defend the Jews at the same time was fantastic. Mondolfo knew for a fact that Lenin had been Jewish; he had tabulated the number of Jews in the upper levels of the Soviet Bolshevik government; he had made lists of the German Jews who had been members of the German Communist Party before the Nazis had the sense to suppress it; he had read police reports on the Jewish membership of the now-underground and therefore dangerous Italian Communist Party. All you had to do, Mondolfo thought, was scratch a commissar, and there'd be a Jew underneath the red.

The Jews were using Bolshevism for their own ends: to overthrow and destroy the Roman Church they hated, wipe out Christianity itself, and reach their final goal of world domination. They'd never possessed such a weapon as the perverted philosophy devised by the Jew Marx. And the Church couldn't overcome such power by herself; she needed, as every strong Pope in history had known, the alliance of a strong secular arm. And the Germans were without doubt the strongest power in Europe, perhaps in the world. The democracies were worthless in the struggle.

It was perhaps true, Mondolfo reflected, that the Germans had been guilty of some excesses against the Church. But they'd never denied her right to exist, as the Jews and the Bolsheviks did. And in any case, the Church had a long history of bending secular power to her will, even if the alliances seemed unlikely at first. There would come a day when Hitler would submit to Rome, just as the Emperor Henry had been forced to do centuries ago.

But the Bolsheviks would have to be vanquished first. And the only nation in Europe that could possibly do that was Germany. Like it or not, Berlin and the Vatican were on the same side. Pius was blind not to see it. So was Pacelli. Blind, or perhaps worse.

Mondolfo wondered briefly whether Pacelli was in fact Jewish. It

would be like them, to infiltrate one of their own into such a position of power, where they could corrupt from within. He'd have to look into it. In the meantime. . . .

It wasn't common knowledge, but Pius wasn't well. Last winter he'd nearly died of a combined attack of heart weakness, arteriosclerosis, and asthma. If he died before he published whatever he was planning, the danger might be over. Pacelli wouldn't necessarily become Pope. If the Curia saw reason, and the necessity of a temporary alliance with the Germans, a man who promoted such an alliance would have a good chance at the succession.

A man like Cardinal Giuseppe Mondolfo, for example. He'd already considered what name he might take. Clement, perhaps: the Merciful.

His future, and probably that of the Church, would be in ruins if Pius made a direct attack on the policies or, worse, the legitimacy of the Nazi and Fascist regimes. The old man had to be stopped, for the sake of the Church and the future of Catholicism. There was, unfortunately, no mechanism for removing a Pope from office.

Or, to be exact, no mechanism except death.

Mondolfo did not blink at the thought. If matters came to a choice between the life of a Pope and the life of the Church, there *was* no choice.

Although, he thought, it hasn't come to that yet.

He locked his desk drawer and got up. It was time to continue his own thread of diplomacy, the thread he'd been developing ever since the *Burning Sorrow* encyclical.

He left the Vatican by way of the Museum entrance on the north side, without anyone noticing him particularly, and walked up the Via Ottaviano to the branch post office near the church of Saint Rosario. In the post office he placed a telephone call.

"Ja?"

"You must meet with me," Mondolfo said in Italian.

"Very well," the voice said, in the same language, although slightly accented. "Where?"

"The second of the three places. At six o'clock. Is that possible?"

"No difficulty."

Mondolfo hung up and left.

About thirty minutes later, the telephone rang in Heydrich's office in the Prinz-Albrecht-Strasse. He listened for a few seconds and then said, "Good. Let me know what happens, but by courier. Don't use the telephone or the coding devices."

He replaced the receiver and returned without hesitation to the file he'd been reading.

Trieste—Palestine

August 28—September 3, 1938

Rossi sat at the splintery pine table near the open door of the warehouse. Through the door he could see the long finger of the Venezia Wharf stretching out into Porto Vecchio, the harbor of Trieste. On the side of the wharf, and looking dilapidated enough to sink at her moorings, was the slab-sided and rust-pocked hull of the *Olympia*. The freighter was far from aptly named; of no more than two thousand tons, her keel had been laid down at Tyneside in Scotland at least thirty years ago. She had the traditional turn-of-the-century profile of a tramp steamer: a high forecastle and a high poop, each of which was separated from the center island and bridge structure by a well-deck. A pair of dirty buff masts bearing cargo derricks rose above her scabbed black funnel, which was adorned with the colors of the Greek shipping line (if a two-ship concern could be called a line) that owned her. Her worn-out engines could just drive her at a torpid twelve knots, if she had a following wind. She'd been chartered through Greek intermediaries by the Mossad, and aboard her at this moment were some two hundred and thirty-six Jewish refugees from Austria and Germany.

Rossi chewed angrily at the end of his fountain pen and withdrew his gaze from the rusting freighter to consider the young man before him. The man was the last of the line Rossi had been processing; the other three Mossad men taking the exit interviews were almost finished, as well.

"Sit down," Rossi said, indicating the chair at the side of his table. "I speak adequate German. I assume you're from Germany."

The young man sat down. "Yes." He was thin from lack of food, and gray with exhaustion. His voice was tremulous, both from anxiety for himself and from fear for those he'd have left behind. Almost everyone who came through the Trieste escape route had left someone behind.

Because of his three months' absence from the escape lines, Rossi had lost some of the protective callous he'd built up in Turkey. "I need to ask you some questions," he said as kindly as he could. And then he added quickly, as the young man's face took on a hunted look, "It's so we can try to protect anyone you know back in Germany." Rossi never said *back at home*; there was no home any more behind these people.

"Oh. Yes. Please ask."

"What's your name?"

"Samuel David Levy."

"Where are you from?"

"Altgarten. It's forty kilometers from Regensburg. About. To the southwest."

Rossi wrote on the blank sheet of paper in front of him. The information he gathered on this sheet, along with that on thousands of others like it, would be used to identify Jews remaining at risk in the Reich, and also to document the severity with which they were being treated. Rossi had taken hundreds of such depositions, but wasn't yet jaded enough not to be outraged at almost every one.

"When were you forced to leave?"

Levy told him what had happened, from the time the trucks rolled into the ghetto square in Altgarten, until the time he reached the transit camp outside Trieste.

"You don't know what happened to the three men who were with you on the train?"

"No. I'm sorry."

"I didn't really expect you to," Rossi said. It was common for people to try to get valuables out of the country. Often confiscation was all that happened, but occasionally the Germans decided to make

an example. They didn't like liquid funds to be removed from the Reich. A watch would be set to see what happened at the trial, if there was one, if the manpower could be spared for the watch. Mossad was short of people who could work inside the Reich. "So you are the only Altgarten Jew to be allowed to emigrate? As far as you know?"

"As far as I know. My wife and father. . . ." Levy closed his eyes and his face contorted. "My wife is expecting a baby."

"We'll look for them," Rossi said. "We'll try to get them out. Do you know where they were taken?"

"No. The SS man only mentioned a temporary camp. There were only about sixty of us in Altgarten."

Sometimes, Rossi knew, inhabitants of such temporary camps were overlooked or ignored for months, all the time at risk from typhoid and malnutrition-related diseases, not to mention pneumonia in the wintertime. "We'll look for them," he repeated. "I promise. You've told me everything you can think of?"

"Yes," Levy said, and then, shyly: "What is it like, in Palestine? Would my wife like it?"

They all asked that question, and Rossi always gave the same answers. "You are illegal immigrants," he told Levy. "The British will try to stop us from getting you ashore, but once ashore you will normally be able to blend into the established Jewish communities. There is some danger to the communities. The Arabs don't like us, and there have been some murders. However, you will be safe from organized persecution such as the Germans use."

"Don't we need forged visas or identity papers?"

"Anything you need like that will be supplied after you're in Palestine. I have to tell you, though, that there's a lot of unemployment."

"I'm a kosher butcher," Levy reminded Rossi. "People have to eat. Surely there'll be somewhere for me."

The other interviewers were packing up. "I don't know," Rossi said. "You'll have to find out when you arrive. Now take your things out to the ship. That one, over there, with the black smokestack. The gangway's on the far side. You'll be assigned a place." He stood up. He had to get aboard *Olympia* himself; he was the debarkation controller on this voyage, and had to ensure that the freighter's

captain reached the Palestinian coast without taking unnecessary risks with British naval patrols, and that the refugees weren't abused or dumped on a deserted stretch of beach, as had sometimes happened.

"You'll look for my family?" Levy pleaded, as he stooped to pick up his cracked leather valise.

"Yes," Rossi assured him. "We'll do everything we can."

The *Olympia* sailed just before sunset. The evening air was still sweltering, and few of the refugees had taken advantage of the shelter offered by the hold, which stank of bilge gases, coal, rotten fruit, damp rust, and ancient dried fish. Rossi was on the starboard bridge wing, watching Saul Aaronson organize the distribution of food and water to the refugee men and women and children in the forward well-deck. There were two other Mossad men besides Rossi and Aaronson escorting this shipment; one of them, Mandel, would be staying behind in Palestine with the reception team, to help move their charges inland to a safe area.

The wheelhouse door slammed and *Olympia*'s captain stamped out onto the bridge wing to join Rossi. The captain's name was Papagos, or something like it. Rossi didn't speak Greek, but Papagos, happily, was fluent in Italian.

"We'll be well out to sea by dark," Papagos said, and spat a gout of tobacco expertly over the bridge rail into the waves below. The Greek was heavy-set, jowly, and about fifty, with thinning gray hair on which sat a stained blue officer's cap. Despite the heat, he was wearing an equally stained uniform jacket over a fray-collared and tieless white shirt. "You want to be off the coast north of Netanya at two in the morning, right?" he asked.

"Right," said Rossi. He thought he smelled the aniseed odor of ouzo on Papagos's breath, but he wasn't sure. "Six days, you said," Rossi added pointedly. There was no more than enough food and water for that length of time.

Papagos spat over the rail again. "Assuming the engines don't break down. Ten knots is almost as much as this old whore will

make." He obviously didn't look on his ship with any particular affection. "And assuming good weather. We might get autumn weather early, you never know."

"Yes."

"My crew isn't paid to help look after these people of yours," Papagos added. "Except to row them ashore at the other end. If you ask my men to help while we're underway, they'll demand extra pay. The ship owners won't stand for that."

"We won't ask for help. We already discussed that."

"Just making sure you remember. You have any more business on my bridge?"

"No," Rossi said, taking the more-than-hint. He left the rail and went down the companionway to the boat deck. He didn't like the look of the boats. The davits and davit blocks were thick with paint slapped on over the years; the paint would have to be chipped out of the blocks, or the falls wouldn't run through them to lower the boats. There was no chance the crew would do it, although it was certainly their job. He'd have to talk to Aaronson tomorrow about getting the work done.

He continued down to the after well-deck to see how matters were going there.

The next five days passed in a procession of good weather and stunning monotony, except for Rossi's low-level feud with Papagos. The man didn't want to provide tools for freeing the boats. When Rossi and Aaronson assured him that they and some of the refugees would do all the work, he wanted a deposit on the tools in case any were lost or damaged. They scraped up the deposit, which Papagos accepted with grumbling and ill grace. While the work was going on, the crew—a mixture of Greeks, Italians, and Lascars—hung about watching and passing scathing comments about the incompetence of the landsmen. After it was done, Papagos tried to pretend the deposit had been a rental. Rossi came close to threatening him before the Greek handed the money over.

On the third day, one of the fresh-water condensers broke down

and drinking water began to run short. The crew got first call on it, in spite of the dehydrated condition of several of the children aboard. Fortunately one of the Hamburg refugees had been a steam fitter, and after several hours' work got the condenser going again. Papagos hadn't tried to extort a deposit that time, likely because he didn't want to pay for the condenser repairs when *Olympia* reached port.

The food was starting to go bad when the morning of the sixth day came, because the ship's refrigeration plant had stopped working and Papagos hadn't bothered to tell the Mossad escort about it. Rossi and Aaronson decided against a confrontation, because the ship was only a few hours' sail from the Palestinian coast, and Papagos, if he were sufficiently annoyed, could cause no end of trouble in debarking the passengers. He might conceivably put his ship in the way of a British patrol; Rossi had privately sworn to throw the man overboard if this happened.

The last day at sea passed with the speed of slow torture. *Olympia* was approaching Palestine from the northwest, on the shipping lane from Famagusta in Cyprus, as though she were nothing more than a tramp steamer going about her usual business. But because of the danger of British patrols, the refugees had had to be battened down below the hatch covers, in the stifling belly of the ship; a Royal Naval destroyer spotting a tramp with her decks full of people would know exactly where such a vessel was bound. Rossi and the other members of the escort spent a lot of time in the holds, reassuring the refugees and trying to make sure their basic needs were met. It was a losing battle; there were four cases of heat prostration, which couldn't be relieved until the sun went down and the victims could be brought up on deck. Rossi twice noticed the young Jew from Altgarten sitting quietly by himself, uncomplaining and quite alert in spite of the heat. For all his scrawniness, Levy seemed to have deep reserves of stamina.

Darkness fell at last and the canvas hatch covers were dragged back, allowing cool air to sink into the holds. Rossi had demanded a look at the charts, and Papagos, likely relieved to be almost rid of his troublesome cargo, had obliged. The freighter was about sixty kilometers off Netanya, a relatively new settlement isolated among its sand dunes where the Plain of Sharon ran down to the sea. The

refugees were to go ashore a few kilometers north of the settlement, near an even smaller place called Kefar Vitkin, where the British were unlikely to catch them among the half-drained swamps of the coastal plain.

The engines thumped steadily as *Olympia* drew nearer to the shores of Palestine. There was no moon, only starlight, and the ship's navigation lights were turned off. Rossi waited on the bridge with Papagos, looking for the faint black line of the coast against the dark sea. There was little swell tonight, which would be a blessing when the time came to load the refugees into the ship's boats. Use of the boats was part of the charter deal, and Papagos hadn't been in a position to complain about it.

There the coast was, finally, a shadow on the sea. Rossi went out onto the bridge wing and called down to the boat deck. As he went back into the wheelhouse he heard Aaronson and the other men of the team start working the two lifeboats clear of their chocks.

"Go in to two kilometers," Rossi ordered.

Papagos muttered an instruction to the helmsman and *Olympia*'s bow swung a little to port. If Papagos's navigation was correct, Kefar Vitkin should be a couple of kilometers to the south of their present position.

Rossi was carrying a flashlight, which he shone for an instant at his wristwatch. Five to two. The men ashore would burn a blue light for three minutes every hour on the hour until dawn, as a landing mark. Even so short an exposure risked attracting the attention of the British seaward patrols, but the lights were essential. It was too dangerous to have exhausted and frightened refugees blundering ashore on the wrong part of a swampy coast; armed Arabs were a peril, as were the swamps themselves.

There. A blue gleam. Rossi went back onto the bridge wing, aimed the flashlight, and pressed the switch twice. The blue light went out.

"Get them aboard," he called softly to Aaronson. Sound traveled a long way over water on a still night like this. "We're in the right place."

He heard the muffled tread of feet on the deck planking, and low exclamations and whispers. At thirty people per boat, the debarkation

was going to require four trips. Two hours. Maybe there were boats ashore that could help; sometimes there were.

"Hold position a thousand meters off shore," Rossi said to Papagos. "There's enough water under the keel, isn't there?"

He saw Papagos nod in the starlight. The captain was more than usually agreeable, likely because he had a skinful of ouzo. Rossi had been breathing it at second hand ever since he'd joined the Greek on the bridge.

The freighter slowly came to a stop. Her engines thumped just enough to keep her in place against the current flowing along the shore. Papagos, whatever his faults, was a good navigator and ship handler.

Rossi joined Aaronson on the boat deck. "Lower away," he said.

The pulleys squeaked as the lifeboats inched down toward the water. Rossi and Aaronson watched the ship's crewmen to make sure they didn't foul the lines or drop either end of the boats too quickly and spill the occupants into the sea.

The first load was afloat. Under the direction of the Mossad pilots, the crewmen in the boats began pulling for the shore a thousand meters away. Rossi waited, watching to seaward. There was no sign of any other shipping, specifically the luminous bow wave of a British destroyer.

The boats returned twice for further loads; the party ashore didn't have any boats of its own, unfortunately. One more trip and *Olympia* would turn her bows for Brindisi in Italy, carrying Rossi and Aaronson.

Rossi turned his attention shoreward in time to see the two lifeboats returning from their third run. They reached the side of the freighter and the crew attached the falls for hoisting to the level of the boat deck, where the last of the refugees would be loaded.

Something was wrong at the port boat, the one Aaronson was overseeing. Rossi joined the other Mossad man at the rail. "What's the matter?"

"Mandel's sprained his ankle helping people off. He can't walk at all."

Rossi swore under his breath. "Get him out. I'll take the last load in."

"What about moving them once they're ashore? Mandel was supposed to stay."

"I'll talk to the shore party."

"Fine."

Rossi waited until the last refugees were in the boat and then clambered in himself. He recognized Levy on the thwart next to him, but the young German didn't say anything. The four crew members at the oars swung the boat and began rowing for the dark and featureless shoreline. No one in the frail vessel spoke; even the children were silent. The boat surged and dipped in the light swell, which as always was more pronounced than it appeared from the level of a ship's deck. The oars squeaked in the locks, beating time.

Without warning they were in the light surf of the sloping beach. Rossi could make out dark knots of people against the paler sand. The lifeboat lifted and then bumped down as the keel hit bottom. Rossi jumped over the side into mid-thigh-deep water, and began guiding the bow up the shore, being careful not to let the heavy boat run over him. One of *Olympia*'s crew had gotten out on the other bow and was helping. Not all of them, at least, were like the captain.

The lifeboat grounded; Rossi and a couple of male refugees began helping the others overboard into the low surf, through which they waded up to the sandy beach. Rossi could see the other boat unloading a few meters away. When everyone was ashore he said to the crewman on the other side of the bow, "Wait until I come back."

He saw the man nod in the weak starlight. Rossi trudged through the warm, breaking waves to the beach. The head of the shore party was waiting for him, his features no more than a faint blur in the darkness.

"We're short one man," Rossi said in English. "Can you get them to Kefar Vitkin?"

"Yes." An American accent. Rossi wondered where the man was from. "If they keep together," the other added. "There are some bad spots of swamp just inland."

"Good. Good luck."

"Good luck. We—"

Brilliant white light bloomed in the sky above them. The sand was

suddenly lit by illumination as bright as daylight. Rossi saw the faces of the refugees lift to look in astonishment at the parachute flare as it began to descend toward them; in the surf the white lifeboats gleamed like cakes of ice. Rossi saw the crewmen frantically swinging the bows around to pull out to sea.

"British!" shouted the leader of the reception team. "Inland! Run! Go with them," he yelled at Rossi. "Help them through. A hundred meters, turn right. As many as you can take!"

Rossi ran toward the nearest knot of refugees; they were from the boat he'd been on. "Come with me!" he shouted at them. "Quickly! Quickly!" At least, he thought as he herded several of them up the beach, it's not Arabs. They'd be shooting.

He heard a voice calling through a megaphone, in a plummy English accent. "Everyone stay on the beach! Do not move! You are surrounded!" A pause, as though for thought, and the same voice repeated the orders in German.

Go to hell, Rossi thought as he pelted up the sand toward the dunes behind the beach, following his tiny flock. He'd managed to collect half a dozen people, three women and three men. No children. One of the men was Samuel Levy. In spite of the soft sand Levy was running easily, as though he'd trained for it.

One of the women, just ahead of Levy, stumbled and almost fell.

"Help the women!" Rossi called. Levy reached out smoothly as he passed the one who'd faltered, seized her by the arm, and dragged her up the face of the dune.

They reached the top as the parachute flare burned itself out. Rossi heard a shot somewhere off to the left. Firing into the air, he thought. I hope.

He counted swiftly, straining his eyes to see; the flare had destroyed his night vision. His flock of six had formed itself into three couples, so the men could assist the women through the foot-dragging sand. Because of the loss of his night sight, Rossi couldn't tell what the land was like on this side of the dune. The man on the beach had warned of swampy patches.

Another flare burst in the sky. *Thank you*, Rossi thought as the light revealed the back of the dune sloping away from them, dotted with scrub thorn here and there, and clumps of broom. At the bottom of

the dune the land leveled out, with more low, wind-racked vegetation among scattered rocks. He couldn't see any of the British patrol, but there were shouts and yells from the beach over his left shoulder. The Englishman with the plummy voice was bellowing through the megaphone again, but Rossi couldn't make out the words.

"Come on," he said. "Farther in. Then we head for Kefar Vitkin."

He heard their ragged breaths behind him as he set an even pace inland. None of the refugees were fit for this; the six days on the ship and their privations beforehand had left them too weak for even fear to sustain their flight for long. They made it all this way, Rossi thought as he slogged his way through the sand. And now the British will put them into a camp, or try to send them back to Germany if they can. The bastards.

The little group of fugitives had reached the flats on the landward side of the dunes when the flare went out. Rossi heard a splash and a sucking sound, and stopped, spinning around. One of his couples, running to the left of the others, had blundered into a crusted-over patch of swamp and were floundering about, up to their knees in stinking, brackish mud. Rossi hurried back, stumbling over scrubby bushes in the sudden dark. He sensed rather than saw the others halt, as well, and then he'd gotten the two mired people out of the bog and was pushing them on ahead of him. Levy and his charge were a couple of meters away on the right.

Pop.

Another parachute flare, behind them this time. It was obliging of the British to light their way like this. Rossi and his group had obviously penetrated one of the gaps in their cordon. He and the refugees seemed well away from the soldiers, now.

"*Halt!* Halt or I'll shoot!"

Not so lucky after all, Rossi thought as he cut right, away from the source of the voice in front of them. Levy's woman stumbled in exhaustion and her arm tore away from the young butcher's grip. Levy seemed to hesitate, saw Rossi nearing him, and tried to get the woman to her feet again. Rossi took her other arm, but she was as limp as a bag of the sand that surrounded them. He looked over his shoulder. The other refugees had vanished, but he saw three men in

uniform running toward him and Levy and the woman. They were
about a hundred meters away.

"I can't run any more," the woman was sobbing. "Go on. Go *on*."

Rossi hesitated. If they tried to save her, the British would catch
both him and Levy. But they couldn't leave her behind, not after she'd
come all this way.

She must have sensed his indecision, for with what had to be the
last of her strength she wrenched her arm out of his grip and
staggered toward the soldiers. There wasn't anything he could do
without throwing himself into the arms of the British. He turned and
ran toward a rock outcrop, glimpsing Levy already well ahead of him.
The butcher had decided to save himself.

Rossi caught up with him on the other side of a stony ridge, just as
the flare glimmered into extinction. He could hear Levy gasping for
breath, just as he was. He wondered if the soldiers were going to
follow them. He thought Levy and he had been on enough rock to
make tracking difficult.

"Stop," he gasped in German to Levy. The other obediently halted.
Somehow the man had managed to hang onto his valise. "*Was?*"
asked Levy.

"We have to turn toward Kefar Vitkin." Rossi tried to orient
himself; with all the running and dodging, he wasn't sure where they
were in relation to the sea.

"What's there?"

"Safety. I think. It's one of our settlements. They'll hide us from the
British, if they can."

"Whatever you say."

Rossi swore at himself for not having a compass, and studied the
stars. After a minute he thought he had it. "This way, I think."

They trudged into the night. Rossi's throat was burning with
thirst. How far to the settlement? It couldn't be more than a couple
of kilometers.

Half an hour later, he wasn't sure any more where they were. They
were still slogging through the scrub and thorn, occasionally running
into patches of bog, which they had to skirt carefully because of the
danger of quicksand. It was well past three in the morning. When the

sun came up, Rossi decided, he'd find a patch of higher ground and try to locate the ocean.

"Are we lost?" Levy asked. He hadn't spoken for a long time.

It was necessary not to alarm the man, although he'd borne up very well for someone of his background. "Not very. There are settlements near the coast. Come daylight we'll find a place with no difficulty." And hope it's not Arab, he thought.

"Can we rest?"

Rossi's own knees were beginning to feel wobbly. His long convalescence had diminished his stamina rather more than he'd wanted to believe.

"I suppose so."

They sat down by a patch of scrub broom that was struggling for a foothold in an outcrop of rock. "I wish we had water," Levy said plaintively.

"So do I."

"Do you know what time it is?"

"Nearly five. There'll be light soon."

"Oh."

"You're a butcher, you said?" Rossi asked.

"Yes. In Altgarten."

"I remember talking to you in Trieste. I'm from America. New York."

"That's the accent you have, then."

"That's right."

A silence. Levy seemed to have no desire to talk, which upon reflection wasn't surprising. He'd had a lot to cope with in the past few weeks.

"Have you been in Palestine before?" Levy asked suddenly.

"Twice, but only for a short time each time. Tel Aviv, and before that, Haifa."

"Never Jerusalem?"

"No."

"Tell me about Haifa and Tel Aviv."

"Haifa's the main port of Palestine," Rossi explained. "Tel Aviv is just outside Jaffa, which is an old Arab city. A lot of Jews have settled in Tel Aviv. It's built mostly on sand, but there's always construction

going on. Sometimes the Arabs come from Jaffa and cause trouble. They've killed a lot of Jews. We've killed some of them, too."

"Oh." Levy's voice was subdued.

"Try not to run into armed Arabs when you're alone," Rossi said.

They sat in silence for a while, both too thirsty to talk further. Eventually Rossi saw a pink streak over the eastern horizon. Now that he had a direction, he realized that they'd been going northeast instead of southeast, as they should have been.

"Dawn's coming," he said. "We ought to get moving."

"Very well."

They picked themselves up and headed southward. The rest hadn't done Rossi a lot of good; his legs still felt rubbery. Levy didn't seem to be much better off.

"Are we anywhere near a road?" Levy asked after a few minutes. The sky was now quite light.

"I'm not sure. I've never been this far inland around here." Privately, Rossi was wondering whether they might run into any more British patrols. They might still be looking for stragglers.

They trudged along. The sun came up in a hurry; the temperature began to rise and with it a wind out of the west.

After an hour they entered a region of low rock ridges, free of sand but cut by shallow dry watercourses. Rossi climbed to the top of one of the ridges, but the air was already hazed with heat and with dust blown up by the steady wind, and he couldn't see much of anything. They tried to stick to the ridge tops for a while, but the going was so rough they returned to the watercourses and tried to keep a more or less southward direction.

The worst happened so suddenly that Rossi almost didn't have time to react. He and Levy came to a bend in the watercourse they were following; right at the bend, two shallower tributaries entered the ravine. They stepped around the bend and there in front of them, not a dozen meters away, were three Arabs armed with rifles. The Arabs were looking straight at them.

"Run!" Rossi yelled, and threw himself to one side to start racing up the right-hand ravine. He heard clatters behind him, of boots on stone, but didn't dare turn to see who it was. A shot banged, echoing from the stone walls of the ravine. The ravine began curving away,

more to the west; Rossi blessed it for the cover the bend gave him. He risked a glance over his shoulder.

He was alone in the ravine. Levy must have gone the other way, up the other tributary.

If Rossi had been armed, he would have gone back, but he was no match for three rifle-carrying Arabs. He could only hope that Levy had gotten away up the other watercourse and would be able to evade the Arabs among the ravines and ridges. It wasn't much of a hope, though; a Jew from a small town in Germany wouldn't have a chance of escaping from Palestinians on their home ground.

Neither did he, for that matter.

The watercourse was rising and becoming shallower. When he reached its end he'd be exposed on the ridge line. He had no choice, though. He couldn't go back. He'd keep low and try to scuttle down the other side of the ridge without being seen.

Rossi scrambled up the last meter of slope before the crest of the ridge, and hit the top in a running crouch.

He stopped, stunned.

Lying before him were the neat irrigated fields and cinder-block houses of a Jewish settlement. He could see men and women working around the buildings and out on the farmland. Rifle-carrying guards were posted on the perimeter. One of them saw Rossi and raised his gun. Rossi put his hands into the air and ran down the slope toward the guard. He was safe.

As Levy would have been, if he'd turned the same way Rossi had.

Rossi slowed to a walk and lowered his hands to his sides as he approached the guard. Dejection flooded through him. Of the six he'd tried to save, five were captured, and the wan little butcher from Altgarten, who had come so far with so much pain, was almost certainly dead.

Starke crouched behind the mass of rock rubble that partially blocked the entrance to the cave. The cave mouth was about five meters up the ravine's steep side, and overhung by a lip of rock that threw the opening into deep shadow. By peering carefully around the boulders in the entrance, Starke could see the far wall of the ravine and a patch

of its floor. A little way behind Starke, the cave narrowed into a half-meter-wide cleft that ran for some unguessable distance into the bedrock.

He knew they weren't far behind him, although the curve of the ravine had hidden his desperate climb up its steep slope to the cave entrance. All three Arabs had taken off after him, much to Starke's fury. At least they hadn't been shooting, after the first round. Short of ammunition, most likely, and wanted a sure thing. If only they'd all gone after the Jew, or even split up—

No help for that now. He had to either escape or kill them as quickly as possible, and be on his way. They might miss seeing the cave mouth. If they did spot it, the cave was the best ambush site he'd seen in his five-minute flight up the dry ravine.

His breath was becoming more even. He watched the ravine floor. They knew he wasn't armed, and it would make them careless. Moreover, they thought he was a Jewish refugee, not someone likely to put up a serious fight. They'd be approaching him with the attitude of a pheasant shoot.

He saw them. All three Arabs were trotting up the ravine floor, not hurrying, trusting to their knowledge of the land and their endurance to wear down their quarry. One of them was scanning the ravine walls as he went. Starke ducked back out of sight.

He heard one of the Arabs calling to the others. He's seen the cave, Starke thought. He willed the man to come up.

Voices again down below. Starke risked a peep. Two of the Arabs were proceeding on up the ravine, while the third, head down to keep his balance, was climbing toward the cave.

Perfect, Starke thought. He stood up, gripping the club-like sliver of granite that was serving him as a weapon, and pressed back against the rear face of the rockfall. Silence reigned in the cave.

He heard a clink from just outside as the Arab's foot dislodged a stone. Then the light in the cave dimmed; the man was standing at its entrance. He said something into the darkness, a tone of command. Starke could see the muzzle of the Arab's rifle poking past the edge of the rockfall.

Come in a little farther, Starke commanded silently. Come in a meter farther.

More of the rifle appeared as the Arab stepped gingerly into the cave. Starke could now see the man's left hand as it gripped the forestock of the rifle. The morning was bright outside, and the Arab's eyes wouldn't have adapted yet. Starke was as good as invisible behind his wall of stones.

The Arab said something guttural and stepped into full view. The German stepped forward and slammed the granite club down onto the side of the man's head. The Arab's knees buckled and he started to fall. Starke grabbed the rifle from him before he hit the ground; the sound of metal on stone might bring his comrades back.

Starke waited, aiming the rifle at the cave mouth, just in case. No one came. Now he had to move quickly. The other two Arabs would expect their friend to be following them in short order.

He checked the Arab's pulse. The heart was still beating weakly. Starke laid the rifle down and broke the man's neck with one expert twist. Then he quickly assessed the weapon. It was an 1886-pattern French Lebel infantry rifle, and very dirty. Starke discarded it in disgust; it would be as likely to jam as not, and God only knew what condition the sights were in. More useful was the curved knife the Arab wore in a belt sheath. Starke whipped the weapon free and threaded it onto his own belt, heading for the cave entrance as he did so.

The ravine outside was empty. Instead of scrambling down to its floor, Starke went up to the top, and found himself on a windy ridge. He began following it in the direction the other two Arabs had taken, keeping away from the lip of the ravine. Every so often he paused and listened, straining his hearing to separate the sound of the wind from the rattle of footsteps on loose stone.

Suddenly, he heard voices below him. He threw himself flat and crept to the top of the ravine to peep down into it. The two Arabs were right below him, arguing and pointing back the way they had come. Obviously they were wondering what had become of their companion. As Starke watched, one of them turned and set off toward the cave, holding his rifle across his left forearm ready to fire. The other, more nonchalant, sat down on a stone to wait. He was facing up the ravine, surveying the direction he thought his quarry had taken.

Starke slithered away from the top of the ravine, got up, and ran back the way he had come. He had to reach the cave before the Arab did.

He barely managed it. The man was approaching the loose scree below the cave mouth when Starke arrived on the overhang above the entrance. The German took up position behind a low ridge of stones and located a chink that gave him a view down into the ravine. Then he became still as a stone himself, watching.

The Arab was nervous. Before he started up the slope he looked all around, shading his eyes with his hand against the bright morning light. Seeing nothing, he began to climb toward the cave mouth. Like his now dead companion, he tended to keep his head down to judge his footing on the steep incline.

Starke waited, tensing his muscles. The knife was ready in his hand.

The Arab stopped midway up the slope and raised his face to the ridge above, studying it intently. Then he opened his mouth and quietly called:

"Narouz!"

The sound echoed within the ravine and vanished into the rustle of the wind among the stones. The Arab nervously clicked his rifle bolt to make sure he had a round chambered, and resumed his climb.

As all but the top of his head disappeared under the rim of the overhang, Starke crawled silently over the pile of stones and crept toward the edge of the rock, keeping the man's *keffiyeh* just in sight. The Arab was almost under the overhang—

Now.

Starke dropped out of the sky right on top of the Arab. His weight slammed the man to his knees, and the rifle went clattering to the ground. The Arab drew in a breath to scream, but Starke's knife was already slicing deep across his windpipe and jugular vein. The man, bubbling through the blood pumping from his gashed throat, collapsed onto the stones. Starke sat on him until his struggling ended, wrinkling his nose in disgust as the man's bowels let go.

When he was quite sure the Arab was dead, Starke cleaned the knife off using the man's dirty robe, and then dragged him inside the cave. The blood was already sinking into the thirsty gravel. Starke finished the job of concealment with more dirt, while he considered

his next move. He didn't think he'd get out of the area if he allowed the last man to remain to raise a pursuit.

The second Arab's rifle was an old British Lee-Enfield, a much better weapon than the Lebel although just as dirty. Starke worked the bolt thoughtfully. He had to decide whether to make a run for it now, or to dispose of the third Arab and then take his time. At first glance, the former was the better way. But Starke didn't know the countryside, and the Arab presumably did. He'd also be able to whistle up more friends if Starke left him alone. But killing him silently would be difficult. The man would be extremely wary now that his companions had mysteriously vanished, and Starke wouldn't find a close approach easy. That meant using the Lee-Enfield, and risking the attention a rifle shot might bring. On the other hand, the wind was strong and blowing toward the sea. It would dissipate the report.

Starke shrugged. He had to have his rear secure, even at the slight risk of a rifle shot.

He chambered a round in the rifle, climbed back up to the ridge, and ran in a crouch parallel to the ravine, keeping well back from its edge. When he calculated he'd come far enough, he dropped to the ground and moved, elbows and knees, in the rifleman's crawl to the rim of the gully.

The third Arab was where Starke had left him, but now was gazing anxiously back along the ravine, toward the location of the cave. He was looking away from Starke.

It was an easy shot, no more than forty meters. Starke adjusted the backsight, put the rifle into rest, aimed carefully, and fired a single shot. The detonation rebounded from the walls of the ravine and was lost in the moan of the wind. When silence returned, the Arab lay on his face on the gravel of the ravine floor, a hole punched in the back of his head.

Starke dragged him to the cave and put him into it with his two companions and all of the firearms, although he kept the knife. A half hour's work with loose stones, and the cave mouth was blocked and invisible. Then Starke set off inland, toward the morning sun.

Berlin—Rome

September 12, 1938

The oaks in the great Tiergarten park were beginning their autumn transformation from green to gold. Among the heavy trunks to the left of the path, Heydrich glimpsed the blue shimmer of water. Over there lay an arm of the Neuer See, the small lake that the landscape architect Lenne had incorporated into his redesign of the park at the end of the last century.

Heydrich looked down at the woman walking beside him. "Let's go down to the water," he suggested.

Sofia von Falkenberg nodded compliantly. Heydrich noted with approval that for this meeting she had worn conservative clothes, a gray dress covered by a light fall coat. He himself was in civilian clothes. At this hour on a Monday morning the park was almost deserted, except for a few nannies out with their perambulator-borne charges, and the meeting was in no danger of being observed.

Especially, Heydrich thought, since all the observers in Berlin are now mine, and I know where they are.

As they ambled across the grass under the oaks, he glanced sideways again at the beautiful face beside him. Sofia could have served as a model for a Madonna in a quattrocento painting, one perhaps by Andrea del Sarto. Perhaps del Sarto's models also had the private tastes that afflicted Sofia, Heydrich mused, tastes unbetrayed by their appearances either in paint or in flesh. He was aware that he could have Sofia with a crook of his finger, but he'd never considered giving in to the temptation. His marriage to Lina was too strong, to

begin with, but he also knew that sleeping with Sofia could be professionally disastrous. A man involved with her would find it all too easy to lose control of his actions; she had that much female magnetism. There were scores of people who would be delighted to use such a slip by Heydrich to bring him down.

This is one of those situations, Heydrich thought as they neared the lake, where virtue and advantage neatly coincide. But even if that were not the case, I'd still refuse her. No man can rule others who cannot rule himself.

They stopped at the margin of the lake. A duck and a drake floated near the far bank, dibbling for waterweed. "Look," Sofia said. "A couple. Do you suppose they're man and wife?"

"I don't know," Heydrich said. It was a measure of her breeding and sophistication that she didn't speak archly. She had never even attempted to flirt with him, let alone seduce him. Nevertheless, she somehow made it plain that she was there if he wanted her.

She became businesslike. "Herr Heydrich, you wanted to see me about work?"

"Yes," said Heydrich. The ducks were both upside down now, tails in the air. "I want you to prepare to leave Berlin for a while. Without your husband, if at all possible."

"Where are you sending me?"

"Rome."

She knit her brows in concentration. "Helmuth will not be any trouble. He knows how I like Italy. And his business . . . well, he prefers it to myself."

Heydrich nodded. The dossier on Helmuth Kardel von Falkenberg was several inches thick. The man was twenty years older than Sofia, and homosexual to boot. He was extremely discreet about it, though. A lot of homosexuals were spending time in Sachsenhausen; but unlike Sofia's husband they were neither pro-Nazi artistocrats, nor wealthy.

"When do you want me to go?" she asked. "I should try to be in Berlin for Christmas. There are appearances. . . ."

"I'm not sure," Heydrich said. "It won't be until late in the fall. Perhaps not until January. But I want you to lay the groundwork with your husband to spend an extended time in Rome. Natural enough

for someone from an old Catholic family like yours."

"Yes, Herr Heydrich. I will do that."

He'd better get it out of the way now. "You remember Herr Dorf, the man I sent to you at the end of May?"

"Yes." Perhaps there was the ghost of a smile at the corners of the perfect mouth. Heydrich still was not sure of her motivations in working for him, apart from the obvious one of sex. It might be the thrill of clandestine work that she craved. He'd seen that often enough in men, but it seemed rarer in women.

As rare as a woman who could keep her mouth closed while her legs were open, he thought, intentionally though silently crude with her. He didn't like being unsure of her purposes. He was used to seeing people's wants clearly, even wants they didn't know they had, and manipulating these to his own ends.

She was regarding him expectantly. "I am to work with Herr Dorf?" she asked.

"Yes. But I must emphasize something to you. No matter what you are assigned to do with regard to him, *do it*. Don't be surprised at any order. No matter how unlikely it may seem."

"Very well. May I ask why?"

He'd never have accepted such a question from anyone else, not even from Starke. Starke would have known better than to ask, anyway. But she didn't seem to care.

"You may ask," Heydrich said. He'd originally decided not to tell her, but had reconsidered on his way to this meeting. If she knew, the knowledge might steady her resolve at critical moments.

"But will I receive an answer?" she said blithely.

He nodded, and told her. She gave a microscopic start and said, "Oh, I see." Heydrich watched her intently for further reaction, half-expecting disgust. None was evident.

"Be ready at a moment's notice," Heydrich said. He was satisfied with his judgment of her. "I'll get your instructions to you in the usual way."

The atmosphere in Donati's dining room was heavy with gloom. Donati toyed with a heel of bread while Teresa the housekeeper removed the dessert dishes. Rossi, sitting across from Julia, emptied his wineglass and half-filled it again. He offered the bottle to Julia, but she shook her head silently.

"Not a cheerful homecoming, Marc," Donati said after Teresa left the dining room with the stack of plates. "I'm sorry."

Rossi had returned to Rome that morning, after an exhausting journey back from Palestine. Trapped ashore without the visa that would let him leave the British Mandate legally, he'd had to return by one of the clandestine routes Mossad used: small boat to Crete, on to Corfu, and then across the Tyrrhenian sea to Brindisi, down on the Italian heel. He'd been traveling night and day.

And he'd returned to Rome to discover from Julia that Mussolini's government had driven one more nail into the coffin of Italian Jewry. On September 3, the day Rossi reached Palestine, the government had announced that foreign Jews could no longer establish residence in Italy, and that those already in residence were to leave within six months. But worst was the last provision of the new laws: all Jews who had been nationalized after the beginning of January 1919 lost their citizenship. They were now foreigners, and would have to leave. Several of Donati's friends, and therefore their families, fell into this category.

"And it will get worse," Donati said, as though he had been reading Rossi's thoughts. "There are rumors that as well as the citizenship laws, there are even more stringent ones coming."

"What do you think they'll do?" Julia asked quietly. She looked wan and drained. Rossi suspected she hadn't been sleeping well. He'd been somewhat surprised to find her still at Donati's on his return, thinking it likely that she'd have gone back to the States by now. Apparently she'd taken over the paperwork Rossi had gratefully left behind. She'd been coolly polite with him, as he with her, both remembering their collision the day before he left for Trieste.

"If Mussolini goes on modeling himself on Hitler," Donati said, "I can imagine exactly what they'll do. Sanctions against property ownership for Jews. Restrictions on the professions. Mine, for example. Jewish lawyers only able to represent Jewish clients. And

they've already begun closing off the public education system to Jews. I am afraid it may get worse."

"Camps, like the Nazis?" Julia said.

"In time, perhaps." Donati looked down at his wineglass, found it empty, and refilled it. "Look at this table. Once it belonged to the household of the Dukes of Parma. It's three hundred years old. My family has been in Italy nearly two hundred years longer than that. There are Jews here who never even thought of themselves as Jews, we've assimilated so completely. Now the so-called Aryan Italians have decided we're not Italians at all, but some kind of disease inside the body of the state."

"Surely Mussolini can't go as far as Hitler has," said Julia.

Donati sighed. "It's true a lot of Italians don't like what's going on. But given time. . . ."

"What is the Pope going to do?" asked Rossi. He'd been itching to ask during the meal, but Donati's melancholy had prevented him from doing so. He knew that Donati and Julia had had an audience with Pius while he was away, but Julia hadn't volunteered any information, and he'd been reluctant to ask her outright.

"I saw Cardinal Pacelli this afternoon," Donati told him. "The Church is doing nothing about the citizenship laws. Pius evidently feels the time is not right to speak." He glanced at Julia. "We saw Pius while you were on the way to Palestine," he told Rossi. "He's promised to condemn the Nazis in Germany, their persecution of minorities. That will include Jews. He will also, presumably, condemn what the Fascists are doing to us here."

"When?" Rossi said eagerly. With the Pope as ally against the Germans and the Fascists, a great deal might be accomplished.

"He wouldn't say. Pacelli swore us to secrecy. You're the only one besides us who knows of this. Outside the Vatican, of course."

Rossi felt a wave of disappointment sweep through him. "I see. He may never do it. Politics."

"Yes."

Donati said, "I think he wants to. But he's under such pressure. There are plenty of pro-Germans in the Curia who don't want a repeat of *Burning Sorrow*. They see the Germans as the best defense against the communists in Russia. There are also anti-Semites, like Cardinal

Mondolfo. And Mussolini can make life hard for the Vatican, if he chooses to do it." He paused. "Also, I think Pius is not well. Pacelli let something slip about his health today. I don't know if it was intentional or not."

"Not well?" Julia cried. "But if he dies, and a pro-German becomes Pope—" She stopped, aghast at the prospect.

"Who has the best chance at the Papal chair?" Rossi asked.

"Pacelli. But the Germans aren't comfortable with him. After him, Mondolfo. He's the one the Nazis and the Fascists would like. It could happen that way, especially if something happened to turn Vatican opinion more against the Jews."

"Like what?"

"I have no idea. They might manufacture something, I suppose."

They all remained silent for a few moments, staring down at the old wood of the Duke of Parma's table. Rossi thought: what things have been planned around this wooden slab, over the last three centuries? Has it ever heard anything like this?

Probably. None of this is new. Only the scale.

"I'm fearful," Donati said slowly at last. "I believe there is going to be a war, if not this year then next. When that happens, the borders all over Europe will close. Just now, we can save many of our people by getting them out, helping them emigrate. When we can no longer do that, when they're trapped inside Germany. . . ." Rossi looked up in time to see him shudder. "I think the Germans will begin to kill them systematically," Donati said. "I feel it in my bones."

"They *couldn't*," Julia said in horror. "No civilized country would do that."

"Who would stop them, if they decided to do it?"

A silence.

"The fact is," Donati said, "that we may not have a lot of time left, unless Pius acts in our favor. An encyclical condemning the Nazis would buy us time, because the Nazis would then have to spend their energies getting back the support of German Catholics. There might even be enough turmoil to bring Hitler down. At the very least, we'd be able to extract more of our people from the Reich."

"But if he dies," Julia said, and left the sentence unfinished.

"I'm worried about that," Donati said. "What also worries me is the

possibility of something happening to alienate the Vatican from us. Pius and Pacelli both detest violence. If Jews here or in Germany began taking the law into their own hands, acts of terrorism for example, the Nazis would be delighted. I suppose that's what I meant earlier, when I talked about Vatican opinion turning against the Jews."

"So we aren't even permitted to defend ourselves," Julia said, with a savagery in her voice that made Rossi look at her in surprise. "In case we offend the old men in the Vatican. So that we can go on waiting for them to act. And waiting. And waiting."

"Julia," Donati said quietly, "I know. But right now there is no other way. Pius is one of our best hopes. We can't do anything to put that hope in jeopardy."

She put her elbows on the table and rested her head in her hands. "I realize that. But it makes me feel so horribly futile."

Rossi didn't think the conversation was going anywhere. "Have you found out what's happened to the *Olympia* refugees?" he asked Donati.

"Yes," Donati said, clearly grateful for the change of subject. "About half got away from the British. The rest were rounded up. The British are sending them back to a holding camp on Cyprus. You can imagine what it's like in there. What they're going to do with them after that, I don't know."

"Can you check to see if there is a Samuel Levy in either group?" Rossi said. "I need to know."

"Of course. Why?"

"He may be dead," Rossi said simply. He told Donati what had happened in the ravine, and afterward. "We searched for him," Rossi ended. "But there was no sign of him. The Arabs must have killed him and hidden the body somewhere. I should have been taking better care of him, damn it."

"He might turn up later," Julia said, in an effort to be consoling. The gesture grated on Rossi. The Arabs had gone in pursuit of Levy, and there wasn't the slightest chance the butcher could have escaped from men who knew the country. She should have been perceptive enough to realize that. She was naive.

"You said he was one of the Altgarten Jews?" Donati asked. "I read the exit interviews of the *Olympia* refugees."

"Yes," said Rossi. "He was the only one the Germans let out."

"Do you think it odd the Germans promised exit papers to the whole Altgarten group? And then hung onto them?"

"No odder than other things they've done," said Rossi. "The Germans never do anything without papers. The people from Altgarten may be stuck because of a misplaced file somewhere in the Reich Emigration Office. We have to try to find out where they are now."

"I'll put that in motion," Donati said. "Now, another matter, I'm afraid. Marc, there'll be another ship ready to leave at the end of September. A very small one this time, but it's all we can manage. That'll be the last over-the-beach run till spring, because the bad weather starts in October." He frowned. "Even this run is a little late for my liking. Anyway, we want you to go over on it."

"Do you want me to come back on the same ship?"

"That's just it. You're going to have to get out of the country for a while. The new residency laws are going to be enforced strictly at first, and it'll take time to find ways around them. My . . . friends at the passport control office know you stay here, and they're perfectly well aware that you're Jewish, as well as American. I've been lining their wallets for them to give Mossad freedom of movement here in Italy, but the new laws are making them nervous. The police are pressuring them to point out American Jews, and if they catch you, you'll probably be deported. Then it will be very difficult for you to get back in. They might even jail you, if they wanted to set an example."

"What do you want me to do?"

"The Haganah needs men to help with the defense of our settlements in Palestine."

"I see," Rossi said. Haganah, the Jewish defense force, had been established just after the World War, following Arab attacks on Jewish settlers in Galilee and Jaffa. For several years it had been small-scale and amateurish, but with the outbreak of the Palestinian Arab revolt in 1936 and the widespread murder of Jews and destruction of Jewish farmland,

it had turned into a tightly organized militia of part-time soldiers. But it was always short of men and weapons.

"Moreover," Donati went on, "we have information that the Grand Mufti is planning a major terror offensive for later this fall. His men have been building up to it all this year."

"Pardon me," Julia said, "but who exactly is the Grand Mufti? I've heard you mention him before, but I'm still not clear."

Rossi said, "His name is Haj Amin el-Husseini. He's the spiritual leader of the Palestinian Arabs, the Grand Mufti of Jerusalem. Or he was, till the British kicked him out of the Mandate last fall, for organizing the Arab revolt back in 1936. Unfortunately, the French let him into Lebanon. From there he went to Syria, and he's been coordinating attacks on us from Damascus. He has two guerilla groups, about ten thousand men in all. One group operates out of the hills of Galilee, and the other's in Samaria. He also has a big terrorist organization, with headquarters in Damascus and Jerusalem. Altogether they've murdered more than two hundred of us since the beginning of the year. Men, women, and children."

"The Mufti's people tried to kill Marc in Istanbul in the spring," Donati said to Julia. "He was here to recuperate from his wounds."

"Oh," Julia said, almost apologetically. Her eyes said to Rossi: *I'm sorry. I didn't know that.*

"Part of the shipment to Palestine this time will be weapons," Donati told Rossi. "Haganah needs them desperately."

"I'll get them across," Rossi said. "I'll stay in Palestine for the winter. When the weather improves in the spring you can bring me back, if you can get around the passport authorities and the police."

"Good. That will work well."

"I'm coming, too," Julia announced.

Both men looked at her in astonishment. "What are you talking about?" Rossi said when he got his wits back.

"I just told you. I'm going with you. On the ship."

"No, you're not," Rossi said.

She turned on him angrily. "What good am I doing *here*? The Pope won't see me again. Claudio's dealing with Pacelli. Do you suggest

I sit here on my fanny, pushing paper around, until the Italian police get around to deporting me? I'm as Jewish as you are, or had you forgotten?"

"It's too dangerous," Rossi said. The woman had no idea of conditions aboard the refugee ships. She probably thought it would be like crossing the Atlantic on the *Queen Mary*. He wished she'd never set foot in Rome.

"*Dangerous?* What has that to do with anything? Of course it's dangerous. Do you suggest I run from danger every time it raises its head? What about the women and children on the ships? Why should I be exempt from what they face?"

"They have no choice," Donati reminded her. "You do."

Her eyes remained on Rossi. "Then I choose to go. What use will I be, if I go back home now? Let me tell you something. Hardly anyone back in the States has any real idea of what's happening over here, how bad it's becoming. They don't want to believe it, they tell themselves it's all propaganda, that the Nazis and the Fascists can't really be doing these things, it's all stories to sell newspapers. Somebody has to push the reality into their faces, somebody who's seen it with their own eyes."

"Like you, for example," Rossi said.

"Yes. Like me." She fell silent, cheeks flushed, nostrils dilated.

She's a goddamned loose cannon bashing around on the deck, Rossi thought. God knows what she'd get up to if we let her.

"She has a point," Donati said thoughtfully.

"*What?* Claudio, you can't be serious. I can't nursemaid a woman—"

His words were cut off by the slam of Julia's flattened hand on the tabletop. That must have hurt, Rossi thought fleetingly.

"*Don't* you patronize me," she hissed at him. "Who do you think you are, to judge what I can or can't handle? You don't even know me. What makes you think you're an expert on me? Or on any other woman, for that matter?"

Rossi took refuge in silence. Eventually she'd shut up and go away. He glanced at Donati for support. He thought he saw a flicker of amusement in the lawyer's dark eyes.

"As I said," Donati resumed, "Julia has a point. She has important

contacts in the American Jewish Conference, and it's true that our problems here seem very abstract to non-Jewish Americans. It's isolationism, I suppose. They don't want to believe what's happening, because then they'd feel constrained to do something about it, and they don't want to get involved. Could you get an eye-witness report on the refugee ships published widely in the United States?"

"Yes. I could."

Donati turned to Rossi. "I think we should let her go on this run. It may well be the last clandestine one before spring."

"Claudio—"

"Marc, please," Donati said. "It's important that this be done. Take her as far as Palestine. Let her see what it's like. She can return on the ship with one of the other escorts."

"As long as that's what happens," Rossi said.

"Julia?"

She nodded reluctantly. "Thank you, Claudio. I'll *try* to avoid being a burden to you, Mr. Rossi," she added.

"Perhaps you two should declare an armed truce before you board the ship," Donati said mildly. "You'll be at close quarters for some time."

"I'm sure Mr. Rossi and I will have very little to say to each other," she informed Donati. "Thank you for this, Claudio. Please excuse me."

She pushed her chair back, stood up, and left the dining room. When she had gone, Donati favored Rossi with a wide grin.

"Be careful, Marc."

"Why?"

"She likes you."

"Claudio," Rossi said, "for an intelligent man, you sometimes talk the most god-awful drivel."

PART TWO

1939

Northern Palestine

January 13, 1939

A chill wind was blowing out of the night, a north wind from the mountains across the border in Lebanon. The rush of air flowed down the deep ravine cut through the bedrock by the narrow Quren River, along whose bank Rossi and the other men of the ambush team were slogging uphill toward the ruins of the fortress.

Rossi took his eyes from the boulder-strewn riverbank for a moment, and looked ahead and up. Above him, outlined against the stars, was a great spur of rock crowned by the massive curtain wall of the Crusader stronghold of Montfort. Rossi's tireless interest in the nooks and crannies of history had led him to a few scraps of information about the place, abandoned for nearly seven hundred years: built by the Crusader Count Joscelin of Courtenay, it had been stormed, sacked, and destroyed by Sultan Saladin in 1187. Rebuilt by the German Order of Knights some fifty years later, it had again fallen to the Moslems in 1271, and since then had been slowly falling into ruin, foresaken and empty.

Tonight there would again be armed men within its grim perimeter of stone. If matters turned out as they should, there would also be fighting, and men would die.

The more it changes, the more it stays the same, Rossi thought as the squad leader began leading the team up the steep slope toward the southern side of the castle. I wonder what the old Christian ghosts here think of us?

His rifle bounced against the small of his back as he climbed, and

he could feel the weight of the two hand grenades dragging at the pockets of his leather jacket. The weapons were British, but the ambush team wasn't. Its members were Haganah men, as Rossi was, and they were out here to fight the Arab terrorists on their own ground. Until a year ago, the defense of Jewish settlements in dangerous areas of Palestine—which now meant most areas—depended on palisades, sentries, and weakly armed garrisons. The Arabs came, attacked, and left as they pleased. Then, annoyed by increasing Arab terrorism against British targets and short of men, the British had reluctantly begun to consider using Jewish help against the raiders. The idea would probably have come to nothing, though, had it not been for the tireless dedication of one Orde Wingate, an intelligence captain in the British Army. Captain Wingate, who had become a fervent supporter of Jewish hopes for a national homeland in Palestine, had decided that the terrorists could only be checked by carrying the battle to their own doorsteps. He trained Jewish Haganah men to travel and fight by night, and during much of 1938 his mobile ambush teams had intercepted, killed, or captured dozens of terrorists.

The work was so successful that the British Foreign Office took fright. Jews were actually taking up weapons, training for combat, and turning into deadly and efficient soldiers. The Arabs would be enraged at the prospect of Jews defending themselves. The Arabs would blame the British for this unprecedented behavior. If there was a war, the Arabs might be angry enough at the British to help the Germans, and there was no telling where that might lead. Jews were supposed to *put up with things*. They always had. Why should they complicate diplomacy by not continuing to do so?

Captain Wingate had been recalled to England in October.

The British acted too late. The men Wingate left behind knew that his superiors wouldn't allow him to come back. They took up where he left off, set up even more intelligence nets to track Arab movements, and continued training soldiers. Rossi was one of them. This was his third operation.

And it would probably be his last for a while. He'd received word this afternoon that Donati wanted him back in Rome as soon as possible. Mossad was opening up the clandestine escape routes again,

despite the weather. Pius still hadn't acted, and the millions of Jews remaining in Europe were in deadly peril. As many of them as possible had to be removed from the grip of the Nazis, whatever the risks.

Rossi paused at the top of the slope and caught his breath; it had been a long climb. From the position of the stars he estimated that it was about midnight. The vast mass of masonry that was the ruin of the castle's keep loomed above him. Part of the ambush team was to take up positions here, overlooking the ravine through which the Quren flowed. On the other side of the ravine was concealed a blocking party, which would cut off escape in that direction. The Arabs they were intercepting were part of Fawzi Kawakji's band, the same group that had murdered nineteen Jews in Tiberias last September. Kawakji was operating from a base just across the border in Lebanon, and intelligence indicated that a raiding party of twenty of his men was on the way into Palestine for a strike at Kibbutz Hanita. The Arabs were trying an indirect approach this time, infiltrating past Montfort and along the course of the Quren.

Rossi unslung his rifle—a British Enfield—and chambered a round. He heard faint metallic clicks as the other Haganah men near him did the same. There were eight of them including Rossi on the height near Montfort's keep, and four in the blocking party on the ravine's far side. The Arabs outnumbered the Jews, as usual, but everybody was used to that. Rossi found a good position among the rocks from which he could see a hundred-meter stretch of the riverbanks in the ravine below.

Gideon Laski, the lieutenant commanding the squad, was working his way along the firing line to make sure everyone was properly in position. Laski had trained directly under Wingate, and had absorbed the English officer's professionalism. He was a Polish Jew of thirty-one and had been in Palestine for ten years.

"Everything all right, Marc?" Laski whispered after making sure Rossi's field of fire was where he wanted it. Laski spoke in English, which because of Wingate's influence was the working language of the ambush teams.

"Everything's fine, Gideon," Rossi whispered back. Nobody paid much attention to the formalities of rank. Even Wingate's men

had addressed the Englishman by his first name when they were in the field.

"Now we just have to wait," Laski said softly as he went on down the line. "Keep your eyes open."

They might be waiting for a long time. Rossi put one of his spare ammunition clips on a rock within easy reach, and tried to find a more comfortable position behind his boulder. Three meters away he could see the rounded hump of Nathan Bein's shoulders as Bein also peered into the depths of the ravine. Water tinkled over the rocks below. The noise would hide the sounds of the terrorists' approach, so everyone would have to keep a sharp watch. Laski had put pickets out in case the Arabs detected the main Haganah force and tried a counter-ambush. With luck, the pickets would detect the enemy force before it reached the ambush, and give Laski time to adjust his dispositions if he needed to. For some inexplicable reason, the Arabs rarely used reconnaissance scouts and pickets. The omission had cost them a lot of men.

After an hour, a quarter moon began edging its way above the horizon. Its light rimmed the stones of the ancient fortifications with a ghostly luminescence. Rossi felt himself getting sleepy, despite the probability that the Arabs would be coming soon. They'd want the moonlight to help them on their way.

To keep himself alert he thought about Julia. He had long since gotten over being angry at her for the incident on the beach back in September. The anger, in fact, had been replaced by embarrassment at the way he'd behaved.

There had been a moon like this one, in a clear sky, but the surf on the beach was high and rising. They'd brought most of the refugees ashore without losing any, and then the last boat capsized and spilled its passengers into the breaking waves. Rossi and the shore party ran into the surf and started dragging them out of the tumbling water. It wasn't until Rossi hauled the last gasping and choking refugee up onto the sand that he noticed, first, that it was a woman, second, that she was extremely tall, and third, that it was Julia.

He almost dropped her onto the shingle. "What in hell are you doing here?" he shouted at her over the rumble of the surf.

"I'm staying," she said, brushing hair and water out of her eyes.

"What? That wasn't what we agreed. You're supposed to go back on the ship!"

"You and Claudio agreed. I didn't." She had some kind of leather bag slung across her shoulders, and began rummaging anxiously inside it.

The sailors from the ship had managed to right the lifeboat and were clambering back aboard to bail it out. "Get back in the boat," Rossi said. "You can't stay here. You haven't any papers. The British will throw you out."

"I've got my passport." She finished rummaging in the bag and triumphantly held up a dark rectangle.

"What good will it be now? It's soaked."

"I put it in oilskin. It's fine."

"We've got nowhere to put you," he snapped, feeling desperation rise in him. She was dragging him into something *again*. "You haven't got a visa from the English."

"I brought money. I'll manage. And why should I need a visa? Your refugees haven't any."

"Good God Almighty," he swore. The exhaustion and nervous tension brought on by the appalling voyage and the dangerous run ashore, added to what Julia was putting him through, snapped his temper. He grabbed her by the left forearm. *"Get back in the boat!"*

A moment later he was lying on the sand, looking up at the moon. His jaw hurt. He couldn't believe it. She'd hit him and knocked him down.

"Sorry," she said, a tall dark shape leaning over him. She didn't sound even slightly repentant. "But if you try to put me back on that boat, I'll hit you again."

He sat up, rubbing his jaw. She hadn't really hit him all that hard, he thought; he must have been off balance. "Why in hell are you so determined?" he said angrily. "You don't need to do this."

"Oh, but I do," she said. "I have to find out exactly what all this is like. So I can write about it, to make other people understand. I won't write about something I haven't gone through myself. And why in *hell* should you be able to tell *me* what to do?" The words came out of her

in a rush. "Do you think you're the only committed person in all this? Thousands of other women have come to Palestine, without your objecting to it. What are you picking on me for?"

He got to his feet, trying to think of an answer. He couldn't find a good one. "Claudio expects you to be taken care of," he mumbled. "You're important."

"Claudio can go to hell, if that's what he thinks. So can you. Do you think anything that happens here can be worse than that god-awful ship we came on? And I can take care of myself."

The worst of it was that she was probably right. The crossing from Trieste had been a particularly bad one: the ship hardly bigger than a trawler, packed with refugees, the water bad and the food worse, the weather foul for most of the run and everyone seasick, vomiting over the decks and each other. One lavatory for ninety people. She'd leaked, and the pumps ran constantly. Between Cyprus and Palestine Rossi had been sure she was going to sink, and there were only two lifeboats.

Through it all, Julia had moved as serenely as a woman traveling first class on a Cunard transatlantic liner. Seasick for the first day, she'd quickly acquired her sea legs and begun helping with the women and children, many of whom were already malnourished from the hardships they'd endured in Europe. She'd rapidly become an authority figure among the refugees; by the time they were halfway across they were looking to her for support more than to Rossi or to the other Mossad escort, Saul Hausner. Hausner in particular admired her. A German Jew originally from Dresden, he thought it wonderful that a rich American woman could be willing to share the torment of the refugees. Rossi pointed out to Hausner that anyone could put up with anything, if he or she knew there was going to be an end to it in a few days. And Julia was going back to Italy, via plane from Cyprus, as soon as the refugees were landed.

Except that she wasn't. The ship's crew had now bailed the lifeboat out, collected the oars, and were starting to row back to the tiny vessel beyond the surf.

"It's the refugees who need our help," he said. "You don't. You're using up resources we need for them."

For a moment he thought she was going to hit him again. Then she

said quietly, "You were glad enough to have *my* resources when everybody was sick and you thought we were going to sink."

He hadn't realized she'd known he'd been worried about that. "Okay," he said. "You're right. I apologize." He was furious, nonetheless. She had a way of blundering about in his life, and then making him say he was sorry for what had happened.

"Fine," she said. "That's settled, then." She turned away from him, stuffed her passport back into her bag, and started walking inland.

They'd both ended up in Jerusalem a week later, Rossi to make his connection with the Haganah, and Julia to find work with the Jerusalem office of the Kuppat Holim, the organization that provided medical service for the Jewish workers of Palestine. Rossi had only seen her once since then. He'd gone to Jerusalem to help move a clandestine shipment of arms up north, and had encountered her, quite by accident, in the street. To his considerable surprise she'd told him where she was living, and invited him to come for coffee that evening; it was as though she'd forgotten the incident on the beach. Rossi hadn't, and felt in some obscure way that he needed to make amends for his behavior. He also thought she looked lonely, and so he accepted the invitation. But the arms shipment left earlier than planned, and he had been unable to go meet her. He also hadn't been able to tell her he wasn't coming.

She's really going to think I'm a boor because of that, Rossi thought as he squinted along the barrel of the Enfield at the river flowing through the ravine below him. But it can't be helped. Maybe I'll stop and see her on the way back to Rome, if I can manage it. I could call her from Nazareth just before I leave. Assuming she's still with the health agency.

Suddenly he thought he saw a movement up the ravine, where it curved around the base of the crag under the outer curtain wall of Montfort. It might have been his eyes playing tricks in the uncertain light. He squinted. No, there it was again, a black shadow on the paler stones of the riverbank.

"Rossi," a voice hissed from a couple of meters away. It was Nathan Bein, the tailor's son from Dusseldorf. "Did you see it?"

"Yes. It's them."

He sensed rather than heard Laski behind him. "They're coming,"

Laski whispered. "The outposts reported them. About thirty. Aim very carefully."

The back of Rossi's neck tingled. It was a big raid. Enough men to outnumber the Jews by two to one. It didn't matter. They had to be stopped, regardless of the cost. In Tiberias others like them had stabbed Jewish women and children and thrown them, still living, into the burning synagogue.

Laski crept away along the firing line. As the Arab raiders came nearer, Rossi could see that they were traveling in a single file. He selected a target and laid his sights on the man.

There was a soft *pop* off to his right, and a white Verey light soared into the night sky, bathing the ravine of the Quren in a harsh flare of radiance. From both sides of the ravine, the ambush party opened fire. Muzzle flashes stabbed through the darkness. Rossi squeezed the Enfield's trigger and the man he'd selected threw up his arms and fell. Rossi switched his sights to another target and shot again, but thought he missed. Some of the Arabs had thrown themselves to the ground and were trying to return the fire that was coming from the heights above them. They were aiming at the muzzle flashes, and Rossi ducked as a bullet clipped the stones thirty centimeters to his right. Several other Arabs—about half the raiding party—were running along the ravine, back the way they had come. Rossi kept shooting at them and saw several fall, trapped in the crossfire. Shouts and screams echoed from the walls of the ravine.

The firing pin of Rossi's Enfield snapped on nothing. Jammed? No, he'd fired off all the ammunition clip. He ripped the empty clip out of the rifle and slammed a fresh magazine into the slot. Laski had fired another flare; it bobbed above the Quren's torrent, its light glittering from the dark water. The fleeing Arabs had vanished, either shot down or escaping into the night toward Lebanon. The Jewish outposts upstream might account for a few more while hurrying the rest on their way.

A few Arabs were still on the riverbank, though, pinned down but still fighting back. Rossi heard another bullet snap overhead. They were firing too high, common when one was shooting uphill. Somebody else threw a grenade at the Arabs, which exploded on the stones in a hail of metal and rock splinters. Rossi squeezed his trigger

again, aiming at a suddenly moving shape near the water, and the Enfield jolted against his shoulder. He seemed to have missed, and tried again. Once more the dry snap of an empty chamber. It surprised him. He hadn't realized he'd fired so many shots. Reload. Three or four grenades had already detonated. If the grenades didn't kill the Arabs, they would at least drive the raiders from cover so they could be shot at.

Rossi was pulling the spent clip out of the rifle when the flare went out and, simultaneously, the Arabs in the streambed roused themselves for a desperate charge up the hill at their tormentors. Rossi saw them coming and fumbled in his ammunition pouch for a full clip, cursing himself for having kept only one spare magazine within quick reach.

He suddenly saw that he wasn't going to be able to reload in time, because an Arab was rising out of the ground not six meters away. Somehow the man had managed to use ground cover to infiltrate almost to the Jewish firing line. In the dark, Rossi couldn't tell how, or if, he was armed.

The bright tongue of a muzzle flash from the Arab's hip, and something tugged hard at Rossi's jacket. A rifle or pistol.

Rossi leaped up from the ground, holding the Enfield at trigger guard and forestock, sweeping the butt end of the weapon up and to the left. The Arab fired again, but again missed. Rossi felt the heavy stock of the Enfield slam into flesh and bone, but not solidly enough. He'd caught his attacker no more than a glancing blow under the right armpit.

It was enough, however, to make the Arab lose his grip on his rifle. Rossi heard it clatter to the stones and drew his own weapon back for another blow, but the Arab was on him before he could swing. The man's weight knocked him to the ground and Rossi released the Enfield. It was useless at such close quarters.

He saw metal glint in the moonlight above him and twisted just in time to avoid the downward sweep of the knife. The blade clanked against stone beside his shoulder, sparks darting from the impact, and then the Arab was drawing himself up for a more accurate strike.

Rossi, almost flat on his back, kicked the man in the testicles. The Arab screamed, but didn't drop the knife. He lunged clumsily at

Rossi, but his aim was thrown awry by pain. Rossi easily avoided the blow, grabbing up a fist-sized stone as he did so. He slammed the jagged rock into the Arab's face. Bone crunched. The Arab screamed again in a bubbling way and turned to stagger away down the hill, still screaming. Suddenly he threw his arms into the air and fell down, silent. Somebody had shot him. Rossi looked frantically to see what had become of the rest of the Arabs' charge, but no one was standing up except him. He dropped hastily to the ground and rolled into cover, head uncomfortably lower than feet because of the slope of the hill, and managed at last to reload the Enfield.

All shooting suddenly stopped, the echoes dying away into the night wind. Rossi heard footsteps crunching on loose stones behind him, and twisted around, Enfield at the ready.

"Careful," he heard Laski say quietly. "It's me."

Rossi found that he was shaking from reaction. "It's over?"

"I think so. I couldn't shoot the one attacking you till you drove him off. He was too close. Sorry."

"Doesn't matter now," Rossi said. He drew a deep breath. "How many did we get?"

"Let's look." Laski blew two sharp bursts on a whistle: the all-clear. Then he started down toward the rushing waters of the Quren. Rossi followed.

There were seven dead Arabs and eight wounded, three of them very badly hurt by grenade explosions. None of the ambush team had so much as a scratch. They buried the dead men under a cairn of stones and patched up the wounded as well as they could. The three seriously hurt were put on litters for transport back to the Haganah base, while the other five were bound and made to walk as much as they could. Rossi helped with one of the litters. The man was very young, not more than twenty, and had been half-disemboweled by a grenade fragment. Rossi knew he'd die within the next forty-eight hours. A gut wound like that always turned septic. It would be an agonizing death as the poisons slithered through the young Arab's flesh.

Perhaps, Rossi thought as they set off and he lurched over the stones with the litter's weight dragging at his arm, this is one of the

men who threw our children into the fire at Tiberias. Alive, after using his knife on them, so they couldn't crawl away.

The thought gave him a savage satisfaction. He burned with righteousness. He wanted to stop the column, persuade Laski to shoot the prisoners and leave them for daylight and the carrion birds.

Then the emotion passed, leaving him feeling cold and sick and violated. It's in me too, he thought with loathing. Lust for death and killing, the deep, foul delight. Why are we made this way?

He looked up at the grim ruined battlements of Montfort on the crag above him, and found, as he had expected, no answer.

Jerusalem—Tel Aviv

January 17-18, 1939

Starke had a room in a house in Mea Shearim, the down-at-heels Orthodox Jewish enclave on the northwest side of Jerusalem, outside the walls of the Old City. The house was a twenty-minute walk from the brickyard where he'd found work back in October, after making his way down from the north.

The first part of that journey, with Starke moneyless and on foot, had been hard and dangerous; Palestine was simmering with terrorism and violence, and it seemed to Starke that he'd spent more time hiding off the road than walking on it. His in-country supply point was Haifa, where there was a German colony that had been planted there back in 1868. Much to Starke's relief the SD dead drop was loaded, and after clearing it he had money, a weapon, and a forged immigration certificate in his Levy identity. The certificate, true to Heydrich's attention to detail, was indistinguishable from the papers the Jews themselves produced for their people: a forgery of a forgery.

After clearing the drop and finding something to eat, Starke set off, as per instructions, for Jerusalem. It was a big enough place for him to get lost in, but small enough for him to be identifiable later as Levy, after the mission was completed.

Whenever that was to be. Starke had resigned himself to an indefinite stay in this pestilential country while Heydrich arranged the approach to the target. The resignation might have come easier if Starke had known the identity of the target, but he didn't.

Palestine was in such a state that the cross-country buses were wearing sheet iron armor, to fend off Arab attacks. British patrols seemed to be all over the place, but from the damage anyone could see in the Jewish areas, they appeared to be having little effect. Twice, once outside Nazareth and once near Nablus, the British stopped the bus Starke was riding on to make identity checks. His papers passed each time. One young man was caught without papers, and bundled off the bus into a waiting British truck. The Arab passengers on the bus jeered; the Jews screamed abuse. A tiny civil war seemed about to break out on the vehicle as it moved away from the checkpoint, until the driver pulled over to the side of the road and refused to go farther until the noise stopped. Pragmatism overcame emotion and the bus lumbered onward, under its carapace of sheet iron, toward Jerusalem.

That was one minor example of the confused state of the country. Starke had needed some time to figure it out. Not all Arabs wanted to kill or expel the Jewish settlers; many Palestinians would have preferred to live in peace, so one had Arabs and Jews, for example, riding on the same bus—although under some circumstances tempers and abuse could flare. But there were also plenty of Arabs who *did* want to drive the Jews out of Palestine, and these would kill.

On the other hand, although most Jews wanted good relations with their Arab neighbors, there was again a substantial number who wanted to reclaim all of historical Israel as a purely Jewish nation, and these wanted to throw the Arabs out. The British occupying forces and Mandate government fell into three categories: those who favored the Arabs, those who favored the Jews, and those who wanted to drop the whole explosive mess and leave. There were thus at least seven sides to the conflict, and the number of possible alliances and enmities was bewildering. Starke didn't think it could be solved short of one race annihilating the other.

On his arrival in Jerusalem, Starke had obtained work in the brickyard near Mea Shearim. This had been purely by his own efforts, without any assistance from Heydrich. Most of the available work for Jews was arranged through the Histadrut, the Jewish General Federation of Trade Unions, and security prevented the SD from helping him out. Housing had been more of a problem. Starke

didn't want to risk his cover unnecessarily by close contact with German Jews, so his choices were somewhat restricted. It was only after a week's search that he found an elderly couple, Polish Jews, who needed to make ends meet by renting out a tiny room off the courtyard of the house they themselves rented. Starke's opinion of Poles in general and Polish Jews in particular wasn't raised by the fact that the toilet was in a shack in the courtyard, and the kitchen a tin lean-to not one meter from the toilet. His landlady was still ecstatic because the British had recently put in piped water, and she no longer had to boil the dirty liquid from the communal cistern up the street. The cistern, Starke suspected, had been constructed while Palestine was still part of the Ottoman Empire.

At this particular moment, Starke was trudging along the narrow street toward the house. He'd just finished his ten-hour shift in the brickyard and he was thirsty, tired, dirty, and hungry. He was wondering, for no good reason, what the old woman had prepared for the evening meal. The diet was Polish, staple, and monotonous: barley or oatmeal porridge in the morning, bread and soup in the evening. Sometimes there was a tiny amount of meat in the soup. Vegetables in season, or dried ones in the soup. The Poles—their name was Koubski—had accepted Starke's presence in the household only because of their need for money, and kept their distance from him. Part of it was that although he was (as they believed) Jewish, he was also German. This suited Starke perfectly. He wanted no intimacies. If Frau Koubski had tried to make a pet of him, he would have moved on.

He reached the door to the courtyard and pushed it open. The door was barred at dusk, which was now only a few minutes away; if Starke got home later than that, he had to bang on it until Herr Koubski, with much ill grace, came and opened it.

Three damned months, Starke thought, as he stepped into the courtyard and closed the gate behind him. How much longer? Heydrich, what the devil are you waiting for?

The courtyard was dim under the smoky orange sky of a Jerusalem winter evening. Odors from the privy and the open kitchen lean-to mixed in Starke's nostrils. He wrinkled his nose in distaste. The

brickyard was dusty and gritty, but at least its dirt was inorganic. All he'd need now was to contract dysentery. That would be as disabling in his profession as a gunshot wound.

Frau Koubski wasn't in front of the oil stove, as she usually was when he came home. The soup pot was on one burner, but the fire was off. Starke halted in annoyance. Was he going to get cold food again, as he sometimes did when the oil ran out?

Then he noticed that the cracked wooden door to his room was standing half open. One thing the Koubskis never did was enter his room. He'd buried the pistol from the Haifa dead drop under the dirt floor, but if the old woman had been snooping around—

He walked carefully and silently over to the open door of the room. No sound except the usual street noises, the rumble of a truck to the north on the Jaffa Road. At the door of the room he paused, listening.

Someone coughed softly inside. It didn't sound like a man. Frau Koubski, damn her. What did she think she was looking for? Now he was going to have to move. And if she'd found the gun. . . .

He pushed the door wide and stepped into the tiny dark room, which was lit only by the open door and the small glassless window next to it. His eyes took an instant to adapt to the lack of light, and then he saw her.

She was sitting on the stool which, apart from the rope bed and the decaying wooden table, was the only furnishing in the room. She raised her head when he came in, and he realized with a jolt that she wasn't Frau Koubski at all. She was much younger, and he'd never seen her before.

"What are you doing in my room?" he asked angrily, speaking in the Yiddish he'd learned from the old Jew in Berlin.

"I'm sorry," she said in Hebrew. "I don't understand."

Starke's Hebrew was minimal. "Deutsch?" he asked. Who in hell was she? She was pretty enough, he could see that even in the poor light. And tall, and dark. Italian-looking.

"Kein Deutsch," she answered. "English?"

"A little part," he answered in the same language. The real Levy had taken English in secondary school, Starke remembered, just as he

had. Starke was quite fluent, which was one of the reasons he'd attracted Heydrich's attention a few years ago. But he was more fluent than Levy would be. He'd have to allow for that.

"Good," she said. "Are you Samuel Levy?"

He was careful not to show any reaction. He was considering how to dispose of her body if he had to. It would be best to wait until after midnight and then move the remains, suitably cut about, to an Arab district. But there was always a risk of British patrols. Killing her would be a last resort.

"Perhaps I am," he said. "My papers are in order. Who are you?"

"Julia Belmont. I work for Kuppat Holim."

The Jewish health service. Starke relaxed fractionally. "Why do you come here?" he asked, taking care to thicken his accent.

"I wanted to find out if you were all right." She was smiling, as though about to present a child with a birthday surprise.

Starke grappled with the idea, and could make no sense of it. "Why? I'm not *krank*. Sick."

She laughed. Starke felt a jab of sexual urge. On closer examination she was gangly and long-limbed, not graceful, but there was an allure to her body. A primitive part of Starke suggested using her here and then dumping her for the British to find in the morning, but he rejected the idea out of hand as being unprofessional. Besides, she'd have told people where she was going.

"I know you're not ill. You look quite well to me. We were worried about you. That is," she said, looking suddenly concerned, "if you're the Samuel Levy from Altgarten, who came here on the *Olympia*."

He nodded. How in the name of Christ had they caught up with him? And why? "I am," he said. Delay making any decisions until he found out where this was going.

"I asked your landlady to let me wait for you here," she said. "I hope you don't mind. But I thought it was important. You see—well, you remember Marc Rossi? The man who was with you when you ran from the British on the beach?"

"I never knew his name," Starke said carefully. "But I remember him."

"He thought the three Arabs you met inland had probably killed you. Men from the kibbutz searched the area the next day, but there

was no sign of you. Or the Arabs." Starke stiffened at that one, but she didn't notice. "Marc will be very happy that you made it," she went on. "Escaped. How on earth did you get away?"

"I ran hard," Starke said. "There was a cave. I hid a long time. Then I found a road. A man drove me to Haifa, gave me some money. I came here with a bus. I found work."

She looked around the squalid room. "It's hard, isn't it?"

"Yes," Starke said. His mind was racing. Damn the Jews, the way they tried to keep track of everybody. Never mind, this could have advantages. Later, his false identity would be supported by this woman's evidence. He wouldn't have to kill her.

But he didn't want to meet Rossi. This Julia Belmont, if she didn't know the country up north, would accept a story like the one Starke had just told her. But Rossi might not. The Mossad man had been there in the ravine with Starke. A conversation with Rossi was just what Starke didn't want to have.

"I'm glad Herr Rossi escaped," Starke said. "I was afraid he was also killed. Is he here now?"

"Somewhere in Palestine. I don't know exactly where. He called me from up north a few days ago. He's coming here in a while. Would you like to see him again?"

He could hardly say no. "Yes, of course. But I have to work long hours. It might be difficult. But please. Have you any word of my family?"

Lay it on thicker, stupid. Starke blinked rapidly, as though holding back tears. "I write often to the Reich Emigration Office, I call on everyone I can think of, I go to the German Consulate here, and there is nothing. Why are the Nazis keeping them? What use they are for the Nazis?"

"I'm sorry, Herr Levy," she said gently. "I don't know. But I promise, now that I know you're here, I'll make a special effort to find out. And let you know as soon as I can. Would that help?"

Starke nodded, apparently wordless. He had in fact made the contacts he described, as would have been normal for the real Samuel Levy in his position. Furthermore, the letters to the Reich Emigration office provided a handy and secure conduit to let Heydrich know what Starke was doing and where he was. An interception watch was being

kept by the Reich postal service for his letters, which upon being identified were sent directly and unopened to Heydrich's desk.

"Thank you," he said at last.

Julia Belmont stood up. "I should go now," she said, "while it's still light."

"Wait," he said. "You came here alone?"

"Yes." It didn't seem to concern her.

"It's dangerous for a woman alone at this time. It is soon dark. Let me come with you." It might be useful to know where she lived.

She considered. "I only have to go a little way to find a bus."

"Please," he said. "I would be greatly distressed if you were hurt because of coming here."

She suppressed a smile. "I'd be distressed if I were hurt, too," she said. "Perhaps it would be safer. Is it safe for you, though?"

"Yes. I'm strong. Brickyard work. Is that how you found me?"

"Yes. Histadrut records. I pestered them until they looked you up, just to get rid of me."

"Oh," he said. This woman was extremely determined. Starke added that fact to the mental file he was building on her. There was an odd vulnerability under the determination, though. He sensed, as he sometimes did with women, that she was drawn to him. She might not even be aware of it herself. Females, Starke thought with ironic amusement, instinctively recognize the power of the dominating male. Even when it's hidden under the cloak of a Yid brickmaker. "*Also*, let us go then," he said quietly.

They walked along the narrow alley toward the Jaffa Road. "Where do you live?" Starke asked.

"Near the new YMCA building. I share three rooms with another woman who works for Kuppat Holim."

"Are you from America?"

"Yes. Have you ever been there? Your English is very good."

"No. I have never been to America."

"It's a very good country."

"Is it good for Jews?"

Her expression was indistinct in the last evening light, but Starke thought she was frowning. "Not always. There are people there who don't like us. But it's not nearly as bad as Germany is now. Can you

imagine, once Germany was a *refuge* for Jews who were persecuted in the rest of Europe? And now the Germans are worse than everyone else put together. Hitler. How can any civilized nation let itself be ruled by a creature like *that*?"

He firmly didn't allow himself to become angry. She was a Jew. Dogs barked, pigs grunted, and Jews moaned about their fate, especially when it was justified. One might as well be angry at a cow for not understanding Nietzsche.

"He's mad," Starke agreed, and added silently: a God-given madness. Divine inspiration, a breathing-in of genius. The Jews are angry because they thought they had a monopoly on it. They'll soon find out differently.

The streetlights were coming on when they reached the intersection of the alley with the Jaffa Road. A bus was growling up to the corner in a cloud of grit and dust. Julia waved at it and it pulled to a stop.

"You don't have to come all the way," she said, pausing with one foot on the step. "I'll be all right from here on."

"I insist," Starke said, and also put one foot on the step. She moved ahead instinctively, allowing him to board with her. The door closed and the rattletrap vehicle lurched into motion.

Most of the ride they passed in silence, Starke because he didn't want to put up with any more Jewish maunderings about the injustice of fate, and Julia for whatever reasons of her own. Starke did notice, however, that she didn't stand quite as far away from him as she could have. Once or twice, when the bus lurched, her hip brushed his. He caught himself wondering if sleeping with a Jewish woman really should be a crime under the Reich racial-purity laws.

Not that there was any chance of that. He'd need a good wash and a shave before any woman could be expected to look at him. Wearily, he turned his mind to business and began to think about Rossi. What was to be done next?

The man was dangerous. There was no question in Starke's mind about that. Rossi was coming to Jerusalem, according to this Belmont woman, and in the busybody way of Jews with their coreligionists, he would want to see Samuel Levy with his own eyes. Then he'd want to know how Levy had escaped the Arabs up near Kefar Vitkin. He

might be suspicious about that, especially if the bodies had been found, and they might have been by now. On the other hand, if Levy simply vanished again, there'd be even more cause for suspicion. The real Levy would be anxious to meet Rossi, to find out if there was any hope of getting his family out of Germany.

The crux of the matter was that Starke didn't want an encounter with Rossi, and he couldn't afford not to have one if it was offered. The solution was simple, at least in theory. If Starke couldn't be removed from the equation, then Rossi had to be canceled out of it.

There had to be an indirect method of managing the cancellation; Starke didn't want to have a part in it himself. He considered possibilities until he had what he thought might be an answer. Then he said to Julia:

"When did you say Herr Rossi is coming to Jerusalem?"

"In a few days." She peered past Starke, out the front window of the bus. The YMCA building was just ahead; she'd be getting off in a minute. "I don't know, exactly."

"Will he be coming to see you?"

Her face took on an odd expression: anger mixed with a softer look. She likes him, Starke thought, but he's offended her in some way.

"Yes, I think so. He's on his way back to Italy."

Italy. Starke decided to probe a little deeper. "You know him well, Herr Rossi?"

"Fairly well. We had a disagreement. I wanted to patch things up last fall, but he didn't come. Then he called me the other day. To apologize, I think."

"Patch things up?" Starke asked. He hadn't followed the idiom. The bus was slowing for her stop.

"Make friends again."

"I see," said Starke. He was marveling at the openness of Americans. She'd hardly met him, and she was talking to him like a friend of ten years. But then, she thought he was Jewish, like her.

"This is my stop."

"Let me come the rest of the way with you. I have to turn around, anyway."

"I'm sorry to drag you all the way over here like this," she said as

she descended to the curb, with Starke following. "I didn't expect to be coming back this late."

"I am not troubled."

She laughed. "You have a curious way of expressing yourself."

"I'm sorry. I don't speak English very often."

"It's very good English," she said. "Just different. I live up here on the right."

The house was perhaps twenty meters up the narrow side street, a two-story place with the ground floor windows heavily barred. Its entrance, a heavy wooden door, was dimly lit by a streetlight at the corner of the main road. She took an antiquated iron key from her bag and unlocked it. "Thank you for bringing me home, Mr. Levy," she said. "I appreciate it very much."

"You're welcome," he said. "Will Herr Rossi perhaps be able to help with my family?"

"We will ask him. Good night."

"Good night."

The door closed behind her. Starke, musing, walked back to the bus stop. He had decided what to do.

First light was Starke's usual time of rising; work in the brickyard started early. He dressed and went out to the courtyard where the Koubski woman was preparing the inevitable porridge. Her stringy gray hair overhung the bubbling iron kettle as she stirred the mess.

"No dinner last night," she snapped at him. "Late."

She didn't have to tell him that, since the house had been dark and the stove cold when he returned. "I am sorry," Starke said in Yiddish.

"Are you going to be having that woman here?" she said angrily. "She was from the health agency, or I wouldn't have let her in. Are you sick?"

She'd be worrying that he'd lose his job through illness and not be able to pay the rent. Starke thought: The only thing worse than a Pole is a Polish Jew. One of these days we'll deal with the lot of them. "I'm not sick," he said. "She won't be coming here again."

"Good. This is no social club." She slapped porridge onto a chipped plate and thrust it at him.

He ate standing alone in the courtyard under the brightening sky. When he had finished and made sure the old woman was out of the way, he returned to his room and excavated quickly in the packed earth under the narrow bed. The automatic, a Walther PPK, was wrapped in oiled cloth inside a small aluminum box. There were two extra clips, as well as a roll of currency for emergency use, and a good Swiss watch. Starke checked the pistol for corrosion, found a fleck of rust on the exterior of the barrel, and cleaned it off. Then he pocketed the weapon, the money, and the watch, reburied the box, and left the house.

He did not set out for the brickyard, but instead made his way to the main bus station, where he bought a ticket for Haifa. The bus departed at seven, leaving him with only five minutes to wait. Starke noted his timing with satisfaction. He occasionally worried that the enforced idleness might make him slightly rusty, as the Walther had been. He didn't think he could afford any rust.

The bus left, somewhat to his surprise, on time. Like the cross-country vehicle he'd ridden back in October, this one had sheets of iron bolted to the sides and over the windows, with only small slits cut in the metal for light and ventilation. It was all the engine could do to haul the added weight up some of the hills, and by the time the vehicle reached Nablus, it was already running an hour late. Starke didn't fret. There was nothing he could do about the delays, so he ignored them.

Besides Starke there were only a few passengers, all Jewish, on the bus. By now the Arab terrorist raids had made cross-country travel dangerous enough to discourage all but essential journeys. There was only one woman, and no children. Two of the men were armed with rifles. They'd got on in Jerusalem and were still aboard at Nazareth. Haganah men, Starke thought. Guards. The Jews are getting ready to take over the country.

The bus reached Haifa in mid-afternoon and three hours late. Starke had allowed for that. He went to the central railway station across from the new deep-water harbor the British had built for their

naval base, noting with interest the long gray hulls of several Royal Navy warships swinging at anchor out on the water.

He found a telephone booth and placed a local call. A man answered. "Yes?"

"Avraham Gellner, please."

"You have the wrong number."

"Is this not Haifa 2-5437?"

"No."

Click.

Starke hung up, satisfied. He had just arranged a face-to-face meeting with the SD station chief in Haifa, the man who had loaded the dead drop for him back when Starke was on his way to Jerusalem. A few hours to wait. He'd find something to eat, and then put himself somewhere inconspicuous until dusk.

The western sky was streaked red over the Mediterranean, and a chill wind was blowing in off the sea. The windchill was worse up here on the ridge than it had been down in the town. Starke pulled the collar of his jacket up and thrust his hands deep into his trousers pockets. Until he'd arrived, he'd thought of Palestine as a land of perpetual warmth. But here on the western ridge of Mount Carmel, the temperature wasn't more than ten degrees Centigrade, and the wind off the sea made it worse.

Starke looked at his watch. Time to move in.

He walked into a nearby grove of trees to a position from which he could watch the front of the Carmelite Monastery. The building was sharp-edged against the dusky sky. Nearby, the Stella Maris lighthouse flashed rhythmically.

Starke saw the slowly approaching figure. He drew back into the shadows of the trees, and waited. When the man reached a point opposite him, Starke stepped into the open as though he'd been walking through the wooded area. The other man stopped. He was keeping his right hand in his trousers pocket.

"Excuse me," Starke said in German. "I seem to be lost. Can you tell me the way back to Shderot Hacarmel Street?"

"It's a longer way than I'd want to walk," said the man. He took his hand out of his pocket, empty.

"But it's a good evening for a walk," Starke suggested. The words were the correct ones.

"Only if you're fit," said the other, filling in the rest of the exchange. "Where do we talk?"

"Come into the trees."

The SD man joined Starke under the branches. Starke studied him briefly: strong face, dark hair, about forty years old. Starke hoped he'd be competent. The stress of field work could turn even good agents erratic or sloppy, and Heydrich would have no way of knowing it until too late.

"What do you want?" the man asked. "This is extremely dangerous for my position. Drops are one thing, meetings are another."

"Yes," Starke agreed. "But it's an emergency. There is someone I need removed, and I can't do it myself."

"We're intelligence," protested the other. "Not assassination and espionage."

"I realize that. I'm not asking you to do anything like that. I want some information passed. I presume you can make contact with the Mufti's organization?"

"Yes. But I can't tell you how, if you're going to ask that."

"I don't want to know. Listen. North of here, near Netanya, three Arabs were killed. It was in early October. Their bodies may not have been found. Did you hear anything about that?"

"Yes. They vanished. One of them was the nephew of Naif Zobi."

"Who is Zobi?"

"One of the Mufti's officers near the Lebanon border."

"I presume Zobi wants to know what happened."

The SD man gave a snort of laughter, but very quietly. "That is an understatement."

"I know where they are, and who killed them."

The other German eyed Starke curiously. "Do you, indeed?"

"Yes. They're in a cave in the side of a ravine a few kilometers from the beach. I made you a map of as much as I can remember. The

bodies aren't important, though. What's important is the identity of the killer."

"Which you can furnish?"

"Of course." Starke permitted himself a smile. "It was a Mossad man, a Jew, one of the people bringing other Jews to Palestine. His name is Marc Rossi."

The SD man gave a start. "Rossi?"

"The name's familiar?" Starke frowned. "Why?"

"The Arabs have been looking for him since the spring," the SD man said. "I gather he killed all of one of the Mufti's attack squads, up in Istanbul."

"How do you know this?"

"The Arabs are aware of the interest we take in Mossad. A representative from the Mufti asked me to watch for a man named Rossi. In exchange for the promise, I wormed out of him why they wanted the Jew."

"Can the Arabs identify him because of Istanbul?" It would be perfect if they could. Starke was reluctantly willing to point Rossi out to the Arabs, but if he didn't have to, so much the better.

"I believe so. They didn't ask for information on that score. Where is this Rossi?"

"He'll be in Jerusalem within a few days," Starke said. "I am sure he'll be visiting a certain address. But I don't want the Arabs to know exactly where that is. Too dangerous for me. Tell them to look around the new YMCA, and around the headquarters of the Jewish health organization."

"You're sure of this?"

"Yes," Starke said. He frowned. "Do you think it will work? If it won't I'll have to dispose of Rossi myself, and I don't want to do that."

The SD man nodded. "It ought to work easily. Once Zobi knows his nephew's dead, and who did it, the revenge code will make him do everything he can to destroy Rossi. That would be the case even without Rossi's killings in Istanbul."

"How soon can you get word to Zobi?"

"Early tomorrow. I think. Yes, that should be possible."

"They'd better move fast. Rossi is leaving soon for Italy. How long will it take for Zobi to get men into position?"

"Not long."

"Good," Starke said. "One other thing."

"What?" The SD man was shifting nervously about. Plainly he wanted to get away. Starke was remorseless. He'd come all the way from Jerusalem; let this desk-sitter twitch for a few more moments.

"There may be a woman with Rossi when Zobi finds him," Starke said. While on the bus, he'd come to a decison about the Belmont woman. She was a loose end that could profitably be clipped off, if there was an opportunity to kill both her and Rossi with the same stroke. "If she is, they should eliminate her as well. Tell Zobi something to make him want to do it."

"No difficulty," said the German. "She tempted the three men up north so that Rossi could kill them from behind. Arabs think women are the gate to hell. Zobi'll be delighted to believe it."

"That's perfect," Starke said.

Jerusalem

January 23, 1939

Rossi got off the bus and stood for a moment to look up the side street where Julia lived. He was feeling a combination of frustration and annoyance: frustration that he hadn't found her at work, and annoyance at himself for feeling compelled to see her before he left for Italy. He'd called her from Nazareth the day after the night ambush, to tell her he was coming to Jerusalem. She'd sounded cool even over the bad telephone line, but hadn't bluntly refused to meet him. Even with himself, Rossi was skirting the fact that he was in Jerusalem because of her; his ship left from Haifa, and there wasn't any real reason for him to be in the ancient city.

This morning he'd expected to find her at work, but the woman with whom he'd spoken at Kuppat Holim said that Julia had left the office about half an hour previous to Rossi's arrival. Rossi had had some difficulty prying from her the information that Julia had gone home. Was she ill? he had asked.

"I don't know," the woman said stubbornly. "She didn't tell me."

Rossi didn't know what kind of papers, if any, Julia had been able to acquire. "Is she in some kind of trouble?"

"I don't know. You should ask her."

"She went home, you say."

"As far as I know."

That had been as much as he could find out. So now he was standing on the curb of King George Avenue in the bright morning sunlight, debating whether or not to go and knock on her door or

turn around and catch the next bus for Haifa. The ship didn't leave until tomorrow, but he could find some way to pass the time in the port city.

Oh, hell, he thought. I'm here anyway. I might as well go through with it.

He set off up the side street, which wasn't much more than a lane with a narrow raised walk on each side and rough paving down the middle. It was crowded with vendors' stalls and customers haggling with the stalls' owners, and smelled of bad drainage and decaying vegetables. Most of the people were Jews; there weren't many Arabs in this part of the city.

An almond seller reached into his sack and waved a fistful of pale nuts at Rossi. Rossi, preoccupied, gestured the man away and went on, delving in his memory for the directions Julia had given him back in October. To his chagrin, he discovered that he couldn't remember them clearly. Was it the third courtyard entrance on the right? Or the second? Perplexed, he stopped in the middle of the street to consider what he should do next.

He happened to be looking at the third door when it opened and Julia came out of it, not six meters away from where Rossi was standing. She was carrying a fiberboard suitcase in one hand, and a leather satchel was slung over her left shoulder. She turned to pull the heavy door closed behind her, her movements hurried and nervous. Then she looked anxiously up and down the street, as though expecting unwelcome visitors. Her eyes flicked over Rossi, and then flicked back with surprise as she recognized him. "Marc?" she called disbelievingly.

He hurried forward and stopped a meter away from her. All of a sudden he didn't know what to say. "Like a bad penny," he said awkwardly. "I arrived today, but I missed you at the office. Are you moving out in a hurry?"

She wearily set the suitcase down on the pavement. "I have to," she said. "They're after me."

He felt an instant stab of fear. "Who? Who is? Arabs?"

"No, not Arabs. The British. They're going to deport me."

"What for?"

She looked quickly around. "Come inside for a minute. I've got a little time."

She led him back through the doorway into the courtyard and slammed the heavy door behind them. He could see that her hands were shaking. "What's this about the British?" The possibility of encountering them made him nervous. They'd be more than interested in why he was carrying a Browning automatic pistol in the inside pocket of his leather jacket.

She leaned against the wall and closed her eyes. "I've been collecting information on the way the British are treating us in comparison with the way they deal with the Arabs. One example was the massacre at Tiberias. There was a whole British battalion in the old Turkish fort in Tiberias that night. They didn't lift a finger to help the people the Arabs were killing." She opened her eyes. "A lot of other things, not as bad as that, but bad enough. I sent some of the information back home, and it got into the New York papers. Somebody was careless. My name was on one of the articles, as author."

"So the British started looking for you."

"That's right. But I guess we have somebody in their security system somewhere. I was warned they were going to pick me up today, kick me out of the country."

"Claudio's told me to come back to Italy," Rossi told her. "You could come too."

She blinked at him. "I know. He wrote and told me. But that's not the point. The British are also going to confiscate all the documents I've collected." She hefted the leather satchel. "I've got the papers in here. They make the British look dreadful. Not only dreadful, stupid. They don't want such things being made public. So I'm going to turn the stuff into a book just as fast as I can. If they confiscate it, I might as well have stayed in Rome. I *have* to get it out with me. That's why I'm running."

"I could take the papers," Rossi offered before he could stop himself. "You could meet me in Rome and get them back."

"I wouldn't want to burden you. They're heavy. Besides, aren't you kind of a suspicious character yourself?"

"Maybe," Rossi admitted. Now she didn't trust him to deliver the

documents safely. Or was she letting him think as much so that he'd insist on doing it? Damn the woman.

"No matter what we decide," she said practically, "we've got to get out of here." She leaned over to pick up the suitcase. Rossi anticipated her. The case felt almost empty. She had the sense to travel light, at least. "Where are you going?" he asked.

She frowned. "I don't know, yet. I was going to save that problem for after I got away from the British."

He sighed. "Okay. I may be able to help you. What identification are you carrying?"

"My passport, and a visa. The visa's not real."

"Come on, then."

He opened the courtyard door and poked his head out to look up and down the street. There was no sign of anyone hostile, British or otherwise, only the throngs around the vendors' stalls, and the street hawkers crying their wares. Rossi motioned to Julia and she followed him out into the street. He heard the courtyard door thump closed behind them.

"Where are we going?" she asked as they threaded their way through the crowd toward King George Avenue.

"A place where you can get help," he said. They reached the intersection of the side street and King George. Rossi paused to scrutinize the boulevard before entering it. Midday was approaching, and the street was crowded with pedestrians, peddlers' carts, battered cars, and dusty, clattering buses. A British Army open-topped truck with a squad of soldiers riding in it was rolling along the pavement not twenty meters away. Rossi didn't think the British authorities would send a truckful of men to arrest one American woman, no matter how politically dangerous she might be. He made himself ignore the truck and its soldiers, although he was suddenly very conscious of his hidden Browning and its weight resting lightly against his ribs. The vehicle with its sunburned young men passed the intersection and went on toward the southeast.

"It's okay," he said over his shoulder to Julia. "Let's go."

"Bus?"

"We could. We're going to the far end of King George. I can carry the documents, if you like."

"Thanks, but I can manage." She paused and added, "Let's not wait for a bus. I don't like standing still in the open."

They set off along the street, Rossi still lugging Julia's suitcase. After a few dozen meters he began to feel peculiar. For a minute or two he tried to ignore the sensation, but then identified it as the same sense of being followed that he'd experienced in Istanbul the night Cohn and he were attacked by the Mufti's assassins. His subconscious was picking up danger cues and trying to warn him.

"By the way," Julia said.

"What?" Her words broke his concentration, and the sensation vanished. Rossi tried to regain it, to no avail. He wanted to tell her to shut up so he could listen, but then he'd have to explain himself.

"Samuel Levy. I found him."

"Who? You mean the one—"

"You thought was dead? Yes."

He could tell she was very pleased with herself. "You found him here in Jerusalem?" Rossi asked, hearing the incredulity in his voice. He'd given Levy up for dead months ago, another Jewish casualty returning anonymously to the dust of Palestine.

"Yes, he's here. He's working at a brickyard just outside the city. I saw him a few days ago. He asked me to remember him to you."

"That's astonishing," Rossi said. "I was *sure* the Arabs caught him. How in hell did he get away?"

"He said he hid in a cave, and they couldn't find him. Then he managed to get as far as Haifa, and came on to Jerusalem. He's been trying to find out what's happened to his family, and the rest of the Jews from . . . what was the name of his town?"

"Altgarten, I think."

"Anyway, he's had no luck." She bit her lower lip. "I promised to help him, but now, with this . . . I won't be able to. Damn. I hate breaking promises."

"Can't be helped," Rossi said absentmindedly. He was thinking about Levy escaping like that. The Arabs couldn't have known the land as well as Rossi had believed at the time. The man had been stunningly lucky.

"He'd like to see you, if you can manage it," Julia said. "I don't

know exactly when you're leaving, but I can tell you where he lives, if you want."

"I'll see," Rossi answered. The warning sensation was creeping back into his mind, nagging at the edges of consciousness. Julia and he had now almost reached the grounds of the Ratisbonne Monastery on the left, and a little way beyond the grounds was the next main intersection, King George and Bezalel. They'd put behind them perhaps a third of the distance they had to go.

"Julia," Rossi said as they neared the intersection, "I want you to drop your document case."

"I beg your pardon?" She'd been about to press him on the matter of meeting Levy, and was taken aback.

"Please just do as I say. Let your bag slip off your shoulder, as though you'd dropped it. Let me pick it up."

She didn't miss another beat. "Okay," she said. "On my count of three. One. Two. Three."

She stopped suddenly as the heavy mass of papers in their leather bag slipped off her shoulder and thudded to the pavement. Rossi gave an exasperated gesture for the benefit of their assumed watchers, and stooped to pick the satchel up. As he did so, he looked surreptitiously but carefully back the way they had come. No one appeared to be paying any particular attention to himself and Julia.

He was *sure* there was someone there. Pretending to find something wrong with the straps that secured the flap of the satchel, he knelt on the pavement. His eyes slid sideways again.

There. It was the almond seller Rossi had passed when he went up the street to Julia's house. Rossi had hardly noticed him, assuming he was a Jew. The man was still carrying his sack of almonds, but he wasn't trying to sell them. One hand was buried deep inside the bag.

He has a gun or a knife in there, Rossi thought. Why didn't he go after me when he had the chance back there in the side street? Too many Jews around, likely, too hard to get away. Or he was waiting to whistle up reinforcements. Or both. It's those bastards from Istanbul. That photograph. They've tracked me down somehow, damn them. Thank God I've got the gun. If I get a chance to use it.

Unless it's Julia they're after. No, not likely. They'd have no reason to be interested in her. I'm the one they want.

Time was moving very slowly. Rossi had loosened and refastened

one strap of the satchel, and now was working on the other. Were there others?

Yes. At least one. A man wearing an Arab *gelabiyeh* had stopped a few meters behind the almond seller, and was standing on the curb as though trying to flag down a bus.

Rossi finished with the satchel and slowly stood up. Out of the corner of one eye he saw the almond seller begin to saunter toward him. After a couple of seconds the man in the *gelabiyeh* followed.

Now what? They certainly knew Julia was with him, and he didn't dare flee and leave her behind. But she might slow him down if he tried to drag her in his wake; unencumbered, the Arabs would find it an easy chase. He had to dispose of them, somehow, now. He handed the satchel back to Julia and picked up her suitcase, this time with his left hand.

"What's the matter?" Julia asked.

"There are two Arabs behind us. I think they're after me because of what happened in Istanbul."

Julia and he were now almost at the intersection of Bezalel Street and King George. "Oh, God," she said. "To kill you?"

"Likely. Revenge."

"Run for it, Marc. Leave me. I'll try to get help."

He should have remembered the foolhardy courage she'd displayed against the blackshirts in Rome. "No. They might kill you too, just for being with me. We have to lose them."

"How? What are we going to do?"

He was scanning the traffic at the intersection ahead. Now he was hoping to see a British foot patrol, but of course there was none. They needed cover, something to hide them while they put some distance between themselves and their pursuers.

Like a heavy truck, for example. One was approaching the intersection from the left, lumbering along Bezalel and slowing as it neared the heavier traffic along King George. Its open bed was piled high with crated vegetables. If they could reach its other side in time, cling to it out of sight as it crossed King George Avenue or turned right down King George, they might slip away. If it turned left, though, they'd be exposed. Never mind, cross that bridge if they came to it.

"Hurry," he ordered her. "The truck, there. When it stops for the

crossing. We'll go to the other side, hang on when it moves off. But we have to keep out of sight. Use the rear wheels for cover. But *don't* look like we're hurrying. They don't know we've spotted them."

She nodded. "All right."

He heard the tremble in her voice. Rossi hoped that fear wouldn't make her clumsy. At least it wasn't crippling her ability to act.

They reached the corner just as the truck was pulling up to it. Rossi wanted to look around to see where the Arabs were, but he didn't dare. And he could be overestimating their caution; maybe the next thing he'd feel would be the impact of a bullet between his shoulder blades, a knife in his back.

Neither happened. The truck stopped in front of them. It was an English truck with right-hand drive, and the driver was signaling a right turn, his arm lolling out the window. Perfect.

"Wait till it starts moving," he muttered to her. "Then around the back, grab onto the other side, stay behind the wheels."

He *had* to know where they were. He looked back and forth along Bezalel, and then over his shoulder down King George, as though searching for a break in the traffic. He glimpsed the almond seller, only about six meters away now. They must be getting ready.

The truck was just starting to roll as he turned back. "Let's go," he told Julia. He positioned himself on her left and took her upper arm in his right hand.

They hurried into the street, elbowing their way through the crowd of pedestrians also making the crossing. The truck's tailgate was moving very slowly away from them. They reached the far side of the vehicle. "Go," Rossi urged.

He shoved her toward the slowly turning rear wheel. She reached up with both hands and grabbed the slats of a vegetable crate, pulling herself off the pavement, the satchel dangling from her shoulder. Rossi was encumbered by her suitcase, but for some irrational chivalrous reason couldn't bring himself to abandon it. He clamped onto a crate slat with his right hand and levered himself off the ground, feet searching for a hold on the underframe of the truck. The vehicle was moving sluggishly, at no more than the speed of a slow walk.

Hurry up, damn you, Rossi thought at the driver. Hurry up. Get on with it and turn right, hurry up.

The truck began to swing left. The driver had changed his mind. Rossi and Julia were exposed and vulnerable. Worse, Rossi realized in a flash, the Arabs knew that he and Julia had been trying to get away, that they were no longer unsuspecting targets. The pursuers would go for the kill without another moment's hesitation.

He was already dropping from his handhold as he thought this. As he hit the ground he shoved his hand inside his jacket and seized the butt of the Browning. Where were the Arabs?

Not more than five meters away, but they'd been careless, probably because they hadn't known Rossi had spotted them earlier. Only now, as he landed bent-legged and fought for his balance, were they reacting. The *gelabiyeh*-clad man hadn't been looking at the truck, so the almond seller was a couple of seconds ahead of him. His gun was already out of the sack and swinging toward Rossi, who hadn't yet freed the Browning from his jacket.

Rossi threw the suitcase lefthanded at the almond seller. The man flinched instinctively as he fired, and the bullet whipped by Rossi's ear as he brought his own gun up, snapping the safety off with his thumb. The suitcase hit the Arab on the right forearm, spoiling his aim again, and before he could correct it Rossi shot him. Without a pause for thought, Rossi turned the Browning on the other Arab and pulled the trigger. The bullet hit the man in the right eye. He tumbled over backward, a gun flying lazily into the throng of pedestrians.

"Run!" Rossi yelled at Julia. Somebody in the crowd screamed, and men shouted. Several people, conditioned by months of sniping and terrorist warfare, were dropping to the pavement.

She was already off the truck, which had stopped. The driver must have stalled it as he reacted to the shots nearby. But instead of fleeing away up the exposed street, she leaped onto the truck's running board and wrenched the door open. "Bomb!" she yelled into the cab. "Get out, quick!" She reached into the cab and Rossi, incredulous, saw her drag the driver out by the arm and shove him into the road. Then she hurled herself into the truck and slammed the door closed behind her. "Marc!" Rossi heard her shout from inside the vehicle. "Come *on!*"

The truck's engine roared into life and the transmission grated and clashed as she forced it into gear.

The driver shouted something in Hebrew and scrambled to his feet. But before he could reach the truck's running board, Rossi hit him from behind and knocked him flat on his face. Before the driver could get up again, Julia took her foot off the clutch and the vehicle jolted forward, dropping several crates of vegetables over its tailgate as it did so. Rossi, on the running board by now, clung desperately to the door handle and the window frame as the truck roared up King George Avenue, pedestrians scattering before it.

After a moment he managed to wrench the door open and get inside. Julia found third gear with a gnashing protest of metal gear teeth, and reengaged the clutch with a jolt that snapped Rossi's head back against the rear of the cab. He hastily clicked the Browning's safety on.

"What now?" she shouted at him over the protesting clatter of the engine's valve train. Her cheeks were flushed.

"Get off the main street," he shouted back. "The next turn, try left. We'll leave the truck and go on on foot. The British will be all over the place in minutes. The truck's too conspicuous."

"Okay."

She took the corner with enough speed to lose another few crates of produce. "Have you ever driven a truck?" he yelled.

"No. But it's easy."

He winced as she accidentally raced the engine between gears. Wisps of steam were whipping from under the hood. The oil gauge showed next to no pressure. The engine had likely blown a gasket, unsurprisingly, given the abuse being inflicted on it.

"How well do you know Jerusalem?" Rossi asked over the racket of protesting, ill-lubricated metal.

"Not this part."

"Me neither. Turn into the lane ahead. We'll leave the truck there. It's not going to last much longer, anyway."

"Right."

She slowed to a sedate pace and turned into the narrow street. It wasn't much wider than the truck, and fortunately wasn't a shopping area. A woman glanced curiously down from a second-floor window

as the vehicle rumbled past, but there was no one in the street itself. An alley led away to the left.

"Let's leave it here," Rossi said. He pointed to the mouth of the alley. "We'll go up there on foot. If nobody got a good look at us, we're okay for the moment."

"Okay."

Rossi said, after a pause, "You did brilliantly back there. I was underestimating you all the time. I hadn't thought of using the truck."

"You tend to do that," she said as she slowed the truck.

"What?"

"Underestimate me."

"I know," Rossi admitted. He decided not to pursue the matter further. It had the makings of yet another row between them. "I'm sorry I lost your suitcase."

"Never mind the suitcase," she said as she disengaged the clutch and switched off the ignition. "I've got the documents, and that's more important than a change of clothes. Where are we going?"

"I want to find a restaurant," Rossi said. "It's lunchtime."

Forty minutes later, after getting lost twice in the labyrinth of unmarked streets east of King George Avenue, they were almost at their destination: the intersection of Histadrut and King George. Rossi poked his head out of the alley they were following and looked up and down Histadrut. No patrols were visible, but he and Julia would have to move fast before one turned up.

"I've kept quiet up till now," Julia said from behind him, "but are you sure we need lunch? I can think of several more important things to do. Or are you being funny?"

"No, I'm not being funny. We're going to Fink's. It's a dozen meters away from here."

"What's Fink's?"

"A restaurant. It's also a Haganah *sleak*, a secret arsenal and a communications center. We both need help, and that's the place to find it on short notice."

"You've been to this Fink's before?"

"Yes. Come on."

He darted out into the street and hurried along the sidewalk to the entrance of the restaurant, Julia following close on his heels.

The restaurant was packed and noisy, and the clientele, not surprisingly, was all Jewish. Most of the crowd was men, with perhaps three or four women scattered through it. Cigar smoke hung in the air, mixed with the scent of thick sweet coffee and spilled beer. The room was no more than eight meters by five, with a few tables jammed into it, and a tiny bar with wooden stools where Moshe Fink, the Hungarian founder and proprietor, was drawing beer into glasses. Rossi looked hurriedly around, searching for familiar faces.

"Who do you know here?" Julia asked him in a low voice.

"Everybody knows Moshe Fink," Rossi said. "I'm looking for Leon Meisl. He set up my training with the night patrols. I don't see him." He started elbowing his way toward the bar, dragging Julia in his wake. A few of the men glanced curiously at Julia as she passed. The looks aimed at Rossi were more guarded; he wasn't well known at the *sleak*.

Rossi reached the bar and managed to get Moshe Fink's attention. "I remember you," Fink said. "You were here last October with Meisl." He took in Julia's disheveled look and Rossi's expression of worry. "What's the matter?"

"We're on the run from Arabs. It's more than coincidence. I need to talk to Leon."

"He's supposed to be in in about half an hour. Come with me. You can wait in the back room."

Fink came around the bar and led them to a tiny room behind the restaurant. In it were two tables, a few chairs, and not much else. Cooking odors wafted from the nearby kitchen. "I'll send in some food and beer," Fink said. "You hungry?"

Rossi discovered that he was ravenous. "Yes, thanks."

"Could I have some coffee?" Julia asked. "Beer doesn't agree with me."

"Yes, yes," Fink said. "Soon. Sit down and wait. I'll tell Meisl you're here as soon as he arrives."

He bustled out. Julia thankfully slipped the document satchel from

her shoulder, put it on the table nearest her, and sank down onto one of the hard wooden chairs. "Safe," she said. "Thank God."

"For the moment," Rossi answered, also sitting down.

"I didn't know you were carrying a gun," she said.

"Good thing the Arabs didn't, either. That was beautiful, what you did with the truck. You ought to be in the Haganah. Can you use a rifle?"

"No. I've never handled guns."

"Are you afraid of them?"

"I don't know. Let me see yours."

Rossi pulled the weapon out of his jacket. "This is a model 1910 Browning automatic pistol," he told her. "The bullets are carried in a magazine inside the butt. It can fire nine shots before reloading. This is the safety catch, so it won't go off by accident. The catch is engaged now." He handed the pistol over to her. "To disengage it, you flip it with your thumb." He showed her. "Okay, now it will fire each time you pull the trigger. Flip the catch back on."

She did so. She handled the gun gingerly at first, and then with more confidence. "It's not as heavy as I thought it would be," she said, hefting it. "How far will it shoot?"

"Quite a long way. But a pistol is very inaccurate at ranges of over twenty meters or so. It's hard to aim one precisely because the barrel's so short. It's a close-in weapon only." He showed her how to remove the magazine, and then had her dry-fire the Browning several times, demonstrating how to aim. "It also recoils when it's fired," he added. "You have to hold it firmly, or the recoil will throw your aim off. But don't hold it in a death-grip, because that can spoil your aim, too."

She handed the gun back to him. "You're showing me this for a reason."

"Yes," he said. "You might have to use one someday."

"I wish I'd had one when those blackshirts were beating up those people in Rome. I'd quite cheerfully have killed them."

He found himself half-believing her. "That wouldn't have been a good idea. They don't often execute women in Italy any more, but you'd have spent a long time in a Fascist prison."

"I suppose."

She started to say something else, but was interrupted by the arrival

of Moshe Fink with a tray of food: borscht, sausage, bread, beer, and coffee. "There's more if you want it," he said, and bustled out again.

They ate in silence for a while. "I didn't think I'd ever get used to this coffee," Julia said as she pushed her empty plate aside and picked up the cup. "It's nothing like American. Now the stuff we drink back home seems really insipid."

"Everything's more intense on this side of the Atlantic," Rossi agreed.

"What have you been doing since I saw you last fall?"

Rossi told her a little about it. She listened intently. "Are we winning?" she asked, when he finished.

"Not yet. It's a standoff. We need weapons, better training, supplies, vehicles . . . everything."

"Why can't we and the Arabs live in peace with each other?" she demanded angrily. "There should be enough for everyone here. The land's fertile, if it's drained where it's wet and watered where it's dry."

"The Arabs are afraid we'll swamp them with numbers and make Palestine over as a Jewish place. According to the Grand Mufti, anyway. He's widely believed."

"Is that who's after you?" she asked. "Here, and in Istanbul?"

"I think so."

"What exactly happened in Istanbul?"

He told her that, too. When he'd finished she looked down, cheeks hot with humiliation. "I'm sorry for what I said that day in Rome," she said miserably. "When we met the Fascists. I had no idea then, the sort of things you were doing. Claudio hadn't said anything, and I thought you were. . . ."

"A paper-pusher?"

"I guess so. And then you looked so angry with me all the time. I got angry back. So when I found you were helping run the escape routes, I still didn't say anything. I'm sorry."

"It's okay," Rossi told her.

"And then you didn't want me to stay in Palestine, when we came ashore that night. I shouldn't have hit you. I'm sorry about that, too."

"I deserved it," Rossi said. He was feeling magnanimous all of a sudden.

"Yes, you did deserve it," she said. "But I still shouldn't have done it."

He was startled. "I deserved it? How?"

"For always thinking I couldn't take care of myself. You treated me like a child, or the village idiot. The innocent American abroad, who doesn't know how to keep out of trouble. Part of the reason I was angry with you was that you were always so patronizing."

"I wasn't patronizing," Rossi said hotly. "I was being realistic. There were things you didn't know about."

"But you wouldn't tell me what they were. You just acted superior, because you knew them and I didn't." Her flush of embarrassment was being replaced by one of anger. "You didn't want me to worry my pretty head about them, was that it?"

"I never said anything like that!"

"You didn't need to. And how do you think I felt on that ship, holding buckets for people to throw up into, trying to do something with rotten food and bad water, while you pretended I wasn't there?"

"I did just as much as you did!"

"Not quite as much. But that wasn't the point. You didn't acknowledge what I *was* doing. And then you had the nerve to try to pick me up and throw me back in that damned boat when we got here. As though I hadn't earned my passage just as much as you did. Where did you get that kind of nerve?"

"I was trying to protect you, damn it."

"That's the most patronizing thing you've ever said to me," she snapped. "It just makes me want to spit. What you're protecting is your superior opinion of yourself. If you'd only admit it."

"Oh, to hell with it, then," Rossi growled. "Forget it. It doesn't matter now."

"God, that's like a man. As soon as you start losing an argument, you try to pretend there isn't one."

Rossi began a hot retort, but closed his mouth as the door to the bar opened and Leon Meisl came through it. He was a tall, saturnine man with deep pouches under his eyes. "Hello, Marc," Meisl said, closing

the door firmly behind him. His eyes flicked to Julia, then back to Rossi. "You two are having some kind of difficulty?"

"Yes," Julia snapped. Meisl blinked at her with surprise. "Marc will tell you all about it," she added.

Rossi suppressed an almost irresistible urge to snap back at her. "Okay," he said. "A pair of Arabs tried to kill me, and Miss Julia Belmont here, this morning. Down King George Avenue, near the Ratisbonne Monastery. Julia's also in trouble with the British. She's got documents they don't want her to publish." Rossi recounted the events leading up to their presence at Fink's, as well as the attack on himself in Istanbul.

When he had finished, Meisl whistled. "You really managed to land yourselves in the borscht pot today, didn't you? I already heard about the two Arabs. They're both dead. The British are swarming all over the place. They'd got things simmered down here in Jerusalem, and now this happens right under their noses."

"Sorry," Rossi said.

"You did what you had to. It's a war. Marc, you say you were going back to Italy by steamship from Haifa?"

"Yes."

"You can't do that now. Not from Haifa. The Mufti's people will be watching for you there. And as for Miss Belmont, the British will be asking themselves pretty soon whether she was mixed up in the shootings today. It would be safest if you both got out of the country. Italy would be easiest, since Marc's supposed to go there anyway. Is Italy all right with you, Miss Belmont?"

"Yes. It's fine. I can go back to the States from there."

"Good idea," Rossi said.

"Go to hell," she told him.

Rossi thought he saw the ghost of a grin at the corner of Meisl's mouth. "I can get you both as far as Italy," he said. "It'll be uncomfortable and dangerous, but I can do it. You'll have to go by way of Egypt. Palestine and the Lebanon are too much inside the Mufti's sphere." He stood up. "I'll ask Fink to keep you near here until I can make arrangements. You both have American passports? Good. We'll get you to Cairo as soon as possible, and then to Port Said

or Alexandria. It may take a couple of days to put together. Please," and he eyed them both, "be patient. All right?"

"All right," Rossi said.

Meisl left. "There," Rossi said. "Satisfied?"

"Yes."

"Good."

A look of concern passed over her face. "What now?" Rossi asked her.

"I was thinking about poor Samuel Levy. When we get back to Rome, could you try to see what's happened to his family?"

"My, God," Rossi said in exasperation. "You never quit, do you?"

"No," she answered. "I don't."

Tel Aviv—Jerusalem

January 24-25, 1939

Starke was feeling extremely short-tempered. He leaned on the railing of the public promenade that overlooked Tel Aviv's sandy beaches, and gazed morosely at the horizon. A drizzle had fallen throughout most of the morning, and the sun had broken through the clouds only an hour before. On the strand below Starke's vantage point, a scattering of Jews strolled about, taking advantage of the noon mealtime to absorb some of the sun's warmth. The promenade itself was quite crowded, for the same reason. Starke absent-mindedly judged the air temperature to be about twenty degrees. He still hadn't gotten used to a warm January.

Starke straightened up from the railing, feeling another surge of annoyance. He had no desire at all to be in Tel Aviv, no matter how good the weather or how pleasant the vista of the seashore. The German SD man in Haifa had no business at all calling him to a meeting in this city full of Jews. The sheer mass of them made Starke's flesh crawl; at least in Jerusalem they were diluted by other races and nationalities. And if it were time for Starke to be on his way, there was no reason the Haifa dead drop couldn't be used to transmit orders and documents.

Unless, of course, something was wrong with the drop. Or the Haifa SD man might be worried about British counter-espionage having gotten onto him. What with the rising tensions in Europe, the British were likely taking a keen interest in the doings of the

German colony in Haifa. At least, they would be if they had any professionalism or even common sense.

Starke sighed to himself and regarded the low breakers along the sandy shore. He'd simply have to wait and see. The letter from Haifa, which he'd picked up from the general delivery at the Jerusalem post office, had contained only coded instructions to be here at one P.M. today. It had also told him to carry a copy of the *Jerusalem Times*, which he was obediently doing.

Well, he was here, but the SD man wasn't. Because of his irritation, Starke had begun to refer to the man mentally as Herr Scheisskopf. Shithead.

Starke looked over his shoulder, back across the promenade and into the stretch of greensward bordering it. Beyond the narrow stretch of grass was a street, and beyond that the city itself. The area was full of Jews but there was no sign, as Starke put it to himself, of anyone resembling a German spy. Starke wondered idly whether the Arabs had disposed of Rossi and the Belmont woman yet. Not that it mattered much, if Starke was about to leave Palestine. In a few weeks, maybe, he'd be back in Berlin, mission accomplished. If he were particularly pleased with Starke's accomplishments, Heydrich might provide him with another rest and recuperation night at Chez Kitty. The thought of Sofia made Starke's breath shorten. Then he replaced her image with that of the Belmont woman. That was just as good, if not better. He wondered if he could somehow get the Belmont woman into Madame Kitty's stable for his personal use, and then dismissed the idea as a pointless fantasy.

Keep your mind on business, Erich, he instructed himself. You're still a long way from Berlin.

He returned to his contemplation of the Mediterranean. Starke wasn't the only person leaning on the promenade; it seemed to be a favorite vantage point for looking at the ocean. Below him, a few hardier individuals were splashing about in the light surf, shouting to each other in Hebrew. It was a dead language once, Starke reflected. With some effort we can return it to that condition.

He sensed movement at the rail beside him. Out of the corner of his eye, he recognized the profile of the man from Haifa. Scheisskopf was

right on time. He was carrying a light raincoat over his left arm, and, like Starke, a copy of the *Jerusalem Times*.

"Hello," Starke said out of the corner of his mouth. To an onlooker, there would have been no obvious connection between the two men.

"Hello," said the man from Haifa.

"Why didn't you use the drop?" Starke said in a hiss, without further preamble. "I don't like this."

"I don't like it either," Scheisskopf said. "But the drop's been destroyed. Construction."

"Why didn't you set up another one and send me there?"

"I didn't dare. I think the British are watching me."

Starke barely prevented himself from turning on his heel and walking away. "You half-wit. You think that, and you bring me to *meet you?*"

"It's safe," said the SD man. "I made sure I was clean when I left Haifa. But I had to get the documents to you."

"I'm to move?"

"Yes. Italy. Come a little closer. Ask me the time. Exchange newspapers."

Starke did so. Under cover of looking at his watch, Scheisskopf gave Starke his own newspaper and took Starke's. "The documents you need are in there. And the contact point in Rome."

"What am I to do there?"

"How the devil should I know?"

At least there was *that* much security.

"By the way," the SD man said.

"What?"

"If you were having trouble with that Jew Rossi, you've still got it. The Arabs missed him. He's gone underground. Also the woman."

Starke swore. "Where did they go?"

"To the Haganah, likely."

"Surprise me again. Where in location, damn it?"

"The Jews have a post office at Fink's restaurant on King George Avenue. Try sending Rossi a letter that way, if you like." Scheisskopf's voice was heavy with sarcasm.

"How do you know this? About the restaurant?"

The SD man sneered. "You don't think we're the only two German agents in Palestine, do you?"

"Do the British or Arabs know about it?"

"I don't know. I don't think so. Neither of them watch it, anyway."

"Why haven't we told the British or the Arabs?" Starke asked.

"What for? The more trouble the Jews cause the British, the better for us. The more trouble the Jews cause the Arabs, then the more trouble the Arabs cause the British because of it, and the better for us. The Reich thrives on chaos here, Herr whoever-you-are."

It made sense, of a sort. "Very well," Starke said. "Good-bye."

"Good-bye."

Starke tucked the newspaper under his arm and walked away from the man from Haifa. After he had crossed the promenade he glanced back, as though for one last look at the sea. Scheisskopf was just moving away from the railing, settling his raincoat over his arm.

He should have waited until I was out of sight, Starke thought, and turned to go on. He was just beginning to cross the grass beyond the paving when a tall young man with a mustache stepped in front of him. Starke looked up at the bony face in very natural surprise.

"Excuse me, sir," the man said in English. "British Army Intelligence. We would like to ask you a few questions." Another man, no older, was standing just behind the first. He had brown hair and blue eyes and was considerably brawnier than the one who was accosting Starke. If they were carrying weapons they were keeping them concealed. Starke's own Walther was pushed into the waistband of his trousers, at the small of his back.

Scheisskopf, you asshole, Starke thought. Clean from Haifa, oh of course. "What?" he asked in Hebrew.

"I assume you speak German," the intelligence officer said in that language. "If you're a German Jew. Who was that man you were talking to?"

"What man?" Starke asked querulously, switching to German. He looked over his shoulder. Three men had collared Scheisskopf and were searching him. "The one by the rail? I don't know. I only asked him the time."

"May I see your identity papers, please?"

The heavier man watched Starke's hands very carefully as he fished his papers from his jacket and gave them over. A small crowd of Jews was gathering by the curb, observing the proceedings and muttering ominously. The British, characteristically, ignored them while the mustached officer perused the identity documents. "Herr Samuel Levy. Very good. Herr Levy, may I see your newspaper, please?"

The Englishmen both leaned forward and their eyes, both pairs, switched from Starke to the newspaper. It was all Starke needed. He slammed the heel of his hand upward to strike the mustached Englishman under the nose, driving the man's nasal cartilage and sinus bones up into the forebrain. Blood spurted from the smashed face.

Wide-eyed with surprise, the other Englishman was already reaching under his raincoat, but it was the wrong move and far too late. Still holding the newspaper, Starke slammed his fist into the man's face with every ounce of strength he could muster, and felt bone crunch under his knuckles. The man groaned and fell over backward. Starke leaped over his body and sprinted for the buildings on the far side of the road, darting among the vehicles and bicycles toward a temporary safety. He risked a glance over his shoulder. Two of the men who had been holding Scheisskopf had seen what happened and were running after Starke.

Somehow the Jews who had been watching the incident seemed to get in their way without meaning to. The British intelligence men were slowed down somewhat, but then burst through the human barricade and came hammering after Starke. He put his head down and began running as fast as he could up a side street. He knew he didn't have much chance of getting away. They'd know the city, and he didn't. It was probably going to come to a last stand, until he'd used up all the rounds in the Walther. What angered him most, oddly, was that he wouldn't be able to go to bed with Sofia again.

After a few dozen meters he heard, through the pounding in his head and over his heaving breath, the sound of footsteps close behind. One of them must be a champion runner. Maybe he'd isolated himself. Starke reached under his jacket at the back and pulled out the Walther, spun to fire.

It wasn't the Englishmen at all; it was a boy of about sixteen. Starke's pursuers were still a good seventy meters behind. "No, no!" the boy hissed. "I'm with you! Run!"

Starke did so. The Englishmen had seen him draw the gun, though. A pistol cracked and a bullet whined over Starke's head. It was only a warning shot; the man didn't fire again.

"Haganah?" the boy got out between breaths as he pulled alongside Starke. He could run like a deer. "I saw what happened back there."

Starke nodded. There was hope, a little. "Yes. Haganah."

"Follow me. I'll get you away!"

The boy plunged into a narrow lane between two apartment blocks. Starke followed. Construction equipment and packing crates littered the space between the nearly finished buildings. The boy suddenly turned again, and Starke found himself scrambling down a steep rubble slope into a ravine bordered on one side by the building's foundation wall.

"Sewers!" the boy gasped. "They're still hooking them up. Down here!"

A black hole was undercut into the bank of sandy soil. It was about a meter high. The boy disappeared into it. Starke doubled over and followed, into pitch blackness. "Keep moving!" he heard his companion call back to him, very quietly. "There's light ahead."

When they were a good thirty meters into the tunnel, Starke glimpsed a faint glow ahead. It strengthened, and after another fifteen meters he saw that the glow was coming down a manhole shaft from a metal cover high overhead. The boy scrambled into the shaft and stopped.

"We'll wait here," he whispered. "If they find the entrance, we can go on."

They waited. No sounds penetrated from the way they had come. After five minutes the boy relaxed. "They missed us," he said quietly. "You're safe for the moment."

Starke was regaining his breath. "What about you?" he asked.

A shrug. "They didn't see my face." The accent was Austrian. "They'll never find out who got you away."

"Thank you," Starke said. Now that he was at least temporarily out

of danger, he began to savor the irony. Rescued from the British by a Jew. Not for the first time: Rossi had been the first. Maybe there was something, after all, to the idea that there were gods, and that they were on the side of the Reich. "What's your name?" he asked the boy.

Again the shrug. "It isn't important. But you can call me Yakov."

"You have a good sense of security."

"It only makes sense."

"Yes," Starke agreed. He began to wonder what he should do next. His Levy papers were gone, although he still had the escape documents. Not that he dared use them now. He didn't trust Scheisskopf to hold up under interrogation. The asshole might very well tell the British where Starke was going, bargain Starke away for a promise of leniency. If the British didn't hang him, though, Heydrich eventually would. For criminal incompetence.

Now how was he going to reach Italy? It was just about the only thing he could do, anyway; even if the operation was aborted, he still had to get home somehow. Italy. He was beginning to have the glimmer of an idea.

"Why did the British want you?" the boy asked suddenly. "Have you killed some of them?" He looked interested, in the manner of youth.

"No," Starke said. But I might have, he thought. That first blow was a killing one. "Just Arabs."

"Oh. They're even worse. Good. Very many?"

"A few."

"Is *that* why the British are after you?"

"I don't think so," Starke said. It was time to feed an adolescent fantasy. "I can't tell you why, but I can tell you that your rescue of me is going to make a huge difference to the fate of all Jews." Which is quite true, Starke thought with amusement, although not in the way this young fool would wish. "But to finish what I'm doing, I have to reach Jerusalem."

The boy was impressed, although making a transparent effort to appear tough and knowledgeable. "Jerusalem," he said. "It's not so far. But they'll be looking for you on the buses."

"I know. I need a private car."

"Why don't you get help from the Haganah here?"

"I would, but the British are watching everywhere, and I don't dare endanger anyone else."

"Of course." Yakov nibbled at his lower lip. "I have an idea. It's not a car, but it might do. . . ."

"What is it?"

Yakov told him.

Dusk was already far advanced as Yakov led Starke out of the dry storm sewer. Starke had spent the afternoon and most of the evening in the hiding place, alone, while the young Jew was out reconnoitering the proposed escape route. While waiting, Starke had looked at the escape documents. They would have taken him as far as Rome, but there the route ended. The most useful thing left was a Roman telephone number. Starke was to call it and identify himself with the code name *Rienzi*. The correct response was *Tannhauser*. He had memorized the number and the names and slipped out for a moment to bury the documents in the sand at the sewer entrance. More time passed, and Yakov had finally returned at about seven with a heel of bread and a couple of oranges. He apologized for having brought so little. Starke assured him that it didn't matter, although even after eating the food, the German was still ravenous.

The lights of Tel Aviv were already on as Starke and the boy made their way south by side streets, keeping to pools of shadow. Starke, apprehensive about trusting his safety to an adolescent, asked Yakov what his parents thought he was doing. Yakov shrugged.

"My mother's dead. She caught typhoid a few months after we came here. My father works all the time. I want to go and join a *moshav* or a *kibbutz*, but he won't let me. He wants me to be a rabbi, he says, not a farmer. He doesn't think we should fight, he doesn't like the Haganah. He doesn't know anything about the real world. Not how I feel, either. I don't tell him anything about what I'm doing, if I can help it."

"Where does he think you are?"

"He went to the synagogue. He doesn't know I'm out."

Starke relaxed a little. He hadn't decided yet whether to dispose of the boy. The fact that no one knew Yakov's whereabouts was moving Starke in the direction of doing so. He was reluctant to leave a possibly talkative adolescent behind him, one who might boast to his friends—or worse, to his father—about how he'd helped a Haganah man on the run. Starke put the decision aside for later; right now he needed Yakov to point him in the direction of escape.

After a good hour's furtive travel, twice ducking into hiding to avoid the notice of British police patrols, Starke heard the *huff-huff* of a railway switching engine not far ahead. They were near the south station, where the Tel Aviv-Jerusalem line started, and the freight yards associated with it.

"Not far now," Yakov muttered to Starke.

"How do you know there's a Jerusalem freight leaving tonight?"

"I like trains. I come down here to watch them a lot. I know some of the railway men. In Vienna, when I was ten, I had a clockwork train. But we had to leave it behind. Anyway, a freight leaves every night at ten for Jerusalem."

"Isn't it guarded?"

"Yes. But the soldiers get on at the edge of the yards. If you get on as soon as they make the train up, you'll be ahead of them."

"Good."

A high wire fence separated the street they were now on from the freight yards. The wire looked rusty, and in places the fence was poorly lit. Yakov selected one such place, where the fencing kinked to miss the wall of a building. He pulled at the bottom of the mesh, and a section peeled up.

"Through," he whispered. "I'll hold it for you."

Starke scrambled under the fence and in turn held it up for Yakov. On the other side of the fence, almost invisible in the darkness, was a stack of railroad ties. Beyond the ties were the tracks of the freight yard. Several strings of rolling stock, with and without engines, stood on the tracks in the dim glow of scattered electric work lights mounted high on poles. The air smelled of coal soot, creosote, ash, tar, and dust. The switching engine chuffed steadily somewhere beyond the stationary

railroad cars, and Starke could hear the clank of couplings and the squeal of metal wheels on rails.

"The train you want is beyond these tracks," Yakov murmured. "Over there is the main Jerusalem line. Come on."

Starke followed obediently. The boy was good at moving in concealment. An excellent sneak, Starke thought. Typically Jewish. But one has to use the tools at hand.

Yakov led him to the lines of stationary freight cars and without hesitation ducked underneath one to cross the tracks. Starke went after him, with a momentary twinge of anxiety about being cut in two by an unexpected shift of the rolling stock. The huff and thump of the switching engine was now louder. Yakov crawled under another freight car and stopped beneath it. Beyond were two runs of empty track, and on the third a freight train made up of boxcars and flatcars. The flatcars were stacked with wooden crates, some of which were covered by heavy roped-down tarpaulins.

"There it is," Yakov hissed, peering out into the dim light of the yards. "It'll be leaving for Jerusalem soon. You could get into one of the boxcars, or get under a tarpaulin."

"Where do the soldiers ride?"

"On the engine and tender. Sometimes there are a couple on the last car of the train."

"Are you sure that's the right train?"

"Almost. It's the right track."

It was a fine time to be expressing uncertainty. Worse, Yakov might be making a wild guess, unwilling to look ignorant in front of a Haganah man and adult.

Starke decided to make the best of it. Having gone this far, there was no point in turning back. If it was the wrong train, he could try to find the right one. At least he was in the right place to do so, which was infinitely better than the storm sewer.

"Good. I'm going to go—"

He stopped, looking southeast along the line. There was someone down there, flashing a light around. "Wait," Starke whispered. "Who's that?"

Yakov peered around the car's running gear. "Maintenance crew. Checking the wheels and things."

Starke squinted. "Three of them?"

"I don't know why they'd need three."

"The British," Starke muttered. They'd be checking the trains, of course, looking for a suspected German spy.

"Maybe they won't come over here."

"Back," Starke whispered. The light was drawing nearer. He and Yakov scuttled away in the direction they'd come from, and hid under the line of boxcars farthest from the Jerusalem freight. The glimmer of the light passed slowly by their earlier position. Starke could hear English being spoken, but couldn't make out the words.

The men passed on down the line. "Try now?" Yakov whispered. "They might come back up this way."

Starke nodded in the darkness and slipped under the lines of cars toward the freight. He reached their original vantage point just as a whistle shrilled to the east, toward what was presumably the front of the train. A rumble passed down the long line of cars as the couplings took up their slack. The wheels squeaked and began to turn.

"It's leaving!" Yakov hissed urgently. "Quick!"

Starke hesitated for an instant. If he was going to kill the boy, he'd have to do it now. But there was no time to hide the body, and Yakov might be found within minutes by the men searching for Starke. That would be as good as a map for them: their quarry was trying to leave for Jerusalem by train. Yakov would have to live.

"Good-bye," Starke muttered, and scrambled from under the boxcar. He ran in a low crouch across the intervening tracks, caught the rearmost ladder of a flatcar as it creaked and groaned slowly along the tracks, and clambered aboard. The car was stacked with crates. Starke wormed his way between two of them, under the covering tarpaulins. Inside the stack was a narrow gap running the length of the car. It would conceal him well enough from a cursory search. He drew the Walther, just to be on the safe side, and settled down to wait.

The freight reached a speed of perhaps ten kilometers an hour and maintained that for a few minutes as it rattled over switches and cross rails. Then it slowed with a shrieking of steel on steel and a crash of couplings, and stopped. Starke heard the hiss and pant of the engine, and voices calling back and forth. Someone—presumably a soldier of the train's escort—trotted by outside, boots crunching on the

cinder track ballast. Starke gripped the butt of the Walther tightly and waited.

Another minute or two passed. Then the couplings banged again, and the freight jolted into motion. This time it gained speed steadily. Starke relaxed, and put the gun away.

Major Dalloway put the telephone receiver back in its cradle and sat quite still for a moment, staring at it. From the other side of the desk, Captain Bateman regarded him anxiously. He had entered the intelligence office while Dalloway was still on the telephone. At last Bateman asked, "Sir? Was that the hospital?"

"Yes," Dalloway said tiredly. "Lieutenant Purcell died of his head injuries twenty minutes ago."

"That bastard Levy," snarled Bateman. "Or whatever his name is." He looked around the bare office angrily, as if searching for something to break. "Is Rupert going to be all right?"

"He'll need facial surgery," Dalloway said. "But he's in no serious danger. Is there anything from the search parties?"

"No, sir, I'm sorry. He's dropped out of sight completely. We haven't got anything out of Golz yet, either, I'm sorry to say. He insists he was in Tel Aviv on business. According to him, this person Levy did no more than ask him the time. He denies he ever saw him before in his life. But I'm certain there was an exchange of newspapers. Levy is a German spy. There is no doubt in my mind about it."

Dalloway steepled his fingertips and regarded them attentively. "I wonder what was in the newspaper."

"Golz has refused to talk, sir. So far."

"We have to catch Levy," Dalloway observed. "Spying is bad enough, but to murder a British officer without giving him a chance to defend himself . . . by God, isn't it just like a German? They're either at your feet or at your throat."

"Quite so. Should we publish an arrest bulletin on the grounds of espionage?"

Dalloway drummed his fingertips on the desk. "I don't believe so, actually. I'd prefer to keep the spying end of things quiet. The less the Germans know we know, the better. By all means let's publish a

bulletin, but we'll do it through the civil authorities. Make it on suspicion of murder, for one Samuel Levy, address unknown. Issue what description we have. I don't suppose the man *looked* especially German. Blond Aryan superman, and all that?"

"No, sir, unfortunately. According to the reports of the men he eluded, he wasn't particularly tall, and he had brown hair. Rupert may be able to add some more when I see him tonight."

Dalloway sighed.

"Major," Bateman ventured after a short silence, "I'm sure Golz knows far more than he's admitting. So far our questioning has been extremely mild. I hesitate to suggest this, but if we were to apply a certain additional amount of coercion—"

He trailed off as he found his superior regarding him coldly. "Do you propose," Dalloway queried acidly, "that we apply the same principles to questioning suspects that the *Germans* do?"

"No, sir, not at all," Bateman said hastily.

"I'm glad to hear it. Carry on."

Dalloway studied the door after Bateman had closed it behind him. He hated to admit it, but Bateman's suggestion held a certain amount of appeal. Nonetheless, it couldn't possibly be acted upon. Once one began that sort of behavior, there was no telling where it would end. But certainly it wouldn't end in a way suitable to the reputation of the British officer class.

He sighed regretfully, and went back to work.

Starke, despite his determination to remain awake until the train reached Jerusalem, had drowsed off. He came to with a start, and experienced a few seconds of disorientation before he recollected where he was and where he was going. He had no idea what time it was, but the freight was still rumbling along, and inside the stack of crates it was still pitch dark, too dark to see his watch. Jerusalem and Tel Aviv were only fifty kilometers apart as the crow flies; Starke mentally doubled that to allow for the meanderings of the railway, and then tried to estimate from the sounds of the wheels how fast the freight was traveling. It wasn't moving very quickly. But he

didn't think the trip to Jerusalem could last much more than a couple
of hours.

His stomach grumbled at him. He was still hungry. Starke dis-
regarded it, cleared his mind, leaned his head back against the
rough wood of the crate behind him, and began planning. Minutes
slipped by, then an hour. Starke reassessed the course of action he had
devised. It involved all sorts of risks, but it was the best he could
do.

The freight seemed to be slowing down. Starke listened as the
couplings banged back and forth against each other. Then the brakes
began to screech deafeningly. Starke wriggled his way back along the
alley between the crates, and looked carefully around the corner of one
of them to peer out into the night. Lights were passing, but that could be
no more than a nearby village. Then he saw a railway spur peeling away
from the line he was on, and then another. When there were four sets of
tracks parallel to each other, he concluded that they were entering the
Jerusalem freight yards. Red lights and green lights passed: signals.

Starke withdrew from the opening between the crates to think.
The freight yards and the main station were in the southwest corner
of Jerusalem, and from the configuration of the lights on the skyline, Starke concluded that that was where he was. He had made it
this far.

He looked out again. About fifty meters farther on, a boxcar was
standing on the tracks next to the main line. It would provide cover
when Starke jumped from the train, so that the soldiers he presumed
were riding the last car of the freight would be less likely to spot him. He
readied himself and waited. The freight was only moving about ten
kilometers an hour now. The distance to Starke's jump point
diminished with agonizing slowness.

Twenty meters to go. Fifteen. Ten.

At no more than five meters from the rear of the stationary boxcar,
Starke slid feet-first from between the crates and hit the ground in a
running crouch. He wasn't in the open for more than a few seconds. He
reached the boxcar, ducked under the couplings, threw himself flat on
the ground beneath the car's axle, and compressed himself into an
inconspicuous ball in the shadows between the rails. Then he waited.

The freight on which he had been riding lumbered and screeched interminably past, and he began to worry that it would stop so that the last car, bearing the soldiers, would stop right next to his hiding place.

It did not. The rear car rumbled past. Starke heard voices speaking English above him, arguing over a card game. Ordinary soldiers were the same everywhere, he reflected. Only the best were careful not to let their guard down too soon.

After the freight had gone, Starke carefully observed his surroundings for some minutes, and then slipped from under the boxcar. He was going to have to go to ground until morning. He'd already decided on a hiding place, one of several refuges he'd marked out during his months in Jerusalem: a dry medieval cistern in a patch of waste ground near the old Turkish caravanserai, just a few hundred meters from the railway station.

He reached the cistern without incident, and felt his way down the crumbling steps to its rubble-strewn floor. He moved very carefully in the dark, not daring to risk a twisted ankle, or worse, a fracture. At the bottom of the cistern a section of the wall had fallen away, forming a deep alcove that was out of sight from above. Starke wriggled into it and piled a few rocks at the entrance to conceal himself more thoroughly. Only then, with the Walther ready by his side, did he allow himself to doze off.

Starke woke to sunlight filtering through the cracks of his makeshift wall. By his watch the time was ten to seven, and he could hear the morning noises of the city, although the sounds were muffled by the depth of the cistern. He stretched and spat from a dry mouth; although he was cold he was extremely thirsty, and his body ached from the stones of its rough bed. He also felt dirtier than he had since Spain. More than almost anything else, he wanted a hot bath, a good meal, and a stiff drink.

But I'm not likely to get any of those for some time yet, he thought as he climbed stiffly out of his hiding place and stretched some of the ache out of his back and legs. Never mind. I am at war, and this is my battlefield. There is not, and should not be, any comfort in

war. It softens one. The only way to victory is through hardness
and strength.

He considered the matter of the gun, which he had tucked back into
his waistband. He couldn't take it all the way to his destination, and he
might have trouble getting rid of it on the way there. Reluctantly, he
decided to leave it behind, and concealed it under a pile of stones inside
the alcove. If necessary, he might be able to return for the weapon.

He left the cistern and made his way to King David Street. He didn't
really expect the pursuit to have been raised in Jerusalem yet, and it
hadn't. No one paid him the slightest attention on the bus he took north
along King George Avenue; despite his shabbiness, he wasn't
remarkable among the early morning crowds.

Deciding to reconnoiter the last few dozen meters on foot, he got
off the bus where King George intersected with the Jaffa Road,
and went on northward, not hurrying. Now that the crisis point was
near, he found himself worrying that Rossi might have already been
spirited out of the country; or even that the Mufti's killer had got him. It
would actually turn out to be a stroke of luck for Starke if
they hadn't.

There it was, just a little way ahead: Fink's restaurant. Starke scanned
the pedestrians and traffic in front of it with a practiced eye. He saw no
signs of surveillance, either British or Arab. Scheisskopf had been right
about that, at least: nobody knew what the place really was except the
Jews and the Germans.

He didn't hesitate at the entrance, but went right in. Judging from the
smells of coffee and hot bread that hung in the air, the place had been
open for a while, although there were now only three customers at the
tables. Starke's hunger returned, redoubled.

No one was behind the bar, but Starke went to it anyway and stood,
waiting. He could feel three pairs of eyes boring into the space between
his shoulder blades, and mentally slipped into the part he'd composed
for himself.

A door behind the bar opened and a man came out. He eyed
Starke with some suspicion. "What can I do for you?" he asked
in Yiddish.

Starke struggled with the language for a moment; he'd expected

Hebrew for some reason. "I need to see a man named Rossi," he said quietly.

"There's no one by that name here."

The man was lying; Starke could see it in his eyes. "Please," he said, letting a quaver slip into his voice. "I have to see him. He knows me. The British are after me. I need help."

The man's eyes narrowed. "Where do you know this Rossi from?"

"He brought me to Palestine. On the *Olympia*, it was. I know he's in Jerusalem. A friend of his told me."

"What friend?"

"A woman. An American woman. Her name was Belmont. Young, dark hair. Please, I *have* to have help."

"What for? What did you do?"

"I think I may have killed an English soldier. I didn't mean to, I was frightened—"

He felt a presence at his elbow: one of the men who had been at the restaurant tables. "Wait, Moshe," he said to the man behind the bar. "There may be some truth in this."

The man named Moshe scowled. "If you say so."

"Who are you?" asked the other man. He was taller than Starke, gaunt in the face, with prominent pouches under his eyes.

"Samuel Levy. I came from Germany. Herr Rossi was on the ship, he helped me get away from the British when they tried to catch us after we landed."

"And they're after you again?"

"Yes. I don't know where to turn. It was an accident."

"Rossi can identify you?"

"Of course. Do you know where he is? Please, I need to see him."

The tall man's eyes narrowed. "Very well. But I warn you, if he says you're someone other than Levy—"

"I *am* Samuel Levy. He knows me, I tell you." Starke felt a wave of exultation, which he sternly repressed. So Rossi *was* still in Jerusalem.

"And you know a woman named—"

"Julia Belmont," Starke supplied. "She came to see me a week or so ago. She told me Herr Rossi was coming to Jerusalem. When I got into trouble, I thought he could help me. So I came here."

"What made you do that?"

Starke shrugged helplessly. "One hears rumors. I didn't know where else to start."

"I hope the British don't hear the rumors," snapped the man behind the bar. "Who exactly did you hear about this place from?"

"I don't remember. It might have been someone at the brickyard where I work."

"You work in Jerusalem?"

"Yes."

"Very well," said the tall man. "Come with me." The man behind the bar made a gesture of protest. "It's all right, Moshe," the tall man said. "He's on the run. I heard something this morning to make me believe him."

Starke suppressed a start of surprise. The Haganah intelligence net was better than the British. He wondered if it was better than the German, and hoped not.

The tall man was leading him around the bar and through a door into the rear of the building. Beyond the door there was a room with a table and a few chairs in it, and in the far wall another door leading onward. "Wait here," said the man. "I'll bring him to you."

He left by the far door and Starke heard a lock snap over. Starke tried the door by which he had entered. That was locked, too. They weren't taking any chances with him. He sat down on one of the chairs and tried to ignore the hunger pains in his stomach, which were being made much worse by the cooking odors floating through the air.

He waited for perhaps ten minutes before hearing the rattle of the lock in the rear door. It opened and the tall man entered, followed by both Rossi and Julia. Starke allowed his face to brighten. Next was to come the most difficult part of his entire scheme.

"Herr Rossi!" he exclaimed in German. "Thank God you were here. Fraulein Belmont." He switched to his stilted English. "I am so glad to see you again."

"Hello, Mr. Levy," Julia answered. Starke noted that she looked sleepless and rather disheveled.

Rossi sat down at the table. "Hello," he said, speaking German. "I gather you're in some kind of trouble. What?"

"I was in Tel Aviv to look for a better job. An Englishman stopped

me in the street. He said he was from the British Army and wanted to see my papers. There was something about them he didn't like, and he was going to arrest me. So I hit him and ran away." Starke put his head in his hands. "I didn't mean to hit him so hard."

"You said you were afraid you killed him," the tall man said. He was standing, arms folded, against the back door of the room. "Why do you think that?"

"I looked behind me once. He was lying on the ground. He wasn't moving, and there was blood."

Rossi looked at the tall man and said, "Leon?"

"There was a scuffle like that in Tel Aviv yesterday," the man named Leon answered. "We don't have any details, except that an English intelligence officer was taken to hospital."

"It was you who did that?" Rossi asked.

"Yes," said Starke. "It must have been."

"What're you saying?" Julia asked. She'd been looking from one man to another as the conversation proceeded in German. Rossi told her.

"But if they took him to hospital, he couldn't have been dead," Julia pointed out.

Starke shot her what he considered a grateful look. "I hope that is true," he answered in English.

"You speak much English?" Leon asked suspiciously.

"*Nicht fliessend.* Not fluent. It is from the high school. I was good at language."

"I see. How did you get back to Jerusalem so quickly?"

Best to use the truth. "I went to the rail yards and hid on a train. I didn't know where it was going. It came here. I was in luck."

"Yes, you were. What do you expect us to do?"

"I wish Mr. Rossi to bring me to Italy with him."

Leon covered the length of the room in two strides and had Starke by the collar and half off the chair before the German could react. *"How did you know he was going to Italy?"*

"*Gott in Himmel,*" Starke gasped, struggling ineffectually to free himself. "Miss Belmont told me. Days ago. Please let go. You did, didn't you, Miss Belmont? When you to see me came, the evening I you home took—"

Julia frowned, trying to remember. Then her face cleared. "Yes. Yes, I did. He's telling the truth, Leon."

Leon relaxed his grip and Starke dropped back onto the chair, rubbing his neck where the shirt collar had dug into him. "Thank you, Miss Belmont."

Both Rossi and Leon were regarding Julia with angry disbelief. "You told him I was going back?" Rossi asked. "Why in the name of God did you do that? Don't you know anything about security?"

"You told me yourself when you came back from the north," Julia snapped back hotly. "And so did Claudio, in that letter. Neither of you said anything about it being some kind of secret. If you're going to be sloppy, don't blame me if I can't figure out whether you're underground or not."

Rossi turned red. Leon leaned over him and muttered in his ear. Starke couldn't make out what he said. Rossi nodded, and Leon left the room.

Rossi, still looking humiliated by Julia's pointing out his own security breach, had put aside the matter of Italy and was studying Starke. "Why do you want to go to Italy?" he asked in English, presumably for the Belmont woman's benefit. "The Fascists are only slightly better than the Nazis when it comes to dealing with us."

Rossi had accepted him as a real Jew, then. Good; that was the most essential step out of the way. "I have been thinking about this for many weeks," Starke explained. "Now that the British are hunting me, I have to flee somehow, anyway. I want to look for my family. I've been trying for months, but nothing is happening, no one can discover out anything about them. I want to return back to Germany and search for them, at least discover out if they are still. . . ." Starke closed his eyes and reopened them. "Alive. My wife and father are there. Not knowing what is happening to them is sending me mad. From Italy, I may be able to reach Germany."

An expression of sympathy and concern spread over Julia's features. "I'm so sorry, Mr. Levy," she said. "It must be terribly painful for you."

"I'd like to know how you got away from those Arabs who chased us," Rossi said. His voice was neither accusing nor admiring, just neutral.

Careful, Starke warned himself. "I think they were not really interested in finding me," he said. "They chased me for a few minutes, but there were a lot of big rocks. After shooting the first times, they did not any more. I found a cave and hid in it. It was deep. I think they looked into it, but they did not come in after me. I stayed for some hours. When I came out, they were gone. I found a road when the sun was going down, and a man in a truck stopped for me. He was going to Haifa. He gave me some money, a little bit. So I came to Jerusalem." He stopped. Rossi would either believe him or not. If he did not, Starke would try to disable him before Leon came back, and make a run for it.

"You may be right," Rossi said slowly. "Perhaps they weren't serious about catching us. But you should have tried to find me."

Starke shrugged helplessly. "I know. But I was frightened, and I did not know where you had gone."

"All right," Rossi said. "I understand."

The door opened and Leon reentered. He didn't say anything, but resumed his former stance at the back door. Rossi explained what Starke wanted to do.

Leon shook his head decisively. "No. We can't spare the resources. Mr. Levy may have to stay out of sight for a while, that's all. If the Englishman isn't seriously injured, they'll lose interest after a while. They have bigger fish to fry than an assault and battery case."

"But suppose he's dead?" Julia asked. "What then?"

Leon frowned. "That would be a different matter. I'm trying to find out how things stand. Be patient."

Starke sent a determined look at Rossi, and then at Julia. She would sympathize with him more than the men. Despite his assumed awkwardness in the language, he continued to speak English so she could understand. "If you will not help me," he announced, "I will try to reach Germany by myself. You cannot *make* me stay here."

"You'd never even get into Italy," Leon told him. "Even if you managed to leave Palestine."

"Are you so sure? I have lived by my wits ever since I reached Palestine. My wits are not dull yet. Herr Rossi, Herr Leon, I can be useful, remember. Do you not need men to help others escape from

Europe? Let me go back. I can help you. I speak English as well as German, I know Palestine now. I am not afraid to fight. You know that from what happened in Tel Aviv."

"It's true," Julia observed, supporting him as he'd hoped she would. "Mr. Levy is a survivor if ever there was one."

"We're short-handed in Italy," Rossi said. "That's why the man in Rome wants me back now."

"It'd be better to use an Italian Jew in Italy," Leon pointed out. "Levy would spend all his time hiding."

"Not in Germany," Starke said.

"It might be worse in Germany," Leon told him. "You've no papers, to start with, no place of residence. The Germans are much better organized than the Italians."

"We do need men, Leon," Rossi warned. "If Samuel is willing to take the risks."

"Look," Leon said, "I realize all that. But it's going to be hard enough getting you out of Palestine under cover. We didn't expect to have to ship a third body."

Starke looked from Rossi to Julia. "Are you in trouble as well?"

"Some people want me dead," said Rossi. "The British are after Julia."

"Oh," Starke said, nonplussed. He could not imagine why the British wanted the Belmont woman. It worried him a little. Eluding the Mufti's Arabs wouldn't be extremely difficult, but the British were another matter.

There was a knock at the door. Leon went to it and put his head out. Starke heard mutters. Leon closed the door and turned around to look at them. "What?" Julia asked.

"Matters have changed for the worse," Leon said grimly. "There is a British arrest warrant out for Samuel Levy. On a charge of murder."

"Oh, no," Julia cried. "They couldn't."

"The intelligence officer died last night," Leon said. He looked at Starke. "You did hit him harder than you thought."

"What will happen if they catch him?" Julia asked.

Leon gave a bitter laugh. "When we and the Arabs kill each other,

it's usually a long term of prison. If an Englishman is killed. . . ." He shrugged. "And an English officer, into the bargain. They might put it before a military court. They'd probably hang Samuel."

"But it was an accident!" Starke exclaimed. He had noted Leon's use of his first name. Matters were improving. "How could they hang me if it was an accident? I understand prison, but—" He gestured helplessly.

"To make an example," Leon said.

"That settles it," Julia said. "We can't leave Samuel here for the English to hang."

"It's not that easy," Leon said. "They'll really be looking for him, now."

"They're looking for me, too," Julia pointed out. "If you can get me away now, you can do the same for him."

"Marc," Leon said, turning to Rossi. "If you travel with Samuel, the danger's going to be worse."

"It's true, what Julia said," Rossi answered. "I didn't get Samuel all the way to Palestine for the British to hang him at the end of a rope."

Leon looked pensive. "We can do it," he said. He looked at Starke. "In return, we'd expect you to work for us in Europe."

"I have already offered that," Starke said with dignity.

"Yes. Very well. I will make arrangements immediately. It will require another two days. Marc, Julia, are you willing to wait that long?"

"Yes."

"So be it, then."

"Thank you," Starke said, with complete sincerity.

Berlin—Rome

January 26-27, 1939

Reinhard Heydrich, in a display of fury unusual for him, slammed his palm down flat on the polished surface of his desk. He immediately regretted the loss of temper, not least because his palm stung painfully. Shaking his tingling hand, he stared moodily through the office window at the black and frost-rimed branches of the trees outside.

Golz was taken by the British.

Heydrich returned his attention to the message flimsy on the desk and reread it word by word to see whether there was the slightest chance he'd misinterpreted it, or whether the decoding might have garbled it. He knew very well that neither of these things had happened, and that he was indulging in what he most warned his subordinates against: wishful thinking.

Needless to say, his anger hadn't changed the words by a single syllable. Golz was indisputably under lock and key in a British jail. Unfortunately the message, which was from the German consulate in Jerusalem, didn't tell Heydrich what he most wanted to know: whether Golz had been able to issue Starke's orders and documents to him before being captured.

But then the consulate wouldn't, and couldn't, know about that. The consulate, in fact, thought Golz was exactly what he pretended to be: an innocent German businessman operating in Haifa. Heydrich didn't run the Palestine operations out of the consulate, and his agents normally went nowhere near it. This was for two reasons. First, the

185

British watched the consulate as a matter of course, and second, the Reich Foreign Ministry under von Ribbentrop refused to permit its embassies and consulates to serve as SD support or basing locations. This was because von Ribbentrop had ambitions of being a spymaster himself, and didn't want a competing intelligence organization using Ministry resources. The man's lack of cooperation caused Heydrich and the SD no end of annoyance. To obtain information von Ribbentrop should have provided freely, Heydrich was forced to spy on the Foreign Ministry's communications and break its diplomatic codes just as though it were an enemy. It was such an intercept that had provided the information about Golz, who naturally had requested consular assistance after his arrest.

Golz had his own transmitter, of course, but he was in no position to use it.

Heydrich mused on the matter. There were three possibilities, as he saw it. First, Starke didn't know Golz had been captured, but had the documents, knew that he was supposed to go to Italy, and was doing so. Whether he managed it would hinge on Golz keeping his mouth shut under interrogation. There was nothing Heydrich could do about that.

Second, Starke hadn't made the contact, had neither instructions nor documents, but knew about Golz's misfortune. He wouldn't know enough about the operation to carry on—Heydrich had briefed him only as far as Palestine—and would assume as well that it was laid bare to the British. Bereft of support and direction, he would try to make his way back to the Reich without further ado. There was nothing Heydrich could do about that, either.

Third, it was possible that Starke had his instructions, but had found out that Golz was in British hands. Under those conditions, he would have to assume that his travel plans and destination were known to the British. He might either abort the operation, or try to carry it out by alternate means. Knowing Starke as he did, Heydrich favored the latter possibility. As with the other two cases, however, there were no useful measures Heydrich could take until Starke reached Rome. If he did.

Heydrich loathed enforced inaction, but he was going to have to live with it. All he could do was alert Rome that Starke *might* arrive

from some unexpected direction, at some uncertain time. Unless Starke turned up in Germany instead. Or found himself a captive of the British.

Heydrich's eyes fell on his desk calendar, and the date. He wondered how long Starke would need to do whatever he was doing.

Sofia von Falkenberg stood in the long reception room of the apartment and surveyed herself in the ornately framed mirror. She was correctly dressed to receive a prince of the Church: all in black, her shoulders and arms covered, hemline at mid-calf. The image amused her with its demureness. It would be wonderfully perverse to appear so during one of her sessions at Chez Kitty. Perhaps she could add this little act to her repertoire when she returned to Berlin.

Whenever that might be. In the mirror, her mouth pursed with annoyance. She'd expected to be in Rome for a couple of weeks at most, but here it was the beginning of the third, and still Heydrich left her hanging. There was a limit to the amount of social life she could indulge in without her husband present, and she was beginning to be bored. Moreover, the weather was dreadful, day after day of leaden skies and intermittent cold rain. Sightseeing was impossible, and she took little interest in it anyway. Helmuth and she had spent a number of summers in Italy over the nine years of their marriage—if it could be called that—and she had seen everything she wanted to see.

She considered finding a likely man in the street and amusing herself that way, but rejected the idea without hesitation. She was supposed to be here as a good Catholic woman, for the good of her soul, and for priestly instruction. That was the cover.

She wondered whether Helmuth had believed it. He'd made little fuss about her going off to Rome by herself, and had seemed less than interested in why she was doing it. Of course, he had his own reasons for failing to object. Her absence would give him a freer hand with his peach-bummed boys. He thought she didn't know about them, the old fool. Not that she minded; if she'd had a normal husband she'd have been forced to suppress her own inclinations. From her point of view she and Helmuth had the ideal arrangement.

Nevertheless here she was, stranded in Rome with no way to pass the time. She knew that Hans Becker, Heydrich's man in the German embassy here, would be glad to help her pass it, but she wasn't going to compromise her position for Becker. Sofia had two servants here in the big rented apartment on the top floor of the Villa Zelotti, an eighteenth-century palazzo now transformed into a *pensione* for the very wealthy. She had chosen the housekeeper and cook herself, but knew perfectly well that servants always watched, and always talked. She had given them no subject for gossip but the visits of the priest, and that would draw little attention. On this occasion, however, she had taken the precaution of sending both servants out of the apartment for a couple of hours. She didn't want any ears or eyes at keyholes this afternoon.

Not that they had any idea who the priest actually was. Cardinal Mondolfo, fortunately, had never been in the public eye.

Sofia sighed, adjusted the line of an eyebrow with a dampened index finger, and sat down on one of the damask sofas to wait. A decanter of sherry and some biscuits were laid out on the sideboard should Mondolfo desire refreshment, although on his other two visits he had declined both food and drink. Sofia permitted herself a smile at the memory of their first encounter. Although Becker had told him who he was to meet, the cardinal had clearly been expecting a woman much older, and not nearly as attractive. Heydrich had taken a calculated risk by sending Sofia instead of a man; there had always been the possibility that Mondolfo would refuse to work with a female, especially a relatively young and attractive one. Probably Heydrich's quirky sense of humor had something to do with the choice. Making a Catholic cardinal swallow the humiliation of taking direction from a woman would appeal to him.

Anyway, the ploy had worked. By the end of the first meeting, which was merely to provide an introduction and a precedent for a series of visits, Sofia knew she had Mondolfo at her fingertips. It wasn't through sexual appeal, although that was certainly a subconscious factor on Mondolfo's part, but through Sofia's presentation of herself as a passionate defender of the Faith and an enemy of Bolshevism. In addition—according to Becker—Mondolfo wanted the Papacy, and thought that with German help he might get it.

During the second meeting, Sofia had played on both those themes: the horrors the Bolsheviks would inflict on the Church if Germany wasn't there to stop them, and the need for a strong, vigorous Pope who would unite Europe spiritually against the communists as Hitler and Mussolini were uniting it militarily. Mondolfo had listened with a ready ear. He was convinced that she was speaking for the government of the Reich. He was ready, he told her, to act.

It was not quite time, she had said. The man they needed had not yet come. He would arrive within a very few days.

But he hadn't. Sofia picked angrily at a loose thread on the damask. Dorf was supposed to be here by now. She'd been horrified, yesterday, when she decoded the message Heydrich had sent to her through Becker. Dorf had vanished, the message said. Whether he would reappear was problematic, but if he did it would be without warning. The priest should be told to be ready at a moment's notice. And his commitment should be confirmed absolutely. But he should not be told about the problem with Dorf. It might make him draw back. As soon as Dorf appeared, Sofia was to contact Berlin for final instructions.

The bell jangled in the outer hall. Sofia jumped up and hurried from the reception room to open the apartment door. Mondolfo entered, shaking drops of rain from his flat black hat and shapeless overcoat. Sofia smelled camphor and incense, both of which she hated.

"I am so glad to see you, Monsignore," she said as she closed the door behind him. "I have sent the servants away for a while, so that we may talk undisturbed."

"Good," said Mondolfo in his rusty voice. He removed his coat and hat and hung them on the hall coat tree where they began to drip onto the inlaid marble floor. Sofia led him through the hall into the reception room, with its frescoed walls and ornate pilasters painted to look like green marble.

"Please be seated, Monsignore Mondolfo," she said. "May I offer you some refreshment?"

Somewhat to her surprise, he nodded. "If you have some sherry?"

As she poured a glass for him she noticed that he seemed somewhat

distracted. He kept stroking the large mole on his right cheek. He has something on his mind, she thought. What?

She brought the glass to him and, while he took his first sip, seated herself at the other end of the sofa. "Is His Holiness well?" she asked.

"As well as can be expected given the state of the weather," Mondolfo said, setting the glass down on an inlaid rosewood table. "In fact, his chest is troubling him slightly."

"Is it serious?"

"It could turn to that."

"I see," she said. "Monsignore, you seem troubled. Is something bothering you?"

"Yes," Mondolfo said. "It is. Pius is intending to issue an encyclical against the government of the German Reich."

She put a hand to her throat. "Oh, no. Not now. How can he be so *foolish*?"

"Well you might ask," Mondolfo snarled, causing Sofia to sit upright. She hadn't seen this much savagery in the old man before. "It's the devil guiding him in this, not God," Mondolfo went on. "Or at least, God has withdrawn his hand from him. The old man is about to divide our Church from those who can defend us against Bolshevism, and Pacelli won't lift a hand to stop him. They're both cursed."

"I am afraid so," Sofia answered. "Why must we all suffer because of one man's inability to see the truth?" She was thinking rapidly. Heydrich would want to know this at the earliest opportunity.

"I would much prefer that he regain the right path," Mondolfo said. "But I doubt whether he'll do that."

"When is this encyclical to be published? What does the Pope say?"

"It was to be at the end of this month. Now, a little later, because he's not well enough to work on it steadily. As to its contents, I am not sure. He and Pacelli have been very quiet. But I know enough to think that it will make *With Burning Sorrow* of two years ago look like a tap on the wrist. He will condemn everything the German and Italian governments have done to defend Europe against the Bolsheviks, and he will insist that singling out the Jews as bad elements is wrong

and un-Christian. As if everyone didn't know they're behind the communists and the socialists and atheists like that. Europe seems to have forgotten what the Jews are, they're the Christ-killers. Pius should be reminding people of that, not attacking the German and Italian governments for defending us against this plague of atheism. Even though Germany has treated some Catholics roughly in the past few months."

"I agree wholeheartedly," she told him. "And it's true the Church has had difficulty with some over-zealous authorities in Germany, but I've been told to assure you that the Fuehrer deplores such conflicts, and is taking steps to discipline the men responsible for them."

"Good." Mondolfo half-emptied his sherry glass. "Now, as to further action. But perhaps I should speak with Becker, as well as with you."

"No," she said. "I'm sorry, but it's not safe, and I have to follow my orders. Herr Becker and you should not meet any more. I am responsible for your contacts, as well as for instructing the man who will come soon. For your safety and everyone else's, there can be no more direct contacts."

"And this man who is coming? I will not see him, either?"

"Not until it is time."

Mondolfo nodded. Sofia detected relief in the cardinal's lined and withered face. She thought with contempt: he is too squeamish to spend any time with the man who'll do what he himself can't stomach doing. But he will take advantage of the results. No wonder Christianity is so weak and useless. When the time's right we'll crush it without mercy. It deserves it.

"When is he coming?"

"Soon. Please be sure that everything's ready."

"How soon is soon?" Mondolfo insisted.

"I'm sorry, Monsignore. I have not been told myself."

Mondolfo looked annoyed. "I provide this avenue, but I am not permitted to assist further. Do you not trust me?"

"It isn't a question of trust," she said. "I simply don't know."

"Does Becker know?"

"I don't believe so."

"Ask him."

"Even if he did and I did ask him, Monsignore, he wouldn't tell me."

"I see. This is how you work?"

"Always."

"It may," Mondolfo said slowly after a moment, "not be necessary, finally. Pius's illness might become worse."

"Yes, it might. If it doesn't, are you sure you are prepared to carry on?"

He nodded once, abruptly and decidedly. "Yes. I have prayed long over this, and God's answer has been clear. He does not want this schism for his Church. Pius is no longer doing the work of God. The voice that told me this was very plain. And in comparison to the life of the Church herself, the welfare of one human who has willfully forsaken God to give aid to the Devil's henchmen. . . ." Mondolfo gave an expressive Roman shrug. "Do I need to say more?"

The man's insane, Sofia told herself with a slight shock. He hears voices that tell him what he wants to hear. I wonder what kind of Pope he will make? "No," she answered. "The choice is quite plain."

Mondolfo stood up. "I must go. I presume you'll pass along what I've told you about the encyclical? We may have less time than we think."

"I'll make sure it's known. Bless me, Monsignore, before you go."

She bent her head while he made the gestures above her and mumbled the benediction. When he finished, she got up and accompanied him to the door. "We communicate as before?" he asked on the threshold.

"Yes. No change."

He nodded and left. Sofia closed the door and fanned the air rapidly with her hand to disperse the odors of wet cloth, camphor, sherry, and incense. The hall was filled with it, from his wet coat and his brief presence on the way out. To escape the reek she went back to the private salon behind the reception room, where a coal fire burned low on the hearth. It took the dampness out of the air and warmed the room pleasantly. Sofia opened the liquor cabinet, poured two fingers of Scotch whiskey into a shot glass, and gave it the briefest of splashes from the soda syphon. She gulped half of the drink and then threw

herself onto the chaise longue near the fire. She stared moodily into the flames.

Where was the man named Dorf? Dead? Imprisoned somewhere? Or on the way to Rome, and unable to communicate? Even Heydrich had no idea.

Dorf didn't know what was awaiting him when he arrived, assuming he did. It would be interesting to watch his face when she told him. But as soon as he laid eyes on her, he'd have sex on his mind and be expecting to get it. She wasn't going to allow that, but she'd have to tread carefully. If Herr Dorf was going to assassinate Pope Pius the Eleventh and get away with it, he was going to have to keep his concentration pure and undivided.

Trieste—Rome

February 6-7, 1939

Julia huddled in the after part of the boat, icy salt spray dripping from her hair into her eyes and slithering in cold drops down the back of her neck and under the collar of her overcoat. Ahead of her, almost invisible in the gloom, two crewmen from the freighter hauled at the oars, driving the ship's boat slowly toward the unseen shore ahead. At the tiller behind Julia a third crewman, some junior officer or other, was steering. A kilometer and a half to Julia's left a beacon flashed off and on in the darkness, marking the rocky point where the Gulf of Trieste curved north toward Monfalcone, but the boat was too far north of Trieste itself to enable her to see the lights of the port city. Rossi had told her they were going to come ashore a little way south of Sistiana, and make their way into the city from there.

She could see him up there in the bow of the boat, a dark form against the slightly lighter shade of the planking. Samuel Levy was sitting on the thwart astern of Rossi; even in the near-darkness Levy appeared, to Julia's eyes, miserable and in need of comfort. Unlike Marc, who never seemed to need anything at all, least of all either emotional or physical comfort. No man she'd known back home in New Jersey even faintly resembled him. She tried to picture him out at the country club, cleanshaven in a jacket and tie and with his hair trimmed, but failed. At least he had good table manners; that she knew from observing him at Donati's house in Rome.

If we could just meet in ordinary, civilized circumstances, she thought as the boat crested a roller and slid down the other side.

194

Instead of being cold, wet, exhausted, and grubby, the way we are now. I must look absolutely god-awful. That ship. . . .

They'd been aboard the freighter for a week, as it churned its smoky, rolling way from Port Said in Egypt up the Adriatic toward Trieste. To Julia's surprise and relief the journey by truck and then train from Jerusalem to Port Said had been without incident; no Arabs had attacked Rossi, and the British hadn't spotted either Levy or herself. At Port Said they'd been taken aboard the freighter at night, by small boat, just an hour before she sailed: another one of Mossad's secretive travel arrangements.

The arrangements weren't luxurious. She and Rossi and Levy slept in the forward hold, with the cargo of Egyptian cotton; they used the same sanitary facilities as the crew, and ate the same food. Neither were up to much. She had next to no clothes—the dress in her satchel and the overcoat she was now wearing over a pair of baggy trousers and a denim work shirt—to replace the ones she'd lost in Jerusalem, and washing them was next to impossible. That hadn't bothered her as much as Rossi's behavior. It was true that they hadn't fought, as they usually seemed to do when together for more than ten minutes, but that was because he was even more taciturn than he had been when they were hiding out in Jerusalem. He spent most of the time on the ship's fantail, gazing back at the wake; when Julia spoke to him, he answered politely and volunteered nothing.

Levy was far better company. He asked her a great deal about America, which she was glad to talk about, as she was having one of her attacks of homesickness. The thin Altgarten butcher was especially eager to know what life was like for Jews in the United States. She talked to him for hours, remembering what it was like. He didn't like talking about Altgarten and his family, though; she'd gently tried to get him to open up about what had happened, but the questions so clearly upset him that she dropped the matter. Instead she helped him with his English, and taught him some Italian. He was remarkably quick at languages.

It had all come to an end at midnight, when one of the ship's officers told them to get ready to disembark. The boat was swung out; they boarded it, and were lowered into the heaving water below. Julia had no idea how they'd have reached shore if the sea had been too rough

for the boat. Likely, she reflected as it dug its prow into a wave and threw spray at her face, Rossi had an answer for that problem, too. He seemed to have an answer for anything that physically threatened him. Julia was honest enough to admit that she was glad of it. He might be cold, inscrutable, and horrifyingly self-sufficient, but he was on her side and he made her feel safe.

Levy was more of a mystery, perhaps because he was a German. Julia knew she attracted him; that was plain enough from the way he looked at her when he didn't think she was noticing. But there was something else, buried deep inside him, that she couldn't quite fathom. It almost seemed to her like a streak of ruthlessness, even violence, although she couldn't imagine why she thought that. Perhaps it was because he'd killed a man, although his remorse for having done so was evident. He was younger than she by a couple of years and she felt protective toward him most of the time, almost maternal. But sometimes she noticed how gracefully he moved, like some kind of dangerous feral animal, and if she was honest she had to admit that at those times she felt a primitive physical response deep inside her. The contradiction was disturbing.

Suddenly, she could see dashes of white ahead in the darkness, and beyond them a darker loom. The land was near. Rossi called something back to the helmsman, and the rowers lay on their oars for a moment until the helmsman shouted at them and they began to pull again. The line of the surf drew nearer, and Julia could hear its boom. They were going to get wet. She realized that she was already shivering, although under the overcoat her clothes were still mostly dry.

If I'd been told a year ago I was going to be doing things like this, she thought, I'd never have believed it. I still can't believe it. I must be tougher than I thought I was.

She nervously checked the waterproof covering of her document satchel. After bringing the papers all this way she hated the thought of having them ruined by a dousing in the Adriatic. Her shoes—sturdy leather ones Meisl had gotten for her before they left Jerusalem—were draped around her neck, tied by the laces with her socks stuffed inside. Rossi had told her not to get the shoes wet; once ashore, they'd need to be dry-shod. Her only other clothes, the underwear

and dress she was wearing in Jerusalem when the Arabs attacked, were stuffed into the satchel along with the documents.

Without warning the boat plunged into the white tumble of the breakers. The surf wasn't high, but it was heavy enough to heave the boat off course and pour dozens of liters of water over the gunwale. Julia heard the helmsman cursing the rowers as they struggled to straighten the swaying craft. Another wave caught the stern and spun the boat even farther around, so that it was lying almost parallel to the beach. It heeled steeply, throwing Julia against the inwale. She felt a stab of fright, imagining for a split second the boat capsizing with her trapped in the dark underneath.

But the wave passed before the boat quite went over, and in the following trough the helmsman managed to bring her bow-on to the beach again. The rowers heaved at the oars. Julia heard sand and shingle grate under the keel.

"Go, go!" the helmsman was calling to her. "Over bow, go!" He didn't want to bring the boat any farther in for fear the waves would drive her too far up the beach and pin her there.

Julia gave the satchel strap one last check and scrambled forward, past the rowers, into the bow with Rossi and Levy. Rossi was watching the lift and fall of the waves. The boat steadied for a moment in the backwash of a breaker.

"Now!" Rossi called out. He swung himself over the gunwale into the knee-deep, foaming water below. Levy was doing the same on the other side of the bow. Julia clambered gracelessly over the side of the boat, dropped, and felt icy water clamp around her calves. To her surprise, Rossi was waiting for her. He grabbed her arm and hauled her toward the beach. The sand, sucked from under her bare feet by the backwash, shifted as she trod on it and she almost fell down, the shoes swinging clumsily against her chest. Rossi dragged her roughly to her feet. It was hard to run in the receding water, and she could hear the hiss and roar of another roller breaking behind them. Then the surge around her calves stopped and reversed direction, pushing her shoreward. Water roared behind her. Rossi hauled mercilessly at her arm.

The breaker hit her in a tumble of icy water and almost knocked her off her feet. It was to her knees, to her thighs, dragging at the skirts

of her overcoat. Then, as she was deciding she was going to have to swim to save herself, it began to draw back. Now, however, it wanted to take her with it. She struggled gamely on, digging the balls of her bare feet into the sand and shingle to make ground, Rossi still trying to help but having his own difficulties despite his strength. She glimpsed Levy on her left, still upright, still moving toward the land.

Suddenly, without Julia quite knowing how it had happened, they were out of the breakers and on rough sand and shingle above the waterline. Sharp stones cut the soles of her feet and she gave an involuntary gasp of pain. Rossi was still holding her arm and heard her. He let go quickly.

"Socks and shoes," he said. "We'll put them on here. We'll have to climb some rocks above the beach."

She knelt and started putting on the footgear. Her feet were chilled through and wet, making the socks hard to draw on. She managed everything finally, after a struggle with the knots in the shoe-laces. Levy, a few feet away, was doing the same. Rossi had already finished and was standing up, doing something with an object in his hands.

It's a gun, she realized. He came armed.

Rossi appeared satisfied with the weapon, and put it away. "Are you ready?" he asked her as she got to her feet.

"Yes. Where now?"

"Beyond the beach. I think we're in the right place."

She knew roughly where they were going. Rossi had said there was a tumbledown house between the beach and the coast road, where they'd wait until daylight. Then they'd walk into Sistiana, where there was a morning bus to Trieste. She'd asked him why they weren't landing nearer the port itself, as that seemed easier; but apparently the freighter's captain was worried about anti-smuggling patrols.

"You know this coastline?" Levy asked Rossi as they began slogging up the beach inland.

"Somewhat. I made it my business to. We've used this stretch for coming and going before. Did anyone get their documents wet?"

Julia didn't think she had and said so; so did Levy. He was traveling on a genuine German passport Mossad had obtained from some-

where; his name was now Franz Bittner. Matters were simpler for Julia and Rossi, who were using their own passports. Because of the way they had reached Palestine and returned from there, it appeared that they had never left Italy at all. Their visas had almost expired, however. Julia assumed Donati would fix that when they got back to Rome.

Unless, she reflected as they left the sea farther behind them, she decided to go back to the United States. She hadn't made her mind up whether to do so or not. But she wasn't sure what use she would be to anyone in Italy. Perhaps Mossad could find a niche for her. That might mean continuing to work with Rossi. She didn't know whether she could endure that. Anyway, she wanted to turn her documents into a book or at least a series of magazine articles, and doing so would be easier back home.

It's too early to think about it, she told herself as they reached a more level stretch of ground well above the beach. I'll worry about it later. My God, I'm freezing.

She was drenched from the waist down, and the wind was cutting into her. Her teeth had begun to chatter uncontrollably, almost painfully. She knew you could die from cold, even if the temperature wasn't below freezing. Rossi helped her over a large rock, and she was disturbed to feel him shaking too. Levy surprised her. He trudged on through the darkness like an automaton, not speaking, alone with his thoughts.

"I know where we are now," Rossi said quietly. "Follow me. It's hard to find."

Obediently, Julia and Levy fell in behind him. She kept her eyes fixed on the dark blur of his leather jacket, wondering if he ever wore anything else. Suddenly, the jacket disappeared. Julia stopped, nonplussed.

"Down here," said Rossi's voice, apparently from the ground in front of her. His voice echoed, as though he were speaking into a barrel. "Step down. Be careful, it's steep."

She felt a hand grasp her ankle and place her foot securely on a flat stone surface. "Okay now? Watch your head as you come down. The roof's low."

She felt her way down, realizing that she was following a flight of

stone steps. Something brushed at her hair and she thought, Bats! before she realized that it was the low roof Rossi had warned her about. Finally there were no more steps. Pitch blackness surrounded her, and she stopped. She heard Levy's boots scrape on the stone behind her. "Marc?" she said doubtfully.

The darkness was split by the flare of a match, blinding her. Her eyes adapted a little and she saw Rossi searching about on the stone floor of whatever structure they were in. He found what he was looking for: a stick with a pitch-soaked rag around it, a torch. Rossi applied the match to it and after a few seconds the rag caught fire, filling the space around them with a smoky orange light. Julia saw that they were in the lower story of a tumbledown stone building set back into the hillside, so that the building's landward wall was not masonry but the bedrock itself. The stairway angled down it from what was once the upper story.

"There's undergrowth all around here," Rossi said, holding the torch up so that the smoke could escape through the gaps in the stone vault above them. "It's safe to make a fire. We'd better, before we all catch pneumonia. There's wood over there."

Someone had piled dry wood against the back wall, perhaps some of Rossi's colleagues who knew he was returning this way, the same people who had left the torch. Within minutes Rossi had the fire started and the chill was beginning to leave the air in their stone burrow. Julia sank thankfully down beside the blaze.

"It's going to be hard lying, I'm afraid," Rossi told them. "Just the floor to sleep on."

"Are there fir branches outside?" Levy asked. "We could make bedding."

"No. This place has to stay looking deserted. If it were day, we couldn't even have a fire. Smoke."

"Oh. Did they leave us food?"

"I'm afraid not. They didn't know exactly when we were coming."

"I'm too tired to eat, anyway," Julia said. "And I'm just glad to be off that damned ship."

Rossi looked at his watch. "We should try to get some sleep. It will

be light in four or five hours. It'll take us an hour's walking to reach Sistiana. But we ought to be in Trieste by noon."

"Good," said Levy. He sat down a meter from the fire and leaned against a fallen roof-slab. "I will sleep, then."

"Should we stand watches?" Julia asked.

"Yes. I'll take the first two hours, and wake Samuel."

"I can watch," she said.

"It's not necessary."

She bit back a retort. They were edging toward another fight already. "Whatever you like."

"Get some sleep."

She stretched out beside the fire, using the document satchel as a pillow on the hard stone floor, and wrapping herself in the overcoat. I refuse to be angry at him, she thought. It's not worth it.

Despite the myriad sources of discomfort, she fell asleep almost immediately.

Rossi woke Levy up at four in the morning and set him to guard the hiding place, although he didn't give Levy the gun. He didn't think the man's education would have included firearms. Levy didn't ask for it, anyway, and Rossi dropped into a deep sleep, broken only once by the sound of the other man adding wood to the fire. He was dreaming about New York when he felt Levy shaking him gently.

"It's dawn," Levy said. "Should I let the fire burn out? It's not smoking much now."

Rossi looked up. Gray was filtering through the holes in the vault of the roof. According to his watch it was twenty past six. His body ached all over from the hard surfaces he'd been sleeping on.

"Let it go out," he said. His mouth felt dry and rough, and he was very thirsty. They'd have to get water inside them soon, even if they couldn't manage food. He looked over at Julia, who was still sleeping quietly in her cloth cocoon. She'd stood up remarkably well, he thought. He'd tell her so when the moment was appropriate. Unless Levy did it first. She'd spent so much time with the German aboard ship that Rossi was beginning to wonder whether she was falling for

the man. Rossi didn't care one way or the other if she made a fool of herself, but he didn't want the pair of them distracted from more immediate matters, like getting to Rome as soon as possible. Once she was back in civilization, she'd see how impossible a fling with Levy was. The pair of them weren't well-matched at all, as far as Rossi could see, and besides, Levy was married.

He levered himself off the ground and stretched painfully. Julia opened her eyes. "Time to get a move on," Rossi told her. "I don't know about you, but I'm thirsty and I want some breakfast."

"Good," she said, wide awake all at once. "So do I. Damn it all, I'm stiff as a board."

It was, as Rossi had expected, an hour's walk to Sistiana. They reached the town without incident, bought bread and cheese with the Italian money Rossi was carrying, and drank a quart of water each. Rossi passed out some bills and coins, in case they became separated. The bus left for Trieste at nine, but they stayed away from the stop until five minutes beforehand, not wanting to attract any attention from the village police force. The bus was only ten minutes late, but was crowded with villagers going up to Trieste, and they had to stand up. Julia's trousers drew disapproving attention from a pair of old women in black dresses and kerchiefs; they muttered between themselves about her attire for most of the way to Trieste. Julia ignored them. So did Rossi, after a while; he was still reluctant to attract attention. Levy had retreated within himself once again.

They reached the port city just after ten and decanted themselves from the rattletrap vehicle into the square in front of the bus station, which was located a stone's throw from the railway station. "Now what?" Julia asked.

"Now we go to the place you and I stayed before we went to Palestine. We all need to clean up before we go near a train."

It was true. They all showed the effects of rough travel. Levy in particular was beginning to resemble a hobo.

"Do we walk?" Julia asked. "I can't remember where it was from here," she said.

"We'll get a cab. There's a rank at the train station over there."

Rossi didn't have a key for the apartment, so they had to go down to the docks to the Mossad office to get one. When he returned to the cab he was looking grim.

"What's the matter?" Julia asked as he told the driver the address. Rossi looked pointedly at the back of the man's head and said, "Later."

The apartment was in a nineteenth-century building on the edge of the Old Town, near the recently discovered remains of an ancient Roman theater, and was overlooked by the warren of narrow lanes climbing the hill of San Giusto. The apartment was at the rear of the building; its narrow windows looked out on a vista of crumbling stucco and brick, with washing flying from clotheslines over dingy courtyards. "Not a room with a view," Rossi told Levy. "Sorry."

Levy shrugged. "What was the matter back there?" he asked. "Julia was asking."

He'd started calling her Julia instead of Miss Belmont while aboard the freighter. For no clear reason, it grated on Rossi.

"Nothing specific," he said. "Things in general. Did you know about the race laws they brought in here last November?"

"I knew they did it, but only of a few things in particular."

"Julia?"

She nodded. "Yes. I was worried about Claudio. How strictly are they enforcing them?"

"It's erratic, according to Chaim down at the office. There's a good deal of maneuvering around them, but if you hit a dedicated Fascist official things can be awkward, apparently. We'd better be careful till Claudio fixes us up with new visas."

"Am I all right?" Levy asked anxiously.

Rossi emitted a short bark of laughter. "I'm not sure how the man in the street here feels about Germans, but as far as the Italian government's concerned you're certainly more welcome than Americans."

"Good."

Rossi eyed the Altgarten butcher for a moment. The man was an odd mixture: seemingly timorous at times, and at others decisive and capable. He'd certainly reacted fast enough when the British tried to

pick him up. And before that, when the Arabs were pursuing both him and Rossi the night they landed in Palestine. By rights he ought to be dead, or in a British jail. There was more to him than met the eye. Rossi thought he might well be useful in the escape lines, especially now that the war clouds were gathering. With experience he could become a valuable Mossad asset.

"There's a train at eleven, with connections for Rome," Rossi said, turning away from Levy. "We'd better get cleaned up."

To Starke's pleasure, Rossi bought first-class railway tickets, saying that they were less likely to be molested if they were traveling that way. Starke's estimation of the Mossad agent had risen considerably during the time they had been traveling together; Rossi was obviously extremely competent, and courageous into the bargain. He would also kill if he had to, as proven by his escape from the Arabs in Jerusalem. Starke could not help smiling at the irony of that escape. He'd set the Mufti's assassins on Rossi to prevent the Jew from searching too deeply into his cover, and yet here was Erich Starke traveling quite comfortably with the man he'd tried to have killed. As it had turned out, Rossi wasn't suspicious at all.

That, Starke reminded himself as the train whistled and puffed its way through the outskirts of Trieste, was partly because of the circumstances of Starke's own flight, and partly because Rossi didn't know what had happened to the Arabs near Kefar Vitkin that morning back in October. If Rossi knew that all three of them had been killed . . . but he didn't. Everything had turned out, fortuitously, for the best. If Rossi had indeed been killed, Starke might still be trying to wriggle his way out of Palestine.

Although there was room for six in the first-class compartment, they had it to themselves. Julia and Starke sat with their backs to the engine, with Rossi facing them. Julia had changed into the dress she'd been carrying with her in the satchel; the garment was wrinkled, but presentable, although it clashed somewhat with the sturdy leather shoes she was wearing. None of them looked prosperous, but neither were they scruffy enough to attract unwelcome attention. Starke at

first had been curious about what the satchel contained, but when Julia told him he promptly lost any but simulated interest. What the Jews did to upset the British was no concern of his.

The day was fair, and the train rumbled through the bright winter sunshine over the coastal plain. Starke began to think about Rome, and plan what he would do when he reached the city. He could not make up his mind whether to stay with the other two and take advantage of this Claudio person, or simply drop out of sight as soon as they reached the capital. Eventually he elected not to decide; he would wait and see what opportunities were offered.

"When do we reach Rome?" Julia asked.

"We have to change at Padua. We get there a little before three. There's a Rome express leaving at four. It gets in about one A.M. Claudio's expecting us at his place."

"Myself as well?" Starke asked, in his persona of Levy.

"Yes. Of course."

Starke nodded, satisfied. He'd go that far with them, at least. He didn't want to be wandering around Rome in the early hours of the morning, trying to reach his contact.

They reached Padua on time, one of the positive achievements of Mussolini's government. There was time for a hurried meal in the station buffet, and then they boarded the Padua-Bologna-Florence-Rome express. The train was more crowded than the one from Trieste had been, and a middle-aged Italian couple shared the compartment with them. The man attempted some conversation with Rossi, but Rossi pretended not to speak Italian. Disappointed, the man fell asleep. His wife read a religious-looking book until she did likewise.

The train rumbled through the gathering twilight. Darkness fell. The Italian couple roused themselves at Bologna and got off; no one replaced them. The train bored on through the night toward Florence and Rome. Now it was climbing into the great craggy spine of Italy, the Apennines. Even where there were villages, Starke could see only the occasional glimmer of a lantern. The moon was not yet up and the mountains were visible only in his imagination, looming unseen in the night above the passes through which the train panted and hissed. Starke mused on the journey: somewhere ahead of him lay some kind

of destiny, one whose nature he did not precisely know; except that there was death in it for someone. He imagined hanging suspended and disembodied outside the window of the train, looking in at himself in the yellow-lit compartment: death riding the train to Rome. Somewhere in the city ahead of him there was a man (assuming it was a man) who was even now going about the business of living, eating or laughing or making love or simply sitting by a fireside, a man who had not the faintest suspicion that death was riding over the mountain passes to meet him somewhere in the streets of the ancient city.

I am larger than life, Starke thought. I am fate, and destiny. I am Death.

His stomach twinged. Something he'd eaten at the buffet in Padua wasn't agreeing with his digestive system. He dismissed his fantasies, and went to use the lavatory.

When he got back to the compartment, Rossi had fallen asleep and Julia looked heavy-eyed. Starke resumed his seat between Julia and the window. "Would you like to sit here?" he asked suddenly, remembering his manners.

"No, thank you," she answered drowsily. "I'm nearly asleep, and there's nothing to see, anyway. Not until we reach Florence."

"It's on the other side of the mountains?"

"That's right."

"Perhaps someday we can go there and see it as it should be seen."

She smiled briefly. "Perhaps." She laid her head back against the seat and closed her eyes.

Starke felt his own eyelids growing heavy. He normally needed little sleep, but the stress of the last couple of weeks had taken its toll. He hoped vaguely that he'd have time to get his full edge back before Heydrich sent him into action. Probably he wouldn't; at any rate, he'd better not expect to be able to do so. He'd simply have to make allowances for not being quite at his peak.

He drifted, not exactly awake but not asleep either. For some reason Heydrich had gotten onto the train and was sitting across from Starke, beside Rossi. Heydrich glanced at Rossi and put a finger to his lips: don't wake him.

"You must have got on in Bologna," Starke said to Heydrich.

"Perhaps," Heydrich answered. "Do you know what you are to do yet?"

"No. You haven't told me."

"Would you like to know?"

Starke suddenly wanted that more than anything else in the world. "Yes. Please tell me."

"It's not yet time," Heydrich said, smiling so that his teeth showed. "But I will tell you anyway. You are to bring back the bones of Saint Peter."

"Very well," Starke said. "Where are they?"

"Under St. Peter's, where else?" Heydrich raised his slender white hand and clenched it into a fist. "Once we have them, nothing can prevent our complete and ultimate victory. They possess a power no one knows about but myself, and now you."

Of course that was what he was to do. Starke couldn't imagine why he hadn't realized it before. It was so obvious, and at the same time so marvelous. He'd always known there was a key to everything, and now Heydrich had shown him what it was. He felt a flood of exultation, and closed his eyes with the fierceness of it. When he opened them again, Heydrich had gone. However, Sofia was sitting in his place. "Are you supposed to be here?" Starke asked. He wondered if she knew about the bones. He'd better not mention them.

"I just decided to come," she said. "You haven't forgotten me, have you?" For some reason she was wearing a silk bathrobe and little else; her feet were bare. Starke found himself worrying that the conductor might come along and ask her to leave.

"No, of course not," he said. "Are you going all the way to Rome?"

She didn't answer. She was undoing the robe. Starke leaned forward to stop her, but instead of seizing her wrist he somehow found himself sitting on the opposite seat, with her naked on his lap. Beside them, Rossi slumbered on. "We can't do this here," Starke told her.

"Yes we can," she said. "They're asleep."

"But so am I," Starke told her. He'd just realized it. Sofia seemed to evaporate, and he found himself back on the other side of the compartment in his seat next to Julia. He'd fallen asleep with his head

against the window frame, and the angle had put a crick in his neck. Starke raised his head gingerly and looked around. Rossi was still asleep, and so was Julia, with her shoulder pressing against Starke's as the train swayed back and forth.

He was half-aroused from the dream, and the presence of Julia next to him did nothing to dispel the feeling. He badly needed a woman. Sofia, in fact, was the last woman he'd had, and that had been months ago. Starke gritted his teeth in frustration. If they'd been alone on the train, he might have approached Julia when they reached Rome; she might well be attracted enough to him to give in. But he didn't want to try anything as long as Rossi was around.

It was too bad Rossi was present last night in the ruined farmhouse outside Trieste. If he hadn't been, Starke mused, he'd have spread Julia whether she was immediately agreeable to it or not. He expected she would have come round. Women had their seasons too, and Julia probably needed a man from time to time. It would have been intriguing to find out.

The train was rounding a curve, and the sideways force began to press her harder against his side. Damn the bitch, didn't she realize what she was doing to him? Not likely; she was asleep. Or was she?

Her head fell sideways onto Starke's shoulder. She *was* asleep, then; she wouldn't make a play for him with Rossi sitting there across the compartment. Enough of this. They must be near Florence, anyway; the train was running along the level, and there were electric lights visible in the darkness outside. Starke shifted in his seat, jolting the head of the sleeping woman.

Julia started and sat up abruptly. Starke glanced sideways at her. Her cheeks were pink; she knew she'd been sleeping on his shoulder. Rossi must have sensed something, because he was blinking, slowly coming awake. Starke looked out the window, his arousal diminishing rapidly. They were definitely nearing a large population area, judging from the number of lights, and the train was slowing down.

"I think it's Florence," Starke said to Rossi. "We don't have to change trains, do we?"

"No," Rossi answered, yawning. "This goes straight to Rome." He looked at his watch. "It's on time, too."

"I will be *so* glad to sleep in a decent bed again," Julia said. "And eat a decent meal. Thank God for Claudio."

"Who is Claudio?" Starke asked. "You have several times mentioned him, but I have not wanted to be curious."

"A friend," Rossi said. "A lawyer in Rome. He's Jewish, like us. I work for him in the escape organization."

"I see," Starke said, filing this away for Heydrich's future reference, although he imagined the SD chief already knew about Claudio. "Can he help me return to Germany?"

"I expect he can send you to someone who will, if he can't help you himself."

"Thank you."

"Thank Claudio."

"Yes. Does he know I am with you?"

"I don't believe so. He's expecting me and Julia, though. There'll be room for you for a while."

"Do you still wish me to work with you, in Germany?"

"I've been thinking about it. Let me talk to Claudio first."

"Yes. Fine. But I would very much like to help."

Rossi nodded. The train was drawing to a halt under the dimly lit arches of the station; on the platform outside the window, porters and travelers scuttled up and down through clouds of steam. Across the platform Starke saw another passenger train begin to pull out, people still moving around inside as they looked for seating. Thuds and bangs and footsteps echoed down the corridor of their own car as passengers boarded and got off. The car jiggled.

"Changing locomotives, I think," Rossi observed. A pair of nuns looked into the compartment, looked doubtful, and hurried on. A few seconds later they returned, came in, and sat down. One of them immediately began telling her rosary, muttering under her breath. The other took a heel of bread out of a straw hamper and began eating it fastidiously, in very small bites that she broke off with her fingertips. Neither of them showed the slightest interest in their fellow passengers.

That's another lot we'll get rid of someday, Starke thought as the doors slammed and the train began to pull out of the station. Nuns

and priests. Parasites. Clinging to their bloodless, nerveless, sexless
Christ. How can anyone with any courage or strength be taken in by
them? They're enough to make you throw up.

The lights of Florence fell away behind as the train rolled down the
valley of the Arno toward Rome. For a while it paralleled the main
south road, and Starke could occasionally see vehicle headlights
over on the highway. Then either the rail line swung away from the
road, or there were no more vehicles, and the night became
black again.

"How much farther?" Julia asked.

"Three-four hours. The dining car should still be open. Does
anyone want to eat?"

"Not for me," Julia answered.

Starke shook his head. The bad food at Padua was still disagreeing
with him.

"Okay. I'm not hungry, either."

"I think we're all too tired to be hungry," Julia suggested.
"Tomorrow we'll be ravenous."

"Probably."

No one felt like talking. The nun who had been eating finished her
bread, but the one with the rosary mumbled on and on. And on.
Starke had decided to rip the thing away from her and toss it into the
corridor, when she stopped. He felt Julia give small sigh of relief
beside him. She put her lips to his ear and whispered:

"She must have done something very wicked to need to say that
many Ave Marias or whatever it was."

Starke grinned. Rossi was watching them with intense curiosity.
"She must have," Starke said, not bothering to lower his voice. "I
think it is likely dangerous to ride in the same compartment."

Julia gave a snort which was actually a strangled giggle.

"What?" Rossi asked.

Starke told him, speaking very fast in German in case the
nuns had some English. The bread-eater was staring at him with
plain disapproval.

Rossi gave a faint grin. "Should we move?"

"I think not. I believe we can deal with them should it be required.
However, one of us should remain awake at all times."

Julia snorted again. Starke realized that she, and perhaps Rossi and himself, were badly overwrought from exhaustion. Starke nodded politely to the nun with the rosary. She pursed her mouth and turned away. That seemed to diminish the joke. Rossi closed his eyes. "Wake me up when we're in Rome," he said.

A few minutes later, Julia had also fallen asleep. Starke followed her not long after. This time he did not dream, or if he did he did not remember what it was he dreamed.

Again, the train was on time. It steamed into Rome's Termini Station at eight minutes after one in the morning, exactly as advertised. Mussolini had ordered reconstruction of the station the previous year, and after getting off the train, Julia, Rossi, and Starke had to pick their way among piles of building materials to reach the main entrance. The air smelled of coal smoke, steam, brick dust, and damp mortar. Outside in the Piazza Cinquecento, a cold wind was blowing down from the Esquiline hill. Rossi noticed that Julia was shivering.

"We'll be there soon," he said. "We'll try to find a cab."

"I hope we can."

Starke said nothing.

Rossi had spotted a cab a dozen meters away and was about to start for it when a shadow detached itself from a pile of brick rubble and stepped toward him. Not here, he thought, disbelieving. They couldn't have tracked us all this way.

He was reaching for the Browning when he recognized something in the walk. "Claudio?"

"Yes." The low voice was full of relief as Donati stepped forward into the dim glow of a streetlight. "I wasn't sure it was you." Doubt entered Donati's voice. "You have someone else?"

"Yes. A friend."

"All right. Quick, follow me, all of you. We have to get out of sight."

They hurried after Donati as he trotted across the Via Marsala and into the shadows beside the church of St. Cuore. The lawyer stepped into an alcove behind a buttress and stopped.

"What's the matter?" Julia asked in Italian.

"I intercepted you at the station to keep you from coming to my house. It's not a safe place for you any more. The problem is papers."

"But our visas are in order," Julia protested. "Aren't they?"

"Yours is for the moment. Marc's was until this afternoon. Just after lunchtime my friend in the immigration office was arrested for accepting bribes. Everyone does it, but somebody decided to make an example of him. The police will be going through his files to see who he made special arrangements for. That might include you, Marc, depending on what records my friend kept. I can't take the chance."

"What will happen if they catch him?" Julia asked.

"At the very least, deportation. At worst he might be charged with trying to bribe an official, which is serious. They couldn't make it stick, Marc, since I did the bribing, but they could keep you in jail for quite a time while they investigated. I don't know which is more likely to happen. Assuming you're in the files."

"Oh, shit," Rossi swore. "Why now?"

"What about you?" Julia asked Donati.

"I don't know. My name wasn't on paper anywhere, as far as I'm aware. It will depend on what they get out of my friend if and when he's interrogated."

"How bad is it here overall?" Rossi asked. "We heard things in Palestine, and when we got to Trieste, but not much detail."

"They brought in more race laws on November 17," Donati told him. "That hyena Mussolini, trying to ingratiate himself with Hitler. We cannot marry non-Jews any more, we can't own factories that employ more than a hundred people. We can't own land over a certain value or serve in the armed forces. We can't work in banks or insurance companies or the government. Jewish lawyers can only have Jewish clients. And we can't employ non-Jewish domestics. Teresa, my housekeeper, has had to resign." Donati gave a quiet, bitter laugh. "I do not enjoy my own cooking very much. All that in addition to the restrictions on education they brought in last summer, and the citizenship changes in September. It's mad. We Italian Jews were the most assimilated in Europe. Some of us even belonged to the

Fascist party, for God's sake. Two of us have been prime ministers of Italy. I thought I understood human nature, but now—"

He broke off, unable to say more. Rossi asked: "What do you want me to do?"

"My car's nearby. I've a safe place, I hope a safe place for you until I find out exactly how much danger you're in. I have to ask who your companion is."

"Samuel Levy," Rossi told him. "The man I was with when we went ashore from the *Olympia*. He's in trouble in Palestine, so we brought him back here. He wants to get back into Germany to look for his family."

"I see." Donati didn't sound especially pleased at Levy's presence. "What papers does he have?"

"German passport and visa. He's better off than I am."

"All right. Julia, I'd ask you to stay with me, but if I get into trouble, they might bring you in for questioning too. I don't want that. I think, if you're willing, you'd better stay with Marc. There's room for three where you're going, but it'll be cramped. I hope you don't mind."

"It's fine," she told him.

They jammed themselves into Donati's Fiat and he started driving southwest, keeping to the back streets. "How did you know we were going to be on that train?" Rossi asked.

"I called Trieste right after I found out my friend was arrested. They told me."

"You found us a safe place in a hurry," Julia said from the back seat.

Donati grunted. "I got my hands on it last November, through an acquaintance. I thought it would be needed sooner or later."

"You were right," Rossi said.

They were still speaking Italian. Levy asked plaintively from behind Rossi, "Is there something wrong?"

"Yes," Julia said. She explained in English while Donati navigated the narrow streets. Levy didn't comment when she had finished.

"This is the place," Donati said, pulling up to the curb. "Do you know where you are?"

"I think we crossed the Via Cavour," Rossi answered. "Near Saint Maria Maggiore somewhere?"

"Yes. This is Via Sforza." Donati got out of the car. "You're on the ground floor, at the back."

He led them under an arched passage into a tiny courtyard and unlocked a door at the courtyard's rear. Inside was a small furnished apartment: a bedroom, a bathroom, a sitting room, and a scullery-kitchen. There was no electricity, only oil lamps. "The kitchen door opens onto an alley," Donati told Rossi when they had finished the inspection and were back in the small sitting room. "It's a bolt-hole, if you need it. I hope you won't. There's bread and cheese I brought today, and wine. If you want hot water, you'll have to heat it on the stove. There is kerosene for the stove under the sink."

"Thanks. We'll be fine."

"For the moment, anyway. I'll come tomorrow if I can and let you know what's happening. But if I don't turn up until the day after that, don't be surprised." Donati took a deep breath and looked at Rossi and Julia in the dim golden light of the oil lamp. Levy hovered in the shadows. "Avoid going outside, if you can. Signor Levy will be safer to send, if you need something urgently. Now I have something to tell you. The news is not all bad."

"Yes?" Julia asked, hope in her voice.

"Pius is going to speak at last. Pacelli has told me. The encyclical will be published on February 10. Pacelli would not tell me exactly what it says, but he gave me to understand that it will be much stronger than *Burning Sorrow*. It will list the persecuted peoples, and demand that all such persecution cease. Including that of the Jews."

"That's wonderful," Julia said. "At last." Her eyes were bright.

"How much difference will it make?" Rossi said thoughtfully.

"I think it could avert the coming war, or at least delay it until the democracies are better prepared to meet Hitler and Mussolini. It will certainly undermine the Fascists here. And Hitler cannot ignore the millions of Catholics in the Reich who will have been told he is a criminal, and told by the Pope himself at that. It will divide Germany badly."

Levy had been trying to follow the conversation, obviously without success. "May I tell Samuel?" Julia asked.

Donati hesitated. "Very well. Except the date. But it must go no

further. I wouldn't permit telling him at all, except that there are already rumors."

Julia told Levy what had been said. His eyes took on a strange intensity in the lamplight. "Good," he said when she ended. "That is perfect." He paused. "Perhaps the Nazis will release my family then."

"Perhaps," Rossi said, not wanting to raise Levy's hopes too high. A good deal of time could pass before the Reich government gave in to Catholic pressure, if it did. Again, Rossi found that Levy puzzled him. There was something *odd* about the man's expression. There was gratitude and delight in it, yes, but they were mixed with something else. Anticipation? No. Glee? That was closer to the mark.

He was too exhausted to consider it any further. Donati, sensing their fatigue, turned to go. "I will try to come tomorrow," he repeated. "Or the next day, at the latest." He glanced at Rossi. "If it goes badly here," he went on, "you realize you both may have to go back to the United States. Or leave Italy again, at least."

"I know," Rossi acknowledged. Julia nodded reluctantly.

"Here's the key," Donati said, handing it to Rossi. "Good night. I'll go out by the alley." He turned and left the circle of lamplight, and Rossi heard the lock of the alley door click shut behind him.

"What are the sleeping arrangements?" Levy asked suddenly.

Rossi couldn't follow for a moment what he was talking about. Then he understood. There was a couch here in the sitting room, and a double bed in the bedroom. He was about to say he'd take the couch and Julia could have the bed, but then realized that would leave Levy on the floor.

"I'll take the couch," Julia said practically. "It'll fit me better. You two can use the bed."

"But that is impolite," cried Levy. "The lady should be able to use the bed."

"But that means one of you will have to sleep on the floor," Julia pointed out. "Unless you're suggesting that I share the bed with one of you."

"But that also would be not suitable," Levy said plaintively. "Also, I am a married man."

"We'll draw straws for the couch or the floor," Rossi told Levy. "Julia can have the bed."

Julia emitted an odd sound. With a start, Rossi realized that she was laughing at them. "Look at you both," she said. "We've been living in each other's pockets for days, and all of a sudden you're worried about my honor because of a bed."

Rossi felt himself flush. "That was out of necessity."

"Getting some decent sleep is also a necessity," she told him, "and that won't happen if you're lying on the floor. Use your heads. I spent six nights with you two in the hold of a ship, and my virtue's still intact. It's stupid to waste half of a perfectly good bed because of some idiotic notion of chivalry. Either let *me* sleep on the couch, or draw straws for the other half of the bed, if that's what you want to do."

Levy prodded the couch doubtfully. "It is very hard. With many bumps."

Julia threw up her hands. "I give up. I'm going to bed, *in* the bed. You two do what you please."

She picked up her satchel and the oil lamp and stalked into the bedroom, leaving the door a quarter open behind her. Levy and Rossi looked at each other in the sudden gloom. "She's right," Levy said. "It is stupid to sleep on the floor. I am married. I will take the couch."

"Fine," Rossi said irritably. She'd made him feel like an idiot again. As usual. She probably thought he *was* an idiot.

He tapped at the bedroom door. "What?" she asked.

"It's Marc. I'll sleep in here."

"Just a minute." He heard the slither of cloth. "All right. Come in."

He left the door half open behind him. She was already under the rough country-homespun blankets, lying on her side facing the wall. The bed was also Italian country-style, so wide it almost filled the tiny room. Julia's dress was hanging from a coat tree.

"I can put my trousers back on if you'd prefer it," she said, seeing him look at the garment. "They *are* still damp from getting ashore, though. I don't want any more wrinkles in the dress, it already looks bad enough."

"It doesn't matter," he mumbled. He sat on the opposite side of

the bed and peeled his socks and shirt off. Then, still in his pants, he got under the blankets. Lying down, even on the coarse sheets, felt wonderful.

"May I blow out the lamp?" she asked.

"Yes."

A puff of breath, and the room was plunged into darkness. Rossi closed his eyes. He wondered why sleeping half a meter apart in the hold of a ship should be so much less suggestive than sleeping half a meter apart in a bed. Married couples slept together in beds. Maybe that was it. This was a little what being married to Julia would be like.

It was a thought that had little to recommend it. Rossi tried to ignore the soft breathing on the other side of the mattress, and listened instead to the noises of the night city. Actually, Rome at this hour was fairly quiet. Some cats were fighting in the distance. Rossi wondered vaguely what they were fighting about.

"Marc?"

He snapped back awake. "What?" He managed not to make it *What now?*

"Will you go back home if you can't stay here?" she whispered.

"I don't know."

"I don't know, either. Would you go back to Palestine?"

"Maybe."

"I might do that. I could sneak back in. Work in the country, so the British wouldn't catch up with me."

"It's a hard life."

"I know. Harder than this?"

"I suppose not." He wished she'd shut up so he could get some sleep. His feet were just beginning to feel warm again.

"What would you do if you went home?"

"I don't know that, either."

"Settle down?"

"You mean, find a wife, raise a family?"

"I suppose so."

"I think I'd be bored."

A longish silence. "That would be boring?" she asked.

"Not for some people. Maybe for me."

Another silence. "I never got married," she said. "I was too busy. It was my mother's despair."

He really didn't want to talk about it. "I'm sorry."

"Sorry for who? My mother?"

"No. Yes. I don't know, dammit."

"You're getting annoyed again," she observed.

"No, I'm not. I just need some sleep."

Another pause. Then she said softly, "You really don't know much about women, do you?"

He refused to answer. She didn't say anything else, and before long he heard her breathing even out. Rossi breathed a prayer of gratitude, and promptly fell into oblivion himself.

Rome

February 7, 1939

Thin February sunlight was trickling in through the bedroom window when Rossi awoke. Julia was still asleep beside him. He moved carefully, so as not to wake her, and looked at his watch. Ten past nine. He hadn't slept in so late for a long time.

He eased himself from under the blankets and pulled his shirt and socks on. Julia stirred and muttered in the bed, but didn't waken. Rossi left the bedroom, closing the door quietly behind him.

Levy wasn't on the sofa, but the door to the bathroom was closed. That was where he was, unless he was in the kitchen.

He wasn't. Rossi drew the muslin kitchen window curtain aside and peered through the cloudy glass into the alley, which in daylight he could see was narrow and shadowed. The stucco on the building across from him was coming away in yellow-gray slabs to expose rough brown brick underneath. A heavy iron-bound door and a tiny grilled window stared back at Rossi.

He sighed and dropped the curtain. He badly wanted a cup of coffee. After some searching he located a sealed bag of coffee beans, a grinder, and a coffeepot, all cheap but new. Donati must have furnished the place expecting a protracted stay for someone.

He had lit the kerosene stove and was just putting the coffeepot on it when Julia entered the kitchen, yawning and rubbing her eyes. "Morning," she said. "Are you making coffee? Wonderful."

"Ask Samuel if he feels like breakfast. I'm famished myself."

She looked at him in surprise, and then around the kitchen. "But I thought he was out here."

"He was in the bathroom a few minutes ago. Go and bang on the door."

"But I was just in there myself. He's not in the sitting room, either."

"What?" Rossi went and looked in the sitting room, and then the bathroom. No Levy. He came back to the kitchen. Julia gave him what he was beginning to think of as a Julia-look. "I told you he wasn't there," she said.

"Sorry," Rossi answered, not sorry at all. "What the hell does he mean by going off like that without telling one of us? Donati won't like it. I don't like it, either."

"He's got the German passport," Julia pointed out.

"Even so," Rossi said, and trailed off.

"You don't suppose he's already heading for Germany?" Julia asked. "He seems to do things on impulse."

"Like killing a British army officer?" Rossi said sharply. "Yes, I suppose he does."

"You don't like him, do you?" Julia observed.

"I don't care either way. He's just there."

She eyed him knowingly. Rossi said, "You're kind of fond of him, aren't you." It was a statement, not a question.

"I'm awfully sorry for him. It makes me feel protective, I guess."

"I don't think he needs protection."

"Women see things men don't."

"He's killed a man, Julia. How much protection do you think he needs?"

"Everybody needs somebody to care about them. Even you."

"What's that supposed to mean?" Rossi asked. He refused to meet her eyes. "We were talking about Levy."

"Were we?"

"I thought so."

She sighed, as though accepting some kind of defeat Rossi couldn't identify. "Never mind. Are you going to go out and look for him, or what?"

"No," Rossi answered. "There're too many places he could be in a city this size. We'll just have to wait for him to come back. Assuming he does. Maybe he's just sightseeing. If he *does* come back, though, I'm going to tear a strip off him a yard wide."

Levy was not sightseeing; he was Erich Starke again, and he was looking for a public telephone from which to call the number the SD man had given him that hair-raising day back in Tel Aviv, when the British almost caught him. Starke hoped that the telephone was still manned. Heydrich would long since have learned of the near-disaster in the Jewish city, and might have decided to close down the operation.

Starke hoped not. It would be the crowning achievement of a career such as his. He had never suspected his target might be the Pope, not until last night when Julia translated what the Jew lawyer had told her: the old nun-fucker Pius was going to try to turn good Germans against Hitler. With her words, the deviousness of Heydrich's plan became clear to Starke.

A Jew named Levy was going to murder the Pope. The Christ-killers, so far from being remorseful for what they had done two thousand years ago, were willing to do it again by murdering Christ's representative on earth. Whatever sympathy anybody had for Jews was going to vanish with that atrocity, and disposing of them one way or another would be much less likely to raise an international outcry. Moreover, and perhaps even more important, Pius's driveling old mouth would be stopped for good. The next man to sit on the throne of Peter might be far more sympathetic to German destiny. He would certainly not be sympathetic to Jews.

Starke found himself grinning as he finally spotted the facade of the railway station ahead. Heydrich had outdone himself this time. Anyone who wanted to could trace the path of the Jew Levy from Germany to Palestine to Rome to the Vatican. As a lucky bonus, it could also be shown that Levy had been brought to Rome by friends of Donati. Donati's influence with the Vatican, however great it was, would vanish.

Starke reached the railway station and went in to search for a public telephone. He speculated for a moment about how Heydrich would make sure Levy was identified as the Pope's assassin. Probably by using the real Levy, or more likely his body, with appropriate documents on it. That was why the orders in Tel Aviv had been so insistent on Starke's bringing all his papers with him from Palestine to Rome. There was no substitute for the real thing. He'd told Rossi he'd thrown them away, but they were inside the shoulder lining of the jacket he was now wearing.

Starke saw a bank of telephones outside the main station hall, and hurried toward them. The contact, assuming the operation was still on, would tell him how Levy was to be maneuvered into position. Or maybe the contact wouldn't tell him; Starke would simply do the job and get out, with somebody else attending to the logistical details. Either way suited Starke.

Starke was still carrying the money Rossi had given him in Trieste. After redialing a couple of times and cursing the Italian telephone system, he heard a ring. It went ten, eleven times. Starke was about to hang up and try again when the receiver clicked in his ear. Then a woman's voice said, "Three seven five, two three nine."

Starke pressed the connect button. "This is Rienzi."

A fractional silence. Then the woman responded, "Tannhauser."

"I'm in Rome," Starke said.

"How good to hear from you," answered the woman. "Please come round right away. The address is the Villa Zelotti, the pension on the upper floor. It's on the Via Rasella, number 36. Will you be able to find it?"

"I'm at the railway station," Starke said. "I don't have much money."

"How much?"

He counted, and told her.

"That's enough for a cab. Get here as soon as you can."

"Is there a doorman or concierge?"

"I'll take care of it. Just come."

Starke hung up and hurried out into the sunlight. He'd expected a man. A woman made him uneasy. But she was probably only

the cutout, and the operation would be run by a man. He'd know soon enough.

He had no trouble finding a taxi at this hour of the morning. He gave the address and the cab set off southwest along the Via di Viminale. Starke wondered whether Rossi was awake enough yet to miss him. He hadn't yet decided whether to return to Donati's safe house; that would depend on what he learned from his contact. If he did go back, he'd tell Rossi he had gone out to look at the Eternal City. That would be natural enough. And Julia would intervene for him, if Rossi decided to get nasty. Starke half hoped he would. He'd welcome an opportunity to flatten the self-possessed shit. Although beating the daylights out of Rossi would be hard on his cover. Starke sighed. He'd have to forgo the pleasure, at least for a while.

The cab turned right along Via Agostino Depretis, this time heading northwest. Starke wondered whether the driver was going to try to give him the tourist's runaround, but after a few minutes' travel the driver peeled off left into a side street, just short of the vast bulk of the Palazzo Barberini. A few meters down the street he stopped and half-turned in the seat.

"Villa Zelotti, Signore."

Starke handed him the wad of bills, not bothering to count them, and got out without waiting for change or complaint. The Villa Zelotti was a three-story pile covered with cinnamon-colored stucco; tall windows with stone cornices looked down into the street. The door was large, wooden, and solid, with a bronze handle and iron latch. Starke pressed down on the latch and pushed and the door squeaked ponderously open. Inside was a tiled foyer lit by windows on each side of the door. A stair led upward in front of Starke, and on his right was a cubicle with a half-door separating it from the foyer. There was no one visible in the cubicle.

A place like this would have a doorman-guard, Starke thought as he started up the stairs. Not an unbribable one, though. The rich can pay for discretion.

He reached the top of the stairs, and a landing on which were two paneled doors, black with a couple of centuries of polish. She'd suggested she had the whole top floor, so Starke arbitrarily rapped on

the right-hand door. It was too thick for him to hear anything on the other side of it, so when it opened he was caught somewhat by surprise.

"Hello, Herr Dorf," Sofia said. There was amusement in her eyes, which she was going to no great lengths to conceal. "Please do come in."

Starke pushed brusquely past her and waited until she had closed the door and locked it. If this was Heydrich's idea of a joke, he wasn't amused. Not nearly as amused as Sofia appeared to be.

"Herr Dorf," she said. "You don't seem surprised to see me. I thought you would be."

He regarded her. She was wearing a white silk blouse with long sleeves and a high neck, and a flowing red skirt. Thin gold bracelets encircled her wrists, and there was a large cameo clasp at her throat. "Is there anyone else here?" he asked, ignoring her statement.

She became businesslike. "No. I have two servants, but I sent them away for the morning. The doorkeeper I bribed to notice nothing. I hope that meets with your approval."

He nodded. "Let's get started."

"Come this way, please."

She led him through the reception room into a smaller, more comfortable one where a coal fire whiffled to itself in the grate. He observed the height of the ceilings and the quality of the furnishings and said, as he sat down in a wing chair next to the fire, "I see Heydrich provides you with a generous expense account. Or does this come from your earnings?" There was no harm reminding her what she was.

She laughed, untroubled. "No. It comes from my husband's earnings. My full name and title are Countess Sofia Eloise von Falkenberg. You may have heard of the family."

Starke blinked. He had. He resolved to behave a little more politely. "My apologies. I spoke without thinking."

"It doesn't matter," she said. "I do receive a stipend from the SD, but it's no more than hat money." She arched her eyebrows at him. "I do the work for the love of it. Like you, I'm dedicated. Unlike you, however, I don't look as though I'd been sleeping in a barn. Where have you been?"

"There was some difficulty with the travel arrangements," Starke said cautiously. "I had to come by an alternate way, and it took longer. I wasn't in a position to let Prinz-Albrecht-Strasse know what was happening."

"Please be more clear."

"No. I'm here. Arrange for me to speak with Heydrich. You must be able to do that."

There was a long silence, which she broke. "Let's get one thing perfectly clear," she said. "You are to tell me everything. You are not to hold anything back. If you do, Heydrich will punish you severely. I was sent to Rome to direct you according to his orders, and I will not put up with obstruction from you. Heydrich told me you might act like this. This is his message to you: Follow orders, or pay the consequences."

Starke raised his eyes in supplication to the heavens, and then lowered them. "All right. This is what happened."

He told her, beginning with the aborted meeting with Golz and ending with his journey to the railway station last night. However, he left out what Donati had said about Pius's encyclical. If he was wrong and the target was somebody other than the Pope, Sofia had no business knowing such acutely sensitive information.

She was looking thoughtful when he ended. "I'll have to pass this on to Heydrich as soon as possible," she said. "It's likely one of the things he's been waiting to hear."

"In the meantime," Starke asked pointedly, "what am I supposed to be doing?"

She was sitting in a wing chair opposite Starke's, on the other side of the fireplace; now she leaned forward and, taking up the poker, stirred the coals a little. Sparks flew up the chimney and a piece of coal cracked with a *pop*. "You are to assassinate Pius," she said.

"Oh," Starke answered flatly, without emotion.

She sat up, still holding the poker, and stared at him with disbelief. "This doesn't surprise you?"

"No. I had already decided it must be that."

She replaced the poker in its stand. "When did you realize?"

"Yesterday evening." He told her what Donati had told him through Julia, about the encyclical.

"You weren't going to inform me of this?" she asked angrily, when he had finished.

"It was irrelevant to what you needed to know at the time." He intentionally made his tone patronizing.

"I'm warning you, Herr Dorf—"

"Of what?"

She decided not to pursue the matter. "If this is true, then Heydrich will want you to move as fast as you can. Within twenty-four hours."

It was Starke's turn to be surprised. "You can get me close enough to Pius on such short notice?" He had had visions of a long stalk.

She was nodding. "Yes."

"It's brilliant," Starke said admiringly. "What Heydrich's doing, I mean. Making it look as though a Jew's killed the Pope. How are you planting the real Levy in the right place?"

"That's not something you need to know," she told him. "Follow orders, and don't worry about the rest. Heydrich's arranged everything."

"Do you know how that part is to be done?"

"No. And I haven't asked. I suggest you do the same."

Starke suspected that she wasn't telling the truth, but short of torturing her he had no way to make her confess it. If she hadn't been so close to Heydrich he would have used some force on her, but as it was he didn't dare. "Very well," he said. "What weapon?"

"None. You are to break his neck. As he sleeps, preferably."

"I'm not to take any kind of weapon in with me?"

"No."

Starke thought it was peculiar, but also that Heydrich must have his reasons for the order.

"I presume," Sofia said, "that you brought with you the Levy papers?"

"They're inside my jacket lining."

"Please give them to me."

Starke eased them out of his jacket and handed them over. As he put the jacket back on he asked, "Who is taking me in?"

"A priest."

Starke grinned savagely. "Some of His Holiness's flock have teeth, do they? Good. What's in it for this one?"

"He wants to be Pope. Heydrich thinks he would be a good choice for us. Anyway, he will take you to the Pope's chambers, and leave you. After you've killed the old man, leave by the same way. Someone will meet you at the place you entered the Vatican, and get you away. There's no danger."

Starke raised his eyebrows. "Only from the Noble Guard, the Palatine Guard, the Swiss Guard, and the Papal Gendarmes as well as some plainclothesmen. Are they all going to stand by with eyes front while I saunter past them in the wake of this would-be Pope? Wouldn't he be just a little bit of a suspect afterward?"

Sofia made an impatient gesture. "Of course it's nothing like that. He says there is a secret way into the Papal quarters, very old. It's not guarded. Only a few people know of it."

"That in itself will point a finger at him, afterward. Isn't he worried about that?"

"He has ways to point the same finger at others. Once the Pope is dead and the Jews have the blame for it, it doesn't matter to us what happens in the Vatican, anyway. So much the better if they're all looking over their shoulders at each other. They'll have less time to interfere with Germany."

Starke nodded. It made sense. "Good. Where am I to go to meet this raging sheep?"

"Tomorrow evening. Go to this address: 27, Via Vespasiano. Memorize it. It's a bar near the Vatican, to the northeast."

Starke committed the address to memory. "I have it. Go on."

"Don't go into the bar. Go around the corner onto the Via Degli Scipioni. You'll see a church a block farther on, the church of Saint Rosario. Wait just inside the doors. You are to be there at eleven o'clock. Your guide will meet you there. Follow him, but don't make any obvious contact until he indicates it's safe to do so."

"What's the recognition signal?"

"How good is your Latin?" she asked.

"I remember a little from school. Horace. Virgil."

"That will be enough. The signal is the first line of Virgil's *Aeneid*. You say the first half. He completes it."

" 'Arma virumque cano, Troiae qui primus ab oris,' " Starke quoted. "Yours are the first three words."

"All right," Starke said. "Do you have money for me? I'll need it for transportation. There may be other things."

She went to a sideboard and took out some bills and a small rubber packet, which she gave him. He inspected the packet; it contained thin surgical gloves.

"Wear those inside the Pope's quarters," she said. "Heydrich's orders."

"Fine," Starke agreed. As he folded the bills and pushed them and the gloves into the heel of his sock he asked, "Do you wish me to stay here until I have to meet the contact?"

She frowned as she sat down across from him again. "No. The servants. Is it safe to go back to your Jews?"

He considered. "Yes. I believe so."

"You're sure they have no suspicion who you are?"

"I'm sure." Starke grinned. "They think I'm a harmless Jewish butcher from Altgarten." His eyes dropped to her blouse. He wasn't sure, but he suspected she was wearing nothing underneath it.

She'd seen the look, and her eyes were fixed on his. "I assume you've had no connection with the Jewish woman. You know how the Reich feels about sexual relations between Aryan men and Jewish females."

"No. No connection."

"Not even aboard that ship all that time?" she asked. "Surely you must have been tempted. Are you sure you and this Rossi weren't taking turns with her? She is American. They're free and easy with their favors. Or so it's said."

He gave a short bark of laughter. "Not that free and easy. Even Rossi wasn't sleeping with her."

Sofia leaned forward. "Really? Cooped up like that . . . you both could have done whatever you wanted with her. I'm surprised you didn't take the opportunity."

"It would hardly have suited my cover," Starke pointed out. In spite of himself, he was becoming aroused. "And Rossi has illusions of being a gentleman."

"Don't tell me you didn't consider spreading her."

Starke shrugged. "Think whatever you like."

She stood up. "You may go now."

She was dismissing him like a servant. Starke felt anger rising in him. That, and his previous arousal, left him suddenly and rigidly erect.

She was already moving toward the door to the reception room. He got up and followed her. Sofia opened the door. Starke took two long steps to catch up with her and seized her from behind, by the shoulders.

"Not so fast. We're not finished." He pulled her toward him, feeling against his palms the smooth skin under the blouse.

She twisted from his grip and backed away. "Not so fast yourself, Herr Dorf. I haven't invited you."

"I'm not waiting for an invitation." He stepped forward. Sofia backed away from him again, into the reception room. Her cheeks were flushed and she was breathing rapidly. Starke's eyes flicked to her blouse. The white silk over her breasts showed two small bumps; her nipples were erect. Starke took another step toward her. She held up a hand warningly. Starke only grinned.

She turned and ran away from him, around the end of the sofa. He ran after her and caught her beside an ornate marble-topped table next to one of the tall windows. She tried to squirm out of his grasp but only succeeded in getting her back to him. Starke pushed her forward over the table, pinning her against it with his hips. He held her there with one hand and with the other pulled up her skirt. Sofia attempted to break his hold but was unable to do so. With his thumb Starke found the waistband of her underwear, and yanked both it and her stocking suspenders down over her thighs. She gasped and tried to stand up.

"Stay put," Starke growled. He undid himself, making ready, and then slipped his hand between her legs and probed. She was extremely slippery, as he'd suspected she would be. She would submit now. He drew back, preparing to insert himself.

Without warning Sofia shoved herself backward, throwing him off balance and breaking his grip on her. She almost eluded him then, but he grabbed her by the upper arm as she lunged for the door to the sitting room, and she stumbled and half-fell to the floor. Starke

followed her down, and in the confused tumble of arms and legs that followed managed to get her stockings and undergarments off. Then he rolled on top of her. She tried to keep her knees together, but he forced them apart.

Once she felt him penetrate her she lay quite still, eyes closed. Starke moved rhythmically and steadily inside her. Half a minute passed. Sofia moaned, gave two involuntary pelvic thrusts, but then regained control of herself. Starke held himself back with some difficulty. He was determined to make her respond.

Another half minute passed, and suddenly he felt her begin to move underneath him. Her arms went around him and she turned her face up to seal her mouth to his. Their climaxes came simultaneously and without warning, uncontrollable. Starke poured himself into her. The spasm was so intense that he almost blacked out.

They lay locked together for almost a minute before he withdrew himself and rolled onto the floor beside her. She looked up at him, a lazy smile spreading over her face.

"You should be an actress," he said.

"I *am* an actress," she answered. She stroked his calf with the inside of her foot. "Poor Herr Dorf. To be without so long, and then to have me refuse you."

"As if it was a real refusal."

"How can you be sure it wasn't?" she asked. "At first?"

"It didn't stay that way."

She sat up and drew her skirt down to cover herself. "No, it didn't. You're very persuasive, Herr Dorf. But the servants will be returning soon. You have to go now."

Starke went down the stairs with mixed feelings. Somehow, despite the fact that he'd made her submit, she'd retained the upper hand. He felt, in fact, as though she'd ordered him to service her, and he'd obeyed.

He didn't like it.

Rome

February 8-9, 1939

Night had long fallen, and after thirty-six hours Donati still hadn't come back to the safe house. Rossi was seriously beginning to wonder whether the lawyer had been arrested.

"Your move," Julia said.

Rossi brought his attention back to the game. Julia had found the chess set, together with a few books, inside the armoire in the bedroom, and set it up on a small side table in the sitting room. As it happened, both she and Rossi played poor chess, so the match was even. The game was nearly over, and the board decimated with Rossi trailing by a pawn. He thought he saw an opportunity to checkmate her, though, if she'd just move her rook into the tempting position he'd left open—

She did. Rossi slid his remaining bishop two squares. "Check and mate," he stated calmly, looking up at her. The three oil lamps burning in the living room gave her skin a rosy glow.

Taken aback, Julia carefully inspected the black and white pieces. "What? Are you sure?"

"Yes."

"Damn. I thought I had you."

"You nearly did. Another?"

She glanced over at the clock ticking on the windowsill. "It's past nine o'clock. No, I don't think so. Do you suppose Claudio's having some trouble?"

So she'd been thinking about it, too. "He might be," Rossi answered.

Levy, on the couch, looked up from the elderly edition of *David Copperfield* that had been in the armoire with the chessmen. He'd been struggling through its rotund Dickensian English, page by page, for the past two hours. "Is there something we should do?" he inquired anxiously.

"There's nothing we can do just now," Rossi said. "If there's somebody there ransacking his files, the last thing he wants is a visit or a phone call." His stomach growled. There hadn't been much food in the apartment. Presumably Donati intended to bring more when he returned, but in the meantime they were all hungry.

"Are you hungry, too?" Julia asked. "Your stomach's grumbling."

"Yes," Rossi admitted.

"I am also hungry," Levy said. "Perhaps I could go out and find something to bring back for us to eat? I would be very careful," he added anxiously.

Rossi eyed him. He judged that Levy was still smarting from the reprimand Rossi had given him yesterday afternoon, after the German returned from his unauthorized sightseeing jaunt. He'd been quiet all yesterday and today, and anxious this evening to help Julia in the kitchen with what supper there'd been. Now, likely, he was wanting to make amends.

"Is there anywhere nearby?" Julia asked. She sounded eager. Rossi now suspected she'd given the men most of what food there was.

"I saw a cafe around the corner when I was coming back," Levy said. "There was sausage and fresh bread. I smelled tomato sauce, and wine. Perhaps they are still open."

Rossi's mouth was watering. There couldn't be any harm in Levy going such a little distance and for so short a time; his papers were in order, after all.

"Is your Italian good enough?" Rossi asked him.

"I know some now. And I can point to what we want."

"Okay," Rossi said. "Let me give you some money. Don't go on any sightseeing trips."

The German look discomfited. "I will not."

When he'd gone, Julia and Rossi looked at each other across the chessboard. "I could eat a horse and chase the rider," she said.

Rossi laughed. "Where did you hear that? I've never heard it."

"I don't know. Somewhere."

She'd washed her hair during the day, heating water on the kerosene stove, and it gleamed black and glossy in the light of the oil lamps. She saw him looking at it.

"I know it needs cutting," she said. "I've looked like a haystack for weeks."

"No," he said, suddenly shy. "I was thinking how, well, good it looked."

"You must be joking. Please don't tease me."

"I'm not," he said. "Really, I'm not."

There was a short silence. She said:

"Do you realize we've been in the same three rooms for nearly two days and we haven't had a fight?"

He gave a grin of embarrassment. "Unless you count the disagreement over the sleeping arrangements."

"It's only a fight if I'm angry," she observed. "I wasn't angry about that."

"Oh," he said. "Good."

Both of them fell silent. Julia picked up a bishop and rotated it absent-mindedly between her fingers. Rossi gazed awkwardly at the thickly curtained window. He had no idea what, if anything, to say next.

"What do you think's going to happen?" she asked.

"I'm not certain," he said, relieved at returning to business. "If Donati's in the clear, we can stay in Italy, for a while, anyway, and keep—"

"Not about that," she interrupted with exasperation. "Why do you insist on being so obtuse? I'm talking about us. You and me."

"Oh. I see."

"Do you?"

"I don't know. I think I know what you're talking about, but—"

"But you're scared to admit it, even to yourself. For fear I'll laugh at you."

"I guess so," he answered. His cheeks and forehead felt hot.

She grinned at him. "You're blushing," she said. "You've gone really pink. I never thought I'd see you do that."

He shrugged, watching the curtain as though there were someone dangerous behind it.

"Look at me," she said. He did so. The smile was gone; her eyes were very large and dark. "Let me tell you the reason we fight all the time. It's to avoid the awkward fact that we've fallen in love with each other. Isn't it?"

Speechless, he could only bob his head.

"Is that a yes or a no?"

"Yes," he said. "I love you."

She sighed with relief. "Good. It was like pulling teeth, but I finally got it out of you."

"And you?" he asked. "What about you?"

"You mean, do I love you? Of course I love you. Madly. You don't think I'd have gone through all these contortions otherwise, do you?"

"No." He was still breathless from the shock. Everything in his life had suddenly changed.

"Don't you think it's about time you kissed me?" she asked.

Very slowly, he leaned over the chessboard toward her. She bent forward toward him.

The alley door in the kitchen creaked open and slammed. "Ah, damn," Rossi muttered. "Levy's back." He brushed her lips with his. "Later," he said, standing up. She sighed in exasperated disappointment.

"Marc? Julia?" came a voice from the kitchen. It wasn't Levy; it was Donati. The lawyer came hurrying into the sitting room. "Marc, where's Levy?"

"He went out to get food. He should be back in a few minutes. Are you in trouble?"

Donati dropped tiredly onto the threadbare sofa. "No. Not now, not for the moment. They let my friend go this evening. Lack of evidence, or he greased the right palms again. I didn't think he'd manage it, but he did. That's not why I'm here."

"What's the matter?" Julia asked.

"I want to talk to Levy."

"Why?" Rossi queried.

"I've had some news from Palestine. There was an Arab attack on

one of our settlements near Kefar Vitkin two nights ago. The place you ended up at the day you lost Samuel Levy, Marc. The settlers beat it off, and captured one of the attackers. The local Arabs had never bothered them before, so they were anxious to find out why the sudden hostilities. The prisoner said that three Arabs from the neighborhood had been found murdered. The bodies had been hidden in some rough ground near the coast. They'd been dead for months. One was beaten to death, one had his throat slit, and one was shot with his own rifle. Two people I know of who were in that area at the time were you and Levy, Marc. Did you do it?"

"Good God, no," Rossi said. "I ran. There were three of them all right, but how could somebody like Samuel Levy kill. . . ." He stopped as the answer became obvious. "Oh, no. He killed a British intelligence officer in Tel Aviv. Then he fled to Jerusalem to find me, he said. We thought it was an accident, that was why we helped him get away. We didn't want the British to hang him."

Donati had been listening intently. "The answer," he said, "is that someone like Samuel Levy *couldn't* do all those things. He couldn't stalk and kill three armed Arabs on their home ground. One, maybe, if he was desperate enough. But not three. That is the work of an expertly trained assassin. If the man we know as Samuel Levy did it, then he's not Samuel Levy. He's somebody else."

"But it might have *been* somebody else who killed the Arabs that day," Julia pointed out. "Maybe Samuel did get away, as he said he did. He said he hid from them in a cave."

"No," Donati said. "I don't think it was somebody else. Perhaps I'd believe that if there weren't so many other oddities. But there are. For example, no one who knows him has so far left Germany. Was this person called Samuel Levy really doing everything he could to get them out? We don't know, we have only his word. And you say he killed a British intelligence officer and escaped from Tel Aviv even while the British were looking for him. Then he managed to get himself out of Palestine altogether. With Haganah help, I might add. This is not the behavior of a butcher from Altgarten. Did he appear to be Jewish to both of you?"

"Yes," Rossi said slowly, "but he didn't talk much, and I didn't question him closely. Neither did Leon, back in Jerusalem."

Donati looked at Julia. She nodded. "I never thought of him as other than Jewish."

"So what we have," Donati said, as though he were summing up a case for the prosecution, "is a man who appears to be a German Jewish refugee, but who is adept at escaping pursuit and who kills professionally at the drop of a hat. A man whose identity is established only by what he says, not by independent evidence. If he is not Jewish, what is he? Coming from Germany, he is likely a German using the identity of the real Levy, if there is one, as a concealment. So we have a professional German killer in Palestine.

"But no one of political importance has been assassinated in Palestine during his stay there. He is at some pains to remove himself after killing the British officer, but the officer was not important enough to be a target for a man such as this. He then decides to take advantage of you to help him get to Italy. This suggests that his target is not in Palestine. Where *is* the target? Consider the probable dedication and determination of this man."

Rossi said unwillingly, "Italy."

"I think so. Now, in all Italy, who is the greatest political threat to the Nazis?"

"Oh, my God," Julia breathed. "The Pope. And we brought him here."

"Exactly," Donati said grimly. "You did. Jews brought him here. And to all appearances, he is himself Jewish. He has left a solid and clearly identifiable trail leading back through Palestine to Germany. Worse, Mossad and Haganah are implicated by our personal involvement."

"That's the intention, then," Rossi said. He felt sick. "To make it look as though a Jew has killed Pius. Make all the Jews guilty by association. No one will ever trust any of us again."

"I fear so."

"But," Julia protested, "why would anyone believe a Jew would want to kill the Pope? Pius has been trying to *help* us."

"But quietly," Donati said. "To the outside world, it appears that he's done very little. We were putting our hopes in the encyclical. If he's killed before it's published. . . . It would be easy to make it appear

that a Jew killed him because he wouldn't help enough. Our enemies are adept at lies, remember, and the bigger the lie the better."

"That brings us to the assassin himself," Rossi said. "If it's a German, what happens if he's captured? Surely he wouldn't go on pretending to be Levy."

Donati gave an expressive Roman shrug. "They'll have some means of getting around that, I'm sure. This shows signs of having been planned for a long time."

"We can't just sit here," Julia cried urgently. "We have to warn Pius. Have you called Pacelli?"

"No. As soon as I worked all this out, I came over here hoping to find Levy. I hope you have a weapon, Marc. He's very dangerous. When should he be back?"

"Soon," Julia said. Her eyes widened. "If he *comes* back."

"He might," Rossi said. "I've got a gun, though. Do we dare wait?"

"I'd prefer to," said Donati. "I don't want to raise the alarm with Pacelli if Levy comes back so we can keep it quiet. But we dare not wait long."

"Ten minutes, no more," Rossi decided. "Then we have to move. Claudio, what will be our first step?"

"We will go to see Pacelli. I don't trust the phones. There may be someone working for the Germans inside the Vatican."

"It isn't Pacelli, is it?" Julia asked.

"I hope not," Donati said.

Starke was well on his way. He'd trotted most of the distance to the Palazzo Barberini, where he'd spotted a cab rank the day before. He climbed into the rear of the first vehicle and gave the driver the address, and as the cab pulled away from the curb he took off his shoe and extracted the surgical gloves and the wad of bills Sofia had given him the day before. There was quite a lot of money, enough to let him lie low for a few days if he needed to. Although, if Heydrich's planning was up to its usual standard, lying low wouldn't be necessary.

Starke shoved the money and gloves into a pocket, and then watched the wet streets and the lighted buildings of the ancient city

slide past outside the cab windows. Compared to the privations he'd had to undergo to kill von Lynchen back in Spain, he mused, this was promising to be exceptionally easy. The death of the target would bring a great deal of reward for very little effort. Little effort on my part at least, Starke reminded himself. Remember the resources Heydrich's poured into this thing. I am the edge of the blade, that's all. But what an achievement. It's too bad we can't be given medals for work like this. On the other hand, you can't eat, drink, or screw a medal. Maybe I can arrange a week with her nose-in-the-air ladyship Sofia von Falkenberg. Give me a week with her, Heydrich, and she won't dare treat me like a stud bull any more. She'll be at my beck and call, not the other way around.

Starke dismissed the matter of Sofia and began to focus himself on the task at hand. He always tried to refine himself to a single point of concentration before a kill, trusting his assassin's reflexes to direct his actions without the need for conscious analysis. It was a little like being in a trance, but a trance in which he was sensitive to every detail of his surroundings.

The cab was crossing one of the bridges over the Tiber; Starke didn't know its name, nor did he feel the need to. He did, however, recognize the vast bulk of Hadrian's tomb dead ahead through the windshield, so they were nearing the Vatican.

On the far side of the river the cab swung left, then right. After several more blocks the driver pulled up in front of a scruffy-looking bar. Dim yellow light trickled from its curtained windows; inside, someone was singing off-key to the wheeze of a concertina. Starke paid the driver and got out, and then waited while the cab sped away into the darkness.

When he was sure the taxi was gone, he walked around the corner, as Sofia had instructed. The church was supposed to be a block farther on. After a few moments' walk Starke saw its facade rising into the darkness above the street, ahead on his right. He tilted the face of his watch to catch the illumination from a streetlight. Twenty to eleven. He'd find a patch of shadow, and wait for the contact to enter the church. Despite Sofia's instructions, only then would he himself go in. He wanted to be sure the man was unattended by followers.

The black mouth of an alley across from the church presented itself

as a possibility. Starke crossed the street and investigated it. The alley smelled of cat urine and garbage, but it was good and dark and offered a clear view of the doors of the church across the way. He slipped into it and settled himself to wait.

Fifteen minutes passed. There was very little traffic on the street, and few pedestrians. A thin cold drizzle started to fall. Starke turned up the collar of his jacket and thrust his hands into his armpits to keep them warm. A couple of drunken men, singing and shouting, approached on Starke's side of the street. Starke withdrew farther into the alley in case they decided to use it as an impromptu urinal. They did not, however, and went on, allowing Starke to return to his vantage point.

There. A figure in a long black robe, looking like a shadow among other shadows, was approaching the steps of the church. Starke could see a flat, wide-brimmed hat but the face was obscured by the brim. The man moved as though he were not actually walking, but gliding over the ground. Starke found the motion eerie. He waited while the figure ascended the steps and entered the church. The street seemed empty. Starke put his head out of the alley and looked up and down. Still no one.

Starke had no intention of actually entering the church. He waited for perhaps two minutes, then another two. Then the door of the church opened and the priest came back out. His motions were less assured than they had been. The man set off down the street, moving very slowly. Starke slipped out of the alley, walked rapidly along the opposite sidewalk until he had passed the priest, and then cut across the pavement to go on in front of the other man. Another alley was just a little ahead. Starke reached it, stepped sideways into the darkness, and waited.

A moment later he heard the soft whisper of cloth and the scrape of shoe leather on pavement. The priest was suddenly visible at the alley mouth. Starke said quietly, in Italian, "Father."

The priest stopped and peered into the alley. "Yes?" It was an old man's voice, dry and pinched.

"*Arma virumque cano*," Starke said, and waited.

"*Troiae qui primus ab oris*," the priest responded, with a hint of relief in his voice. "Do you speak Italian?"

"No," said Starke. "German?"

The man shook his head. Starke was close enough to make out a little of his features, even under the shadowing brim of the hat. The priest was at least seventy, perhaps more.

Starke shrugged emphatically, and motioned for the priest to lead him onward. The man shook his head briefly and did something with the folds of his soutane. Starke tensed. Gun?

No. The old man pulled out a black bundle. It was a soutane and hat like his own. Starke obediently pulled them on; they smelled of old incense and heavy sweat, but they fit, even the hat. The priest regarded him and nodded with satisfaction: good enough. He put a finger to his lips to warn Starke not to speak, and started out down the street.

The old devil has a good deal of stamina, Starke reflected as they hurried along, walking abreast like companions. He's moving as fast as a younger man. I thought he'd be fat and short of breath with too much good living. I suppose there are two types. The fat ones, who want good living, and the thin and hungry ones, who want power. This is clearly one of the latter.

They walked for some ten minutes, straight along the Via Degli Scipione, and then the priest turned left. Ahead, Starke could see the sheer mass of the north wall of the Vatican, the bastioned fortifications completed long ago to defend the Popes and their citadel from men of the sword. Men like me, Starke thought. Much good your walls are going to do you tonight, Pius. Death is coming for you. Although, being who you are, that shouldn't worry you. It should worry somebody like the man next to me here. I wonder how he's worked his treachery out to his satisfaction. More important, I wonder how he's going to get me past the guards.

They reached the Viale Vaticano, the street girdling the Vatican walls. Away to Starke's left, he could see a bastion protruding into the street, and a lighted gate near it. Just ahead, though, the wall was partly shrouded in a fringe of trees that reached some two-thirds of the way up the masonry; above the foliage the wall was lost in darkness.

The priest crossed the road, looked around, and darted between the trunks. Starke also checked to see if they were being observed, and followed.

It was dark under the trees. The priest worked his way to the wall and searched along it. Starke couldn't tell what he was looking for, but after a few moments the man gave a grunt of satisfaction and began pulling on something. Starke realized that it must be a fine dark thread running up the stone into the darkness above.

A few more pulls and a rope's end followed the thread. Starke nodded with satisfaction. The man had planned well. He took the rope from the priest and gave it a tug to make certain it was secure, which it was.

The priest was gesticulating in the near-darkness, but his meaning was clear enough: go up to the top of the wall and wait. I will go in by the guarded entrance, and come to get you. When he was sure Starke had understood, he left.

Starke tossed the priest's hat onto the ground, grabbed the rope, and began to climb. The first part of the ascent was childishly simple because the wall sloped away from him, although at a steep angle. About the level of the treetops the masonry became vertical. In spite of the robes, Starke went up it like a black spider. He took a quick look over the top of the battlements, saw no one, and rolled over the coping-stone to the fighting platform behind. The rope was fixed to an iron staple in the wall. He pulled it up after, coiled it neatly on the masonry platform, and crouched in the shadows to wait.

Fifteen minutes went by. Starke didn't see the priest coming until he was less than four meters away; the old man's soutane seemed to fade into the shadows. "Here," Starke whispered.

The priest saw him and gestured, turning around. Starke followed obediently. They proceeded along the wall for a little way, and then the man seemed to disappear from in front of the German. He'd gone down a steep stairway that descended from the rear of a massive bastion to ground level.

At the bottom Starke found himself in a grove of trees, part of the vast gardens of the Vatican. The priest, who obviously knew the place well enough to be unhindered by the darkness, was hurrying on. Starke hurried after him.

They were skirting some kind of long high building on their left. Unlighted windows gazed blackly down at Starke; he assumed that either no one would be looking out of them, or that nocturnal walkers

in the gardens weren't unusual. Still, he would have preferred to be under cover.

The priest stopped suddenly, and Starke realized that they were in front of a high stone wall. A few steps led down into a sunken alcove cut into the masonry, and at the rear of the alcove was an iron grill. The priest swung it open and motioned Starke to enter. He did so, ducking his head to avoid knocking it on the low stone lintel. Behind him he heard the grill close with a soft sound of metal on stone. A hand took him by the elbow and propelled him a couple of meters farther on, into pitch blackness. Then the pressure stopped. Starke halted.

A light sprang into being. The priest had brought a pair of flashlights, one of which he handed to Starke. Starke flicked it on. They were in a low stone corridor, whose walls gleamed with damp. Underfoot the floor was paved with flagstones, but it was clear of mud and gravel. No footprints, Starke thought. Good.

He'd wanted a good look at the priest for some time. He swept the flashlight's beam from the arched stone roof of the corridor down to the man's face. The priest winced in the light and tried to draw away. Starke seized his arm and held him still.

The face was rather disappointing. Starke had half-hoped to see some recognizable mark of treachery there, but apart from age there was nothing remarkable about the priest's face: a beaky nose, sunken cheeks, sharp chin. The only things out of the ordinary were a prominent mole on the skin in front of the right ear, and a short white scar over the right cheekbone. The man's eyes were shut tight because of the light, so Starke could not tell what color they were.

There's no art to find the mind's construction in the face, Starke reflected as he dropped the priest's arm. The man shook himself angrily, muttering someting.

"*Weiter*," Starke ordered brusquely. He had no patience with bruised feelings. "Go on." He turned his flashlight off to conserve the batteries.

The priest led him a couple of meters farther along the corridor, and turned left. He reached out and touched the wall, leaving a small yellow dot. Starke realized that he was marking the route with a piece of chalk.

So I can get out again, Starke thought. How much of a labyrinth is this going to be?

They came to a shallow alcove in the corridor wall, a niche for a statue or something of that sort. The priest stopped, reached up, and did something between two stones. Then he pressed on the rear wall of the niche. The wall grated and swung slowly back. Starke felt his eyebrows rising. Secret passages, he thought. Well, why not? This place is old, very old above ground, and the foundations are older still. There may be ways through these buildings that everyone has forgotten.

The stone door was heavy and hard for the priest to move. Starke added his own strength, and they pushed it open far enough to slip through. Starke closed it behind them, but not quite all the way, although from the inside the iron release mechanism was obvious. That brought a protest from the priest, but Starke cut it off. He might be in a hurry on his way out, and didn't want to be slowed down with door locks.

The passage on this side of the door was barely wide enough for his shoulders. Mold clung in patches to the stone. The priest swung his light to point ahead of them, and they went on into the dark recesses of the Vatican.

Donati wasn't getting anywhere with the under secretary, or whatever he was. Rossi stood with Julia outside the office of the Maestro di Camera, which was on a mezzanine partway up the stairs that led up from the Cortile di San Damaso. They'd been there for a good half hour, waiting until Donati persuaded the Maestro di Camera to rouse the under secretary, who was now refusing to waken Pacelli. The door to the office was ajar, and Rossi could hear Donati's voice pleading urgently. The guards on the mezzanine looked on, impassive; if they could hear what Donati was saying, they showed no sign of it.

"Why doesn't he just *tell* him?" Julia muttered in a low voice to Rossi. "It's been over an hour since we left. Levy could already be inside."

Rossi nodded. Donati was unwilling to tell the under secretary

exactly why they thought the Pope was in danger, and the man was refusing to take the matter further until he had more information. The bureaucratic mind, Rossi thought. He doesn't want to take risks. He thinks this is some kind of maneuver to get Pacelli's ear again. He's afraid to wake his boss up unless he has everything signed, sealed, and notarized.

Donati's voice rose enough for Rossi to make out the words.

"—I'm telling you, it's true. I think a German is here to kill His Holiness. He may be inside the Vatican right now. You *must* let me see Cardinal Pacelli. You must at least send guards to His Holiness's bedroom. In the name of God—"

The under secretary's voice cut him off. "I have checked with the guards. No one is in the Vatican palace who shouldn't be, and no unauthorized persons have tried to pass the gates. There is no one in His Holiness's study or anteroom. You are afflicted with an overheated imagination. I cannot rouse the Cardinal, much less the Pope, for this. Not without more information."

"That's all I will give you," Donati snapped. "The rest is for Cardinal Pacelli alone. Do you want to risk keeping from him something he very much needs to hear?"

"I do not understand your urgency," said the under secretary. "After all, you are Jewish."

A silence. Then Donati said, "For the love of God, I implore you. It's because I'm Jewish that I'm here. Can't you understand?"

Rossi saw motion from the corner of his eye, on the staircase. He looked around. A man in cardinal's robes was gliding across the marble floor, seeming to have appeared from nowhere. He had a long, pale face with an eagle's beak of a nose and deep-set eye sockets, and he wore small rimless glasses. Rossi noticed one of the guards blink in surprise.

"What is happening here?" the cardinal asked a guard.

"The Maestro di Camera is in the office with under secretary Orano," said the guard. "They are with a man who calls himself Claudio Donati. These two were with Signore Donati. They have been asking to see you, Your Eminence. Under secretary Orano did not wish to wake you."

"I *was* awake," said the man, whom Rossi now realized to be

Cardinal Pacelli himself. "You are Miss Belmont," Pacelli said to Julia. "From America. I remember."

Julia nodded. Pacelli turned his hooded eyes on Rossi. "And you?"

"Marc Rossi. I'm a friend and colleague of Claudio Donati."

"I see," Pacelli said. "Why are you here?"

"We think someone else is already here," Julia burst out. "To kill the Pope."

"What?"

"Yes, Your Eminence. But no one will listen to us—"

Pacelli brushed past Julia and Rossi and threw open the office door. The conversation within ceased instantly. "Your Eminence," Rossi heard the under secretary gasp. "I didn't know—"

Pacelli cut him off. "What is this about, Signore Donati?"

"Your Eminence," Donati said, "if my friends and I could speak with you alone—"

"Leave us," Pacelli said. He looked over his shoulder at Rossi and Julia. "You two. Come in here."

They passed the under secretary and the Maestro di Camera scuttling out. The under secretary shot Rossi a black look as he passed.

"Now," said Pacelli as he closed the office door behind them, "please explain yourselves. This is not to become common knowledge, but His Holiness has a very severe cold. He has been worsening since the beginning of the week. His doctors have been in attendance. I cannot disturb him without urgent reasons."

"This *is* urgent," Donati said. "A man calling himself Samuel Levy has come to Rome from Palestine. We think he is here to kill Pope Pius, to stop the encyclical. We knew where he was until ten o'clock this evening. At that time he disappeared. We think he may already be here. In the Vatican."

Pacelli's face took on a look of alarm. "Here? A Jew come to kill His Holiness?"

"He's not Jewish," Donati said. "He's a Nazi assassin. He has killed at least four men we know of."

Pacelli's eyes narrowed. "You say you knew where he was. How?"

"He came to Rome with Julia and Marc here."

"*You brought him?*"

"Not knowingly," Donati pleaded. "He was using us. We had no

idea. It was only luck that made us suspect him. Please, Your Eminence, there may not be much time."

"Can you recognize him? If he is somehow here in disguise?"

"Yes," Rossi said.

"Come with me."

Pacelli turned in a swirl of robes and opened the door. "You," he called to one of the guards as he hurried out onto the mezzanine, Julia and Donati and Rossi following. "Bring the chief of gendarmes to the office here. Tell him to wait for me." He turned and made for the stairs leading to the second floor.

"But aren't you going to bring men?" Julia asked in perplexity.

"I will not disturb His Holiness with a lot of commotion," Pacelli said. "No one can have reached his quarters. But I still wish to make sure he is quite safe."

Starke knew that without the chalk marks he'd almost certainly become lost on his way out. The passage wound interminably through what must be the thickness of the ancient walls; there were side branches and stairs up and stairs down and what appeared to be blind ends. Twice there had been chinks of light between the stones, peepholes. Starke had peered through the second, ignoring the priest's muttered protests. The hole had overlooked a deserted room whose floor was half covered with broken marble statuary. Starke had no idea what or where the room might be.

Then there was a section of Roman brick wall with a stone tablet set into it. Latin words were cut into the tablet. In the passing glow of the flashlight Starke had made out part of the inscription: MARC.AVR.IMP. Marcus Aurelius, Emperor. The tablet, and presumably the wall, were nearly two thousand years old. Despite his concentration on the coming task, and the discipline he imposed on his imagination, Starke was beginning to feel oppressed by the labyrinth in which he found himself. He wondered what other men had passed through these corridors, bent on what deeds. He would have bet that a number of them had business like his own.

The priest stopped suddenly, causing Starke almost to run into

him. He pointed to the right, into a low black channel. Starke looked
inside. A few feet along he could see the start of a spiral staircase,
going up.

It's a very good thing I'm not claustrophobic, Starke thought as they
entered the channel, the priest leading. This would drive a
claustrophobe mad.

The stairs went up and up in a tight curve, winding around a central
pillar of stone. Starke judged after a while that they were well above
ground level, because the stone was drier here. Both he and the priest
were climbing in a crouch, forced to bend by the low roof. If Starke
didn't keep his elbows in, they bumped against the walls on both
sides. In spite of his excellent physical condition, his back was
beginning to ache.

At last they reached the top. It was a small chamber, with a flat
stone roof no more than a meter and a half above the floor. There was
no sign of an exit. Starke looked around in perplexity.

The priest touched the roof with the palm of his hand. Starke
looked more closely. In the center of the ceiling was a recessed stone
slab. A trapdoor. The priest made shoving motions against the
underside of the slab. It was clearly too heavy for him.

Starke crowded the priest out of the way and put his back under the
slab. If there was someone in the room above, they were about to get a
surprise. Starke had to assume the priest knew what he was doing,
that the room would be deserted. The slab grated slightly in its socket.
Muscles bunching, Starke pushed harder and the stone lifted eight
centimeters. It still wouldn't slide out of its bed. He gave it another
heave, pressing it sideways at the same time. It shifted abruptly,
sliding sideways a hand's-breadth and tilting diagonally. A shower of
smoky-smelling ash dropped through the resulting opening.

It's in the floor of a fireplace, Starke realized. Good thing there
doesn't seem to be a fire.

Very carefully, keeping the movement as noiseless as possible, he
worked the heavy stone to one side. Dim light seeped through from
above. The priest turned off his flashlight. After a minute's work
Starke had the stone aside far enough to admit his head into the
aperture. With extreme caution, he raised himself to look into
the room above.

As he'd thought, the trapdoor was in the floor of a fireplace. The room wasn't large; a wooden desk stood more or less in its center, with a closed door beyond it. The light Starke had seen earlier was from an electric wall sconce by the door. There were four chairs by the desk, and bookcases along the walls. No human occupants.

Starke withdrew his head, and thought for a moment. He didn't want to wear the soutane any longer; its folds encumbered him around the legs. He shrugged it off, took the packet of surgical gloves from his pocket, and put them on. Then he moved the stone far enough to get his shoulders through the opening, and climbed out onto the floor. The priest looked out of the trapdoor. He was nervous, now, Starke noted, eyes moving quickly. And the hand he pointed at the door beyond the desk was trembling. Starke followed the gesture, and raised his eyebrows questioningly. The priest nodded, and put his head sideways on his clasped hands in the universal indication of slumber. Beyond that door, Pope Pius the Eleventh lay sleeping.

Starke regarded the priest, wondering what he was going to do next. The answer was almost immediate. The man gave a stiff bob of his head, as though in farewell, and disappeared down the hole. Starke smiled with amusement. There was another way out of the labyrinth, which the priest knew. Doubtless he'd be in his own quarters in a very few minutes, and no one any the wiser.

Starke decided to give him a minute to get away, and waited calmly beside the trapdoor, arms hugging knees. This was a historical moment, and he wanted to savor it. Very few professional assassins could claim a Pope as one of their kills. This was in a class by itself, even above the assassination of a head of state.

After he judged enough time had gone by, he stood up and crossed noiselessly to the door to the Pope's bedroom. The handle turned silently in his palm, and he very carefully drew back the door until a slit of light appeared. Starke was mildly puzzled. Did the Pope sleep with a light on, like a child?

He applied his right eye to the narrow opening. On the far side of the simple white-plastered room Starke could see a narrow wooden bed, with a sleeping form in it under a blue counterpane. Beside the bed was a low wooden chest, dark with age, on which was a collection of medicine bottles. Starke frowned. So the old man was sick. That

meant a doctor wouldn't be far away. A doctor who might enter the room without warning.

If that happened, he'd have to kill the doctor as well. There might be noise. It couldn't be helped. He'd come a long way to dispose of the Pope, and he wouldn't back away from it now.

He opened the door just enough to go through, and stepped into the Pope's bedroom. The old man was sleeping quietly on his side, his back turned to Starke. There was no sound of the labored breathing one might have expected from him.

Starke crossed to the bed, moving silently on the polished floor. He could hear no noise from outside the room, although he knew that not far away were doctors, churchmen, and plenty of guards. All looking the wrong way.

He was half a meter from the back of Pius's bald head with its straggly fringe of hair. Old men always looked so vulnerable from behind. Starke judged he would have to move the coverlet down a few centimeters to make sure of his grip for the neck-breaking twist. If Pius was as drugged as he seemed to be, there was no danger of waking him up.

The Pope did not stir as Starke gently drew the coverlet down. He raised his hands for the coup de grace, and leaned forward over the sleeping form.

Pius's eyes were open.

Starke was so startled that all his instinctive reactions failed him. For an instant he stood paralyzed above the old man, hands motionless in mid-air.

Then he realized. He put his fingers under the line of Pius's jaw. There was no pulse, and the skin was cool. The Pope was already dead. He hadn't waited for Starke to come for him.

Starke wanted to laugh and curse at the same time. Months of effort, and the old bastard had fooled him at the last minute. Even the doctors couldn't have expected him to go tonight, or they'd have been in the room with him. Now what?

Starke felt the skin again. It was distinctly cool. He'd been dead for perhaps an hour. Never mind. A broken neck was a broken neck, and you didn't get one of those from a cold in the head. Nobody would know exactly when the old man's spinal cord had been snapped, so it

would appear that he'd been murdered, even if he hadn't been. That would have to do.

Starke was reaching out again when he heard noises from the room beyond the bedroom, and low indistinct voices. The door latch clicked.

Starke grabbed Pius's head and twisted, knowing as he did so that he'd rushed and botched it, that it wasn't a clean break. He looked up from the bed to see a man in red cardinal's robes standing in the doorway, speechless horror spreading over his face.

Starke spun from the bedside and threw himself through the door to the other room. He reached the fireplace in two bounds, dropped to the floor, and slithered into the entrance to the chamber below. Turning, he tried to drag the stone back across the trapdoor but it lodged on a piece of charred wood and stuck. He cursed, grabbed up the flashlight from the floor, and switched it on as he plunged into the shadows of the spiral stair.

From behind Pacelli, Rossi saw only the flash of movement inside the Pope's room, and heard the thud of running feet. The cardinal seemed paralyzed. Rossi shoved him aside and burst into the bedroom, taking in at a glance the open door in the end wall and the unnatural angle of Pius's head as it lay on the pillow. Broke his neck, he thought, sickened. How many deaths will that cost us?

He raced through the other door and into the next room. It was a small study. There was no one in it. Rossi stopped and looked around, confused. Then he saw the square stone lying half on the hearth of the fireplace, and the black gaping hole behind it.

"God *damn* it," he snarled. "He came from the inside."

"What?" Donati asked. He and Julia were already in the room. Pacelli had remained with the Pope.

Rossi pointed. "Down there. A tunnel. I need a light. I'm going after him."

Julia looked wildly around. "Where can we get a light?"

"I'll try Pacelli." Rossi hurried back into the bedroom. Pacelli was kneeling by the bed, hands clasped in prayer for the dead. The

posture infuriated Rossi. They needed action, not prayer. "Cardinal Pacelli," he said. "We've found out where he's gone. I need a flashlight, or a lantern, anything. We have to catch him."

Pacelli opened his eyes and got shakily to his feet. Other faces were appearing in the doorway now, priests, officials, guards, doctors, none daring to enter until Pacelli gave the word.

For a moment, Rossi thought that Pacelli, in his devastation and grief, hadn't heard him. Then the cardinal gestured distractedly at the chest beside the head of the bed. "In there," he said. "It's in case the electricity fails," he added with the peculiar gravity of a person in shock.

Rossi rummaged in the chest and yanked out a heavy rubber-jacketed flashlight. Julia was saying, "But aren't you going to call the police?" but Pacelli made only an odd sound in answer. Rossi flicked the flashlight switch; it worked.

Pacelli suddenly seemed to pull himself together. "Bring the Cardinal Camerlengo," he told one of the guards at the door. "And the chief of gendarmes. No one else is to leave. Signore Rossi, don't—"

But Rossi was already racing through the door to the study. He heard Julia and Donati behind him as he dropped to the floor and prepared to slide into the hole through which the assassin had left.

"Wait here for me," he ordered.

"The hell you say," Julia hissed. "I'm coming."

Rossi couldn't spare the time to argue. He reached into his waistband at the back under his jacket and pulled out the Browning, seeing Claudio's eyes widen at the sight of the weapon. No one brought weapons into the Vatican, and he'd never have got it past the guards at the office of the Maestro di Camera had it not been for Pacelli's sudden appearance.

He ducked into the chamber below and saw the entrance to the staircase. There was no other way Levy could have gone. Rossi flew down the steps in a crouching run, scraping his elbows on the walls, the flashlight in his left hand and the gun in his right, hearing the other two clattering behind him.

The spiral stair went on interminably. He tried to work out how much lead Levy had secured. Maybe a minute and a half. If it was a

maze down here they might easily lose him. But as far as Rossi could judge, the German had never been here before, either. If the passages were complex there would have to be some method of guiding him out.

"Look for marks," he called over his shoulder. "He'll need them to find his escape route." I hope, he added to himself.

The stair ended in a short, low passage which in turn led into a somewhat larger one. Rossi paused and shone the light around.

"There," Donati said. "Up there, to the left."

Rossi saw it: a small yellow dot in the middle of the low roof. These stone channels would carry sound. Perhaps they'd be able to hear the assassin ahead of them. "Listen," he said. They all stood quite still, hardly breathing. Nothing.

"Come on!"

They ran along the passageway, Rossi sweeping the light to look for the marks. He glimpsed inscriptions, ancient brick and stone. The tunnel twisted and turned. Once they hit a blind end and had to go back to find the direction mark. Like Theseus in the labyrinth, Rossi thought irrelevantly. Trying to get out. Ariadne's thread. Except Ariadne's here in the labyrinth with me.

He was frightened for Julia in a way he'd never been before. He wanted her to be somewhere safe, not here in this dank blackness with an assassin running ahead of them.

Was Levy armed? Perhaps not. Pius's neck had been broken. But Rossi couldn't assume it. He'd have to expect the worst. He made sure the Browning's safety catch was disengaged.

Up a short flight of stairs and down another. Rossi heard Donati fighting for breath behind him. The lawyer wasn't used to this sort of thing. Where are we? Rossi wondered. Where are we going to come out? *Are* we going to come out? Ambush? But Levy may not know we're after him.

He wasn't sure, but he thought he smelled a breath of fresher air, not the mold and mortar-laden stuff down here in the labyrinth, but something with a hint of rain and damp vegetation. He slowed down. If Levy was going to try to surprise them, it might well be as they came out of the tunnels.

"Stop for a second," he said in a low voice. They did. Rossi

switched off the light and looked for another glow ahead. The darkness was pitch-black, solid, impermeable. Levy was still well ahead of them, then. Or waiting.

They couldn't move in the dark. Rossi flicked the light back on and hurried forward. In the beam ahead he saw that the tunnel ended in a solid stone wall. Another dead end? Had they missed a mark? He aimed the light at the roof. There it was, a small yellow dot. This was the right way, but there was no obvious exit. He reached the wall and shone the light upward.

There it was, an iron bar attached to some kind of swivel just under the roof. Rossi reached up and pulled the bar down. Something clunked inside the wall. "Secret door," he said quietly over his shoulder. "Stay back."

He pulled at the door. It swung open, admitting a fresh outdoor current of air. If Levy was waiting, it was going to be on the other side of this door. Trusting to its rubber covering to absorb the shock, Rossi tossed the flashlight out into the space beyond.

Nothing happened. There might be no one there. Rossi gingerly put his head around the edge of the doorway, gun ready. Still no one. But he could see a rectangle of very faint light a few meters away. He snatched up the flashlight and turned it off. "Come on. We're out!"

An iron grill closed the exit, but it wasn't locked. Rossi pulled it aside and ran up to ground level. Donati's breathing was even more labored, and he could hear Julia gasping as well.

"Where did he go?" Donati wheezed.

"I don't know. Try this way."

They ran along a gravel path beside a long building. At the end of it the Vatican wall loomed against the night-glow of the city. There was a stair here. Rossi looked up it, toward the top of the great masonry bastion that rose above the gardens of the Vatican. He saw violent motion against the sky, heard a muffled curse. In German.

Someone was fighting up there.

Starke knew his luck had turned for the worse. First it had been the cardinal standing there in the doorway, getting a good view of him,

and then the slip as he dropped askew into the chamber at the top of the spiral stair. He hadn't sprained his ankle to the point of immobility, but the injury hurt, and it had slowed him down. But he didn't think there was any pursuit, at least he hadn't heard immediate shouts and running feet descending the stair after him. Not that he'd waited around to find out. He had to get out of the Vatican before anything else went wrong.

He had reached the foot of the stairs to the bastion. The drizzly air smelled good after the dankness of the tunnels and he inhaled deeply. Up to the top, now, over the wall, and whoever was meeting him would spirit him away. Back to Germany. Starke longed to be in Germany again. He was sick of foreign places.

He climbed the bastion stairs as quickly as he could while favoring the ankle. It was a good thing he was going down the wall this time, not up it. He wondered as he climbed the steps how the rest of the operation would be handled, now that the alarm was raised. Heydrich would have some backup plan no doubt, for getting the real Levy—or his body—into the right hands. But, even if that wasn't possible, the Pope was dead, and good riddance.

The doctors might figure out, though, that Pius was already dead when his neck was broken. What would the Vatican do in that case?

It's not my problem, Starke thought as he made his way up the last few steps to the top of the bastion. I did what I was supposed to do, and that's all that matters.

He reached the fighting platform at the top of the stairs. The rope was just along the way. Over the side and down, and that was that. He didn't think there would be any trouble getting out of Italy. Just a little farther to go.

A shadow detached itself from the angle of the parapet ahead of him. Starke halted, his fighting reflexes sending him into a crouch.

"Herr Dorf." A whisper.

Starke relaxed and stepped forward. He'd expected his contact to meet him outside the walls, but never mind. "Yes," he answered in a low voice as he peeled off the surgical gloves and stuffed them into a pocket. "Is everything clear?"

"Yes. Come over here."

Starke advanced, half an ear cocked for the sounds of the Vatican waking up, pursuit. Still nothing. They were disorganized back there, that was obvious. But then they didn't often have to deal with the murder of a Pope. Likely the pursuit had gotten lost in the warren of passages under the palace. But they'd be out searching the grounds soon.

He could see his contact now. The man was big, a lot bigger than Starke. He wouldn't likely have fit through some of the places Starke had just gone. "Let's go, for God's sake," Starke hissed.

The man reached out and took Starke's arm. "This way."

The grip was too tight. Starke tried to shake it off. "You—" he began, and sensed rather than saw the man's other hand coming up seize him by the wrist.

Even in the sudden flash of realization, Starke reacted perfectly. He stiffened his left hand into a blade of flesh and bone, and stabbed his attacker in the solar plexus with it. The man's stomach muscles were tough as armor, but he grunted and his grip on Starke's right arm loosed. Starke tried to knee him in the testicles, but the man was already twisting out of the way. Starke recognized in his assailant the same unarmed combat training that he had himself.

Heydrich betrayed me, he thought, still disbelieving. He was never going to use Levy. It was me he was going to use. Sofia gave this man my old papers. She knew. *She knew.*

Even as he thought it he was trying to break free, jabbing his attacker again in the midriff but slowing him down only a little. The man wasn't trying to kill him, though. He was trying to get Starke down onto the ground, seemingly without damaging him too much.

Starke tried another bone-breaking kick, this time to the man's inner ankle, but his own ankle betrayed him and he stumbled backward toward the unprotected inner edge of the bastion, a meter from the top of the stairs. The man forced him to one knee, then to both, and kicked his legs from underneath him. Starke swore at him as he hit the masonry. He was pinned on his shoulders, in a hold he knew from experience he couldn't break without breaking his own collarbone. He kicked futilely.

His attacker freed one hand for a moment, but jammed his other forearm savagely into Starke's throat. The hand came back into

Starke's view, outlined against the dull orange sky. There was something between the fingers.

A cyanide capsule, Starke thought. Jew kills Pope, kills self, leaves note. No loose ends. Brilliant.

He clamped his mouth shut. Fingers closed over his nostrils. He'd have to open his mouth eventually to breathe. Despair swept through Starke for the first time.

Without warning, a shadow loomed above his attacker. Starke saw a gun in the upraised hand. The gun came down. There was a dull thud and Starke's assailant slumped over him. Instinctively, Starke clamped his hands around the man's neck, thumbs digging into the larynx, and squeezed hard. He felt the bones crush under his thumbs. The man gurgled and his breathing stopped, cut off by the ruin of his trachea. Starke grabbed at the hand that had held the cyanide pill. The tiny glass vial was still in the clenched fingers. Starke palmed it; it was his only weapon. He pushed the body off himself and sat up, hoping that in the darkness his rescuer wouldn't have seen what he'd done.

There wasn't one person, there were three. Even in the poor light Starke could see that the man with the gun was Rossi. Starke began to think very quickly indeed.

Rome

February 9, 1939

Rossi stared down the barrel of the gun at the man he knew as Samuel Levy. He thought about pulling the trigger.

"Don't kill him, Marc," Donati said urgently. "He has the evidence we need."

Starke must have guessed what was passing through Rossi's mind, for he said fiercely, "Don't shoot! Listen to me before you take me back!"

"There's nothing to say," Rossi snarled. This man had brought all their hopes crashing down around their ears. He wanted to kill him. "Get up, Levy."

"My name is not Levy," the man on the ground before him said. He made no move to obey Rossi. "I am SS-Major Erich Starke. I warn you, don't take me back."

Donati was kneeling beside the prostrate form of Starke's attacker. "He's dead," he said bitterly. "Levy's killed him, too."

"Check his pockets," Rossi ordered. "Quick."

Donati rifled the man's clothing, came up with papers and a pistol. "I'll cover him," he said, pointing the gun at Starke. "What are these?" He handed the papers to Rossi.

"We might have expected it," said Rossi after a moment. "Levy's papers from Palestine. And a suicide note in German. 'I have killed the Pope. Let the world take notice that we will defend ourselves. I make this sacrifice for all Jews. Samuel Levy.' " He looked down at

257

the German and switched to that language. "I suppose you can guess what this is."

"A suicide note, and my old papers, yes?"

"Yes." Rossi was thinking hard.

"Don't hand me over," Starke said urgently. "Heydrich planned all this. He was going to have me killed, to look like Levy. He's betrayed me. We can bring him down, I swear I know how."

"Claudio," Rossi asked, "what'll happen if we turn him over?"

"We don't know how deep the plot went," Donati answered. "Ask who let him in."

Rossi did so. "An old man with a mole on his right cheek," Starke told him.

"Cardinal Mondolfo," Donati said in a shaken voice. "That's very bad. He could be the next Pope. He is pro-Nazi and despises Jews. If he became Pope he might go along with the plot. And there may be others with him. If they were to get their hands on Levy and these papers.... Marc, we daren't give Levy up under these circumstances."

"Couldn't Pacelli help us? He's the secretary of state, for God's sake."

"But he's not now," Donati said. "All offices but a few go vacant when a Pope dies. I think he could help, but I'd have to get to him secretly. We need time, Marc."

Heydrich, Rossi thought. We might be able to hurt Heydrich.

He decided. "All right. We'll get him away." To Starke he said, "Up. Carefully. I'll kill you if you try anything."

"They're coming!" Julia exclaimed suddenly. "I see lights over there!"

"How do we get down?" Rossi asked Starke.

"A rope," Starke said.

"Lead us to it. *Move!*"

They ran along the battlements. Rossi noticed that Starke was limping slightly. He hoped it wouldn't slow the German down.

The rope was where Starke had left it. Rossi looked over the parapet. All outside the wall was quiet. The alarm didn't seem to have spread to the streets yet. The Vatican had no jurisdiction beyond the

wall here, and there might be communications problems with the Roman police. He hoped so.

"Can you manage the rope?" he asked Julia.

"I think so. I have to."

Rossi went first, while Donati held Starke at gunpoint on the wall above. Then, with Rossi awaiting him below, Starke was sent down. Julia followed, then Donati. Voices were calling on the other side of the wall, louder and louder.

Pacelli had taken a very long time to react, Rossi thought as he waited for Julia to hit the ground. Perhaps, given what Donati had told him, the secretary of state had been weighing the political consequences of an assassination. Or maybe he'd been waiting for Rossi and Donati and Julia to bring the assassin back. Rossi wondered what Pacelli was going to think when none of them returned. He'd have the Roman police out in force before long.

Julia dropped into his arms and disengaged her hands stiffly from the rope. Rossi gave her a brief hug, not taking his eyes off Starke for an instant. Seconds later, Donati landed beside them.

"We need transportation," Rossi said worriedly. "The car's a long way from here, and we don't dare walk. Levy, do you know how to cross an ignition?"

"Yes. My name is Starke, please. We steal a car, then?"

"We'll have to. Across the street, go! Watch him, Claudio."

They hurried across the Viale Vaticano and into a side street. A few cars were parked along the curb. Rossi tried doors until he found an unlocked Fiat. "This one," he told Starke. "Then into the front seat. Claudio, you drive."

Starke took the flashlight, put the gearshift into neutral, fiddled under the dashboard for a minute; suddenly the engine ground into life. Rossi and Julia got into the back seat, Rossi behind the SS man. "My gun is right behind your head," he told the German. "Sit still. Claudio, where do we take him?"

"The safe house where I put you before?"

"That'll do for a start."

Donati pulled away from the curb. "Aren't we going to talk about Heydrich?" Starke asked Rossi.

"Talk, then," Rossi said. "You said we could bring down Heydrich. How?"

"If I tell everything," Starke said earnestly, "it is only one man speaking. And I don't know enough. But I know of someone who knows a great deal more. She's here in Rome."

"What's he saying?" Donati asked.

Rossi told him. "It's true," Donati observed. "One testimony wouldn't be enough. With two. . . . Ask him what he proposes."

Rossi did so. "I want Heydrich, and there is a woman who can help me get him," Starke said. Rossi could sense the rage and hatred behind the flat voice. "The woman's name is Sofia von Falkenberg. She reports directly to Heydrich. She arranged for the priest to help me into the Vatican. She knows about substituting me for the real Levy. She is of a very aristocratic and powerful family—a countess, in fact. If she confesses, people will have to listen."

"Would she confess?"

"We could persuade her."

Rossi wasn't sure he liked the sound of that. "How?"

"Take her away with us, to the safe house. She'd break down after enough interrogation. At the very least you could hand her over to the Vatican or to the police."

"And you too, don't forget. You're going to have to answer for this."

"I know. I'm a realistic man. I know I'll never get out of Italy, not with Heydrich after me as well as the police." Starke sounded quite calm about the prospect. "This way at least I make him pay for what he tried to do to me."

He's hiding something, damn it, Rossi thought. But what? I can't tell. But we'd better talk to this Countess von Falkenberg woman. Maybe we *can* do something about Heydrich.

"Where does she live?" he asked.

"On the top floor of the Villa Zelotti. It's on the Via Rasella, number 36."

"Claudio," Rossi said. "This is what he wants to do." He told the lawyer what Starke had said.

Donati looked thoughtful. "It can't hurt to try," he said finally.

"There's too much at stake not to try for every advantage. Very well. Let's go."

They sped through the dark, nearly deserted streets. When Donati halted for a stoplight, Rossi heard sirens far off behind them. Pacelli had finally woken up the Roman police.

"Ask him how long to the villa," Starke said. He'd become disoriented. Rossi did so.

"A few minutes."

They rode in silence the rest of the way. Finally Donati said, "It's around the next corner." He pulled the Fiat around the turn and stopped. The drizzle was turning into a slow winter rain.

"Who's here with her?" Rossi asked.

"There is a doorkeeper. Let me deal with him when we're inside."

"No killing," Rossi said. "Not even by accident. I'll be watching you."

"I will kill no one. And my touch is better than that."

They left the car and tramped through the rain to the door of the villa. It was locked. The other three stood out of sight of the covered peephole in the door while Donati rang the bell. After a few moments the peephole slid open. "Announce me to the Countess von Falkenberg," Donati said. "*Subito!*"

The concierge grimaced. Starke pushed some bills at him; the man's face brightened and Rossi heard the door bolts slide back. Donati stepped inside. Rossi, Julia, and Starke burst in after him. The doorkeeper's eyes flew wide as Starke's hand clamped over his mouth. The German pressed the side of his neck for a few seconds, ignoring the man's struggles, and he suddenly collapsed.

They tied him up with his own belt and shoelaces and gagged him with his handkerchief. Then Rossi had Starke drag the man into his cubby and lock the door on him.

"Top floor," Starke said.

"You go up first," Rossi ordered. "I'll be right behind you." The German had shown no signs so far of turning on them, but Rossi wasn't going to take any chances with the man unless he had to.

Starke headed up the stairs. It was a long climb. On the top landing he stopped, listened, and rang the bell. Rossi and the others stood behind him.

A minute's silence. Starke was about to ring the bell again, when there were footsteps on the door's far side and a woman's voice said, "Becker?"

Starke pitched his voice low. "*Ja.*"

The latch clicked and the door swung open. Just inside was a dark-haired young woman wearing a long white dressing gown. She saw Starke and her eyes widened. "*No,*" she gasped, and tried to slam the door in his face.

He pushed it back easily, seizing her by the throat and covering her mouth with his other hand to prevent any outcry. Then he shoved her up against the wall so Rossi and the others could enter. Julia closed the door behind them.

"Be quiet," Starke told Sofia. "We're not here to hurt you. We only want information. Are the servants here?"

Still with his hand clamped across her mouth, she shook her head.

"They're not, eh?" Starke said. He smiled without humor. "And you were expecting someone named Becker. Come to claim his reward for killing me, isn't that right?"

She shook her head, eyes wide.

He squeezed her neck. "*Isn't it?*"

She closed her eyes and, after a moment, nodded.

"Ease off," Rossi growled at him. "There's no use scaring her out of her wits."

Starke gave a short, harsh laugh. "There's not much danger of that." To Sofia he said, "I'm going to take my hand from your mouth now. Don't scream, or I swear I'll kill you. And don't hope for Becker to come and rescue you. He's dead. I killed him not half an hour ago."

He released her mouth, and transferred his grip from her throat to her upper arm. She drew a shuddering breath. Rossi hoped he could keep Starke from killing her if the SS man lost control of himself. He was beginning to suspect that the German was holding himself in by sheer willpower. It was hardly surprising. Starke's loyalty had been shattered by the way his commanding officer had betrayed him, and, from the way he was acting toward Sofia, he'd had some attachment to her as well.

"Herein," Starke ordered in German, dragging Sofia after him toward a door leading off the hallway. Beyond it was a large reception room, lit by a couple of deeply shaded lamps and a fire burning low in the marble fireplace. Starke shoved the woman down onto a damask sofa and stood over her. "Tell us about Heydrich and the priest," he said in a flat voice.

Sofia seemed to Rossi to be regaining her nerve. She looked at him, his gun, and then at Julia and Donati. "In front of these three? Your little Jews from Palestine?" she asked, in her own tongue. "Have you taken leave of your senses?"

Starke raised a hand, and she flinched. But there was fury, not fear, in her eyes. "What, exactly, do you want me to tell them?" she asked.

"Heydrich's orders for the Pope. And about the priest who helped. About Becker. Tell them Heydrich was planning to kill me, to blame the Pope's death on the Jews."

"I decline to do that," she said.

She's got courage, Rossi thought, following the rapid German with some difficulty.

"Fraulein," he broke in as Starke was about to speak again, "we want you to write down your involvement in the assassination of Pope Pius, and sign it. You are going to be arrested in any case. Helping us now might help you later."

If she was surprised at Rossi's command of German, she didn't show it. "I can't," she told him. "Heyrich would kill me. Leave now. I won't say anything until tomorrow. You'll have time to get away."

Starke laughed at her. "The minute we're out the door, you'll be on the telephone to Berlin."

"I swear I won't."

"Your swearing isn't worth spit," Starke said. "You're coming with us, anyway. We're going to tell the world what Heydrich's done, and you're going to help."

She laughed in his face. "You'll never get out of Italy. You're wasting what time you've got, staying here. And even if you do get out, trying to expose Heydrich won't help you at all. He's covered that, too. Even if I wrote out a confession and signed it, it wouldn't do you any good. *There's nothing you can do,* Herr Dorf. You might as well

give yourself up now. Go back to Berlin. Throw yourself on Heydrich's mercy, say you didn't know who Becker was. I'll help you with Heydrich."

"No," Starke snarled. "Heydrich betrayed me. I'd kill him, if I could. This is next best."

"Wait," Rossi said. Sofia looked up at him. Part of him was wondering how so beautiful a woman could be so treacherous. "You told us Heydrich had covered everything," he said to her. "That a confession from you wouldn't help us. What did you mean by that?"

"I don't know how he arranged it. He said there was no danger, whatever happened."

"You're lying," Starke said, very quietly. "Tell us."

"But I *can't*. I don't know." Somehow she had made herself look like a child in distress. A small part of Rossi responded, told him to comfort her, or at least go away and not trouble her further. He found himself thinking that perhaps Starke had made a mistake, that Sofia von Falkenberg was really an innocent trapped in a design not of her own making.

"That's enough," he said. "She's coming with us. We'll get it out of her later."

But Starke had turned from her and picked up a set of wrought-iron tongs from the fireplace. "Starke," Rossi snapped at him. "What in hell do you think you're doing?"

He answered by selecting a glowing coal from the fireplace and turning back to Sofia. Rossi raised the Browning, sighted at Starke's arm. "Stop," he said. "Drop it. Now."

Starke's eyes narrowed, but he obediently dropped the coal into the grate and set the tongs back in place.

"Let's go," Rossi said angrily. "Out, both of you."

Sofia stood her ground. "I warn you. There's no point in taking me. If you make me talk you'll wish you hadn't."

"You'd better spit it out," Rossi said. "Or you're coming with us." He had no intention of leaving her behind, but she seemed so sure of herself that the implied promise might work.

Sofia had a mocking smile on her exquisite face. In it Rossi glimpsed the viciousness under her beauty. "Even if you tell the world

who you are and who sent you," she said to Starke, "you'll play into Heydrich's hands." She took a deep breath. "You see, Herr Starke, since that seems to be your real name, *you're a Jew.*"

There was absolute silence in the room, until a coal in the fireplace snapped softly. Starke was staring at Sofia, his mouth working.

"You're crazy," Rossi said. "That's not possible."

"It's more than possible," she said. "It's so. Heydrich told me himself. This man's grandmother was a full-blooded Jew. She and her husband hid it, but Heydrich's people found out a year ago. That makes Herr Starke, if that's his real name, one quarter Jewish." She was laughing. "A quarter, all, what difference does it make? A Jew is a Jew. Remember, Herr Starke, how I didn't want you between my legs yesterday? You thought I was teasing, didn't you? But I wasn't. It was because I didn't want a dirty Jewish cock inside me."

Starke's face was still again. "You weren't at all reluctant," he said calmly. His self-control was astounding. "But then, I think you are the type of woman who enjoys the stimulation of rape."

"Not by a Jew," she hissed at him. "I pretended it, all of it. You left me cold. I let you because Heydrich ordered me to do it, if I had to. I knew all the time what was supposed to happen to you. Heydrich picked you to kill the Pope because you're Jewish. I knew he was going to kill you afterward. It was only because of the operation that I put up with your Jewish stink yesterday." She was almost shouting. "It'll take at least a hundred men to wash it out of me, you—"

"Shut up!" Rossi yelled at her, but he was too late. Starke, eyes suddenly glazed and mad, seized the heavy iron tongs and smashed them down across the crown of Sofia's head. Rossi heard bone crunch. He threw himself forward and struck with the pistol at Starke's arm, but the German pivoted and slammed his left fist into Rossi's stomach. Rossi doubled over. He heard Julia scream and Donati yell something, then the crunch and thud of two more heavy blows, and then the iron clang of the tongs being thrown into the fireplace. He stood up, trying to catch his breath.

Starke's blows had knocked Sofia to the floor. Blood was pooling around the ruin of her once-lovely head. The German was standing over her with a mad smile on his face. He looked at Rossi. "Hello, brother," he said.

"You bastard," Rossi gasped at him. "You knew I wouldn't kill you."

"Be happy I didn't take the gun. I could have."

"We have to get out of here," Donati said urgently. He was covering Starke with the other pistol. "Someone might have heard."

"Where shall we go?" asked Julia. She looked white and sick.

"Out of the city, we'll hide him till we decide what to do. This makes everything worse. Come *on*."

This last to Starke, who was standing over Sofia's body, looking down at her with a half-smile on his face. Rossi grabbed him by the arm, jabbed the gun into the small of his back, and shoved the unresisting German down the hall and out the apartment door.

By the time they reached the car, Starke had recovered enough to follow Rossi's order to start it. Donati slipped behind the wheel with Starke beside him in the front seat, and Rossi covering him from behind as before. The lawyer began driving toward the Via Appia. After a block, Rossi leaned forward and said to Donati, "You got enough back there to understand?"

"I heard her calling him '*Jude*,' " Donati said grimly. "It wasn't hard to guess the rest. It makes everything else fit. Can he really be Jewish? Does he believe it, do you think?"

Rossi turned to Starke and said to him, "It may not be true. About your being a Jew." He wasn't trying to comfort Starke in any way. Rossi didn't want him to be Jewish. He didn't want to be connected to him at all. He wondered how Starke was coping with it, inside his crazed silence.

"It's true," Starke said lifelessly. "I feel it. It is how Heydrich would work." He slammed his hand furiously against the dashboard. "I cannot be a Jew. *I cannot!*"

"Even if it's not true," Donati observed, "Heydrich would be sure to make it appear so."

"What are we going to do with him?" Rossi asked Donati. He spoke Italian.

"I have no idea. All I can think is that if he vanished, at least part of Heydrich's plot would fail. No evidence of the killer being Jewish. As he in fact is."

"Do you mean," Rossi said, and stopped. Starke knew a few words of Italian. *Morte* might be among them.

"Of course not," Donati said sharply. "We must not be like them. Perhaps he ought to go back to Palestine. We might be able to hide him there."

Starke heard the word. "Palestine?" he said to Rossi. "That would be a good joke. Then I could be completely Jewish. I have had some training." He laughed savagely.

"Heydrich gave you the background?" Rossi asked.

"Months of it. I picked it up quickly. He must have been laughing all the time. Thinking how naturally it came to me."

"Perhaps," Rossi said. "You killed those Arabs when we came ashore in Palestine, didn't you?"

"Yes. I was always worried you'd find out about them. You did, didn't you, finally? That's why you came after me."

"Yes."

"I tried to have you killed in Jerusalem because of those Arabs. It was after your woman tracked me down. I was afraid you'd suspect then. I was glad after that it hadn't worked."

"It was *you* behind that attack? You were going to have Julia killed too?"

"Yes." Indifferently.

"You bastard."

"Perhaps. But it was a mistake."

"What's he saying?" Julia asked.

"He set us up to be killed in Jerusalem."

"Oh, my God," she said. "And then he used us to come here."

"That's right," Starke told her. "It fell neatly into place."

"Is there anything," Julia said wonderingly, "that you won't do?"

"Yes," Starke said. "I would never betray a comrade on the battlefield. That is what Heydrich has done to me. And Sofia. You were my enemies, remember. Now Heydrich is."

"And us?" she asked.

"My enemy's enemy is my brother."

"Don't call yourself my brother," Julia hissed. "I don't care how much Jewish blood you've got in you."

Rossi began to say it didn't matter at the moment, but Donati's voice cut him off. "Ahead," the lawyer said. "Look. They weren't there a second ago."

Rossi looked past Starke through the windshield. A block farther on were three blinking blue lights.

"A roadblock," Donati said. "They've started looking. Of course, they'd put one on the Via Appia first. We should have gone another way. I wasn't thinking."

"Turn around," Rossi said.

"They'll see us doing it." Donati looked in the rearview mirror. "There are more lights back there."

"Is there a side street?"

"I don't see one. And we're driving a stolen car. They may have the licence by now."

"We'll have to run for it," Rossi said. "Get close, then put your foot down. If we can get ahead of them we can ditch the car, find somewhere to hide."

"All right," Donati said. "I suppose I'll be disbarred, and worse." But he kept going.

They neared the roadblock. There were two police cars, and a wooden barrier. Rossi could see *carabinieri* armed with rifles in front of the barrier. At least, because of the glare of the Fiat's headlights, they wouldn't be able to read the licence number until the car was almost on top of them.

Fifteen meters from the barrier. Twelve. Donati shifted down into first gear. One of the policemen put up his hand, palm out, to signal Donati to stop.

"Go!" Rossi ordered.

Donati jammed the accelerator to the floor. The Fiat leaped forward, rear tires grabbing at the rain-slick pavement. Rossi caught a glimpse of the guards jumping out of the way, and saw the striped barrier shatter with a dull crack and thud as the Fiat's grill hit it. Fragments of wood flew into the night. A gun banged behind them as they shot past the stopped police cars, but nothing seemed to hit the Fiat. The engine shrieked as Donati slammed the gearshift into second, accelerating hard, the car's rear trying to fishtail on the wet

asphalt. Rossi looked behind. The *carabinieri* were jumping into their own vehicles.

"How fast are those police cars?" he yelled in Donati's ear, over the engine's roar.

Donati hit third gear and kept the accelerator down hard. "As fast as we are. Maybe faster. I'm keeping to the Via Appia. There are places outside the city we can go, if we can get a lead."

"Where?"

"The catacombs." Fourth gear. The speedometer needle was bumping its peg. Buildings flew by in a blur. Donati didn't slow for stoplights at all, trusting to the lack of traffic at this hour of the morning. Rossi didn't think an Anglo-Saxon could have dared it.

He looked behind again. The police were gaining, slowly. "Do they have radios?"

"Some do."

"What will you do if they catch us?" Julia asked through her teeth, as the car hammered over the uneven pavement. "You've got a gun."

"I won't shoot. There'd be no point."

"Where are we?" Starke asked.

"Via Appia, on the way out of Rome."

"Almost at the San Sebastian Gate," Donati called back to Rossi. "That's where they'll cut us off, if they can."

Ahead, dimly visible in the streetlights, was the great arch of the gateway. There didn't seem to be anyone there to stop them, but the police cars behind were still gaining.

"They're catching up," Rossi warned urgently. "We're losing our lead."

"Only a few hundred meters." Donati sounded quite calm.

The Fiat shot under the great arch. Rossi saw a flash of blue light to his right and heard a shriek of tires. They'd almost rammed another police car, which had been coming up from the southwest to intercept them. Starke was bracing himself against the dashboard in anticipation of the collision that hadn't quite happened.

But the third car was only a few dozen meters behind. As Rossi watched through the rear window, it began to creep toward them.

"We've got to get out," he yelled at Donati. "They'll be alongside us in another minute."

"Get ready," Donati called back. "Three hundred meters—"

Here the ancient Roman road was straight as the edge of a die. The Fiat flashed by some buildings and then there were trees on the right. "When I stop," Donati told them, "run into the trees. Follow me. The catacomb entrance isn't far off."

"All right."

"Stopping now," Donati said.

He jammed the brakes on. The Fiat's tires skidded on the wet pavement. Donati fought the wheel, but the car turned and began to slide sideways. It struck a bump in the road, almost turned over, and straightened out. Rossi was slammed down into his seat as the car's right wheels hit the road again, and he had a confused impression of blue lights flying by on his left. The police cars had overshot, miraculously without running into the Fiat.

The car bounced to a halt. Donati was out the door before the Fiat had stopped rocking on its springs, and the other three were on his heels. Rossi heard shouts and another shot behind them as they plunged into the shadows under the cypress trees.

Starke's ankle was slowing him down. This was no time to worry about trusting him. Rossi grabbed one arm and Donati the other, and they ran as fast as they could in a direction Rossi guessed was south. He could hear sounds of pursuit behind them, and Julia breathing heavily as she ran.

"Just ahead," wheezed Donati. "That building. Inside. Oh, my God. Do you still have the flashlight?"

It was bumping Rossi's thigh as he ran. "Yes," he panted out. He couldn't see much of the structure in the darkness just ahead, but it wasn't very big. Donati knew where the door was, though, and Rossi heard it squeaking on its hinges. They ran inside into blackness. The door thudded shut behind them. "Light," Donati whispered.

Rossi flicked on the flashlight. They were in a small church. Ahead, faintly visible in the flashlight's beam, was a stone tomb. Nearby was a low stone parapet outlining a rectangular hole in the church floor.

"Entrance to one of the catacombs," Donati whispered. "I don't want us to go down there if we don't have to. They go for a long way. There are five levels, and only parts of the top two have been

explored. If you get lost down there and your light goes, it is too dark to get out. Unless someone looks for you, that is, and even then you may be lost for days. People have been found, but they've gone mad down there while they were waiting."

Rossi sensed Julia's shudder. He felt shuddery himself at Donati's words. Starke didn't seem to care. Rossi was keeping the gun on him, but wasn't sure why. The German had nothing to gain now by spurning their help. He wasn't likely to run away.

They waited. Then there were voices outside, approaching rapidly.

"They're coming here," Donati muttered. "Quick, down the stairs! But just to the bottom!"

Rossi, having the light, went first. Julia came after him, then Starke, then Donati. Donati wasn't taking chances; he kept his borrowed pistol trained on the back of Starke's neck as they descended.

The stairs were steep, and went down for some distance. Low niches were cut into the rough tufa walls. Rossi recollected that once the niches had contained the bodies of the dead, sealed off with tile or stone, but these cavities had long been empty.

At the bottom of the staircase they stopped. Rossi turned the light off. But there was light filtering down from above. The searchers were in the church.

"Away from the staircase, quick," Donati whispered.

They backed into the passage onto which the stairs opened. Rossi's back was to the blackness beyond, with the others in front of him. The back of his neck tingled. Five levels, Donati had said.

Did the police know they were down here?

A powerful beam of light shone down the staircase and swept along the stone floor. It couldn't quite reach them. Rossi heard footsteps grate on the stone steps above, a man's voice saying, "Check down there. They won't dare go far if they're there."

There was no choice. Leaving the light off, Rossi grabbed Julia's arm and hurried into the darkness, hoping he wouldn't run into a wall, that the passage wasn't a dead end. He heard the footsteps of the *carabinieri* echoing down the stairwell and into the corridor. If the men reached the bottom before there was a turn to hide the fugitives, the hunt would be over.

Rossi slammed into an invisible wall. For no particular reason he

turned left. Emptiness there; the passage went on. He still didn't risk a light. Julia's shoes whispered on the stone floor behind him; he still had hold of her arm. He wondered about the stairs leading to the lower levels. Were they right in the passage floors, a trapdoor for people walking in the dark? They'd have to have light soon.

Risk it.

He flashed the light for a split second, and saw the corridor leading away ahead of him into blackness. There was another passage intersecting it. It would be best to put another bend between themselves and the men searching for them. Rossi turned into the right-hand passage and stopped for a moment. He heard voices, but they were now very faint.

"We mustn't get lost," Julia whispered behind him. "We have to be careful."

"Yes. I've been keeping track." He thought the voices were louder. Another flick of the flashlight. They were in a chamber about three meters square. Rossi had a brief impression of painted faces, a fresco of a man seated on a throne, garlands. The eyes of the man on the throne seemed to be looking into his. It made Rossi start in spite of himself.

He had also seen the mouth of a staircase leading down.

The voices were definitely louder. "Down," he said. "If we can keep in a straight line it doesn't matter how far down we go."

"Marc," she said, in the beginning of a protest, but the sound of a shout behind stopped her. Rossi held down the switch of the flashlight so they could find the staircase.

"Donati is gone," Starke said from behind them.

Rossi whirled around to cover Starke with the Browning. It was true. The lawyer wasn't with them. "Where?" he asked, stupidly. "Where did we lose him?"

"I don't know," Starke answered. "He touched me just before we made the first turn. After that, nothing. I thought he was following me."

"Dear God," Julia said. Her voice almost broke. "He doesn't have a light."

"He's not far in," Rossi said. "He'll find his way out." Privately, he

was not so sure. He was beginning to appreciate that even on the upper levels one could become lost in very short order.

"I don't know why you keep pointing that thing at me," Starke said. "I have nowhere to go. If you help me, I may escape Heydrich and the Italians. By myself, I am as good as captured."

Rossi considered. The German could have taken his Browning at Sofia's apartment, but hadn't. He could also probably have broken free in the darkness as they were running from the car to the church.

"I suppose you're right." He shoved the gun into his jacket. "Follow me. We have to get out of sight."

Guided by short bursts of the flashlight, they went down the next staircase. The air was colder here. Another niche-lined passage, indistinguishable from the upper ones, lay at the foot of the steps. They stopped a couple of meters down the corridor.

Footsteps and voices, distorted by reverberation, filtered down the staircase. Rossi hurriedly turned off the flashlight. The sounds grew louder. Dim yellow electric light spilled down the staircase. "We could hunt for days down here," a voice said. "We don't even know if they went into the church. Nobody in their right mind would come down here without a guide."

Muttered agreement. The voices sounded nervous. Then they moved off, the words becoming fainter and unintelligible. Then the passages and tombs and staircases fell silent again.

"At least they haven't got Claudio," Rossi muttered into the darkness. As soon as he said it he was sorry he had. That meant Claudio was still down here somewhere, and without so much as a match.

"Could you turn the light on for a moment?" Julia asked. "This is starting to bother me. I need to know where I am."

Rossi was beginning to worry about the batteries, but he obliged. He didn't like the darkness, either. The light showed them the passage, and a low door leading off it. Rossi peered through the opening. Inside was a tomb chamber with more frescoes, Latin inscriptions, and a low stone altar. Seats were cut into the walls.

"Sometimes they celebrated the mass in these places," Julia said from behind him. "Chapels."

"Mnn," Rossi said. He was wondering how long they should wait before making their way back to the surface. What they'd do then, he had no idea.

Julia made an odd noise, and something hit Rossi in the back of the head.

He was stunned for no more than ten seconds, but it was enough. When he sat up, Starke had the Browning and was leaning against the stone altar, pointing it at Julia and Rossi. The flashlight was in his left hand, pointing at the roof, so that it threw a diffuse glimmer over the walls of the tomb chamber.

"Sit still," Starke ordered. "Julia, stand next to him. Don't move any closer to me."

"What in hell are you doing this for?" Rossi said furiously. "Are you out of your mind?"

"No. I understood enough of what you and Donati said in the car to know what you'd decided for me. You then spoke nonsense about taking me to Palestine. I am not so stupid as all that."

"What?" Rossi asked. "What in God's name are you talking about?" He couldn't follow the man's reasoning.

Starke gave a short bark of laughter. "You are not so stupid as all that, either. I suppose I should not have killed Sofia. But with her dead, there is no one to support what I say about Heydrich. Consequently I am of use to you no more. I am also of no use to Heydrich. So if I were to disappear without trace, no one wins, no one loses. You brought me here to make me disappear. Then you go back to the Vatican and say you could not catch me. Nothing at all will happen."

"But the Pope had been *murdered*," Julia burst out. "You killed him. Someone will say something. It won't be dropped, just like that."

"But it will," Starke said. "Because I didn't kill the old swine at all. You'd find that out pretty soon, if I let you take me out of here."

"You lying bastard," Rossi snarled at him. He was measuring the distance to the Browning. It was much, much too far. "His neck was broken."

Starke waggled the pistol muzzle warningly. "I know what you're thinking, Marc. Stop thinking it. And I am not lying. I was quite ready to kill him. I intended to. But he was dead when I reached his bedside. His body was already going cold. I broke his neck for the sake of appearances. If no one had seen me in his room, it would have appeared that he died from the broken neck. But that cardinal spoiled it. Now even the idiot doctors at the Vatican will know he was dead long before I got to him. I might be guilty of desecrating a dead body, but that's all."

"You son of a bitch," Rossi said. "Why didn't you tell us this before? It might have changed everything."

"That is not likely, from my point of view. Heydrich would still have been after me. I thought for a while I could maneuver you and Donati into helping me out, but then I lost my temper with Sofia."

"But," Julia pleaded, "even if there was no murder, you still need us to help you get away from Heydrich. There's no *reason* to do this to us."

Starke gave a wild laugh. "You miss an important point. You know I killed a British intelligence officer. So perhaps instead of killing me here you take me to Palestine, and turn me over to the British. It would be good for Jewish-British relations. Either way I'm dead."

There was, Rossi realized, no good answer to that.

"Besides," Starke added, "even if you didn't plan to do that, I have another good reason for killing you."

"What?" Rossi asked in the ensuing silence.

"Sheer pleasure. I've wanted to kill you for some time, Herr Rossi. Stand up."

For some reason, it didn't come as a surprise. Rossi stood up. "Let Julia go," he said.

"No. What purpose would that serve?"

"What are you going to do with us?" Julia asked in a shaky voice.

"Take you down another level. Or perhaps two. Where no one goes. There are certainly enough holes in the wall. You'll be in good Christian company."

You're going to *bury* us down here?" There was stark horror in Julia's voice.

"Yes. But rest assured I'll be decent enough to shoot you first. At least, I think I will. Now walk. Turn right."

There was nothing either of them could do. Rossi went first, followed by Julia. Starke brought up the rear. They found a staircase.

"Stop," Starke ordered. They stopped. Starke took off his wristwatch and handed it to Julia. "Use the case to scratch a mark in the stone here," he ordered. "I'll need a way out, even if you won't."

He's a torturer, Rossi thought. He likes to do it. What's happened has snapped all his restraints. He's crazy. Is it time to start hoping for an easy death?

He thought of what he and Julia might have had, and mingled grief and fury and horror almost strangled him. Because of this man behind them, they were both going to lie forever down here in the darkness with the rest of the dead, while up above in the sunlight they were slowly and inexorably forgotten until no trace remained that they had ever been.

"Down," said Starke.

The same kind of stairway. At the bottom of this one the floor was noticeably muddy. They were approaching the water table. Starke told Julia to make another mark. She obeyed. "Marc," she began.

"No talking," Starke said. "Or I'll kill the one who hasn't spoken. Look for another staircase."

Rossi noticed that the roof was badly cracked in this section. In a few places, lumps of tufa had broken away from the roof and were lying on the damp floor. He came to an opening in the wall, the beginning of another staircase. If what Donati had said up in the church was true, the bottom level of the catacombs was at its foot.

"Make a mark." Julia did so.

"Down."

Six steps down, Rossi had to stop. "I can't go any farther," he called back. "It's full of water."

"Come back up."

He retraced his steps. At the top of the stair Starke said, "Stand there by Julia." He backed away from them and regarded them speculatively. "What time is it?" he asked Julia.

"Half past four in the morning."

"You know," Starke said, "I have some time to pass before I can go back to the upper world. They may be watching the exit for a while. I have an idea as to how to pass it. If you would be so obliging, Miss Belmont."

"What?" she asked. "What do you mean?"

"I have been thinking about what you said about Palestine. It is just possible that I am mistaken about Mr. Rossi's intention to kill me, or turn me over to the British. Also, I have always . . . the British have a way of saying it . . . fancied you. If you were to give me some bodily indication of goodwill, let's say, I might consider letting you both go. At the surface, not down here."

"He doesn't mean it, Julia," Rossi warned. "He'll kill us anyway. No matter what you do."

"Be quiet," Starke snapped. "Miss Belmont has the bargaining currency, you don't. Julia?"

"You mean," she asked slowly, "if I let you have me, you'll let us go?"

"Yes."

"Marc," she said, "I have to. There's no other way."

"Julia, he doesn't *mean* it. He's just tormenting us. He's snapped. He's paying Sofia and Heydrich back through us." Rossi grabbed at Julia's elbow, but she was already moving toward Starke. Starke shifted to keep Rossi in his line of fire.

"Stay right there, Jew-boy," he said. "No matter what we're doing, I'll be watching your feet. If you move one of them, I'll kill her."

Rossi looked down at the floor. He could not bear to look.

"Remove your underwear," he heard Starke say. "But leave your dress on. I will raise your skirts myself. Now onto the floor. Good. And Marc, remember, whatever you do, don't move those feet. But I order you to watch. *Look up*, Marc! Or I'll put a bullet in her."

Rossi raised his eyes, as slowly as he could. Starke was looking up at him as he lowered himself onto Julia. The Browning was pressed beneath her left ear. The flashlight Starke had placed on the floor, tilted on the rough stones so that its light reflected from the roof.

"She'll be willing soon," Starke told Rossi. "They always are, sooner or later. Won't you, Julia?"

She gave a low moan and her mouth turned up toward Starke's. The fingers of her left hand stroked the side of his jaw.

Her left hand was inside his gun arm.

Rossi held his breath. "In a moment, Julia," Starke said. Her left palm slid up and pressed against his right cheek, her fingers inches from the Browning. Oh God, Julia, Rossi thought, don't do it, he'll be too fast for you, don't try to grab the gun, just let him, maybe he's telling the truth after all, I don't want you to die.

"Almost, Marc," Starke said. "Almost ready to start. I think she's ready, don't you?"

Julia's right hand was on Starke's left shoulder. Reaching up to caress.

"Answer me, Marc."

"I guess so," Rossi said.

"Then we'll start." Starke poised himself for the thrust.

Julia shoved the gun away from her neck with her left hand and plunged her other thumb behind Starke's eyeball.

Starke's scream was enough to split the eardrums. He surged up onto his knees, left hand holding in the remains of his ruined eye. The flashlight went rolling, but somehow the German managed to keep his grip on the gun and pull the trigger. The shot was wildly unaimed and the bullet bounced off the floor half a meter from Julia's leg as she scrambled to her feet. Starke kept screaming but fired again, in Rossi's general direction. Rossi lunged at him, knocking him to the floor, but he couldn't reach the gun hand. The flashlight beam bobbed wildly over stone; Julia had snatched the flashlight up from the floor.

Over Starke's shrieks and curses Rossi heard a thunderous *boom* from above, and then a prolonged grinding roar: stone moving against stone.

"Marc! Marc! The roof! *Run!*"

Starke shot at Rossi without result. Rossi grabbed at his arm again, got it, and wrenched the gun free. Then, pitilessly, he kicked Starke in the knee. The German fell over, sobbing curses.

"*Run*, Marc. It's all falling!"

Thick, damp dust was pouring into the passage. The flashlight

beam was just a couple of meters ahead of him but fading as the air thickened. He raced toward it and collided with Julia.

The roof's coming in, he thought so quickly he wasn't even using words. It was ready to go, and the gunshots set it off. We get away from Starke, and now this.

They staggered along the corridor, groping through the dust billowing up from already fallen rock. A heavy lump struck Rossi on the shoulder. He heard a booming CRACK just behind and above them.

"Faster!" he screamed at Julia. They sprinted. A dreadful grinding sound, so loud it was almost solid, poured into the corridor. Something brushed Rossi's heel. The ground shook as the enormous flat slab of stone, undercut sixteen centuries before by the diggers of the catacombs, slammed into the passageway behind them. Rock shards flew like shell splinters. One hit Rossi in the back of the head and he felt blood welling. Then, mercifully, the catacombs began to fall silent. Falling pebbles tinkled here and there, and then stopped. Silence reigned again, except for their exhausted breathing. The dust began to settle in the flashlight beam. Rossi noticed that the light was distinctly weaker.

"Oh, my God," Julia said at last. "That was close." Then she bent over and began to throw up, great dry heaves with nothing in them. Rossi held her.

"I'm sorry," she said. "It was his eye. I wasn't sure I could do it. But I had to. Was he going to let us go? Tell me, Marc."

"He wasn't going to let us go," Rossi said. "He was crazy, at the end. He didn't need a good reason to kill us. He just wanted to. I don't think he could cope with being a Jew. Maybe he wanted to die."

"He's dead now, isn't he?"

Rossi shone the flashlight on the rock behind them. "Yes," he said. "He's dead. We have to get out of here. The batteries are going."

They made it, just barely. Had it not been for the marks Julia had made for Starke, and the fact that they had not covered much

horizontal distance in their descent, they would have become thoroughly lost. As it was, the flashlight bulb was only the barest of orange glimmers when they reached the foot of the stairs leading up into the small church. Rossi used the last of its light to find a stub of a votive candle near the church altar. There was also, fortunately, an unused match, with which he lit the candle.

"What are we going to do about Claudio?" Julia asked as the small flame sprang to life.

"We can't look for him," Rossi said worriedly. "The flashlight's dead. And if the candle goes out there're no more matches."

"Do you suppose he's already out?"

"Maybe. He might have left a sign in the church. We'd better look."

They found it after five minutes' search with the guttering candle: CD scratched freshly and hurriedly, perhaps with a coin, on one of the door hinges. Rossi sighed with relief. "He's okay, then. I wonder how he managed it? I expect he'll come back for us, if we stay put."

"If he can. If he's not in jail."

"We'd better stay here and get some rest," Rossi said when they were back at the bottom of the stairs. "Starke was probably right when he said they'd be watching the area above ground for a while."

"I don't think we'd better leave before dark, anyway," Julia said. "We look god-awful. Like quarrymen. Or worse. At least the son of a bitch left me with my dress. What time is it?"

"Almost six."

"We should try to sleep."

She huddled in his arms. "This has been a dreadful night. And it's not over."

"The worst is over," Rossi told her. "I think."

"I hope so. I love you."

"I love you too," said Rossi. She closed her eyes. Within seconds she had dropped into the sleep of exhaustion. Very soon after, Rossi did the same.

He was awakened by a light shining in his eyes, and a voice echoing from above him.

"Marc, Marc, wake up."

Rossi felt Julia stirring in his arms. She sat up, blinking. Donati was coming down the stairs, waving a flashlight around.

"Claudio?" Rossi asked. The flashlight dazzled him.

"Yes, come on, quick. Where's the German?"

"He tried to kill us," Rossi said. "We got away, and there was a rockfall. He was under it. It was on the fourth level. No one will ever find him."

"He tried to kill you, did he?" Donati didn't seem surprised. "Why?"

"He thought we were going to kill him. He'd gone crazy."

"Not as crazy as all that," Donati said, leading them up the stairs. "It was the realistic thing to do, although I wouldn't have done it. But I am not sorry he's dead. It makes matters a good deal easier."

"Where are we going?" Julia asked. "Where are the police?"

"There's a car outside," said Donati as he hurried across the floor of the church. Early morning light was seeping in through the high, narrow windows. "Pacelli's helped me make arrangements. We're getting you out of the country as fast as possible. Next plane to Paris. Starke didn't kill Pius, he was already dead. Everything is being swept under the carpet."

"I thought it would be," Rossi said. The thought somehow depressed him. "Starke told us he didn't kill the Pope. What was Pacelli going to do with Starke?"

"Quietly have him sent back to Heydrich, with a warning not to do it again. The Italian police are on the Vatican's side in this one. They don't like Germans operating on our territory."

"Lot of good sending Starke back would have done," said Rossi. "Heydrich doesn't give up. He'll find some other way to settle with the Jews."

"Yes," said Donati sadly. "I suppose he will."

They left the church; outside, the cypresses dripped dismally. A shiny black car was waiting under the trees. Donati got behind the wheel. "Diplomatic plates, courtesy of the Vatican," he said. "We won't be bothered. Here are your exit papers. After Paris, it's up to you."

"How did you get out of the catacombs?" Julia asked him. "We were worried."

"I went the wrong way when you made the first turn," Donati explained. "So I stayed still until the police came down. Then I followed them around, keeping just outside their lights. When they left, I left. It was actually quite simple. Then I went back to the Vatican. That was the hard part. I had to walk a long way before I found a cab."

Julia began to laugh. Tears ran down her cheeks. "Are you all right?" Rossi asked with anxiety. He was worried about her.

"I'm fine." She stopped laughing and leaned against him.

"What did you tell Pacelli?"

"I was going to try to persuade him to accept Starke's testimony without the von Falkenberg woman's corroboration. And I was going to bring Starke to him, in exchange for a guarantee of your safety. I knew we'd be unlikely to get Starke out of Italy, with the hunt that would be raised for the Pope's assassin, so I was settling for the next best thing. As it turned out, Pius wasn't assassinated. So Starke could be sent back, and you were clear, and most of the world none the wiser. I also, by the way, told him about Mondolfo."

"There will be rumors," Julia said.

"Yes," Donati agreed. "There will always be rumors. But the Vatican has been dealing with things like this for twenty centuries. They have more experience then we do. I suggest we leave it to them."

"Gladly," Julia said. "I'd much rather go to Paris. What time does the plane leave?"

"Nine."

"This is a bad time to ask, but those papers I brought from Palestine. The ones for my book. Do we have time to get them?"

"I think so. Yes." Donati turned to glance at Rossi. "Are you quite sure that Starke is dead?"

"Yes," Rossi said. "He's dead, all right."

Starke was not dead.

The torment of his ruined left eye was not easing with the passage

of hours; if anything it was worse. The pain was fathomless; of interminable breadth; of unimaginable length. It was a continent of agony in his head.

From the thighs down he was no better. Through the bolts of pain from his eye he had heard the rock slab grinding down toward him, and he had leaped back from it, but not fast or far enough. Tons of stone and shattered rock had pinned him to the floor. The slab itself had crushed him from his feet to his knees, and from his knees to mid-thigh he was covered in a mass of grit and pebbles and fragments of rock.

He had been excavating at the mass of gravel, very slowly and painfully, for several hours. His fingers were bloody and most of his nails were gone. He almost didn't notice the pain of his hands because of the torment of the eye and his legs. Occasionally he screamed. From the lack of echo he knew he was in quite a small space; in a tomb, in fact. He also knew there was water down the staircase a couple of meters away. He wanted water more than anything except to make the pain go away.

He had finally excavated a small channel as far as the right pocket of his jacket. With extreme difficulty he managed to get three fingers into the pocket, his broken nails dragging agonizingly over the rough cloth inside. He pressed all the way to the bottom.

It wasn't there.

He wept for a few minutes, but the tears so seared his ruined eye that he had to stop. He considered. Perhaps it was in one of the corners of the pocket. He would try that. He had nothing else to do.

It was not in the first corner. He wanted to cry or scream again, but stopped himself. He would try the second.

He felt it. It was there.

Unless what he felt was just part of it. Perhaps it had been broken by the rocks. He felt carefully. It seemed to be intact. He had never felt such relief. Even the pain seemed to recede for an instant.

He inched it, with agonizing care, out of his pocket, terrified that his shredded fingers would drop it among the pebbles on the floor and that in the dark he would never find it again. At last it was at his lips.

He opened his mouth. Let it slide onto his tongue, back to the molars. Between the molars.

Bite down.

His mouth and nostrils filled with the odor of bitter almonds as the cyanide took him.

Epilogue

Cardinal Giuseppe Mondolfo hanged himself in his quarters three days after the death of Pius XII. He was buried very quietly outside the Vatican, but in consecrated ground. It was given out that at the time of his death he was of unsound mind.

Sofia von Falkenberg's death was attributed to murder by persons unknown, probably in the course of robbery. She was shipped back to Germany and buried in the family crypt in Berlin. The church, and the crypt, were bombed out of existence during the Second World War.

Cardinal Pacelli was elected Pope Pius XII soon after his predecessor's death. The encyclical condemning the Nazis and Fascists was never published. Although attacked after the war for not aiding Jews more vigorously, the Vatican did in fact do a considerable amount toward protecting Italian Jews from the Nazis.

Reinhard Heydrich, head of the SD and one of the major architects of the Final Solution, was assassinated by Czech partisans in Prague on May 27, 1943.

Claudio Donati lived in Rome right through the Second World War, managing by going underground to avoid the collection and deportation to Germany of Italian Jews, which began in late 1943.

After the war he was instrumental in helping survivors of the Holocaust reach Israel. He died in Rome in 1958.

Julia Belmont and Marc Rossi returned to the United States, where they were married in October 1939. Rossi returned to university and completed his degree. In 1941 he was recruited by the OSS, the precursor to the CIA, and specialized in Middle Eastern intelligence operations. Also in 1941 Julia published her book on British policy in Palestine, which annoyed the Foreign Office intensely.

They returned to Palestine in 1946, with Julia traveling on a false passport supplied by her husband, since the British refused to let her in legally. Rossi rejoined Haganah, and fought in the War of Independence against the Arabs in 1948. On the foundation of Israel he went back to Mossad, and helped turn it from a refugee-escape organization into a full-fledged intelligence service. He and Julia had two children, both born in Israel. Rossi died of heart failure in Tel Aviv in 1979, at the age of seventy. Julia joined him, as she told her children she would, a year later.

SS-Major Erich Starke lies forgotten in the fourth level of a Roman catacomb. Reinhard Heydrich, although he made some effort to do so, never did find out what had happened to him.

The Jews of Altgarten did not survive the war.